WITHDRAWN

No True Way

Valdemar

Edited by
Mercedes Lackey

DAW BOOKS, INC.
DONALD A. WOLLHEIM, FOUNDER
375 Hudson Street, New York, NY 10014

ELIZABETH R. WOLLHEIM
SHEILA E. GILBERT
PUBLISHERS
www.dawbooks.com

First Printing, December 2014
1 2 3 4 5 6 7 8 9

Contents

The Whitest Lie
Stephanie D. Shaver

—A flash of snow, biting cold, the vertigo of falling. The face of a young boy.—

Herald Wil snapped up his shields and stumbled to his feet. He stood alone in a room lit only by cold moonlight, but a moment before he'd been sitting with his hands resting lightly on the top of a carved rosewood desk covered in ledgers and dust. The ledgers had belonged to the room's former resident, the Bard Lelia. The dust had started accumulating the day he'd forbidden the Palace servants from entering and cluttering it with their lives.

He'd come here to tap his Gift and unwind a nagging mystery.

In the distance, he heard the first cries of the Death Bell.

Now it seemed he had a fresh mystery on his hands.

Unusual for him, he had no name for the face he'd seen in the moment before the Bell began ringing. His Gift usually told him exactly who had died and where, but not this time. One fact stood out—whoever it was had been young. Too young. *Trainee*-young.

:Vehs?: he thought to his Companion.

1

The normally jovial mind-voice of Vehs came back subdued and sorrowful. *:Jalay. Chosen last week.:*

:Last week?: That would explain why his Gift had failed to tell him who and where.

:He's on the Collegium grounds, we just don't know where. We're trying to find him, but his Companion was asleep when whatever happened to him happened and doesn't know where he was.:

:Not in his quarters?:

:No. And his yearmates haven't seen him either.:

Wil's mind flashed to all the awfulness of the last few years—a dead Herald and a tortured Queen's Own, a high-born traitor in the Queen's inner circle, the war with Hardorn, the inevitable war to come. Had young Jalay uncovered something he shouldn't have?

Wil picked up his coat and went for the door. *:I'll see what I can do.:*

His Gift had a few good uses. He had Foresight, yes, but it seemed to span all points in time, not just the future. He'd taken to calling this deviation "Hindsight" and had considered scouring the Archives to see if anyone else had ever exhibited similar Gifts, but he'd never been sufficiently motivated to take the time.

"You aren't even curious?" Lelia had once said to him.

"What does it matter? It works, more or less," he'd responded with a shrug, and his dear Bard had thrown her hands up in the air in exaggerated exasperation. Thinking about it brought a twitch of a smile to his lips, but it also reminded him that he wasn't focusing on what he needed to, so he let the memory go and returned to the present.

Nudges. He needed nudges. He focused on his breathing, reorienting on that every time his mind wanted to wander, and drifted where he "felt" like he should go. Presently he found himself outside the Palace, wandering through snow until he came to the old Queen's Garden, though he doubted Selenay spent much time there. No one did, this time of year.

Except there *were* fresh tracks in the snow, and as he followed them around a corner, Wil's Gift no longer became necessary.

:Send any searchers to the Queen's Garden,: he said, closing the gap between himself and the body in Grays. The boy—the *child*—lay sprawled face-up on the path. The icy, untended, unsalted, highly treacherous path.

Somebody's son, he thought.

People started to arrive. Priests for the body, a Healer to verify how the boy had died. A few other Heralds—Kyril, Queen's Own Talia and her husband, Dirk—appeared and, feeling outranked, Wil prepared to retreat.

"Herald," Kyril said, addressing him. "I've been meaning to talk to you."

"Sir?"

"Not here," the Seneschal's Herald said. "Tomorrow night. Please come see me after dinner."

Wil nodded, his gaze sliding over to Talia and Dirk. Dirk's arm circled his tiny wife's shoulders, the two of them fitting together like puzzle pieces.

:You're staring,: Vehs said softly, and Wil looked away, adopting a quick pace back toward the Heralds' wing.

Lelia. Her smiling face surfaced briefly, but this time the memory didn't elicit a smile of his own. He thought of Jalay's empty eyes, his youth—*a child, somebody's son*—and Wil suddenly needed to get back to his quarters. Someone was waiting for him there.

And though she probably wasn't awake, he desperately needed to see her.

The door opened with only the slightest hiss of metal—the servants had finally oiled the hinges, per his persistent request. He crept in on soft leather soles, the shadowy soul of stealth—

And his foot landed on something simultaneously yielding and hard, sending him staggering across the room.

He windmilled helplessly for a moment and caught himself. Panting from the effort to not break his ankle or—worse—make noise, he bent down and picked up the offending cloth-and-wood dolly.

:How's that Foresight working?: his Companion asked dryly.

Wil poked his head into his bedroom to find his daughter curled into the crook of her uncle Lyle's arm. The Death Bell had gone silent not long after he'd found the trainee's body, so all was quiet once more this side of Haven.

"Thank you again," he whispered as Lyle disentangled himself. Wil covered Ivy with a blanket and briefly rubbed her back, coaxing her once more into the deeper depths of sleep.

"We had fun," Lyle said with a grin. "After three years of war and Circuit duty, she's a breeze."

The two Heralds went out into the main room, where Lyle stoked the fire. Wil collected toys off the floor and stuffed them into a box next to a shelf piled with a mishmash of things. Old reports, bits of gear in need of polish or repair, and Lelia's gittern, Bloom, now safely encased and at the very top, where tiny hands couldn't pull it down. Yet.

Long before she'd lost her voice, Lelia's fingers had stopped being able to pick out the complicated arpeggios and natural harmonics she'd loved to coax from her gittern. She'd made Wil promise to keep the instrument safe and close, in case Ivy turned out to be a Bard.

Not that Wil read much into it, but it did seem as though every time the gittern was within reach, his daughter gravitated toward it like a moth to flame. Then again, it was an unusual object that Daddy clearly didn't want her to have. Such things seemed guaranteed to earn her attention.

"Did you get anything useful?" Lyle asked.

Wil shook his head. "No, the Death Bell put an end to tonight's attempt."

"I keep trying to remember if she told me anything … I just don't know why my sister would have kept secrets from us."

Wil was grateful Lyle had busied himself with pouring them drinks and couldn't see his grimace. "Kyril wants to see me tomorrow night," he said. "I'd bet my Companion's teeth I'm being sent back on Circuit."

:Hey!: Vehs grumbled, sounding sleepy. *:Bet your own teeth!:*

:Go to sleep, you.:

Lyle handed him a glass of Evendim smokewine, then turned his own so that the topaz-colored liquid caught the firelight. He gripped the cut glass tightly with his three remaining fingers. The other two had been taken by a Hardorn soldier's axe.

"If Kyril does," he said, "what will you do with her?"

"There's no 'if.' I've been off Circuit duty . . . what, two years?"

Unspoken between them was the truth they both knew: the Companions were still Choosing at a frightening clip, but the trained and seasoned were in short supply. Ancar had seen to that.

"My little sister has five of her own," Lyle said. "I'm sure there's room for Ivy."

"Your family is . . . near Winefold, right?"

"For now. They roam. We used to go as far west as Zoe, but we haven't in years." He took a sip and coughed. Lyle was still acquiring a taste for smokewine. "It's like drinking a campfire!"

Wil chuckled, and sipped his own draught. "With a soupçon of manure thrown in for good measure." He contemplated the fire a while, then said, "Maresa also offered. And she lives in Haven."

"Mm. Would certainly make it easier to visit when you get back from Circuit."

The firewood crackled as they both toyed with their drinks.

"How many of your yearmates remain?" Lyle asked suddenly.

Wil started a mental calculation, then shook his head. "The hour's too late for that math, Lyle."

"That few, eh?"

"Really, truly—there isn't enough in that bottle for me to go down this road tonight."

Lyle's face stretched in a sad smile. "I always thought it would be Lelia grieving for me. Isn't it the Heralds who die too soon? Aren't *we* supposed to leave mourners, not the other way around?"

"Seems your sister cheated."

Lyle shook his head. "Don't know why I'm surprised."

Wil waited for more, but Lyle had drunk his fill of melancholy. Not that Wil faulted Lyle for wanting to talk about it, even if *he* didn't. She'd been Wil's love, but she was Lyle's twin and had been with him since birth.

"Holding hands during the thunderstorms." The words were hers, and damned if they didn't seem to be whispered right in his ear, in *her* voice. He started and realized he'd begun to nod off. It could be his memory, playing tricks on the borders of sleep. It could also be his Gift, dipping into the past for a shared moment.

"Bedtime," Wil announced, dragging himself out of the chair.

"Will you need me to come by again tomorrow night?"

"If you don't mind. I just can't concentrate with Ivy—"

Lyle held up a hand. "Say no more. I've one more night in Haven. I'll be here."

Wil pushed Ivy over a little as he crawled into bed beside her. They'd tried giving her her own, but as soon as she was able, she'd escape it and sneak back in. Lelia had not-so-secretly loved it, hugging their daughter to her side and murmuring things in her ear. By then soft whispers were all she could do: lullabies, I-love-yous . . . and promises that more often than not were just gentle white lies.

"Any minute, I'll be dancing out of this bed," she'd whispered to them both more than once. "Just watch."

And for all that he'd known the truth from talking to her Healers, Wil couldn't refute her or her desire to live. To stay with them just a little longer.

Ivy sighed and rolled up against him, and his first thoughts, as usual, wandered toward pessimism. He wouldn't sleep. He *couldn't* sleep. Too many puzzles and uncertainties, and his mind too prone to chewing on them like a dog worrying a bone.

Maybe the smokewine worked its magic. Maybe Ivy worked hers. One moment he was seeing runes against his eyelids, and the next—

"Awake, Daddy?" a voice asked in a stage whisper. Something poked his cheek. "Awaaake?"

Mornings were not his strong suit. Even Lelia—frightfully chipper in the morning—hadn't been able to make him warm to the first candlemark or two of waking. She'd learned to stay away from him until he'd had a wash and something to eat. Or at least to ignore anything he said during that time.

But for Ivy, he somehow found the will to be fun. To be human. To be . . . well, a father.

"Grrrr." The sound rumbled out of him like a bear rousing from slumber.

Ivy giggled. "Dad-dee-ee-ee?"

He rolled over. "Mrrrgrrrarrr."

She flopped over him, and through slitted eyes he could see her face hanging in front of his. "Daaaa—"

His tickle assault was sudden and ruthless. She squealed and laughed. Then it was her turn, and though she didn't yet have the art of tickling down, he made high-pitched giggling sounds anyway, mimicking her.

:*Oh, if your yearmates could see you now,:* Vehs chortled.

From there Wil got her dressed, and he washed her face as she squirmed and grimaced. She hated wash-ups, though she loved hot baths. They went together down to the dining hall, he in Whites and she in a brown dress with blue cornflowers embroidered around the hem. A gift from "Aunt" Maresa.

The hall buzzed with somber conversations about Jalay's death. The teachers sprinkled amid the Trainees very firmly squashed any wild gossip, emphasizing that the Trainee had slipped and fallen—nothing more.

Ivy herself seemed more subdued than usual, and it dawned on Wil that she was listening. Together, they fed on cheese and bacon tarts, stewed fruits, and steaming mugs of spiced cider. He ate lightly, knowing their next destination. Bringing a full belly to Alberich's training salle would invite disaster. But it was one of the few places one could take a three-year-old in the winter, and Wil needed practice if he was going back in the field.

"Littles, so full of energy," the Weaponmaster commented as they entered and Ivy began to run back and forth along the salle's length. The scarred Karsite turned a critical eye on her father. "Soft." He poked Wil's belly with a staff. "Time for resting is over, I think."

Wil schooled his face. The Weaponsmaster probably knew, even if Kyril hadn't made it official. "You think?"

Alberich pointed to a rack full of staves. "I think . . . get a weapon."

The meeting with Kyril confirmed his fear.

He had two weeks.

"Understand that if we could, we would give you a position here in Haven," Kyril had said.

Wil knew him to be sincere, even as he knew that two weeks was more time than they could afford. He didn't envy Kyril's job—part balancing act, part puzzle solving, and possibly some knife juggling thrown in for fun. As a Herald, he understood the dilemma perfectly.

As a father, he seethed.

"It may be an option in the future," Kyril had gone on. "If . . . if there isn't another war. And if—"

If.

Every year Wil was in the field was a year he became less a father to his daughter. Time was finite, and Valdemar would eat into that resource with every little nibbling need.

After receiving his orders, he'd gone back to Lelia's old quarters to stare at the ledgers. He didn't bother chasing his Gift. His turmoil would only muddle the signals.

His orders were for Forst Reach sector, where things were—as Kyril had so delicately put it—"going south." Wil had experience there, and locals would remember him, which was part of why he couldn't be spared—his experience and familiarity were in short supply. And with war looming, the last thing Valdemar needed was the lords of Forst Reach shorting the Crown on soldiers when the Queen made her call to arms.

He chewed over these thoughts while flipping through Lelia's ledgers, pages covered in cryptic runes. Heralds had their codes. Who knew Bards did, too? She'd never told him, and he'd only discovered them . . . after.

They were important. His Gift gnawed at him every time he looked at them, giving him nudges.

But he couldn't read them, so the ledgers remained a nagging mystery. And annoyance. *Why didn't she tell me? Or Lyle?* he thought. *What did she have to hide?*

The next day dawned cold, but not so cold it snapped up the breath from your lungs, so he took Ivy down to Companion Field. She ran ahead of him, yelling and flailing her arms, and scrambled over the fence to charge at Vehs, who had the simplest of riding tack on. She didn't quite differentiate between Companions yet, but Vehs had put himself out front and center, so she had no choice but to run to him. She bounced up and down, yelling, "Vehs!"

The Companion knelt, and the girl crawled onto his back, gripping his mane with her mittened hands. Vehs stood and started at a slow trot as Ivy whooped. Other Companions watched, and Wil felt a glow of paternal pride. His daughter. Not more than three and already riding.

:Perhaps there was some truth to Lelia's claim that her family is descended from the Shin'a'in?: Vehs suggested.

Wil snorted. *:And my mother was an Iftel courtier. More likely that* you're *why she rides so well.:*

:Well, I am pretty fantastic.:

:Modest, too.:

"Wil!"

He turned to see a figure in scarlet walking toward him, waving and grinning cheerfully. He nodded and called back, "Maresa. Thanks for coming."

The honey-haired Bard had once been Lelia's handler—finding her work, negotiating contracts, helping her arrange playlists. She'd recently joined the Ruling Circle, helping to earn fair wages for Bards and to raise awareness of some of the less-than-savory employers out there.

She was also the mother of two fine children, and she fostered war refugees who trickled in from Hardorn. Her offer to take in Ivy wasn't just idle courtesy. Wil knew she'd be a good surrogate mother. Moreover, she wanted the job.

:And if Ivy ever shows Bardic talent, she'd have a built-in teacher,: Vehs added helpfully.

:Please focus on keeping my child from breaking her neck.:

"Happy to get your message," Maresa said. "How are you?"

"Contemplating."

She lifted her brows. "About?"

"Your offer, of course." He glanced back toward the field. Vehs did a small "hop," earning a shriek of glee from the (still-seated) Ivy. "Are you sure?"

"Quite sure. And before you offer again—no compensation, I won't hear it. The Applegates have buckets of money."

Wil nodded, not trusting himself to speak around the knot in his throat. Maresa undoubtedly sensed this, as she kept talking in a light, friendly tone. "She'll have the best scholars money can buy—until she gets Chosen or discovered, of course."

He chuckled weakly. "Possibly both?"

"Worked for Herald Jadus."

Out in the field, Vehs pranced and tossed his head. Ivy showed no sign of wear; indeed, she seemed energized, yelling, "Faster! Faster!"

Wil felt a smile touch his lips. It seemed impossible to stay sad too long with Ivy around.

So what happens when I go on Circuit, and she isn't there?

"She's a very happy child," Maresa said, belying his thoughts.

"She gets it from her mother."

"Oh, I'm sure there's some of you in her."

He smirked. "She does have her tantrums."

"Every child does. Ah . . . not to be a Court gossip. . . ."

He raised a brow. "Yes?"

"The Death Bell. Do you know anything about that boy who died?"

Wil considered his words carefully. Maresa Applegate was entirely sensible by Bard standards . . . but she was still a Bard. "A slip on untended ice. We think he was going out to see his Companion. Or tour the Collegium grounds."

"Hmm." She didn't look convinced, but Bards tended not to appreciate the elegant answer. They wanted intrigue and mystery. Wil had had his fill of that with Lelia's ledgers.

Speaking of which. . . .

"Do Bards have a coded alphabet?" he asked.

Maresa gave him a curious look. "What do you mean?"

"Runes." He used the snow to scribe one of the characters he'd seen in the ledger. "Like that one."

She shook her head. "I've not seen such. Why do you ask?"

The Herald shrugged. "Just some books of Lelia's I found. Nothing important." He cleared his throat. "I have a little less than two weeks. We'll start moving Ivy's things over next week, maybe have her spend a night to get used to your home. In the meantime, could you come over and watch her some nights, so she gets to know you?"

Maresa smiled. "I'd be delighted."

He breathed a mental sigh of relief. Lyle had gone back on Circuit, and Wil still had much to try to unravel in Lelia's former quarters.

Maresa left not long after, and he watched as Ivy began to slowly wilt over Vehs' neck.

In the distance, at the outskirts of the old Grove, he

saw a lone white figure. Just one Companion among many. It shouldn't have caught his eye, but it did.

:That's Aubryn. Jalay's Companion.:

:How is she?:

Vehs glanced in her direction. The mare turned and trotted off.

:Defying the odds,: he said. *:Honestly, I don't know. She isn't talking to anyone. Not even Rolan, and I know he's tried. There are definitely some Companions who think she should go Choose immediately, get past this. But I think she needs time.:*

Time. Again, that finite, precious resource.

The one thing we all know Valdemar cannot afford, Wil thought.

He collected Ivy from Vehs' back and carried her to their room for a nap. Later, they would go into Haven and have a nice meal. Tomorrow, he'd get her whatever she wanted—picture books, dolls, wooden swords. Anything.

Two weeks.

He would make what he could of them.

Lelia sat before him, alive, healthy.

One of the ledgers lay open on the desk, alongside her gittern, pens, and a cast-off scarlet cloak. More ledgers rested on the bookcase behind her.

She picked up a pen, a faint smile on her face—

The Vision evaporated, and Wil found himself alone in the darkened room, grasping at shadows.

A steady stream of curses issued out of him as he angrily paced back and forth in front of the desk. Every passing day the imprint of her life eroded from this place, and the Visions became more fleeting. They certainly didn't give any insight on the cypher.

He didn't doubt that Lelia had had the runes in her head—most Bards had incredible memory—but if she wrote it down then she did so with the intent of someone reading them. And he *had* to believe that there was a corresponding code to break the cypher, and that if he could just go back far enough, he'd find it in her past.

But where? Or, alternately, *who* had she intended the ledgers for?

If he knew *that*, the whole thing would unravel.

If his Gift were just stronger. . . .

:Ahem.: Vehs' mind-voice was the equivalent of a delicate cough.

:Yes?:

:You're in the Palace. You're two hallways down from the workroom.:

At first the suggestion confused him. Then realization dawned. *:Would that . . . work? I've been assuming* this *room was the key.:*

:It's worth a try. Maybe all you need is the ledgers and . . . whatever it is that makes the workroom special?:

Wil picked up a stack of the ledgers and headed out. *:Hellfires. Won't know unless I try.:*

He opened the door to the closet-sized space slowly and peeked in. Empty. He set the stack of ledgers next to the crystal sphere and settled onto a padded bench. He knew about the "workroom"—most senior Heralds did—but didn't have much cause to visit it. Amplifying his Gift had never been a desire. If anything, he'd been plagued by Visions *too* strong. He hadn't needed the ancient room and its curious power.

The room had an oddly calming quality to it—as if it muffled some of the constant background chatter of his life. The muscles in his shoulders relaxed. He rested his hands on the ledgers, his eyes on the crystal, and let his thoughts still.

The Vision unfurled instantly.

Lelia sat before him.

No, not in the little room with the crystal. In the quarters Lord Grier had gifted her, two hallways down. He was here but also *there*, in a different *then*—different even from the ones he'd been to previously.

There were no ledgers on the bookcase behind her. The one she opened looked fresh, unused. The first one, he realized. She tapped her lip with her pen, her brow creasing—and then reached for Bloom.

And took the cover off the sound hole.

Her eyes scanned the darkness inside the gittern and, slowly, she started to write crisp, black runes in the ledger.

The first time, he realized. Before she'd fully memorized the code.

She lifted her eyes, and they locked with his. A smile spread across her face, the smile he missed every damn day. His heart pounded like a war drum in his chest.

The Vision, mercifully, melted away. He found himself slumped on the table, half sprawled over the ledgers. His temples burned with the threat of an oncoming headache.

A weak groan escaped him, and then, quite unexpectedly, he laughed.

The gittern. Of course. She'd hidden the code in the one place he'd never look, inside the one object she knew he'd never part with.

Not sure I'll ever forgive you for not telling me about this, he thought, dragging himself upright. *But I also can't deny your cunning.*

He found a burst of energy that carried him back to his quarters, and he dumped the ledgers on a table before reaching for Bloom's case.

"Welcome back, Wil," Maresa said behind him, but he ignored her. He flipped open the case and took the unstrung gittern out. As he'd seen Lelia do in his vision, he twisted off the rosette over the sound hole and peered inside.

Empty.

Nothing.

No . . .

Disbelief rocked him. She'd *clearly* looked *inside* the gittern. There should have been *something*. The headache knocked, pounding on his temples. Something wasn't right, he just couldn't place it. Something. *Something . . .*

The fretboard. The smooth, dark wood. He peered closer at the gittern.

He was no Bard, but he knew that Lelia's instrument, though well-tended, hadn't been this pristine. She'd taken pride in the nicks and bumps, saying it added "texture" to the music. Her nails had worn away parts of Bloom's fretboard—but this one was perfectly smooth.

Someone had replaced Bloom with a copy, albeit one that passed a cursory inspection. Someone had *been in his quarters*.

"Wil?" Maresa looked startled, even a little scared.

"*No,*" he snarled, not to her, but to the impostor gittern. His fingertips wrapped the wooden neck and he focused, *reaching—*

And Saw—

Reality snapped back into place. He sensed Vehs' alarm.

:Should I alert the Guard?: he asked.

:Give us a moment,: Wil thought, focusing his fury on Maresa. She took a step back, her face draining of color, her throat moving in a gulp.

"Maresa," he said, a dangerous edge to his voice. "*Where* is Lelia's gittern? Where did you take it?"

Maresa plastered a placating smile on her face. "Wil— I—ah—I thought I would—"

:No Truth Spell needed here,: Vehs commented dryly.

Wil rolled to his feet. "What the hell is going on, Maresa?" His voice was quiet, icy. The madder he got, the quieter he got. A good thing: Ivy slept one room over. "You replaced Bloom with a copy, I *Saw* you do it. *Why?*"

Her smile evaporated. "You didn't know Lelia as well as you thought."

"Obviously," he growled.

"She spied for the Queen," she said.

Wil felt every fiber of his being still.

:Vehs? Can you verify this?:

His Companion said nothing, but Wil got the sense he was doing as asked. "So the ledgers . . . are her reports?"

"She . . . learned things she wanted to keep *from* the Queen."

With that out, Maresa seemed to deflate. Shaking her head, she said, "You Heralds have Companions, and Healers are surrounded all the time by people reading their emotions. Bards—do you know, I'm amazed we haven't seen more corruption in our ranks."

He frowned. "What do you mean?"

"I mean she believed someone—somewhere—is trying to strike at the heart of Valdemar through the weaker minds in our Collegium, and Lelia used her skills as a Court spy to try to find out *who*. She suspected several Bards—yes, multiple—were acting *not* in Valdemar's interests. Those ledgers are the sum of the last few years of her work."

"And you two were keeping this to yourselves?"

"*She* kept it. She never told me what she learned. Just that she was learning it. And where she kept the cypher's code."

Wil growled. "Trusted you, but not me? Not her brother?"

"Yes, damn it!" Maresa exploded, then seemed to remember Ivy, and lowered her voice again—though her fury and intensity did not subside. "And *she had reason!* Let me just *remind* you that up until a few years ago, there was a senior member of the Council and a Herald's *own uncle* plotting treason and worse. *Heralds* trusted him. *Our Queen* confided in him. And he *used* that *to murder people* and nearly destroy Valdemar! So before you tell me we could have trusted you—you're damn right we could have, but that doesn't mean we could have trusted who *you* trust!"

Wil sat silently. His fury had split—he found himself, surprisingly, most angry at Lelia.

More lies than just the little white ones, eh?

Maresa sighed. "Honestly, now that you know—maybe it is time to let the Heralds in on it. She had hoped she could find it herself, let the Bards deal with Bardic business. But then she got sicker. . . .

"Wil, we think whoever this is—they rank very high. We think they're well-funded, and we don't know *what* they're doing, but occasionally we hear things. Songs that portray the Queen or the Heir in an unflattering light. Songs that suggest it's time for a revolution. The time after a war is a very delicate one—we've seen it over and over in the annals. People love the monarch in the beginning, when the victory is fresh ... but quite a bit less when the war wounded start to come home. Lelia believed someone has figured out they can't get to Valdemar through Orthallen and is trying another approach."

"And these ledgers—they can help find that person?"

"Maybe."

He took a deep breath. "Bring Bloom back to me."

For Vehs to verify Maresa's claim about Lelia, he'd had to talk to Rolan. And because Talia and Rolan could not Mindspeak to each other, that had meant that *Rolan* had communicated to Ahrodie to talk to Dirk to talk to Talia. . . .

:Maresa didn't lie. Lelia was a spy for the Queen. Ahrodie wants us to meet Dirk and Talia in Alberich's office,: Vehs said.

:In the salle?: Wil frowned. *:What about Ivy?:*

The others clearly hadn't thought of that. *:Er ... bring her?:*

Wil muttered to himself, and then—halfway into the bedroom to pick up his sleeping daughter, paused.

Bring her. . . .

:That's an interesting notion,: Vehs observed as Wil scooped up his daughter, wrapping her in blankets.

:Isn't it, though?: Wil replied.

At the salle, Alberich composed a makeshift nest for Ivy out of padded armor, and when Wil set her down, she curled up and went right back to sleep.

Four Heralds gathered around a table with Bloom, a resigned Maresa (who'd been intercepted by Guards and redirected to the salle), and a stack of ledgers. Wil was on his third mug of willowbark tea for his headache, one of the few tonics he tolerated.

His heart leaped when they twisted off the rosette of the gittern and peered inside. Black runes and corresponding Valdemaran letters and words covered the inside of the gittern's body. They needed a spot lantern to make them all out, but within half a candlemark they had the cypher transferred to a sheet of paper.

"Can I just say how much I dislike plots?" Dirk said. "And plotting in general?"

Talia smiled at her husband and patted his hand.

Among the five of them, they translated the first few pages of the oldest-looking ledger and the last few pages of the newest. The tedious work took longer than Wil expected and warranted a fourth mug of tea.

"She's naming names," he noted.

Maresa looked miserable. "All Bards. Every single one has been worrisome to the Circle in some way. Songs that just ride the line of venom, questionable uses of Bardic Gift, shady patrons. Mostly hearsay."

"A gut feeling," Wil murmured.

"That's our biggest problem," Talia said. "We need evidence, not hunches."

"Who . . . is Amelie?" Alberich asked, tapping the newer ledger.

"Lelia's protégé," Maresa said, frowning. "I haven't seen her in months. . . ."

"Might be a reason for that." Dirk pointed to the section he'd translated with Alberich. "Lelia sent her to Forst Reach. Last entry."

"Hunh. My Circuit will take me near there," Wil said.

"Convenient," Alberich said ominously.

"Or not . . . if things are 'going south,' as Kyril put it," Wil said.

Maresa chewed on her lip. "I don't think Amelie knew anything."

"Are you sure?" Dirk asked.

The Bard looked uncertain.

Alberich pointed at Wil. "Send a Herald. Find the truth."

"Agreed," Dirk said. "If there *is* a conspiracy, and it catches wind that we know . . ."

Wil rubbed his eyes. "My thought as well. If I can buy a little time to make some copies, I'll take them and Bloom with me, and leave the originals and the cypher copy with you, Alberich. Gods willing, I'll substantiate what—if any of this—is truly a threat."

"Secret, we keep," Alberich said, sounding simultaneously threatening and weary. "Until secret it no longer need be."

From there the little group broke up. Wil went to pick up his daughter and found her awake and watching him. He wondered how much she had heard. More importantly, he wondered how much she'd understood.

"Daddy," she whispered.

"Hello, dearling," he whispered back as he picked her up.

She hugged his neck. "Don't want you to go."

He rubbed her back. "Me neither."

Wil carried Ivy out of the salle, joining back up with Talia, Dirk, and Maresa. It was past midnight, but Dirk carried a little lantern for light.

As the door shut, Wil said, "Maresa, I can't leave Ivy with you."

The Bard turned, startled. "What?"

"It's not that I mistrust you," he said. "But if this is as serious as we think, I do not want Ivy becoming . . . a liability." He swallowed hard. "I'm taking her with me."

The other three adults stopped and stared at him.

"You . . . can't," Dirk said, confused.

"Why not?" Wil asked.

"Because . . . you *can't*," Dirk repeated.

But Talia looked thoughtful. "You'd be a moving target," she said. "Easier to ambush someone when you know where they sleep, and when. If you're on Circuit, that becomes harder to predict."

"Conflict of interest," Dirk said. "You can't focus on helping people if you've got a baby screaming for attention."

"Vehs can watch her," Wil said.

"*Vehs* is your *partner*. He'll be just as busy as you."

Wil flushed. "I am *not* leaving my daughter to be captured or worse. If Valdemar has a problem with that, Valdemar is going to have to find a new Herald."

:I will watch her.:

The mind-voice hit all of them—the Heralds *and* Maresa and Ivy. Ivy sat up and pointed as a white figure approached. "Vehs?"

:No,: the female mind-voice, a rich, lilting alto, replied. *:I am Aubryn.:* She fixed her gaze on Talia. *:And as I keep telling Rolan, I am* not *ready to Choose again.:*

Talia smiled weakly.

Aubryn looked to Wil. *:Your Companion and I have been talking. I would go with you, if you would have me.:*

The Heralds exchanged looks.

"This . . . might work," Dirk admitted.

"Mm," Talia said. "I admit it'll be an odd sight to see—two Companions, a Herald, and a little—"

:Sounds like a great setup for a joke, actually,: Vehs quipped.

"—but Wil, you'll know that Ivy has someone you trust looking out for her when you and Vehs need to, say, ride all night from a plagued village to a Healer's temple."

Aubryn approached, and Ivy put a hand out to touch her cheek. Aubryn nuzzled her head. The child giggled and wiggled in Wil's arms. He set her down, and she walked over to Aubryn.

And then, between one blink and the next, she was on Aubryn's back.

"She also has a substantial Fetching Gift, apparently," Dirk remarked.

"I could really use that with *my* kids," Maresa said.

If transporting several feet in the blink of an eye bothered Ivy, she didn't show it. She laughed and grinned, and Wil's heart inexplicably swelled.

"I don't know what to say," he said. And then, in Aubryn's direction, "Thank you."

She bowed her head.

"Ivy will need a saddle," Talia said. "And you'll need to bolster your supplies. It'll be a delay, which we needed anyway for you to make copies. I'll personally talk to Kyril, but I think he'll agree that it works for Valdemar." She cocked her head at Wil. "Does it work for you, Herald?"

Something in his swelling heart broke. The realization that Ivy wasn't going away. That for once, he wasn't going to lose what he loved, as he'd lost Lelia, as he'd lost his sister, Herald Daryann. That he could be a Herald *and* a father.

The danger he was potentially putting his daughter in . . . the danger he was keeping her from. The danger Lelia had tried to keep from him.

It all collapsed down on him. He didn't even know the tears were streaming down his cheeks until Talia offered him a handkerchief, and then opened her arms to him.

He wept into her shoulder. At some point, a small hand touched his hair.

"Don't cry, Daddy," Ivy said, tears in her own eyes.

He pulled her off Aubryn and held her tight. Held her, as she held him back.

That first day on Circuit, they stopped earlier than Wil would have liked, but he'd come to accept they wouldn't travel as swiftly as when it was just him and Vehs. A child changed everything, including arrival times.

So when Ivy had gone to sleep, when she was far enough gone that he could disentangle without waking her, he picked up Bloom and looked inside the sound-hole at the characters and then—on a hunch—reached inside and swept his fingers around the chamber.

High up, out of reach of even a spot-lantern's light, he felt the brush of paper. He carefully pried the tightly wrapped cylinder out. Scrawled across it was one word, written in (thank the gods) a familiar hand: *Wil.*

He unrolled it and read.

The whitest lie we ever tell the ones we love is that we will always be there for them. It's a lie we want to believe. Gods know I did. But, as the saying goes, if you're reading this . . . then I've lied to you one last time, and for that, I'm sorry.

   If there is a Havens, I'll tarry. Maybe there are Waystations on that final road? Maybe I'll find one and wait for you.

   I love you,
   — L.

He rolled it back up and tucked it into the gittern.

"I love you, too, Lelia," he said to the Waystation's darkness.

He hoped that somewhere, in whatever Waystation she'd found, she heard him.

Old Loom, New Tapestry
Dayle A. Dermatis

"The Heralds are here!"

The cry resonated through the village square of Blenvane, having started when Heralds Syrriah and Joral had arrived at the village walls. The overcast day clearly hadn't deterred the villagers from keeping a watch on the road.

Indeed, the cry was tinged with a stroke of desperation. The Heralds had been called, although all they'd been told was that there was a crisis—not what the crisis was. Usually when urgent arbitration was required, the Heralds were given information ahead of time.

Syrriah had confirmed with Joral on the ride here how unusual this was.

The village was as pretty as the rolling green hills dotted with copses of trees that they'd ridden through. The whitewashed, thatched-roof houses sat comfortably beside one another, not clustered too close, and it looked as though most homes had ample space for herb gardens and a few pecking chickens. Flower boxes spilled over with riotously blooming flowers in carnelian, cobalt, and gold, their sweet scents filling the air and making Syrriah a bit homesick.

Based on the healthy, thriving livestock and fields they'd seen on their approach, it was clear Blenvane prospered.

So why the deep concern bordering on panic? There was confusion, and a disturbing amount of anger simmering under the surface.

Syrriah's Empath Gift quivered on high alert, and Cefylla, her Companion, snorted and said, :*Remember, be open, but be shielded. You're allowing too much in.*:

Syrriah ran a hand down Cefylla's warm, satiny neck. As much as she adored her Companion, she couldn't wait to be out of the saddle. She ached down to her bones. "Of course you're right," she said. "It's just . . ."

:*This reminds you of who you used to be,*: Cefylla finished her thought.

"Exactly." She raised her voice to include Joral. "Something is definitely wrong here. It's a pot ready to boil over."

Before Joral had the chance to reply, a man approached them. Tall and slender, he struck Syrriah as young to be the mayor, despite the badge on his tunic.

Then again, she'd reached an age when *everyone* seemed too young for their positions.

"Thank you so much for coming," he said. He nodded respectfully to Joral, but directed his words at Syrriah. "I'm Mayor Quentlee, and . . ."

"And I'm Senior Herald Joral," Joral said, swinging off his Companion. "We came as soon as we could."

Quentlee blinked, glancing from Joral to Syrriah, who also took the opportunity to dismount.

The same thing had happened everywhere Syrriah and Joral had stopped on Syrriah's internship ride: the spokesperson (be it mayor, lord, or whoever) spoke first to Syrriah, as if she were the Senior Herald.

Their mistake was understandable, given that Syrriah was twenty years older than Joral.

Nobody expected a middle-aged intern Herald.

Goodness knew, Syrriah hadn't expected to *be* a middle-aged intern Herald.

And she still wasn't entirely sure why it had happened.

Their Companions seen to, Syrriah and Joral joined Mayor Quentlee in his office, a cramped room off one side of the village hall, filled with books and papers and a tabby cat sleeping on the windowsill.

There was hot tea and dense, scone-like biscuits with jam and cream, the perfect combination of warmth and comfort on a gray day after a long ride.

Syrriah couldn't remember when the aches and pains began, the ones she'd heard her mother and aunts complain about. Heraldic training kept her fit, but she still experienced deep twinges, especially after heavy riding. As much as she loved Cefylla, she was grateful to be out of the saddle, even if the wooden chair had no padding to speak of.

"Lord Prothal Blenvane is dead," Mayor Quentlee told them.

Which explained why they'd been greeted by the mayor, rather than the titled head of the manor keep of Blenvane.

"Is there a question of succession?" Joral asked. That happened when a family tree had many branches. The oldest son wasn't always old enough, or the best choice, or even a possible choice.

Quentlee shook his head, crumbling the edge of a scone between his fingertips. "He had a trusted advisor who can handle matters until his first son comes of age. It's his wife, Meriette." He looked up at them, and Syrriah noticed the deep circles beneath his eyes. "She killed him. She went mad and killed Lord Prothal."

The problem, they learned, was that nobody could agree on what to do with Lady Meriette Blenvane.

The facts seemed clear: a knife in her husband's chest, blood on her hands, and, most disturbingly, an emotionless "I killed him."

Those were the last words Lady Meriette had said to anyone since.

She was currently under guard in her suite at the manor keep while the villagers argued her fate.

Some insisted that her admission of guilt without remorse merited her own death. Others had more sympathy, questioning why a quiet, kind woman would do such a thing. Some of those people even suggested dark magic might have been involved.

The Lady's unwillingness (or inability? no one seemed to know for sure) to defend or even explain her actions had made the debate more heated—and brought it to an uneasy standstill.

More than unease, Syrriah realized. This explained the simmering anger she'd felt when they'd arrived.

With Cefylla's assistance, she opened herself, extended and focused her Empathic Gift to seek out Lady Meriette.

Waves of guilt, relief, anger, exhaustion, worry ... and a deep loneliness. It would have been overwhelming if Cefylla hadn't been supporting her.

When she pulled herself back to the mayor's office, she found Joral and Quentlee staring at her, Joral with a line of disapproval between his eyebrows. She was supposed to be learning, paying attention, seeing how a Herald acted in these situations.

Her Senior Herald wasn't wrong. But it wasn't just her Empathy that made Syrriah feel for Lady Meriette—it was understanding, too. A sympathy that spurred her to say, "I'd like to meet with the lady. I think she'll talk to me."

The three of them rode to the manor keep. The looming clouds finally shed their tears, a light, steady rain. Syrriah drew up her hood and focused inward, strengthening her shields with Cefylla's assistance.

Her first impression of the house brought back another pang of familiarity. Made of local, pale gray river stone, the building had clearly been added to over the centuries, with wings and towers almost haphazardly placed, and yet all working together. Inside, she knew, there would be corridors with stairs going both up and down, hallways that turned suddenly, and hidey-holes that children over generations had discovered anew, with great glee.

Inside, she saw both a home and a base of operations, a place where the now-deceased lord could handle the responsibilities of his title while his wife created a welcoming haven for their family and guests.

Syrriah recognized it because, for many years, she had lived in just such a place.

She'd been Lady Syrriah Trayne then, wife of Lord Brant Trayne, and together they'd run the manor keep of Traynemarch Reach.

*　　*　　*

Some people yearn for adventure, dream of being different.

Others, however, find great comfort and joy in hearth and home. Their goal as parents is to raise strong, kind children; they strive for beauty and harmony and well-being.

Syrriah had never been one of the former people.

Her joy had always been a well-ordered household and a happy, vibrant family. A home filled with comfort and beauty: tapestries, pillows, food. Laughter, lively debate, music, poetry. A decorated hearth at Yuletide, Mayday baskets in spring, corn dollies and wheat weaving in autumn to celebrate the harvest. Kindness to the servants—they helped bring her vision to reality.

Her own age had crept up on her like a cat stalking an oblivious field mouse. One minute she'd been beaming proudly through tears as the fourth of her children rode off on his Companion—surely it must be some kind of record to have all four of your offspring be Chosen?— then the next, her beloved Brant was dead from pneumonia after helping the villagers repair a collapsed bridge in a wintry river, taken before his time. Taken just as they'd begun discussing turning the running of the manor and holdings over to her brother-in-law in a few years and enjoying their retirement.

Suddenly she'd found herself middle-aged, the dowager aunt, with nothing ahead but coddling her nieces and nephews, advising her sister—if her sister ever wanted to be advised—and weaving, something she'd always loved and had a talent for.

Something she'd lost interest in. She'd felt alone, adrift, and morose.

And then Cefylla had come to Traynemarch Reach, and Chosen her. *Her.*

The Heralds at the Collegium hadn't quite known how to handle her arrival, either. In the end, they'd essentially had to create a special curriculum just for her. She didn't need classes in history or politics or math. She was already a competent rider. Her sword skills had remained mediocre despite many lessons, but she'd proved to be a fair hand with a bow.

The bulk of her studies revolved around her newly discovered Empathic Gift, one she'd always had to some degree but that had come to its full power when Cefylla Chose her. She'd needed only to learn how to control and use it.

She had a feeling today would be a true test of her Gift.

"Joral," she said quietly, "I'd like to speak with the lady on my own." When he started to frown again, she added, "I was a lady of a manor keep once, Joral. I know what her life is like, more than anyone in this village—including you."

"My job is to teach you, show you—" Joral began.

"Please," she said. "Trust me. You're still the arbiter of the law. I'm just trying to get you information to help you make your decision."

A small smile quirked his mouth. "Very well. This isn't the usual protocol, but you are far from the usual Herald intern. You present a compelling case, Syrriah—and I do trust you."

:If he didn't, he'd have to deal with me,: Cefylla said with a snort, and Syrriah bit back a smile of her own.

*   *   *

The woman who led Syrriah and Quentlee to Meriette's suite was the household chatelaine, the keeper of the keys and organizer of the staff.

"Yes," she said when asked, "I was the one who found the lady and her husband. I've told the story to the mayor and the sheriff, but I've no problem telling a Herald as well. The lady has always been kind and generous to everyone, from the lowest stable boy to the highest-ranking visitor. I don't know what caused her to do it, but she has my support, if that counts for anything."

Syrriah assured her that it did and asked her to give her report to Joral to make it official.

Mayor Quentlee paused at the top of the last staircase, on a landing with a dark-paneled airing cupboard filled, Syrriah knew, with the linens and feather pillows for the bedrooms in this wing.

"Let the Herald enter," he told the guard, "and don't interrupt them."

The guard sketched a brief bow to Syrriah, acknowledging her authority. She raised the latch and entered.

The sitting room was empty; it felt stuffy and smelled of sorrow. Syrriah paused to swing open the casement windows, letting in the fresh spring air. When her children were sick, unless it was bitterly cold outside, she'd open the windows, bring the clean air in, let the stale air out.

The promise of better things.

She found Lady Meriette in her bedroom, sitting in a chair by the fireplace. The woman's reddish-blond hair lay lank along her shoulders, and her skin, unnaturally pale as if she'd suffered a long illness, made her blue eyes look washed out, distant.

She was wan, thin, and had all those emotions swirling

around her. Emotions she used to keep locked inside, Syrriah realized. Emotions that had escaped, and now Meriette couldn't quite fit them back in.

"Hello," Syrriah said, flinging open the casement.

Meriette focused on her, and the lady's eyes widened as she took in Syrriah's whites, the clothing that indicated Syrriah was a Herald. Still, she said nothing.

Syrriah dragged another chair over, a twin to the padded wingback Meriette huddled in. The plump cushions spoke of comfort, and the upholstery fabric, red and gold with blue quatrefoils, spoke of wealth.

It was, Syrriah noticed absently, a tricky and intricate weave.

She took Meriette's cold hands in hers, noting the thinness of the lady's fingers. "My name is Syrriah," she said. "I'm an intern Herald, but I was also the lady of a manor keep until a few short years ago. I ran a household much like yours, overseeing a village much like Blenvane."

She took a deep breath and engaged her Empathy Gift again, surrounding herself and Meriette with as much calmness and peace as she could muster. She couldn't directly affect another's deep emotion—no Herald could—but she could make the other woman feel more at ease. She could influence emotions, not radically change them.

"It's not an easy thing, supporting your husband and maintaining a large household," Syrriah went on. "We carry much of the burden unseen. Our lords are the figureheads, the ones handling the estate, yet we're the most scrutinized. Sovvan gifts are late, an important dinner isn't organized, and our lords are the ones who are judged."

Meriette flinched. She hadn't met Syrriah's gaze yet. A growing horror gnawed at Syrriah's gut.

Among the Heralds, men and women were equal—

age and experience and reputation mattered more than gender. But in outlying villages, the outskirts of Valdemar, patriarchy reigned to various degrees, sometimes in subtle fashion.

Syrriah's husband never made her feel that way; he'd accepted her as his partner. But while she might have had the keener negotiation skills (no doubt a factor of her latent Empathy), her half of the bargain had been the hearth and home, being the hostess.

She had supported him and had been valued for it . . . but in that sense, she'd also been defined by him.

"Raising children, too," she went on. "I had four, all grown now. You have two, they tell me, still young. You haven't been allowed to see them, have you?"

Her children had left her young, but at least she'd known they'd be safe and cared for at Haven.

Meriette shook her head, her ginger hair nearly covering her face.

"That is a tragedy," Syrriah said, more harsh than she intended, letting her own emotions bleed through. But the vehemence in her voice caused Mariette to finally look up at her again, and that was when Syrriah was able to see the almost completely faded medallions of bruises just above Meriette's eyes.

She looked into Meriette's eyes, opened her Empathic link wider than Cefylla—outside, but always connected to her—warned against, and understood the truth.

She'd seen this before, had helped other women in Traynemarch Reach deal with it.

"Meriette," she said, with a gentle pressure against hands that now weren't quite as cold, and a gentler pressure against the woman's emotions, "your husband wasn't a kind man to you, was he? When I was the lady of a manor keep, I saw this happen to women in the village, and I did what I could to help. The Heralds never stand for this. But if we're to help you, you need to tell me what happened."

Meriette took in a deep breath, a deeper breath than she'd probably allowed herself in years, decades. It rattled through her, and when she exhaled, it was as if a window had been opened, releasing the stale, sick air of illness and finally allowing in the sweet, clean air of truth and release.

"He . . . hurt me," she said, her voice a rasp, unused for so long. Possibly for years, really. "I thought . . . I thought for a long time that it was my fault, that I wasn't good enough, and then that it was . . . bearable, because Meri and Ethan were safe."

Her children, Syrriah knew.

"But then—then, he shook Ethan, threatened him, and I couldn't take it—I had to stop him!" Meriette was sobbing now, her words nearly incomprehensible. She didn't need to say any more. Syrriah gathered her up and held her while she wept, a release that had been a decade in coming.

Over the next hour, she coaxed Meriette to speak and also carefully probed her mind with the lightest of touches, confirming the details the lady still couldn't bring herself to speak. Her lord had been well-loved in the community; nobody knew what he was truly like in private, not even the servants. She hid or explained away her injuries, for who would believe her?

In truth, it would still be hard to convince some people, especially only on the basis of Meriette's words. Syrriah went to the door and asked the guard to fetch Joral. For a moment she expected to have a problem asking him to leave his post, but he did so without question, and she remembered: she was a Herald, considered the voice of the Monarch, honorable and just above all.

When Joral stepped into the bedroom, Meriette flinched.

"This is my partner," Syrriah said. "He's a Healer. Will you let him examine your wounds? I won't let him hurt you."

"Very well," Meriette said. Beneath the tired resignation in her voice, Syrriah heard an undercurrent of resilience. She was still, after all, the lady of the manor keep.

Syrriah and Joral worked together, examining not only the fading but still visible bruises, but also using their Gifts to explore more deeply. Old breaks to the collarbone, ribs, forearm. Injuries that could be hidden, or explained away by clumsiness.

Lord Prothal had known exactly what he was doing.

Syrriah kept her anger in check, not wanting to let even the tiniest shred of it influence Meriette.

Joral waited in the sitting room while Syrriah helped Meriette dress and comb her hair. Then the three of them went down to the manor keep's main hall, where Mayor Quentlee waited.

Fires warmed the room from the two great stone fireplaces at either end, and a servant had put out bread, cheese, and sausages, along with slices of juicy melon.

Lady Meriette had taught her staff well.

"Lady Blenvane," Quentlee greeted her, standing and brushing a kiss on her cheek. Her eyes widened, brightened with tears. She clearly hadn't expected him to be gracious.

She'd braced herself for the worst, probably since the

moment she'd stopped her husband from hurting anyone ever again, Syrriah realized.

Joral relayed the facts to the mayor, allowing Syrriah to add details as necessary. Then he gave the verdict, one that would be upheld because the Heralds' word was law.

"Lady Meriette Blenvane acted to prevent a child from being harmed and to protect herself from future harm," he said. "Given those circumstances, she deserves no further punishment. It will be up to the village to decide whether she continue as lady of the manor keep until her son is of age, or whether another should be appointed. Herald Syrriah and I are in agreement, however, that we believe Lady Meriette is capable of handling the duties of her deceased husband."

Mayor Quentlee nodded. "On behalf of the village of Blenvane, I accept your ruling and will inform the village of the decision." He looked at Meriette and added, "Given that no one may question the Heralds' verdict, there is no need to explain the reasons behind your action. That will remain a secret."

"No," Meriette said, and this time the strength in her voice was clear. "I want my story told, and I will be the one to tell it. No woman—no woman, man, or child—should ever suffer in silence as I did, and only by my honesty can I help anyone in this village who finds themselves in need."

Syrriah hadn't wanted adventure, hadn't wanted her life to change. She might have been reluctant, but she'd done her best at the Collegium, done her best on the road with Joral, despite her aches and pains and the desire to be safe and warm in a home of her own.

Being a mother and the lady of the manor keep had been her life, a life she'd loved, but she'd lost her purpose when her children had left and Brant had died.

She'd been given an opportunity for a new life. One where she could use her Gifts and effect more change than in just one village.

For the first time, she felt ready for the adventure.

For the first time in a very long time, she knew what her purpose was.

The Barest Gift
Brenda Cooper

A thin trickle of foot traffic made its way back into Gold-leaf from the ripening fields as the sun finally released its heat and sent long, slanting rays across the road.

Helen sat amid the hedgerows, glancing down the road from time to time, only to be continually disappointed, as it was either empty or held only one or two people she already knew. Some waved at her or stopped to say hello, perhaps on their way to her family's inn, the Robin's Rest.

When she wasn't watching the road, Helen played with a fine, carved wooden Companion her grandmother had given her two years and three days ago, on the day she had turned seven. While she waited, Helen made up adventures for the Companion to share with a small doll she'd made from straw and an old shirt.

She couldn't have told herself why she expected to see a Herald and a real Companion soon. She was certain she had known a day in advance about the Herald and Trainee pair that had come through last year, and right now she felt the very same way. Like there was an itch on her heart.

While she watched, Helen hummed the tune from

"The Innkeep's Daughter," a song about a young woman who saved a field Herald from a band of notorious thieves. She liked to imagine herself being that brave, although she liked to imagine herself as a Herald even more.

The gloaming turned to true dusk. She stood and rubbed the silver hooves clean on the inside of her dress and tucked her doll into a pocket. Before setting out for home, she looked back down the road one more time, finding it empty again.

Inside, she set her toys down on her very own small shelf by the door between the kitchen and the herb garden, breathing in warm air that smelled of soup made with the first of this year's tomatoes and some of the last of the rootstock from the cellar under the inn. Just-browning bread waited in the big, open oven that was the pride of the inn's kitchen.

Helen raced upstairs to kiss her grandmother's papery cheek. The old woman stirred lightly but said nothing. Helen's grandfather sat near his wife, his blue eyes saddened with weeks of watching her fail. He also said nothing, but he and Helen exchanged a smile.

Helen was the youngest daughter of the fifth generation that had run the Robin's Rest, and she and her siblings would eat later. For now, she started preparing plates and bowls of food, moving easily through the dance of meals that flowed from the oven to the long wooden trestle tables. Her mother sweated as she stirred and ladled, cut and chopped. From time to time Helen filled water cups. Her sister Magen handled the mead, fending off good-natured compliments with humor, even though she blushed at a few of them. Helen's brother Dravon snuck in from time to time when he took a break from caring for the horses and stole ends of bread for his favorite dog.

Most patrons were local single men too tired to put together their own meal after a long day in the fields. Three merchants sat quietly in a corner, trading stories. With no Bard or unusual traffic to keep the common room busy late into the night, the room started to quiet only a few candlemarks after the last of the sun faded.

Helen's mother sent her up early to sit with her grand-parents. She had Helen bring fresh water, a single cup of soup, and a piece of fresh bread with berry jam.

Her grandfather took the tray from her. "How are you, child?"

She smiled. "Good. I was hoping we'd see a Herald today, but there isn't one."

"Your grandmother always knew when a Herald was coming," he told her.

Her heart thrilled. Maybe she wasn't imaging the feeling. She thought about sitting by the window, but it had grown too dark to see the road now anyway. She chose a seat on a well-worn couch where she could see her grandfather's face clearly. "*How* did she know?"

He looked at her grandmother tenderly, and then searched Helen's face for a moment, as if looking for a resemblance. "She told me once that it was like having an extra sense, only it wasn't always there. Just when it was needed."

"Like a Healer's gift, or a Bard's gift?" She put a hand on her heart, which still felt itchy. "Or a Herald's?"

"Some gifts are great and noticeable, like the Bard who came through here last winter and warmed us all through the worst of that ice-storm." His voice was still strong, like a younger man's, except he had to stop more often for breath than he used to. "But other gifts are small and seem to appear only when Valdemar needs them."

While Helen thought about that, her grandfather touched his wife's pale cheek and held her hand briefly in his before he took a bite of the bread. Last night, he'd tried to feed the old woman, and she had refused.

Tonight, he didn't even try. That made Helen a little sad, but she didn't say anything about it. Instead, she asked, "Can you tell me about grandmere's extra sense?"

"If you had been alive while she was still running the kitchen, you might have noticed that the best meals always graced our tables on the days that Heralds and Bards and Healers came through town. If women smelled her best pies cooking during the day, they scraped up their pennies to eat with us at the inn."

"Really?"

"Would you like me to tell you a story?"

She nodded. He often told her stories while they sat by her grandmere these last few months.

He looked solemn. "This is a long story. Are you ready to settle in?"

She thought about going down for her horse and doll, but decided she was old enough to leave them. She wiggled around a little and tucked a pillow under her arm. "Yes."

"I loved your grandmother Ella from the time she was twelve, and she loved me. There was never any question between us about who we would marry, except that her eyes always turned a tiny bit over the horizon toward Haven. I used to look as well, hoping against hope that no lone Companion would come and take her away from me.

"None did.

"Even though none came to Choose her, Ella knew

whenever a Herald was headed toward us. She also knew about Bards and Healers and would be sure I knew to be here on those nights. But she lived and breathed for the visits of Companions. She would brighten a day or two before they came, and she would lay out the best feed and clean every corner of the stables. You know the big stall with no door where we put them when they come? She did that herself, pulling out a wall and taking a door off of its hinges, and she used both elsewhere in the barn to make the smaller pens for goats and sheep in storms."

"I know which ones you mean," Helen replied.

Her grandfather acted as if he hadn't heard her interruption, as if he were in some other place and time. "She loved the company of Companions. The best part was that they seemed to love her back. Even though she was never Chosen, it was almost as if she and they were greeting each other as old friends. She would whisper to them, and they would whicker back to her and let her brush out their manes and tails. They would touch her shoulders with their soft noses and bump her lightly.

"Heralds came through once a month or so then, instead of once a year like now."

"Was that for grandmother?" Helen asked.

"No, I don't think so," he said. "The road between Haven and Jackstown wasn't in yet, and so we used to have a lot more traffic through here. More bandits and thieves worked the road when this was a main trade route. Heralds had to work harder to keep the roads clear." He took a deep breath and glanced at his wife's still face, pausing to be sure she still breathed. "Ella always spent a whole day preparing for Heralds. I used to wonder if they timed their travel days to end up here instead of the next town over."

Helen sighed happily, imagining herself sweeping the stable floors and bringing in sprigs of sweet-smelling herbs to decorate the stall doors. If only she didn't have a brother! She would much rather work in the stables than in the kitchen.

"This story is from before Ella was old enough to make the pies and tell the town, and even from before I proposed to her." He leaned toward Helen. "This story is from when she was just a year or so older than you. It starts on a day in the fall, when the wind blew round the inn and scratched at the shingles on the roof and people rushed after any leftover harvest that wasn't covered and dry.

"Ella woke up normally and did her chores. The wind grew stronger, and clouds scudded and piled and filled the sky up. She was standing by the stoop watching the sky darken when she knew that a Herald was on the way. She scrubbed up the stall and went to her grandfather and got him to give her some extra good grain he was keeping against a hard winter. She put on her cleanest shirt and watched by the barn door. The children were all girls that generation, and Ella the only one of them who liked hay in her nose and scritching the barn cats.

"A tinker came in, with his cart full of pots and nails. He settled into the upstairs room. Then a set of three travelers came from the other direction, one of them handing her the reins to all three horses and giving out orders, 'Feed and water them, but leave their tack close.'

"That was a strange command, since the barn had a good, dry tack room in the middle of it. The horses were all so hot and fractious Ella had to work hard to get them properly cooled down and watered and fed. One was a swaybacked nag with a sore hoof, one was far too fine to go with the nag, and the other had clearly worn a harness more often than a saddle from the places its coat was rubbed shiny. The combination seemed as odd as the command about the tack. This put her on edge a little, but before Ella had time to even go in and get a good look at the people who owned the mixed batch of horses, her Herald came in.

"Only he didn't look like one.

"His leather workman's clothes were stained brown and black and had clearly never been Whites. His hair was mussed, and he looked as though he hadn't slept in days. His Companion was just at thoroughly disguised. His beautiful white coat had been dyed black and brown, and his mane and tail had both been turned black as night. Blinders covered his blue eyes, and his bridle had a cruel bit.

"Ella wasn't fooled for a moment. The bit hung too loose in the animal's mouth to cause pain or give the rider much control, and no paint could hide the fine bones and honed musculature of a Companion from *her*. He was the Herald she'd been waiting for, and he looked tired and wary and worried.

"At first he just handed her the reins to his 'horse,' but then he stopped a moment, as if someone were speaking to him. He frowned thoughtfully at Ella and then said, 'Lock him in a regular stall and don't treat him any different,' and pressed a coin into her palm."

"'Lock him?' she asked, aghast."

Helen gasped. Everyone knew you didn't lock up Companions.

"'Yes.' He was very firm with her, and he was a Herald, so she did what he said and treated the Companion like a horse. He acted like one, too, and didn't allow Ella to groom him."

Helen stretched her feet out. "Did grandmother hear the Companion talk to his Herald in his mind?"

"No. She knew when they were coming, but not because they told her. In most ways, your grandmother was a very ordinary innkeeper's daughter." He shifted a bit and looked fondly at his wife. "Ready to settle down and listen to the rest?" He seemed slightly happier than he had for days, as if it were a relief to tell this story.

"Yes, Grandpapa." She tucked her feet under her and rearranged her pillows.

"Your grandmother put the Companion in a stall near the best of the three other horses and far away from the tinker's jackass. She fed him and watered him, feeling edgy all the while, as if the world were simply not right. The painted Companion and the brown-clothed Herald and the three mismatched horses all added up to something bad.

"As Ella was stacking the grain buckets in their corner, hail pounded on the roof and set two of the horses to stamping their feet. The Companion looked up over his box-stall door, head high, scenting the air. Ella stayed with the animals until the hail passed and they calmed, and then she dashed into the common room to grab a bowl of squash and venison stew.

"When she got there, she stood in the kitchen doorway with her bowl. The Herald in disguise sat in the corner of the common room eating quietly, looking as unheraldlike as possible.

"The three men with the three strange horses were eating together. She'd seen the tall, thin one with the cruel eyes when he left the horses off for her to tend. Now she got her first good look at the other two. One was as big around as two men, but girthed in muscle rather than fat. He had a half-moon shaped scar on his right cheek, and he looked as hard and dangerous as the first one. The third man was less noticeable, the kind of man that can blend in with any crowd and look like the least interesting person there. At least that was what he was like until he looked at her, and then she felt a deep, cold evil when she met his eyes.

"Twice, she saw the big one with the scar glance toward the Herald.

"Your great-grandfather didn't seem to like the situation any more than Ella. He was known for having a sense of danger and for keeping people safe inside his inn. As soon as Ella finished eating, he came to her and spoke softly in her ear. 'Go to bed and bar your door.'

"She did, but she sneaked out of the window and went into the stables, where she talked to the restless horses to try to calm herself. She felt as nervous as the animals, with the wind whistling through every hole in every board and keeping the barn cold and uncomfortable in spite of its sturdy walls.

"Even the barn cats paced and occasionally let out sharp whines and yowls that crawled up Ella's neck and made her worry more. She climbed up into the rafters with the hay and the cats, trying to soothe the half-wild felines so the horses wouldn't be worried by them. The Companion was just below her, and she saw him pace and worry.

"She thought about climbing back through her window and listening through the door, or about sneaking into the kitchen and trying to avoid her father, but the fierce rain and worry for the locked-up Companion kept her glued down in the hay, listening.

"When something finally happened, it came between gusts of wind and surprised her.

"The barn door flew open.

"The Companion screamed and kicked at the stall doors.

"Ella's mother yelled from inside the inn, anger and fear in her voice.

"*:Let me out!:* a voice spoke in her head.

"The Companion! Ella had never heard one in her head before, but she knew who it was like she knew her own name. She swung her legs over the edge and started down the ladder.

"The nondescript man stood in the doorway, his face shadowed and his feet spread wide and planted. He held a bow, pulled tight with an arrow aimed at the front of the Companion's stall. The Companion screamed in her head again, this time saying, *:Get out of the way!:*

"She clung to the ladder, watching in amazement as the Companion reared up and battered the door repeatedly with his front hooves.

"The arrow grazed the Companion's face, just below his ear. Blood stained the paint on his coat, and he screamed in pain and anger.

"Ella swarmed back up the ladder and found a bucket. She threw it at the nondescript man. He dodged it, then glanced up and met her eyes long enough for her to feel cold and vulnerable. He reached for another arrow, and she shrank back, but his focus returned entirely to the Companion.

"Another man—one she hadn't seen at all, even in the inn—rushed in through the barn door. He spoke to the nondescript man, crouching low toward the Companion's stall, holding a knife. He was big, and looked mean and cold and angry.

"Ella looked around the hayloft. There was no second handy bucket, no pitchfork. Everything useful was on the floor of the barn. The loft held nothing except a few ragged blankets, bales of hay, and cats.

"She reached for a cat and missed, getting a quick scratch on her thumb. The others scattered.

"The Companion's hooves pounded again and again on the stall door. Wood splintered. Hinges creaked. The door held. As far as she could tell, the Companion didn't see the second man but was still focused on the archer and on getting free.

"She rolled a hay bale, finding it easier than she expected, as if her fear and pounding heart were making her stronger.

"She gave the bale a kick and it rolled a second time, now close to the edge. Stray bits of hay filled the air, and she almost lost her footing.

"A gust of wind blew the big barn door into the wall with a *bang!*

"An arrow hit wood somewhere below her, a *thunk* almost lost in the wind's howl.

"Another thin scream came from the inn, and the door blew shut again, cutting off the sound.

"The man with the knife crouched beside the stall door, just waiting for the Companion to win his freedom. He was just below her, and between the pounding hooves and slamming door and yowling cats, not the mention the storm, he didn't notice she was there.

"Ella was scared, but she was more angry than scared. Nobody should try to hurt a Companion!

"She drew in a deep breath, braced her feet carefully, and rolled the bale the last of the way free of the loft and it fell directly onto him, knocking him down. His knife skittered across the barn floor and came to rest under an old table.

"The Companion broke the door in two. He bounded through the splintered halves and glanced at the man Ella had knocked down. Apparently satisfied that he was no danger, the Companion raced directly into the man with the bow and half-nocked arrow, throwing him to the ground with weight and speed alone. He didn't stop, but leaped past the fallen man and through the door, heading for the inn."

Helen found she'd been clenching her fingers tight around the blanket. She looked at the frail body of her grandmother and asked, "So, she did hear the Mindspeech?"

"Never again. Only that one night."

"Who were the bad men?"

"They were the leaders of the worst bandit ring in this area. The roads were safer for two years after that.

"The Herald had a knife wound in his arm. He had so many bruises that Ella's grandmother fed him soup for two days. Ella washed the Companion clean and brushed out his mane and tail. Her grandfather kept the bandits trussed up in the town jail.

"In two days, a Healer and two Heralds came. They took the bandits and left, although the Healer fixed up a few people in town who needed help as well.

"Before he left, the Herald told Ella that she'd saved them both."

"Of course. If one dies, the other dies."

"Almost always," her Grandfather said. "It's not true for some of the Companions, such as the ones who bond with the King's Own."

"Will you tell me that story?"

"Another day."

"Did grandmother wish she were Chosen?"

"She never told me if she did. But I think so. I think almost all younglings in Valdemar have that hope in their hearts. But most of us grow up and have to be content with the gifts we do get in life. Sometimes it's the barest and smallest gifts that matter, like knowing when a Herald is on the way, or even like knowing when a storm is coming, the way your mom does."

Helen reached out to give her grandmother's hand a squeeze and found it was cold and still. She looked up her grandfather in alarm.

He put a hand on hers, a single tear tracking down his cheek. "I thought she would go tonight and that this would be a good story to be telling when she did. It's okay, sweetheart. She was ready, and she had a great life."

Even though he was saying those words, Helen could tell his heart hurt. His eyes were bright with tears. She walked around her grandmother's still body, touching the cold, stiff toes as she went by. She gave her grandfather a hug and he returned it, his arms shaky.

"She's the woman in the song, isn't she?" Helen asked.

"The Master Bard who wrote it changed the name of the inn and Ella's name so we wouldn't be bothered. The Bards all know, and that's why they stop here so often on their travels, especially the ones in training."

After a while, the other members of the family came up to help out, and Helen went to sleep.

She woke just before dawn, tiptoeing through the quiet and slightly sad inn to the kitchen and stoked the fire.

She made herself tea and stood by the window. As early sunlight spilled onto the road, a Herald and Companion rode up the lane toward the inn. She helped stable the Companion and took the Herald into the kitchen, where her mom and sister were preparing breakfast. Before breakfast was over, a trio of Bards came up on stocky brown ponies, with gitterns strapped to their backs and saddlebags bursting with clothes and food and musical instruments. They all headed for the front door as Dravon took the ponies to the stable.

Helen went to the kitchen and took a hot biscuit directly from the oven. She told them to make at least twice what they were making and to plan on a big lunch. The words came out without her thinking about them. She smiled and went back out to find a spot of shade to watch for more guests. By dinner, there were eight more people from Haven: two Heralds with their Companions, two Bards, and a Healer and her apprentice.

The funeral was held the next day in late afternoon, after the most important parts of the farming were done. The air smelled of warming stew and bread and fresh fruit and mead that people from all over town had brought to the inn, so there could be a feast after the ceremony.

Almost everyone who lived in Goldleaf came, making a small, respectful mob in the cemetery, which was just on the edge of town. The visitors from Haven stood behind the townspeople. None of them spoke a word, although they watched quietly. Even though she'd seen two of the Bards and one of the Heralds and her Companion before, Helen thought it felt like living in a legend for them all to be there at once. She tried to watch them all so hard her neck started to hurt from twisting and turning so many ways at once.

Then the priest started speaking, and everyone quieted into respectful silence. Even though he never mentioned her grandmother's gift, as the priest spoke about how well Ella ran the inn and how she helped so many people, Helen felt closer to her, and she knew how much she'd miss her. She hoped to keep sensing people coming from Haven because every time she would remember her grandfather's story.

After the priest was done with his talk, and after her grandfather said a few simple sentences, the bards started to play "The Innkeep's Daughter."

As she recognized the song, Helen felt her eyes sting with tears. She stepped back a little out of the circle, closer to the Heralds and Companions. She didn't want anyone to notice that the song was making her cry.

One of the Companions came up and put its head on her shoulder lightly, the touch so soft and comforting that Helen felt warmed by it.

Consequences Unforeseen
Elizabeth A. Vaughan

Dearest Father,

This missive is written in haste, and for that I beg your pardon. You may have already received the news, but if it has not reached you yet, I regret that I must inform you that my husband, Lord Sinmonkelrath, was killed in the same hunting accident that claimed the life of Prince Karathanelan. Official word will have been sent through the Court of Valdemar to the Court of Rethwellan. I will write separately to Sinmonkelrath's eldest brother as well, so that he may pass the word within his family, although I fear there was little love lost between his brother and him.

It has been decided that during my period of mourning I should take up residence in the lands deeded to my late lord. Queen Selenay agrees with my decision to depart Haven and has accepted my oath of fealty before sending me on with her best wishes. The carriage awaits, Father. I will send further word when I am able. Please keep me in your prayers.

Your loving daughter,

Ceraratha

The carriage jolted yet again, and Ceraratha braced herself against the wall, the wood rough under her fingers. Alena, her maidservant, lost her balance and jolted against her arm with a murmured apology. Cera was certain they'd be a mass of bruises by the time they reached their destination.

Across from them sat Herald Premlor, looking as jostled and jolted as they were, and almost as frustrated. "The roads," he said with a grimace. "I fear they've not been seen to in the two years since the Tedrel Wars."

Cera nodded, catching her breath, the fear rising in her breast. It was all happening so fast. They'd been days on the road from Haven, and from her impression, they still had a good distance to cover to reach the land of Sandbriar—*her* lands—lands that she'd never even seen.

"You'd be more comfortable on your Companion," she offered tentatively. She might be of Rethwellan, but she knew that Heralds and Companions were . . . special. She'd seen the looks Premlor had cast through the window at the white horse pacing beside them.

His smile was a wry one. "You've much to learn, Lady. And I deem it even more difficult talking through the window of a moving carriage. Let's continue, shall we?" Premlor said. "About the religious laws . . ."

Cera nodded as he started in again. Some of Valdemar's laws she knew as the daughter of a Rethwellan merchant with far trading ties. Others she had yet to fully understand. She settled back, determined to learn even as the carriage jostled on. For she could not, would not fail her oath to Queen Selenay, the woman who'd offered honor instead of disgrace, redemption instead of shame.

The woman who had set her free.

*   *   *

The days of travel blurred together, until one morning the carriage halted at the side of the road. Cera climbed down after Premlor, glad to stand on solid ground.

"Your boundary stone." He nodded at a nearby stone pillar a few feet off the lane. "We are to meet the Circuit Herald here, and she will accompany you the rest of the way." He lifted his head, looking south. "This would be her," he said, bowing to Cera. "If you would give us but a moment, Lady." He mounted his Companion and headed down the road to greet the approaching figure in full Whites.

"Such a height," Alena marveled as she stared up at the stone, her hand raised to break the glare of the sun.

"Has to be, to be seen," the driver said jovially, seeing to his team of horses. "Big enough you can't miss it, true enough."

"So we are close to Sandbriar then," Cera said, not unhappy that they might be quit of the carriage soon.

"Another three days at the most," the driver agreed with a smile. "Two if we push for it."

Cera stiffened, and her eyes met Alena's, filled with a similar shock. Three days? Just how large was this Sandbriar?

The two white figures down the road had stopped, clearly talking outside the range of listening ears. That was fine with Cera, who was happy to walk about a bit, stretching her legs. But it wasn't long before the Heralds returned, riding toward her on their fine white Companions.

"Lady Ceraratha, may I introduce Herald Helgara, Chosen of Stonas, currently riding the Circuit that includes Sandbriar."

Cera looked up to face a middle-aged woman with a

no-nonsense face and a slight wrinkle between her brows. The Companion shone white in the sun, looking as fleet and fierce as her rider.

"Herald Helgara, Companion Stonas. Well met on this sunny day," Cera said, giving both a nod.

"A sunny day that will soon turn to heavy rain." Helgara's voice was deep and filled with gravel. "Stonas' weather sense is sure. We'd best be on our way."

"Rain will make for rougher going," the driver said.

"Soonest started, soonest there," Helgara replied crisply as Premlor prepared to depart. "Let's be about it."

Cera invited Helgara to ride in the carriage with them, not as generous a gesture as it might seem, given the state of the road. Still, it would be easier to talk there than leaning out a window.

Helgara hesitated, then accepted, climbing in after her. The driver urged the horses on with all due speed. Companion Stonas maintained an easy pace beside them.

"Well, Lady." Helgara studied both Alena and her with a skeptical eye. "I've only just been informed of the hunting 'accident.' My condolences."

Cera caught her hesitation and knew she'd a decision to make: go forward with the proper fiction or extend her trust to this woman. It took a heartbeat to decide. She lifted her chin. "My husband was a fool and a traitor to this Kingdom and our Queen." Cera kept her voice calm and level. "Your condolences are appreciated but unnecessary."

"Ah." Helgara settled back on her bench seat. "Perhaps you'd fill in the details for me."

So Cera talked of what she knew, with Alena filling in such servant's gossip as she'd heard. Helgara was a good listener, asking minimal questions, taking it all in with a fierce concentration.

The rain started soon after. The driver carried on, and they shared their noontime meal from the basket that had been placed within. Cera found herself giving more information than she'd been asked for, down to the details of her marriage and her late husband's . . . flaws. She hesitated to speak of the blows and harsh words, lest this strong woman see her as less than capable.

Helgara's eyes were sharp, though.

The driver had been hustling his team, and they arrived at an inn for the night as the rain intensified. Helgara saw to the rooms and took Cera and Alena up to theirs promptly. A fire burned in the hearth, and the beds looked warm and comforting.

"I've not said who you are yet. Best leave that until you are established at the manor house. Time enough to meet your people later." Helgara looked about the room. "This should suit."

"Better than the carriage," Cera assured her. Alena was starting to unpack their bedclothes.

"You were generous with your confidences today," Helgara said softly.

"You are a Herald," Cera said. "And worthy of trust."

"And you trust your servant?" Helgara asked.

"I do," Cera said. "She has been with me since I was a lass."

"We will talk more tomorrow," Helgara said. "Or perhaps I should say that I will talk more. Good night, Lady Ceraratha."

"Cera," Cera replied. "Please."

Helgara paused in the doorway. "In private, perhaps.

But you are the Lady of Sandbriar now, and must accept that role and the title."

"Lady Cera, then," Cera said.

"As you choose, Lady." Helgara replied. "Good night."

"Good night," Cera said to the firmly shutting door.

"There's a decision to be made, Herald," their driver said as they gathered at the inn's doorway in the morning. The rain was still falling, steady and hard. "Either we push on harder, or we maintain the pace. Roads might mire up tomorrow if this keeps up, but if we push, we could be there late tonight."

Helgara got a far-off look in her eyes.

"What of your horses?" Cera asked in the odd silence.

"Good of you to think on them," the driver said. "They'll be ready for a good feed and a rubdown, but a day's rest and they will be well. Worried more about the muck they'll wade through if this rain keeps up. Hard on them, that is."

"Stonas says the rain will continue," Helgara said. "If you're worried more about the mud than the pace, then lets push on for tonight."

"Won't be comfortable," the driver warned. "But it'll get it done."

"We'll be fine," Cera said as she stepped up into the carriage.

She and Alena arranged their cloaks about them as the carriage left the inn yard. Helgara sat opposite, but her posture was more relaxed than the day before.

They hadn't gone a half-mile when she started to speak. "Cera, you are the daughter of a merchant, with a practical bent like my own. I would speak some home truths to you about Sandbriar. But I am a blunt woman not well suited to the likes of Haven."

"Tell me," Cera said firmly.

Helgara looked down at her clasped hands. "I am not sure that those in Haven have done you any favors by sending you here. The land here about is exhausted. So are the people, who are barely able to scratch by."

"Was there fighting here?" Cera asked.

"No," Helgara shook her head slowly. "This was not the battlefield. But the army of Valdemar was large and required much support. Men, livestock, food, all were given freely by the previous Lord, in support of the Kingdom and King Sendar."

"Were you at the battle?" Alena asked, her eyes wide and curious.

"Alena," Cera hushed her.

"I was." Helgara did not look up, her voice flat and unemotional. "Many men died that day, many more were maimed or crippled. Sandbriar paid a dear price for our freedom, including the death of the previous lord and his sons.

"With so many menfolk dead, whatever livestock that is left wanders free or has gone feral. I fear that what crops they were able to put in the ground will not suffice. Last year, the people could glean from the fields. This year . . . I fear there will be hunger. Or worse."

"The Queen gave me funds," Cera said, thinking of the fat purse beneath her clothing.

"Good," Helgara said. "But gold alone will not solve these problems. The neighboring lands are drained as well. There's no trade with Karse, no activity on their side of the border at all, thank the gods. If you have ties with Rethwellan, use them."

"My father would assist me," Cera said. "If there are wares to be sold."

"Then don't hesitate to contact him." Helgara sighed. "But understand, Lady, you are looking at a lot of work with people who are tired and weary and have little hope. Haven didn't tell you that, I reckon."

Fear rose in Cera's heart. This was more than she'd thought, more than she could handle. The fear and grief and, yes, pain reflected in the Herald's eyes mirrored the lands. How was she to cope with this? Deal with all of this?

"My mistress is not afraid of work," Alena interrupted with a stubborn look on her face. "Neither am I."

"No," Helgara said. "I suspect you are not. But you needed to hear the full truth."

Under cover of their cloaks, Cera clutched Alena's hand, more grateful for the support than she could voice. She cleared her throat. "Haven did not tell me," she said slowly. "But then they were dealing with other issues."

Helgara grimaced. "True enough. To be honest, they may not have known. The Heralds in the field are stretched thin as it is. We send the tax records back, but the truth is the entire country is struggling to recover. And out here, things are harder than within the cities. Sandbriar bore the brunt of it, you see. All of it. All of the Tedrel Wars."

Cera took a breath and then another, uncertain of her strength or ability to cope with what was described. Her mouth dry, she focused on the only thing she could. "Perhaps you can give me a bit more information than Premlor provided. Could you tell me of the villages? The people? The land itself?"

Helgara nodded. "That I can do," she said. And while

she talked, describing lands and farmsteads, villages and cots, Cera struggled to keep her fears at bay.

The hours went by slowly, and the chill and the damp grew from the steady rain. As darkness fell, Helgara insisted on riding her Companion. "There are bandits in the area, and our presence will make them avoid us entirely."

"Bandits?" Cera swallowed hard.

"Aye," Helgara said, her eyes fierce and unforgiving. "Not that there's many, but all it takes is a few. Otherwise, I would ride ahead and give the manor a bit of warning of your coming. You may have to sleep in cold beds this night."

"As long as they aren't moving," Alena muttered from under her cloak.

Cera could only agree.

"Open the gates!"

The cry stirred Cera from her stupor. Night had fallen, and every bone in her body ached.

"Open the gates for the Lady of Sandbriar," Helgara called again, and Cera heard women exclaiming, and the grating of wood on wood. Cera's impression was of women, guarding the gate and walls.

The carriage rolled to a stop before a great door, and torches flared as people gathered.

"Herald Helgara?" was the inquiry, but Helgara was having no delays. She threw open the door of the carriage and extended a hand to assist Cera down.

"I bring you your Lady, come from Haven with her maidservant. She needs something hot and then a bed this night. Answers and introductions can wait until we've rested."

"I am Marga, my Lady." An older woman stepped forward with a curtsy, then turned to Helgara. "You'll stay the night, Herald? The Waystation is so far—"

Cera stopped, startled, about to protest.

"Nay, I'll take a bed gladly after I've seen to Stonas." Helgara leaned in to Cera. "No fear. I'll not leave you friendless this night."

Cera just squeezed her hand in reply. She followed the woman through the door and down a confusing maze of hallways and corridors, Alena at her side. In her exhaustion nothing made sense, except a door that opened on a cold room, with a large bed and a trundle at its foot.

"I've mulled cider," an older woman said softly. "We'll light the fire as quick as we can." Their trunks were bustled in, carried by young boys who looked half-asleep themselves. Cera moved stiffly, accepting the warm cup as she watched the fire leap to life.

She remembered little else, other than crisp sheets, soft blankets, and the bliss of a steady surface beneath her as she slipped into slumber.

Cera awoke slowly to a room filled with light and warmth. The fire still burned on the hearth, and light spilled through the shutters. She stretched beneath the blankets, enjoying the comfort. Her fingers found the softness she'd felt the night before, and she marveled at the wool coverlet. She'd never felt wool like that, and she wondered idly what animal it was from. Or maybe they had a special weave?

She drew another deep breath and was content for a moment more, until she truly woke. Sandbriar, she was in Sandbriar. With a rush of energy, she threw back the bedding, her bare toes descending to the woolen rug, and blinked at the room about her as she stood.

Her door cracked open, and Alena popped her head in. "You're finally awake," she said softly with a smile, as she eased in with a tray. "The Herald and the Steward are in the kitchen talking, and the Cook's putting on breakfast. I'm to bring you to the Great Hall as soon as you're ready."

"What are they like?" Cera gulped tea as Alena dug into their trunks and pulled out a dress for her.

"Nice enough," Alena said, but there was worry on her face. "But they're talking more around me than to me, if you know what I mean."

Cera nodded, dressing quickly and seeing to her hair as best she could.

She followed Alena through the hallways to find herself in what had to be the Great Hall, a dark and shadowed affair with a vaulted ceiling and high, shuttered windows. A small fire burned in the hearth behind the high table, or at least it looked small in the vastness of the large fireplace. There were two settings there. Herald Helgara stood before one, dressed in her white uniform.

Behind her, a portrait hung on the wall, a lovely picture of a man and a woman with gentle faces, and two bright-eyed fair boys. The frame was draped in black mourning cloth and tied back with black ribbons. A garland of dried flowers graced the lower part of the frame. A palpable aura of sadness and grief hovered in the air.

Cera walked around the table to stand before her place.

"I'll tell them you are ready to be served." Alena whisked off through a distant door, leaving them standing there.

"Good morning," Helgara said from the far end of the table, a good ten paces from where Cera stood. The Herald had an odd glint in her eye.

"This is ridiculous," Cera said.

Helgara laughed, and then covered it with a cough.

Cera leaned over, scooped up her place setting, and started toward the door. "I think we'd be far more comfortable in the kitchens, Herald."

Helgara had taken up her dishes as well. "As you see fit, Lady."

Cera pushed through the door and into a warm, bright room filled with the smells of baking bread and frying eggs. She'd caught them all in the process of preparing a tray, presumably for herself and Helgara.

"Good morning," Cera said politely. She moved to an open spot at the wooden table and started to set down her dishes. "It makes little sense for me to dine alone in the Great Hall. This would be far more to my liking."

They stood staring at her, although Alena was trying to cover her smile. An older man, a middle-aged woman hovering near him, and a lad with his spoon halfway to his mouth. Various young women, kitchen workers surely, and another stout woman who had to be the cook.

"Lady Ceraratha." Helgara's voice was rich and amused, but ever so proper. "Allow me to introduce you to your Steward, Athelnor, and your Chatelaine, his wife, Marga." Helgara continued about the room, naming all in turn. Cera nodded to each, until Helgara finished, then they all stood in sudden silence.

"I'm famished," Cera said and settled on a stool. "Is there any porridge?"

The room returned to life as they scrambled to serve her.

*　　*　　*

"Herald Helgara has told us of the death of Lord Sinmonkelrath." Steward Athelnor cleared his throat. "I would extend my condolences, my Lady."

They had settled in his office, a small room crammed with documents and the dry scent of papers and ink. Athelnor had moved bundles to allow Cera to sit, and now he hunched behind his desk, his wife hovering at his side. Helgara had waved off a chair and leaned against the doorjamb, her arms folded over her chest.

"Thank you," Cera said.

"My Lady, I have done my best to follow your late Lord's instructions, but it has been difficult," Athelnor continued apologetically. "I've sent the sums he demanded, but—"

"At a cost, you understand," his wife jumped in, her tone holding no apology. "We've closed off rooms, drained our supplies, kept the household to a minimum. If you think to fete guests at this time, Lady—"

"There will be no guests," Cera said firmly. "None but myself and Alena. I have left the Court and will take up residence here. I will not be entertaining."

Athelnor sighed in relief. "We can see to your comfort and amusement, Lady Ceraratha, but I admit it will be a strain on our resources. Our coffers are limited and—"

"Lady Cera," Cera said firmly. "And I do not seek amusement, Athelnor. I wish to ease my grief with work. Money I have, a gift from Her Majesty, which will refill the coffers. What I wish to know are the conditions of the lands and the manor. Let's start with the books, shall we?" She looked over at Marga. "And then I will want a tour of the manor and to see the flocks."

Athelnor looked slightly dazed. "The flocks?"

Helgara coughed behind Cera. Cera ignored her. "The sheep," she confirmed. "And the goats. And where did the wool for my comforter come from?"

Athelnor and Marga just gave her dazed looks.

They left Cera's purse with Athelnor, planning the best way to use the funds.

Helgara followed along on their tour, more from a sense of amusement than an interest, to Cera's way of thinking.

The walk through the manor house was a quiet one. Marga showed her the empty suites and bedrooms, the linen closest filled with perfectly folded blankets and bedding smelling faintly of lavender and cedar chips. Shelves filled with pillows and feather comforters. Beds and furniture covered in dust cloths.

Clothing was carefully cleaned and folded, ready and waiting to be worn. One room in particular struck her. "My Lady's solar." Marga opened the door. "She used it for her sewing and embroidery and tapestry work."

Cera's breath caught in her throat. Fabric. Needles, precious needles. Thread and floss and wool organized in shelves and cubbyholes. A loom filled the center, waiting. Her fingers tingled with anticipation.

Delicate handkerchiefs were piled high, ready for a lady's use. Cera picked one up, admiring the bright golden flowers interlaced with a twining ivy vine. At Marga's nod, she tucked one in her sleeve.

While the unused rooms and bedding were pitiful, worse still were the empty pantries, the bare buttery, the unused storage that should be chock full of supplies. "We consolidated everything into the dessert kitchen, where the delicacies were prepared for the feasts in the Great

Hall," Marga said quietly. "The main kitchens, where the meats were roasted, those are closed and cold."

"Show me," Cera commanded.

And so it was. Great hearths with tall iron roasting spits and great copper kettles that had gone dark with disuse. Empty and sad and . . . lonely was the only word Cera could find that seemed to fit, if kitchens could be called lonely.

"Before the wars," Marga's voice echoed on the stones. "Before the wars, this manor house was filled with people, especially at shearing and lambing seasons. Before the wars . . ." she repeated, and then lapsed into silence. She didn't need to say more.

They ended in the Great Hall, standing in the quiet there, looking at the portrait.

"I'll have it taken down, Lady," Marga said, her voice heavy. "It's been draped since my lady's death, and that was long before the wars even began."

"Leave it," Cera said softly. "Before the war this land may not have been prosperous, but it provided. I would honor their work and their care of their people and build on it."

"As you wish, My Lady," Marga's voice didn't carry much hope. "I'll see to our noon meal, and then—"

"Sheep," Cera said firmly. "And outbuildings. I may need to borrow some boots." She swished her skirts back. "Slippers are not the best in the barns."

Marga blinked, curtsied, and left them standing there.

Helgara chuckled. "I think you will do well here, Lady Cera."

Cera frowned. "There is much to be done."

"True enough, but a good start I think," Helgara said. "I must return to my Circuit, and best be about it."

"Before a meal?" Cera asked, not anxious to lose a friendly face.

"I'll eat on the road," Helgara said, "and be at the Way-station by late tonight. My route brings me back through here in the Fall. I hope to see you well established by then."

"That is my hope as well," Cera said firmly. "But you've time for a warm lunch before you depart. And tell me of these Waystations. I have not heard of these before our arrival. Why do you not house in the manor?"

The Herald was a distant blur down the road when Cera turned to Athelnor. "Where can I find some boots?"

"You were serious," Athelnor looked at her in wonder.

"Steward, I am the daughter of a wool merchant, and I know the trade. Take me, or find me a guide."

"I'll take her." The young boy from the morning popped up. "The herd's in the far fields, and I can saddle the mules."

"Your son?" Cera asked.

Athelnor swallowed hard. "My grandson, Lady. My son—his father—was lost in the war, his mother died not long after." He looked away. "Gareth will take you, Lady, and guide you well. It should be safe enough, so long as it's light. Mind you keep her clear of the worst of the mud, now," he scolded the boy.

"Yes, Grandfather." Gareth pelted off toward the stables, calling back over his shoulder. "There's boots in here, Lady. Bet you can find some to fit."

Cera followed after him, a smile on her face.

Cera frowned at the shepherd. "These sheep have not been sheared."

The field beyond the gate held a fairly sizeable flock. The shepherd was an old man, grizzled and gray, walking with a staff, with three large dogs at his side. It had taken Cera a few moments to realize that his right arm was lifeless, and his one eye sagged.

"Aye," he said slowly. "Few enough to get that done, there is."

"We'll lose them to the heat if we do not," she said.

"Some," he admitted. "Not all."

"One's too many," she said. "Bring them into the barns tonight, as tomorrow we will begin."

"Who's gonna clean 'em?" The man gaped at her. "Who's gonna shear them?"

"We don't need the wool clean, not this year," she pointed out patiently. "We just need the wool off. As to who, I will. Take me some time—"

At this the man guffawed. "You can't," he said.

"The hell I can't," she replied, and left him standing in the midst of the herd.

As she mounted, she caught Gareth staring. "You can shear a sheep?"

"Yes," she said. "What is over there?" she asked, pointing to the tip of a rooftop she could see in the distance.

"That's old Ronal's place. Nearest farmstead to the manor house." Gareth said. "His widow lives there with her kids."

"They know how to shear?" Cera asked, turning her mule.

"Aye, I think," Gareth said. "Why?"

Cera rolled her eyes and kicked her mule, urging it in that general direction.

*　　　*　　　*

It was near dark when Cera rode her mule back through the manor house gates.

"My Lady," Marga greeted her. "We thought you lost. Whatever has kept you—" Her voice cut off as she saw the wagon following Cera and Gareth.

Cera knew it was quite a sight, driven by an older woman and filled to the brim with kids, furniture, and baggage. Tied behind were a cow and a calf, crates of chickens squawked on top of the pile, and a pig with six squealing piglets was tucked in the back .

"My Lady?" Marga asked.

"I visited two of our farmsteads," Cera dismounted gratefully. It had been some time since she'd ridden that distance. "I found two families, one cowering behind stout walls, fearing bandits, another dealing with leaking roofs and collapsing barns. I've brought them here until we can see to their safety and their homes. Makes far more sense to gather together." She straightened her back. "At least four of them know how to shear."

"My Lady," Marga looked slightly horrified as she dropped her voice to a whisper. "They will . . . this is above their station."

"Marga," Cera said patiently, "I will concern myself with that if they are alive next spring, agreed?"

"Agreed," Marga had the grace to look embarrassed. "I will see to this, my Lady."

"As much as I want to start the shearing tomorrow, it might be best to seek out the other farmsteads first," Cera added. "I'll talk to Athelnor."

Within days, Lady Cera had a full manor house, crammed with people and livestock. While there was some resistance, most could see the value. The herds were consolidated and the supplies mustered, and she held a council in the Great Hall to sort out what must be done.

"We will organize as best we can," she announced from the high table. "We must shear to preserve the sheep and goats and then see to the harvesting of crops and the gleaning of the fields that have gone wild. Some must tend the children, who must have their lessons seen to, as the Queen requires."

There were nods all around.

"Now, are there any here who know this kind of work?" Cera held the handkerchief with its gold and green embroidery over her head. Hands shot up around the room.

"Excellent. I wish to speak to all of you afterward, in the solar." she said. "Also, what wool is this?" She gestured to the blanket she'd had set out on the table.

"That's chirra, Ladyship." One of the men limped forward, smoothing the fabric with his one hand. "The Old Lord's great-grandfather, he brought them down from the north country and tried to start a herd. Most of them died of the heat, but some lived and thrived. The Lords always kept the small herd. This here's from the inner layer of wool, and rare as hen's teeth."

"Are there any of the animals left?" Cera asked, trying to hide her anxiousness.

The man grimaced. "See, they make fine pack animals, and the army took 'em when they saw 'em here. None returned that I know of. Might be a cot or two around, and they're mightily shy. Possible they are hiding in the woods, but after all this time . . . I doubt it."

Cera sighed in disappointment, but she nodded. "Still, if anyone sees them or hears of an animal, I'd offer a reward for its return. Make it known to all around, and get word to the neighboring villages."

She looked around the room, at faces filled with new strength and maybe just the hint of hope. "So, to the shearing. No fancy trims, we need to get those fleeces off as fast as we can. It's been many a day since I've tried my hand, but who'll meet and beat my number? A cask of mead for the winner!"

A cheer rose as they headed to their tasks.

Late one afternoon, they gathered in the courtyard, staring at the handcart the boys had dragged in. Spilling over the sides of the cart was the body of a huge, feral boar that had been prowling the woods. The boys had gone after it, with no warning to their elders. "He was after the sows," Gareth offered with a shrug, as if that explained it all.

Marga was pale, her hand at her throat as she stared at her grandson, standing so proudly next to the cart with his fellow hunters. Gareth grinned ear-to-ear, spear in hand, bloodied but unbowed. "It wasn't that hard, but he kept lunging up the shaft and trying to use his tusks."

"That's why . . ." Athelnor had to stop and clear his throat, his expression a mixture of horror and pride. "That's why boar spears have crossguards."

The boys exchanged looks, their hands filled with daggers, pikes, and axes. All of them bruised, filthy, and covered with blood. Gareth tilted his head to look at his spear tip, then nodded decisively. "Think we can affix one to this for the next one?"

"Next one?" Marga strangled out the words.

"I think we could manage," Athelnor said, starting to chuckle at Marga's obvious dismay.

"I think," Cera said gently. "We should be roasting this pig in honor of our fearsome hunters."

The boys all puffed up with pride and started cheering.

The boxes arrived weeks later.

Alena was in the solar, sewing with the women. Marga sent a messenger to Cera to tell her of the delivery and to say that the trunks and crates had been taken to her room. They'd been told their things would be sent on from Haven, so it wasn't unexpected. Cera really didn't think more of it than the need to sort through when she opened the first trunk.

It contained the clothes that she'd sewn for Sinmonkelrath.

She pulled them out slowly, seeing the fine stitching, the lace at the cuffs, the soft silk sleeve, her painstaking needlework that embellished the trim. The faint traces of the expensive cologne he'd demanded. The hours she'd put into the work, isolated in their chambers in Haven.

The beatings. The words. The hateful, hateful words.

Alena found her there on the floor, the clothing wrinkled in her tight fists, weeping uncontrollably. With a cry, Alena knelt, enfolded her in her arms, and tried to offer comfort.

But Cera just shook her head, forcing the words through the tears, trying to make her dear friend understand. "It's not that he's dead, Alena," she sobbed. "It's that I am *free*."

Cera sat in her offices, parchment and pen before her, and smiled. Her windows were open to the warmth of the late summer air, and distant sounds floated to her over the walls. The bleating of sheep, the barks of the dogs and the calls of the shepherds as they herded them to pasture. The halls were filled with the sound of children's laughter and their mothers calling them to lessons.

Better still, the ovens were baking the bread for the evening meal, and the scent filled the room. She sighed with pleasure, then took up her pen. She must finish her letter, for the caravan to Rethwellan's border was set to depart on the morrow.

So, Father, with the grace of Agnetha of the LadyTrine and much hard work, we'll survive the coming winter. Whether or not Sandbriar will thrive is another story, one that I hope I will be able to share with you at a future time.

But onto business. The caravan master who delivers this letter has been well recommended to me. He has been entrusted with five crates of fine clothing that belonged to Sinmonkelrath that I have asked him to deliver to you. The fabric is of the highest quality, and the sewing is all mine, and I know you know its worth. Sell them.

I have also entrusted the caravan master with funds. Use those, as well as any proceeds from the sale of the clothing, for the purchase of foodstuffs such as might make the return journey between Rethwellan and Sandbriar intact. Salted and preserved meats and dried fruits and spices would be most welcome. I trust you to select the best, and assure a good selection.

In one of the crates you will find a parcel containing fine handkerchiefs embroidered in the local fashion. Please see if there is an interest in trade in these items. The handkerchiefs can be provided immediately. I would ask you to be my agent in this, and I of course offer the usual fee for such arrangements. I am still exploring the potential for other trade items as I learn more of my land's blessings.

Lastly, Father, I would ask you kindly to refrain from any speculation as to matrimonial alliances on my behalf. I know that you and Mother were very happy together, but my heart is sore and tired. I have no immediate plans to enter into the wedded state even after my year of mourning has passed. Further, said alliance would have to be approved by the Queen and her Council in Haven, a long and tedious process, I am sure.

Indeed, Father, it is my intention never to marry again.

With much love and affection,

Your daughter, Lady Ceraratha of Sandbriar, the Kingdom of Valdemar

Written in the Wind
Jennifer Brozek

:Today's our birthday.:
   :And the choosing.:
   :Then the darkness.:
   :Maybe. It's foreseen, but not yet written.:
   :It's because of our spark.:
   :I know. But there are still two paths.:

Betta watched her twins stare off into space. They were talking again. Mindspeaking. She could tell by the way their unseeing gazes looked through things. Even though they looked like the rest of the family—dirt-brown hair and doe-brown eyes, with that unfortunate Haldon nose—they were still as strange and fey as the fabled Hawkbrothers of the Pelagiris. Ten years old today, and she still didn't understand how they could've come from her and her husband.

Maybe it was something in his lineage. Highborn he was, even if he was a bastard. But the Lord barely acknowledged him, had sent him away by giving his unwanted son a hold as far as he could from his august presence. The thought still made her angry on his behalf. Then again, at least he got something, even if it was a thing none of the others, the trueborn, wanted.

She squashed her bitter thoughts. The twins would feel her anger, and she didn't want to disturb their birthday. She smiled at the boy and girl who looked like each other and felt a mother's love for them. No matter what, with their special gifts, they would rise above their lot.

"Orun, Milla. Wash up for breakfast. Then we'll have presents."

As one, the twins looked at her and smiled, their faces shifting from the Mindspeaking blankness into childlike joy. Fey and strange they may be, but they were still children, and they loved the brightly ribboned gifts.

The twins' birthday was usually chaotic. Between a special breakfast, the entire family arriving for the gift giving, the catching up, and of course, the unwrapping, the main hall was a riot of people, laughter, and ribbons (carefully collected and saved for the next celebration). In the middle of it all, Orun and Milla sat with their presents around them. A real sword, his first metal one, and a shield for Orun. A new overdress and pretty slippers for Milla. Knitted socks for both. And the carefully carved set of Horses and Hounds pieces and board. Most of the family had chipped in to get the twins an actual game board and pieces, carved from stone, of the twins' favorite game.

It was the thing that had their attention now. They sat huddled, going over each piece, examining and admiring them. Milla held each piece first, turning it over in her delicate hands. *:This one is Margrave.:* She handed over the hound.

:A good name.: Orun took the hound and looked it over. *:I like it. Got dignity.:*

Milla gave him a sly smile. "Yeah?"

"Yeah. A name like a Companion."

The twins gave each other a knowing smile. Then looked up.

:They're here.: Orun looked toward the hall doors a moment before they burst open.

"Companions! In the courtyard. Riderless!" Erbeck, one of the guards, gasped for breath; it was clear that he had sprinted from the courtyard, across the hold, to the main hall. He looked at the twins. "Two of them."

Cedric headed the procession to the courtyard flanked by his children. He walked with a spring in his step and triumph in his eyes. "For you?" he had asked his twins under his breath. Their father had come to trust their foresight flashes. When they had nodded, they both heard his mental cry of joy and wistful thought. *He'll have to acknowledge me now. My children, his grandchildren, Heralds!*

They didn't respond to his joy. They didn't want to ruin the moment for him. All Orun and Milla could do was walk the path, for good or ill, toward their fate.

Where once there were only two, there were now four. Then, the four split back into two again, the twins separating more than they ever had in their short lives as they bonded to their Companions. One look into those sapphire eyes had told both twins that they were no longer alone. No longer dependent only on each other. They still Mindtouched, a habit they were unwilling to break.

Orun clung to Torin's neck in the stable where Companions were given berth. *:I didn't know it would be like this. I didn't know we ...:*

:... weren't alone. No one else has Mindspeech, and we

stopped looking for it.: Milla finished. She and Sorcha were in the next stall over. Sorcha nickered and nuzzled the girl.

:You will never be alone again, Chosen. I will always be here for you.:

Torin's wave of love and care echoed the emotion to Orun. *:Now, Chosen. Tell us why you two feared our coming. You both know who and what we are. We could feel your expectation.:*

:And your dread.: Sorcha's mind voice was tinged in concern.

Without words, Orun gave over control of the telling to Milla. She had always been better at explaining what they both foresaw. Milla took a breath and spoke, not wanting to sully the mental closeness with the imagery. She knew it would be at least a candlemark before anyone came for them.

"All our lives, we have touched mind-to-mind. No one else has the gift of Mindspeech. For a long time, we couldn't understand why they wouldn't talk to us." She touched her head as she leaned back against Sorcha's side. "Then we realized they couldn't. Realized we were different."

She paused, forming their fears into words. "For a couple of seasons now, we've both begun to see what lies ahead. Little things. A lost sheep. A broken bone. A found love. A new baby. Then, we started to see us. Our path. It always starts with joy. Then . . ." Milla stopped, afraid to continue. She bowed her head as Sorcha radiated care, love, and support to her, bolstering her. "There are two paths now. One where we continue, where we have long lives in service. The other . . . darkness takes us."

:Do you know what this darkness is?: Torin's question was colored with his alert concentration.

Orun shrugged. He still hugged his Companion's neck. "No. But it's because of what we can do. A gift not yet born."

:Gift?:

"The spark . . ." Milla groped for the words, trying to explain something she didn't quite understand. "We will do what the songs say Herald Vanyel does on the Karsite border. We can see the energy around us and in the land. You both are shining blue."

:Magecraft,: Sorcha supplied.

"Yes. That. The spark. Something hunts those with the spark."

The twins felt the surprise and shock of their respective Companions. Felt it morph into sudden understanding and determination.

:That explains something we had not yet understood.: Sorcha tossed her head, agitated. *:We need to return to the Palace and tell the Circle.:*

"Explains what?" Milla turned to look into those sapphire eyes.

:Why there are almost no Herald-Mage trainees. What is happening to those with potential and why they have not been Chosen.:

Fear blossomed anew in Milla's heart. "Someone has been killing us before that could happen."

:Yes.:

When it came to arguing with their father, Orun took the lead. He was more apt to listen to his son than his daughter. While Orun and Cedric had words—Orun's quiet and firm, Cedric's rising with frustration—Milla explained the situation to their mother.

"You can't come with us. No one can come with us.

That's not how things are done. Not with newly Chosen."
Milla folded the clothing she would take with her as she
spoke. "Chosen don't have entourages. And Sorcha says
it would look bad on us if we did. We're already unusual
enough with twins being Chosen."

"It means so much to your father. You know why."
Betta packed Orun's things while they spoke.

:Sorcha?:

*:Yes, it's usually highborn who are chosen, but blood
really doesn't matter. It's the heart.:*

:What do I tell her?:

*:That they may come in a moon to see how you are
settling in.:*

"Are you . . . talking . . . to her now?" Betta's voice
was soft and wistful.

Milla nodded, trying to ignore her mother's pain.
"Sorcha says you can come in a moon to see how we're
settling in. That would be best. Plus, we can let the other
chosen Trainees and Heralds know so they can prepare
for Father and you. But you must make Father understand that we belong to the Crown now. Our first duty is
to Valdemar. Besides, Sorcha tells me that they move a
lot faster than normal horses. Instead of a fortnight to
get to Palace, it'll be half that. Father's horses couldn't
keep up." It was an exaggeration—like much of her explanation—but it got her point across.

Betta looked uncertain for a moment, then understood the unspoken message of not wanting to embar-
rass Cedric with his inability to match speeds with the
Companions. "One moon?" Then she nodded. "That will
give us enough time to prepare and to get appropriate
clothing made. Think of it, the Palace!" She finished

packing Orun's bag and hurried off to stop the argument
between her husband and her son.

Milla smiled, but it was false. That would be long
enough for them to make it to the Palace ... or not. It also
would make sure whatever was hunting them wouldn't
get their family.

The attack came on the second night away from the hold
with no warning. No flicker of foresight or even uneasy
dreams. Just after sunset, as they set up their camp, sin-
ewy creatures of shadow and teeth with glowing red eyes,
barely seen in the firelight, appeared. Torin screamed a
challenge and charged the swarming creatures.

:Wyrsa!: Sorcha joined Torin with her own challenge
and flying silver hooves, pummeling the creatures.

Both children reacted to the mental feel of the monsters as much as their visage. Orun wrenched his new
sword from its sheath and set to guard Milla as she dug
for her sling and iron stones. The hold was so far from
the Palace and so near the borderlands, every child was
taught to fight as best they could from the time they
could walk.

One of the *wyrsa* got past the Companions' guard position and came for the children. It dodged Milla's expert
shot and dove for Orun. He swung his sword, catching it
in the shoulder as it clawed his arm. Milla pelted it with a
handful of iron stones, half-panicked, half in response to
Orun's cry of pain. The creature backed off and charged
Orun again, this time avoiding the sword and catching the
boy's already wounded arm in its wicked teeth.

"Orun!" Milla's scream was high-pitched and frantic.
The Companions couldn't help, as they battled the rest

of the pack. Orun punched at the creature as it savaged his arm and raked claws down his leg. Milla grabbed a log out of the fire and thrust it into the *wyrsa*'s side. It screamed its own pain, released Orun, and turned on her.

Holding the burning log like a sword as she had seen Orun do, Milla swung at the creature as it snarled. The fire drove it back, but she knew it wouldn't be for long as the *wyrsa* dodged, charged, and dodged again, trying to get to her.

The sudden slashing of hooves at the *wyrsa*'s backside sent it running to the underbrush, keening in pain. It took one look back, just long enough to see that it was quite alone and both Companions were coming for it, then disappeared into the forest. Sorcha gave chase as Torin came back to guard the twins.

Milla was still clutching the burning log, ready to fight, when Sorcha returned.

:It's gone. It escaped. I don't think it'll be back now that it's alone.:

"Orun. He's hurt."

Torin pressed his long forehead to the boy's brown hair, and a soft glow surrounded them. Milla felt the sympathetic pain in her arm and leg lessen and fade into an itchy sensation. Orun looked up and smiled wanly. Despite the healing, he was still pale under his tanned skin. "We survived." He sounded as if he couldn't believe what he was saying.

Milla matched his smile. "We did survive."

:These aren't wyrsa.*:* Sorcha's mental voice was filled with revulsion. *:They're some sort of demon that look a bit like* wyrsa.*:*

Milla and Orun looked at each other.

:Explains why there's no poison in Orun's wounds.:

Torin walked over to look at the body Sorcha was examining. *:Camouflaged to look like wyrsa?:*

:I think so.:

"Why?" Orun watched the Companions, rather than his sister, who was examining his arm. Unlike the scratches on his leg, it wasn't completely healed.

Torin shook his head, silver mane flying in agitation. *:I don't know. These are blood-fed demons. That means the Mage who called them is still out there.:*

Sorcha flicked the body she had been looking at into the underbrush with a gore-spattered hoof. *:And one got away.:*

"Was it coming for us?" Milla wrapped Orun's salve-covered arm with strips of cloth torn from one of her underskirts.

:Coming for the Mage talented. I don't think for you two specifically. However, now that it knows there are four of us, if the Mage attacks again, he'll summon something bigger, I fear.: Sorcha returned to the fireside.

"Then we'll be ready for it." Orun looked determined as he held his bandaged arm. "We've got no other choice."

They pushed hard for two days, stopping only when they reached a defensible Waystation. The twins, unused to being in the saddle all day at a full run, were exhausted by the time they stopped. Knowing that something was hunting them—that it could, and would, attack at any moment—was as draining as their physical exertion. No uneasy dreams troubled their sleep. They were too tired for that.

On the morning of the fourth day, Milla looked around. "I think . . . I think we're all right. I think we're going to make it. I don't feel the darkness."

Orun shook his head. "I don't know. We saw it for so long."

"We saw two paths. And we fought off the attack. I can't feel anything anymore. Fate is only written in the wind until it's the past."

:The Mage knows you are Chosen now. He could be shielding.: Torin shook his mane. *:He could be readying an ambush.:*

Milla scrunched her face up in a scowl. "Why do you say such things?"

:Because we must, Chosen.: Sorcha's mental voice was gentle. *:It is the lot of a Herald to be in danger.:*

"But we saw two paths. Are we destined to fall to darkness?"

:Destined, no. But it is likely. Herald-Mages have many hard duties. There're so few of them now, with so much to do.:

:And now we know why.: Torin's anger washed over them all before it settled back into its usual determined feel. *:That is our first duty, inform the Palace.:*

"I wish we were Farspeakers." Orun sighed. "Then we could tell them now, and not have to worry about that, too."

Torin snuffled his hair. *:If you knew who to contact, we could bolster you, but . . . :*

"If wishes were fishes, even holders would feast." He touched his Companion's mane.

Milla touched his shoulder. "We'll make it. We've already come to the fork in the path. We've shifted onto the path of duty. The darkness is behind us." She smiled at him and mounted Sorcha. *:Though I wish I could be as sure as I sound,:* she sent privately to Sorcha.

:I wish I could be as well. Foreseeing is a hard gift to

have. Even harder to control. It tells you just enough to scare you.:

Milla leaned forward over the saddle to hug Sorcha's neck for a moment. *:But now I have you.:*

:Yes, Chosen. You always will.:

The next attack wasn't an ambush so much as a wave of evil headed their way. It was so palpable that they felt it long before they saw any sign of it in the dust stirring on the trade route. As one, the Companions turned from the road and bolted into the forest, Orun and Milla holding on for dear life.

:There's a hunter's trail south. We can take it.: Torin took the lead. *:We can use the trail to outrun . . . it.:*

Neither Chosen nor Companion knew what "it" was except that it was wrong in every sense of the word. Whoever was hunting those with the gift of Magecraft had worked a major summoning, and it was coming for them all. For a short while, it seemed as if their plan would work. Then the sounds of breaking branches, heavy footfalls, and snarling calls told them otherwise. Glances back gave glimpses of fang and fur on things almost too big to be real.

"Split up," Orun yelled. "I'll draw them off. They have my scent!"

Milla realized what he meant—the creature that had bitten him, his blood on its teeth. He was going to sacrifice himself for her. "No!"

:Yes.: Sorcha and Torin were in agreement. As soon as they made it to the hunter's trail, the Companions took off in opposite directions. Sorcha back north. Torin to the south.

:I love you, sister-mine. I'll see you at the Palace.: Orun's mind voice was light and false.

Milla knew he was saying good-bye in the only way he knew how. Through tears she sent her farewell. *:I love you, brother-mine. I'll race you. The loser does the winner's chores for a week.:* It was the only thing she could think of to say.

:Deal.:

Then they both hung on as their Companions ran for all of their lives.

Milla screamed and tumbled from Sorcha's back as she felt Orun die by claws and teeth, torn limb from limb. The pain of his death was mercifully short. The pain of his loss was something she would never get over. Curled up on the ground, sobbing, Milla thought she'd die then and there. Sorcha nuzzled her hair.

:Chosen, Milla, we must keep moving. Please, Chosen. Please!:

Only the tone of fear in her Companion's voice brought Milla out of grief long enough to clamber back onto Sorcha. Only the Companion's skill kept the unseeing, inconsolable girl in her saddle as she galloped as fast as she could.

The demon still chased them. It seemed that Torin had killed the rest, but this one came for them when Orun and Torin were dead. This one knew its quarry and would not let it escape. Claws ripped at Sorcha's hindquarters and she gave an all too human scream of pain, then whirled on the demon, hooves slashing at its face and blazing eyes.

As Milla slid from Sorcha's back and hit the ground hard, she saw the demon in all its wrongness. A cross between a bear and a bull, the horned monster had a huge snout full of sharp fangs, a shaggy mane, and glowing yellow eyes. Its claws were as long as her forearm and slashed at the Companion as it went for the girl. Milla stood and stumbled backward. It still caught her side, the claws so sharp Milla didn't feel the pain of the flesh parting until blood was already spilling down her leg.

It focused on Milla. It had her scent now. She knew beyond all doubt, the demon was sent for her and would not stop until she was dead. Even as she continued to scramble away, throwing whatever came to hand, Sorcha pummeled it, cutting with her hooves.

:Run, Milla. Run. Get to the Palace. Tell them everything.: Sorcha's demand was so commanding that Milla could only obey. Her Companion stopped the demon from following, renewing her attack on the creature, even as its claws sliced her open, her hindquarters more red than white now.

Milla ran as hard and as fast as she could, leaving a faint trail of blood behind her. She sprinted through the woods, ignoring her wounded side. She had to get back to the trade road. That was her only hope. Sorcha would meet her there. Eventually. Milla refused to think about her Companion losing the fight with demon.

But, even as she denied the thought she would not think, she felt Sorcha reach out to her with love and regret. *:I'm sorry Chosen, this is the only way. It's . . . too strong.:* With that, there was tremendous noise behind her that made her stumble against a tree. She clung to its trunk, the bark digging in, as the forest grew silent around her.

The silence was also in her mind. Where once Orun had once been . . . and then Sorcha . . . that comforting presence of another, there was nothing. Nothing at all. Milla was completely alone for the first time in her life. Tears streamed down her face. She made no sound except to gasp for air. For a long time, Milla stayed like that, not moving or seeing.

Then she ran.

The only thing that kept her moving through the pain and the grief was her unspoken promise to Sorcha to live long enough to tell the people at the Palace what she knew. It was her last duty in this unforgiving world. Then she would join her brother and Companion in death. For now, she would keep moving until she could move no more.

Hours later, she was back on the trade route, walking and holding her injured side. She didn't look where she was going. Just put one foot in front of the other in time to the beating of her heart and the throbbing of her wound. Milla didn't realize when her steps faltered, then stopped. She swayed for a moment, already unconscious as she crumpled to the ground.

"By the Gods, girl! What happened?"

The voice was far away, above Milla. Then she was scooped up in strong arms and moved to someplace inside. Vaguely aware that she was lying on something more comfortable than the ground, she opened her eyes.

Above her, a concerned face with dark eyes hovered. The man had long black hair, a short dark beard, and a small nose. Above him was the canvas roof of a wagon. "Girl?"

Milla didn't respond. She just looked around. The wagon appeared to belong to a minstrel who played a lute but also did some tinker's work. There were small tools and pots hanging up and a lute case in one corner. The wagon was big enough to have a small stool and workbench in the back. She guessed she was lying on his pallet.

A sudden flare of pain brought her attention back to the stranger. He had peeled back her bloodsoaked, partly dried shirt to reveal the two long gashes in her side. He sat back on his heels with a whistle. "What happened, girl?"

Without waiting for an answer, he turned and rummaged in a bag, pulling out needle and thread. Looked at her again, put them back, and pulled out strip of white cloth. "I'm not much of a healer. Maybe I can get you to one so's you don't scar too bad." He began bandaging her with gentle hands.

The pain was welcome. It meant she was still alive enough to complete her duty. ". . . Milla."

"Hmm?"

"My name is Milla."

"Garth." His fingers worked quickly to bind her. "Where you headed?"

"The Palace. Haven."

One shaggy eyebrow raised in surprised query. "'Cause of this?" He touched the bandage.

The grief of loss overwhelmed her in an instant and tears sprang to her eyes. Suddenly, she was sobbing as Orun and Sorcha's deaths hit her again with renewed strength. Then Garth's arms were around her, holding her to him. He rocked her back and forth, murmuring nonsense words into her hair.

"They killed my brother. They tore him apart. I felt it." Milla sobbed all the more into the man's shoulder, and the story poured out of her in fits and leaps. The birthday party. Being Chosen. The darkness hunting them. Orun and Torin's sacrifice to no avail. Then, finally, Sorcha's sacrifice as she ran.

The whole while, Garth held and rocked her as if he were her father. "Twins," he marveled, his voice soft and triumphant. "Chosen twins. That explains it. I didn't understand before."

Something about the tone of his voice frightened Milla, and she reached out to touch his mind. She recoiled from the touch. His mind was shielded in a way she had never felt before. They were blood-fed shields, feeling very much like the *wyrsa* had felt when they attacked. Milla's stomach roiled as ice flowed through her veins.

"I wonder if the Death Bell tolled for him."

Milla began to struggle, understanding too late that the darkness had come for her after all. Garth's grip tightened, trapping her against him. She never saw the magical dagger that flashed in the wagon's scant light before he plunged it into her back. He held her, tilting her back to watch her face as the life drained from it.

"I wonder if it will toll for you."

Nwah
Ron Collins

All Nwah knew was that she was alone, so very alone, and that her pain felt like fire; that she was lying under a thicket she had crawled into long ago, a thicket that smelled of green wood and mint and the overpowering stench of her wounds; and that more than anything else, she wanted all her suffering to be over.

In other words, Nwah knew only that she wanted to die.

Then she saw the boy.

He was maybe ten years old, and barefoot. He waved a crooked tree branch in front of him like a sword, and he wore a tunic and green trousers that were dirty and thin.

She growled and showed him her teeth.

:Go away,: she said.

But once the boy saw Nwah was no danger, he bent closer instead.

"Who do we have in there?" he asked.

The point of his branch smelled of her blood, and Nwah decided he must have poked her, probably to see if she was still alive. She tried to get up, but her hip was a blood-clotted mass of agony. What had happened? What had she done?

Then she felt the raw, gnawing scrub of loss deep inside her, like a hole where her heart and her innards and her mind had been torn away. It felt as though she were missing an organ, missing a color inside, a piece of herself that she could not touch.

She whimpered.

:Please,: she begged the boy, thinking that perhaps he would kill her now. *:Please.:*

The stick ruffled her shoulder, but Nwah just lay there, her head pressed hard to the ground. She heard a pack mouse as it pushed its nose through dry peat in search of fungus or maybe a beetle or a worm. The scent of the mouse was like a dagger to the gut. She imagined the taste of blood. She gave a slow blink. Tired. So tired. Ants crawled through her fur and dug into her wound. The ground wavered, the edges of her sight faded to a tunnel.

The boy seemed to take off his tunic—a dirty bit of cloth it was, too—but Nwah couldn't concentrate hard enough to follow him.

:Taking his shirt off,: she thought. Boys were so silly. Not like Rayn.

She closed her eyes. The strongest part of her, the part she thought of as her intuition (but was so much more than that), rose up beyond herself, watching as the boy pulled her from the brambles and slid her onto his tunic. The sight scared her. The sensation made her wobbly. Her senses became fully engaged, but she felt nothing as she watched him work. She was nearly his size, she thought, as he dragged the corner of his tunic to slide her along the ground.

Then a dark tint came from the edge of her vision, and she felt more tired than she had ever felt before. She had two last thoughts before the darkness fell completely over her.

Who, she wondered, *is Rayn?*

And why did the mere thought of her make Nwah's entire body throb with anguish?

Upon coming to consciousness, Nwah's first thought was that she would give her first litter for a single tongue of cool water. She was burning up from the inside, and the light of the sun was in her eyes. She heard a heavy scraping. Felt ground slip below her. Voices blurred, conversation came from nowhere. Her body bumped on something, the pain was white hot.

Then:

"That there's a *kyree,* Kade. See the wolf head? See how it's like a cat at the back?"

"I know what a *kyree* is, Pa."

"This one's gettin' ta be a biggun, too. Maybe fifteen, far as I kin tell. Maybe more. Where was it?"

"On over past the trail on the hill."

"Pretty far clip."

"Can I keep her, Pa? You won't have ta do a thing. I'll take care of her."

"Not up ta me."

"What do you mean?"

"*Kyree* choose their own, son."

"How's that?"

"Got no clue. I jus' tend ground, you know? Maybe you go ask that teacher your mum's so fond a. Maybe she kin tell ya. Surprised this one's not already matched." Nwah felt a boot move her paw. "Course, it looks 'bout dead to me."

"I'll take care of her, Pa. She'll be fine. First thing I say,

though, is ta stop calling her 'it.' I figure a *kyree* wants ta
be called right as well as anyone."

"You're right, boy. I'm sure you're right."

In the quiet that followed, despair fell over Nwah
again. The fire in her hip was fierce, but the pain inside
hurt even worse. It was a deep gash that echoed from
places she couldn't imagine. It felt hotter than the sun
beating down, like a roasting oven, like an oven in a
smithy shop. What had she done to deserve this? Why was
she still here?

The man's voice came again. "Take her on back, then.
Find a place in the shack. Clean that leg up good, or she's
gonna lose it."

"Thanks, Pa."

Then ground slipped under her and the world faded
away once again.

Nwah could tell the boy's mum didn't like her.

"That thing's got the mange," the mum said as she
peered down.

Nwah gave a low growl, but the boy rested his hand on
her head to calm her. Kade. Nwah remembered the boy's
name was Kade. How did she know that? She couldn't say.

He knelt beside her and twisted water from a cloth to
flow it gently over her wound. He had no shirt on and was
again barefoot. She smelled animals—a mule, chickens,
and some pigs. They seemed to be in a shelter made of
rough lumber. The ground was dirt, but Nwah was lying
on a ramshackle nest made of cloth and straw. The water
burned at first, but eventually it soothed, and the boy's
touch helped settle her down. His touch brought her a
new image, too—a young woman. It made her cringe,
though she didn't know why.

Nwah peered at him through the corner of her bloated eyes.

Who was this boy?

"She'll be fine," Kade said. "I'm givin' her a bath with the tender leaves every hour."

"*Giving*," his mum said. "There's a 'g' there at the end. 'Giving.' Just because your father's stubborn streak has us living in the middle of nowhere doesn't give you cause to speak without a civilized tongue."

"Sorry, mum."

"I swear you waste more time with those critters than's good for you."

"I like critters," the boy said as he rubbed Nwah's back.

"A *kyree*'s different from others, though," the mum said. "You need to fix it up soon as you can. We don't need Hawkbrothers or other such folks sniffing around here."

The woman leaned in.

Nwah sensed there was friction here, something almost adversarial between the mum and her son that she intuitively didn't feel existed with the boy and his father.

"Wonder what someone would give for her?" the mum said.

"I'm not selling Nwah," Kade said. He put his body between her and his mum. "Pa said I could keep her."

Nwah's ears perked at the sound of her name.

:*How do you know my name?*: she asked, but the boy gave no sign he heard her.

Mum straightened, then shook her head. "So you've gone and named her?"

"Sure," he said.

"Well. I've got better things to worry about than a half-dead animal. We'll speak of it later."

She walked away, which was fine by Nwah.

*   *   *

Kade worked on her later that afternoon and again in the evening. Each time, he soaked her legs with a concoction that smelled of goldenseal and mint and of something else that was so unique but so slight that even Nwah's sense of smell couldn't place it. The boy hummed as he worked. The tune seemed to fill the entire space of the shack, and it filled another place, too—when the boy hummed, Nwah didn't feel the pain inside as deeply as she had before.

:Are you a healer?: she asked him once, though in truth she didn't know how she understood the word "healer."

Kade didn't answer, of course. And in some way Nwah found that his silence hurt her. He was comforting. He was warm. It just felt like she should be able to talk with him, but he did not respond.

And each time Kade left, Nwah found she could not quite remember the melody he had been humming, and each time he left, the deep ache returned to brand her with its fire.

Nwah did not know who (or what) Kade was, but she liked him. He fed her soft food. He made her feel better. He brushed her with strokes that made her think of her mother.

"Your coat is quite nice with all the burrs and brambles out of it," he said to her once.

She tried to Mindspeak with him a few more times, and once he paused at a comment she made about his mum, but that was all there was to that.

His fingers were gentle as they worked her muscles. Gentle, yet firm. His treatments left her relaxed and dozing. It was as if he summoned a river of calmness, as if time stopped when he arrived and started again only when he left. And when he did leave, voices assaulted her, speaking in nightmarish whispers that echoed in places where no one else could ever be.

Useless . . . they said.

Got the mange . . .

Not good enough to make a coat . . .

And somehow, despite Kade's reassuring touch, Nwah knew they were right. She deserved to be punished, deserved to be whipped.

She would never walk again.

She was Mind-mute.

She had this black acid inside her that reeked with thoughts of fear and death, of blood and the venomous ache of eternal loneliness.

She was broken.

She was a waste of the boy's time.

Nwah could neither imagine a future nor remember the past. Perhaps that was best. Perhaps knowing her past would be too ghastly. But *not knowing* was a cancer. *Not knowing* left her free to imagine, and during the moments she lay alone in this nest of straw, Nwah's mind concocted things that grew more horrible every hour. It was these times, when the pain was the worst and the voices their most sinister, that Nwah would put a foreleg into her mouth and bite down, bringing the grinding pain she knew she deserved to suffer.

She wished Kade had just left her to die.

:Yes,: she said to the voices at these times. *:Yes, I am damaged,:* she said to the vacuous pain. *:Yes, I am waste.:*

And the voices grew stronger still.

*   *   *

A few days later, Nwah was amazed to find she could walk again.

The sensation was remarkable, standing tenuously, awkwardly, afraid to step forward but unable to stop herself.

She was stiff, and she had a new pattern to her gait. She could not run. She was even appalled at the momentary lightheadedness she felt at merely making it across the floor and back. She was supposed to be injured, supposed to be in despair. But she had thought her legs were damaged beyond use, and now . . . now she looked at Kade with a deeply profound respect that she could not deny.

The next day, the mum came to the shack along with a man.

The man was tall and gangly, wearing riding clothes and the gnarly, black half-beard of one used to traveling. He smelled of having missed the wash rag for several days, and he struck Nwah as dangerous, though she could not say why. There was just something cold in his gaze, something sinister. Her ears turned toward him, and the fur on her back stood up. She looked for Kade, but the boy was out, probably helping his father.

:Who are you?: she said as she flicked her tail, bared her teeth, and gave a low growl of warning.

The man merely stood there, pulling his beard and assessing Nwah as though she were a sack of grain.

"Ugly, even for a *kyree*," the man replied.

Nwah growled again. The voice seemed . . . familiar.

"I'm thinking she's worth as much as the sword," Kade's mum replied.

"Don't see it. Can't hardly walk, right?"

"The boy says she'll be fine in time."

"Tell you what. Give me the *kyree*, and I'll send Poy-thin and his boys your way. They're always looking for someone who'll pay gold for the things they pick up along the way. You pay for the blade in coin, and if you give me the animal I'll tell 'em you pay well and you keep things on the quiet. Once your name spreads, you'll have more business than you can bear. Not a bad deal for a half-dead animal."

The mum pursed her lips. "Throw in a knife for the boy?"

The man smiled. "I see why you're so good at this."

She shrugged. "He'll probably find another critter to-morrow."

The man slammed the gate open and came for her.

Nwah stood, but her body responded too slowly.

Kade had fenced Nwah in so she wouldn't get into trouble. She didn't like it, but wasn't recovered enough to see that it made much of a difference, nor was she recovered enough to *want* to leave—though that time was coming sooner than she had ever thought possible. Now, though, she wished she could have moved away earlier.

The man hefted her up by the scruff of her neck. Pain of the movement bit into her hind-parts, and she gave a wounded yelp.

"Come on, then," the man said, groaning with her weight.

It was the groan that did it.

The sound of it struck her like a whip. She had heard it before. She flashed on his eyes then, and the thickness of his arms, and she flashed on other things, too—other men, the sounds of footsteps and voices.

She twisted to get his arm, but the man was too quick and too strong. He pulled her along while she squealed and tried to nip at him. He dragged her until they came to a wagon. No. Not *a* wagon, *the* wagon, the one with the front wheel on the right that angled so strangely. She remembered the grating sound it made as it moved. She saw the dark marks, and she smelled the blood that stained its deck. An image of Rayn came over her then, standing tall, her hair tied back, a blade in her hand as the men attacked.

Rayn!

She felt the power of truth as *everything* snapped back in place.

Rayn, the warrior. Rayn, her Mind-pair.

This man had killed her, this man who now threw Nwah into the cage of rusting steel he had loaded onto the back of the wagon, then slammed the door and threw the lock-bar down, this man who then turned to another part of the wagon and gave Kade's mum a package that was long and thin and covered by a soft cloth, a package the mum rolled open to reveal a sword blade that gleamed in the late morning sun.

Nwah growled and pressed a paw against the steel bars, widening her nostrils to take in the blade's cold scent. Her tail flicked against her back. Nwah remembered Rayn's first day with the weapon—saw images of her dancing with it, performing intricate patterns, slicing melons and stabbing straw-filled targets, twirling it above her head as she came to new positions.

"It's a fine blade," the mum said.

"Worth a pretty bit more than a broken *kyree*."

She looked at Nwah.

Nwah growled again.

"Yes, it is," she said as she pulled a bag of coins from inside her apron.

It was too much for Nwah to bear. She gave a howl, a sound that was long and drawn out, full of pain and of longing, and full of all the words she wanted so badly to speak aloud, but would still never have been enough to describe her torment.

She remembered it all now.

She remembered every moment.

She remembered the pairing.

Rayn's daring had saved Nwah and her sister, protecting them from a Hawkbrother raid. Nwah's mother struggled over which of her pups would be the pair-match, but Nwah had been steadfast. Rayn was hers, and she was Rayn's. It was something she felt as deeply as life itself. She had been overwhelmed when Rayn had agreed. The moment of pairing was bliss, something deeper than being together, deeper than family, deeper even than love.

She remembered the next day, seeing the glow of the sun on Rayn's skin as Nwah padded along beside her, feeling the pair-match settle. It was like the day of her first hunt, only many times over. Her chest filled out, and she could smell lilacs and alumroot, briar and the wild leeks that grew all over the forest. She felt Rayn breathing as if it were her own breath. Rayn's passion was like the warmth of a full den. Their link smelled of that passion, that sense of being that permeated her every movement. Her pair-mate smelled bold. That's what Nwah thought. Rayn was bold. Rayn walked with strong, powerful steps, and she sang as they traveled.

Rayn came from a place named Oris, where she

promised she would take Nwah someday. :*It's a sleepy land, though,*: she said with a sardonic smile. :*Nothing to do but chase mice and rats.*: She told Nwah she had always wanted more, wanted to see things, wanted to know what life was really about. That was why she left Oris, she said. That was why she was here.

Nwah had been feeling these very things, lying in her den at night with her littermates, pushing and pawing, growing older and bigger and ready to go someplace, yet not having any place to go. She was due for better things, Nwah had thought.

She was born for a bigger fate.

She remembered Rayn taking her to a smithy's shop to have the blade made.

The whole place glowed orange and white, and it was so heavy with heat that Nwah thought her eyes might boil away. It smelled sharp and dirty, an odor so overwhelming it made her hair stand up. Blades of every kind hung from the walls—hammers, and pikes, and daggers, and scythes, and every other implement of possible terror she could imagine. She kept her ears peeled back, walking beside Rayn in stiff strides, lifting each paw high and placing it delicately, just so.

:*What are you doing?*: Rayn asked.

:*Watching for traps,*: she replied.

Rayn chuckled.

:*You're a silly* kyree,: she said as she ran her hand between Nwah's ears.

Even Rayn's touch had been hot.

She remembered everything about their final trip.

Everything.

:I don't like it,: she had said. *:The trail to Katashin'a'in is lined with Hawkbrothers and renegade clans.:"*

:I know you don't understand,: Rayn replied. *:But it's Stefan. If it's important to him, it's important to me.:*

Rayn spoke the truth, of course. She always spoke the truth; it was part of what made Nwah love her. Nwah felt Rayn's attachment to Stefan, a young man her age, though not from her same litter. Rayn had grown up with Stefan, had shared games with him, and now Stefan had come into ownership of a locket or gem of some type, and he planned to sell it in the grassland markets. He had asked Rayn for her sword as an escort. The strength of that request felt no different than if Nwah's own pup-mates had called upon her.

:Then it is important to me, too,: she finally said.

With that, they were committed to provide security for Stefan's trip through the Pelagiris, over the border of the Dhorisha plains, and into Katashin'a'in. Nwah still worried about the trail, but she had to admit the idea of a land with so few trees sounded remarkable. She wondered what it would look like. She wondered if a *kyree* would find it possible to run forever in a place like that.

Rayn and Stefan hoped their little wagon would be left alone as they traveled   and they agreed they would appear to be newly wedded, if necessary (though that made them both laugh).

They set out, Stefan driving, Rayn beside him, her blade stored behind her. The wagon's flatbed was loaded with pieces of run-down furniture, rugs, and bundles of fabric—all of it a ruse to support their story. Stefan's trinket was wrapped in one of those blankets.

Nwah trotted alongside the wagon, enjoying the coolness of the morning. It had been a few days since she had

run at pace, and the movement made her feel close to
Urtho himself. She remembered her mother and a time
they stood together on a cliffy ridge to stare at a water-
fall in the distance. An owl had soared by, and Nwah had
wondered how it would feel to fly.

:Probably not so good,: her mother replied. *:I can't
imagine not having the ground under my paws.:*

Trotting beside the creaking wagon, Nwah found herself raising her head. She had not responded to her
mother that day because, unlike her mother, she *could*
imagine flying. She could imagine many things, actually,
many things that she knew by then that other good *kyree*
most definitely did not imagine at all. She remained silent that day on the cliffs because she had felt foolish, or
out of place, as if this ability to dream was somehow
wrong. But she remembered then, as she ran alongside
the wagon, that the idea that she was special gave her
such a sense of power that she thought she might well be
able to run forever.

The robbers came the second day, just as the sun was
fading into the dusky clouds. She should have sensed
them earlier, but rather than concentrating on the road,
Nwah's attention had been drawn by a hare out in the
brush of a clearing, and she had been following a drag-
onfly as it buzzed from its nest in a nearby pond. The
forest had so much to see, and she felt Rayn's presence,
and she felt so safe and so complete that she had let
herself go to places she rarely allowed herself to enjoy.

:Hide!: Nwah said.

But it was too late. Men blocked the trail, more filled
in behind.

"What do you have in the back?" the leader said. It
was the man—Nwah pictured him clearly now.

"Nothing but our homestuffs," Stefan replied.

"We'll just see about that."

Hackles rose, and the fur at the back of her neck bunched up. :*Get them away from us*,: Rayn said, throwing off her cover and reaching to her blade as she stood.

Screams came and steel flashed in the gloaming. The smell of blood mixed with sweat. A blade scored her hind leg. Rayn's voice rose, giving orders as she hacked at the thieves who were pulling Stefan away. Nwah leaped to defend Rayn's back, Mind-speaking warnings of men attacking. The crushing blow of a hammer struck her leg, and Nwah fell.

And as Nwah fell, a blade entered Rayn's side.

Angled upward.

To pierce her heart.

Rayn's face froze.

Then the man twisted the blade, and Nwah remembered the greatest pain of all. The pain of ripping. The pain of tearing.

The pain of true loss.

Nwah's howl rose, echoing across the land.

"You best leave before the boy gets back," Kade's mum said.

The man agreed, and got in the wagon.

As they rolled away, Nwah snarled at the man, her heart pounding. She crashed her body against the cage rails again and again, roaring, howling, spitting, reaching her claws out to the man who sat just out of reach. She growled and whined. She scratched at the door until her claws bled. She remembered Rayn's Mind-speak, how it filled her, how it became one with the very essence of her thoughts.

She would kill this man.

She would rip his throat out.

Her injuries had weakened her, though, and a lack of real food had left her drained. She had no stamina, no energy, and raw anger provides power for only so long. By the time they came to camp, she was spent and unable to even lift her head. The muscles of her hind legs burned, and her paws were torn and raw. Still, she growled a low warning and whined as men surrounded the wagon and lifted her cage to the ground.

"Quiet up, ya mutt," one of the men said.

Nwah showed him her teeth. *:I will kill you,:* she replied.

The man poked a blade at her.

She gathered every bit of anger and fury she had left, and threw herself once again at the bars. The cage rattled and crashed as it fell over to its side.

The man returned. "I said ta quiet up!"

He drew a club from his belt loop. The door to the cage swung open, and the weapon caught her alongside the face. Nwah fell back, whimpering. The weapon struck again, bruising her shoulder first, then crashing against the side of her head, bringing blood and the heat of sharp pain.

"Stop it!" the leader said. "No one will buy a dead *kyree*."

"She's got the howling crazies," her attacker said, wheezing with his labor. His stench was overwhelming.

"Looks like you quieted her down enough."

He slammed the door shut, and took some glee in tossing the cage back upright.

They left Nwah alone for the rest of the night, but she didn't have the energy to fight any more. Her body ached. Her jaw was badly swollen, and her paws felt burned. She lay on the bare floor of her tiny cage and cried, softly this time, trying desperately to avoid making a noise that might bring the hammer again, yet unable to keep the river of emotion from flowing. And the voices inside came, too, growing louder and deeper as the sun settled and the darkness crept over the camp.

This time, when she put her paw to her mouth, her jaw hurt so much that she didn't have to bite down to feel pain.

She was done. It was over. She felt it in her wounds, and in her throbbing skull, and in her ribcage that flared with every breath. She tasted it in the blood that seeped over her tongue. She was going to die. Here, in this dirty cage of a band of robbers, Nwah was going to die.

There was a time, of course, when she had wanted that, a time when she would have welcomed it. Now that she was going to do it, though, actually going to die—and now that she remembered all the events of her life— Nwah felt nothing but deep, mind-numbing sadness. She had hoped for so much more.

She began speaking to the darkness, then. Almost random words at first. But she found that when she filled her head with these words, the black whispering quieted, so she continued.

:*I was born fifteen years ago,*: she said to nobody. :*My mother was of the Pelagiris. My father ran off before the litter came.*:

She spoke about her mother and about her pup-mates. She told about learning to hunt, and explained how to stay silent in the woods. She told of her first moments running, and of the time Dair got caught in the poisonous vines down in the valley. She told everything she knew, perhaps everything she would ever know. She spoke her words even if no one else could hear them, because she wanted her story, and Rayn's story, to be told at least one time before they were both gone.

:You're going to be fine,: a voice came through the distant fog.

Nwah sat up with a start. It was dark. Her jaw throbbed and her legs ground bone against bone. She caught a familiar scent and saw a familiar outline in the shadow of the cage, moonlight gleaming off his dark hair.

:Kade?:

:I'm here.:

Her legs shook as she stood. Despite herself, her heart surged at the sight of him, and when he reached his hand through the bars to stroke her coat, she breathed a shuddering sigh of relief.

:You can hear me?:

:Yes.:

:How?:

He shrugged. *:I fix critters. Figured it was just a matter a time.:*

:How did you find me?:

:Wasn't hard. Just followed the path of that power you got in you.:

:Power? I don't have any power.:

:You don't need to hide it from me, girl. You've got magic in you as strong as the Mage that came through a couple months back. Don't lie to me and say you don't know it.:

And she did.

For all her life, Nwah had felt there was something more to herself than others seemed to let on, something special. She had kept it hidden from her mother and her kin, even kept it away from Rayn—afraid her pair-mate would laugh at her as fanciful, or worse, just think Nwah to be a flawed *kyree*. But inside, Nwah had always felt special. She had always felt that she should be able to do things others didn't.

Could Kade be right? Could it be that she had Mage skill?

:I don't know what to do with it,: she said.

It felt awkward to admit it.

:That's why I'm staying with you. I wanna see what it is you got.:

:Staying with me?:

:If you'll have me. We can find someone who can teach you about what you've got. I can help you.:

It took Nwah a moment to understand that Kade wanted to travel with her, to leave his mum and pa and stay with her. And it took Nwah a moment to understand that "if you'll have me" meant he was subjecting himself to her desire, giving her a choice. Those words meant she had value to him.

:You're still a pup.:

:Old enough to be out here now.:

:What of your mum and pa?:

:She's not my real mum. And Pa will make do for now.:

Kade smiled and Nwah leaned against the pressure of his hand as he rubbed her bruised spine. Only the fact that she was afraid to wake the robbers kept her from moaning out loud. She could feel him, too, feel him with a connection that was different from how she had felt

Rayn. This new connection was distant but there, like the smell of a buck out in the woods. Kade would never own her the way Rayn had, and Nwah would never own Kade the way she had Rayn. But she felt him, and the friction of their connection made her heart soar as it hadn't since before the attack.

Nwah jerked as Kade touched her jaw.

:*We need to get you out a here before daybreak, or we'll both be in heaps a trouble. Hold tight. Don't make a clatter.*:

Kade turned the bar slowly, then slid it out of the guide. The gate eased open and Nwah limped out. Her legs shook with the effort, and her muscles ached from her beating, but she could bear it. Indeed, in some ways she felt stronger for the pain, stronger for having withstood it, for having come through.

And she was free.

Nwah smelled the aroma of the dew-covered nighttime, and she heard the sounds of a forest that was forever alive. But mostly, she smelled the man who had killed Rayn, and as she stood there in the darkness, her anger rose, and her lips peeled back.

The man's chest rose in his sleep.

She instinctively lowered herself and stepped toward him, her mouth slavering with a sudden, feral hunger at the idea of sinking her teeth into his throat. Her eyes drew down, and she could see him even better in the shadows. She flicked her tail and slunk forward.

:*Stop,*: Kade said.

He stepped between her and the men.

:*Pa says ya shouldn't do nothin' ya might regret.*:

:*I wouldn't regret it.*:

:*Ain't right to go killing men while they're asleep no*

matter what they done. Besides, everyone will name you
rabid, and they'll hunt you till you're dead.:

Nwah looked at the men as they slept. She understood Kade's advice, but her need for vengeance still
burned against her.

:I can't leave them be.:

:Pa says there's ways to deal with this kind a trouble.:

:And those are?:

Kade shrugged. *:Turn Hawkbrothers onto them,*
maybe. Or the Shin'a'in. I hear they got their own sense a
justice. Or maybe you'll find something to do with that
magic of yours. I don't know. We can find someone to
teach you, you know? Let's leave while we still can,
though, and get enough distance between us that no one
can chase us down.:

He moved back, then, giving her access to the men if
she so chose that direction.

She looked at Kade, this boy who was ten years old
but who seemed so wise, and she sensed that he was
pleading with her now. Hoping, suggesting, but not forcing. He was a healer—she knew that even if he didn't
know it yet himself. And she was, apparently, a Mage
even if she didn't fully believe it yet. They were going to
be quite a pair. Not a pair like her and Rayn. Nothing
could be like her and Rayn ever again. But they would
be a team.

Yes.

They would be quite a team.

Nwah rose up then, and took a breath of nighttime air
thick with clover and peat.

:All right,: she said. *:We'll do it your way.:*

And they turned together, Kade walking as silently as
she did, waiting for her as she limped along, slipping

together into the forest, fading deeper and deeper into the night.

And as they slipped through the woods together, Nwah thought about what a remarkable night it was to be alive.

Spun Magic
Kristin Schwengel

A cacophony of birdcalls emptied the *ekeles* as the whole of k'Veyas crowded toward the northern entrance to the Vale. Stardance's own *ekele* was close by, so she was near the front of the throng, pushed forward next to the Clan Elders.

"Who would be crazy enough to venture out into *this*?" Dayspring's muttered question, asked of no one in particular, echoed her thoughts. Several of the other Elders nodded agreement as he spoke. The icy rain inside the Vale was unpleasant enough, but it was better than the late-season blizzard raging beyond. Six years after the last of the Mage Storms, the k'Veyas Heartstone hadn't *quite* gained enough power to keep the weather fully tempered.

Before anyone else could speak, a snow-covered k'Veyas scout crossed the Veil into the clearing, followed by three exhausted *dyheli* bearing three equally spent riders. *Hertasi* immediately swarmed around, helping the riders dismount and wrapping them with warm blankets. A k'Veyas *dyheli* led the staggering mounts away to join the rest of the herd, which had taken refuge from the storm inside the Vale.

"Miel found their birds. They'd missed the markers in

the drifts and were far off the forest paths." The scout shook melting snow from his head and shoulders, and Stardance blinked. He'd been so covered with white, she hadn't even recognized Nightblade's narrow features and black hair. "They're from k'Lissa." His glance flickered over to Stardance as though he had known where she stood, and she caught a glimpse of something she couldn't name in his dark eyes. Worry, or perhaps anxiety, tinged with something she didn't recognize.

The aging Winternight, the most senior k'Veyas Elder, stepped forward, the rest of the white-haired Elders behind him. "Welcome, friends. Whatever brought you to us through this blizzard can surely wait while you restore yourselves. When you are ready, let the *hertasi* know, and they will gather the Council." The *hertasi* took over, guiding the visitors to the nearest of the guest-*ekeles*.

Stardance slipped away to her own *ekele*, her thoughts racing. She could only guess that their coming had something to do with her, since her father had been from k'Lissa. From Nightblade's odd expression, she assumed he thought the same, even if the strangers hadn't mentioned her. Her thoughts drifted to the bedraggled visitors, trying to remember their features. One was nearly her own age, but had one of the older two shared her unusual gray-green eyes? It was years since she had last seen her father, shortly after her mother's passing, when she had already begun living among the *hertasi* with Triska, her adoptive mother. It had been so long that now she couldn't even guess if he was one of the three who had come to k'Veyas.

It was only a few candlemarks later that one of the *hertasi* tapped gently at the entrance to her *ekele*. This was one of Triska's adult children, who had assigned herself to care for Stardance after the young girl's adoptive *hertasi* mother had died in the Mage Storms.

"The Council is gathering with the visitors, and Winternight has asked for you to join them," Kikara said, then vanished back into the undergrowth.

Stardance pulled out her rain cloak once more and hurried to the Council chambers. The summons didn't surprise her, even though she was not part of the Council. The visitors must have asked for her. They were from k'Lissa, and had traveled for days through this unseasonable weather. She could think of few reasons to do so that didn't somehow involve her.

Fortunately, she was not the last to arrive at the Council. A few minutes later, two others pushed aside the inner draperies at the chamber entrance. Silverheart, the Healing Adept and Stardance's tutor, entered and sat on one side of her. The Mage Windwhisperer sat on her other side, placing his hand on her shoulder with an encouraging squeeze. She gave him a grateful glance. Since the Mage Storms and Triska's death, Windwhisperer had seen to it that she had remained a part of the Clan rather than retreating in grief. His quiet support had often guided her, and his son, Nightblade, had occasionally taken on the role of an elder brother or guardian of a sort.

Winternight stepped forward, his pale features catching the light so that he seemed to glow against the darker wall behind him, commanding the attention of all without a single syllable. "So," he began, "the Council is assembled. Guests from k'Lissa, you may begin."

The oldest of the three stood and looked around the assembled k'Veyas, his eyes lingering on Stardance.

Although all three had been garbed in practical travel gear, he now wore the much more flamboyant robes of a Mage, a dark red embroidered with golden flames that seemed to flicker with his movement.

"I am Firewind k'Lissa," he said, and gestured to the two scouts. "These are Sunsong and Icewing." He paused, his pale green eyes once again shifting over to Stardance, who struggled to maintain her neutral expression. This was her father, although she would not have recognized him. She had been barely six summers old when she had last seen him, and then only briefly before he returned to k'Lissa and his duties there. She didn't remember much of his visit, only that she had not wanted to leave Triska and that the k'Veyas Council had supported her.

"We have come with a plea for aid from Deermoon, our Healer-Mage, who is known to Silverheart." Silverheart gave a brief nod, concern edging her soft features as the assembled k'Veyas turned to look at her.

"He is ill, with a strange sort of fatiguing illness. It has not responded to the Healers' efforts, although they do not think it is fatal. But he is too weak to do the work of the Tayledras, and none of his apprentices are yet strong enough or sufficiently trained to do so. Our other Mages do what they can, but it goes very slowly. It is our hope that one among your Healing-Mages would be able to return with us to assist Deermoon." He sat, glancing again at Stardance as he did.

Winternight was the first to speak. "Is Deermoon expected to recover from this ailment? Will the k'Veyas visitor need to become a part of k'Lissa if he does not?"

"That would be the choice of the one who comes," Firewind replied, choosing his words carefully. "We would, of course, welcome a new member of the Clan, but we would be happy to have a visitor either until Deermoon recovers or until his apprentices are ready to take on the work. He has continued to teach, but he has not the strength of focus to both train his students and rebuild the network of magic. As for his recovery," Firewind gave a tiny shrug, "the Healers are vague. They cannot find or name the source of his weakness, and so they have no answer for it."

Winternight nodded. "We have heard your request and will consider how and if we might be able to honor it. Until the Council has decided, take your ease and recover from your journey."

Firewind smiled ruefully. "The weather was not nearly so foul as this when we left k'Lissa, or we would have waited. We were caught by it nearly exactly halfway between the two Vales, and too late to change direction to k'Onsoya. We decided that it was better to press on and get an answer than to struggle back home with nothing." He stood, as did the two scouts. "We will await your return summons." The three departed the Council chamber, a *hertasi* ready to lead them to the nearest hot spring soaking pools.

Winternight turned to Silverheart. "It should be obvious why k'Lissa came to us instead of k'Onsoya, whose Vale is a little closer to theirs. Stardance's father must be wanting her to return with them."

Silverheart, in turn, looked at Stardance, whose outward calm concealed a writhing mass of uncertainty. She gave her student an encouraging smile. "Deermoon and I studied together with a k'Treva Healer-Mage before we achieved Mastery. He is familiar with my style, which blended well with his, and would expect that any of my students would be equally compatible. Firewind would hope for one particular student."

"Stardance is by far the oldest and most advanced among your apprentices, and you have said she is nearly ready for her Mastery Trial," Dayspring said. "Can she be spared? Should she wait until she takes the Trial? Would any of your other students be capable of assisting k'Lissa?"

Stardance let the conversation among the Elders and the Mages carry on around her, her ears catching occasional fragments of debate over the skills of the apprentices. Her own thoughts drifted back to the stranger who was her father. What would he expect of her, if she were to go? Surely he would want her to stay in k'Lissa, among closer blood kin than she had in k'Veyas. Her mother had had no siblings, and her own parents had died of the same illness that had taken her. If Stardance recalled correctly, her father had children with a partner in k'Lissa, so she would have half-siblings. If she went, would she herself prefer to stay among them? The thought caused a knot to form in the pit of her stomach, as though her own body protested the idea. She glanced over at the statue-like form of Windwhisperer, who was listening to the other Elders, and brought her attention back to the discussion at hand.

The Council seemed to be divided, for several of the Elders resisted the idea of being without one of Silverheart's students, even for a few moons. The arguments went back and forth with no progress being made until Windwhisperer stood.

"It is clear that, among Silverheart's students, Stardance would be the best qualified to aid k'Lissa, even before she achieves Mastery. Perhaps we should ask what she prefers?" He sat, and the full attention of the Council focused on Stardance.

Stardance swallowed, then slowly stood, brushing her white-streaked russet hair back from her face so the Elders could read her eyes. "The longer that Deermoon is ill, the longer the magic around k'Lissa remains wild, which none of the Tayledras want. I am not . . . unwilling to assist them. If Silverheart believes me capable, and believes that k'Veyas will do well without me for a time," she took a deep breath, quelling the knot within her, "I will go." Nearly dizzy with anxiety, she took her seat once more.

Silverheart gave her a smile of approbation. "We will be well. Unlike Deermoon, I am at full strength, and the other apprentices are trained enough to work with me until your return."

After the Council had informed the visitors from k'Lissa of Stardance's decision, she kept herself apart from everyone, retreating to her *ekele*, or even to one of the unoccupied *hertasi* caves. She wanted neither a forced friendliness with Firewind nor a flurry of overwrought emotion from some of k'Veyas, as though she were leaving forever.

One of her *hertasi*, Triska's daughter, Kikara, helped her keep her secret solitude, understanding her continuing struggle with the decision she had made. The peace of the caves helped her think, allowing her to consider the balance of her duties to her Clan with her duties as a Tayledras. For Stardance, the latter now outweighed the former, the command from the Star-Eyed to Heal the broken magic of the world.

As soon as the unseasonable snows ended, Firewind

and the k'Lissa scouts began planning their return journey.

On the day they had chosen to depart, many of k'Veyas came to see Stardance off. Even Nightblade came up to her, giving her an awkward hug before pressing a small, cloth-wrapped object into her hands. "For your eighteenth summer," he muttered, his voice oddly hoarse. "Open it in k'Lissa."

She barely managed to keep from staring at him, mouth agape, as he turned and vanished down one of the paths, his dark gray goshawk soaring overhead. Staring after him, she finally shrugged, unable to find any explanation for his unusually curt manner.

Standing next to Stardance, Windwhisperer watched his son disappear, then gave her a quizzical glance before folding her into his arms for a warm farewell. "*Zhai helleva*, Stardance," he whispered.

"*Zhai helleva*," Stardance replied, tears springing to her eyes. It would be Windwhisperer and Silverheart that she would miss most, and she almost couldn't bear to pull herself out of his supporting hold. A shriek from a bondbird and a call of readiness from the others drew her away, although she didn't dare to meet Windwhisperer's brown eyes for fear of losing her fragile control.

Tucking Nightblade's strange gift into the pack on the back of her *dyheli*, Stardance mounted and joined the three k'Lissa, her father and the two scouts. Kir, her falcon bondbird, swooped down to her shoulder, and the four of them crossed the Veil, hunching against the colder air beyond the border.

The days of travel through the Pelagiris developed their own peculiar rhythm: cursory meals of travel rations supplemented by bondbird kills, sleeping in two small tents when they could not find caves near the marked paths for shelter. Her father tried to engage her in conversation, but Stardance was still aloof with him. Sunsong, the blond younger scout, was the only one with whom she found herself able to talk comfortably. Something about him reminded her of Nightblade, although he was open and cheerful where Nightblade was brooding, and that unnamed familiarity made things a little easier for her. Firewind appeared concerned, green eyes watching her with an uncertainty that seemed to sit ill with him, but she remained separate. She would not force herself into the shape of whatever daughter he might want her to be.

The cold had lessened, the last of the snow melting away as the small group made their final day's approach to k'Lissa Vale. Although she should have been made more comfortable by the improved weather, the increased birdsong, and the pale green spring growth coming up around them, Stardance felt ill at ease. She sensed there was something vaguely *wrong* around her. Even Kir was irritable, snapping and launching herself to the air when Stardance tried to stroke her banded breast-feathers, and the k'Veyas *dyheli* Stardance rode became skittish and unwilling to share Mindspeech. She would have asked to stop so she could sink her awareness deep into the earth to learn more, but her companions were moving ever faster, anxious to get back to their home.

Her father and the two scouts seemed to take no note of the strangeness she felt, nor did their bondbirds or their own *dyheli* seem affected. Was it only she who was bothered, and Kir and her *dyheli* were simply responding to her irritation?

Once their party passed through the Veil, Stardance barely managed to stifle her sigh. The pressure of *wrongness* greatly diminished, although she could still feel an echo of it. Whatever was happening, it was beyond the Veil, not within it, and relief flooded through her. Everyone knew about what k'Sheyna had faced before the Mage Storms, when their Heartstone had been manipulated by an Adept and had gone rogue. Even with the far more limited power that would have gathered in the k'Lissa Heartstone, Stardance knew she had neither the skill nor the strength to face such a disaster.

After a brief welcome from the Elders and Council of k'Lissa, a *hertasi* guided Stardance to one of the guest *ekeles*, where she began to unpack her gear and settle in. She would meet Deermoon and his apprentices in the morning, and she decided that then would be soon enough to explore the strange feeling in the earth. Opening one of the packs, her hand brushed the cloth-wrapped box from Nightblade, and she paused, then pulled it out.

Her actual birth date had passed while they had been traveling, and she had been secretly glad that her father made no mention of it. It didn't feel right to her to distinguish the day when she was away from k'Veyas, away from the friends who should have been with her. Although the Tayledras marked adulthood by one's developing skills and responsibilities, the Clans took every possible occasion for merriment, and the eighteenth year was sometimes celebrated on its own.

Curling up on the low couch below one of the windows, Stardance untied the leather strips and loosened the cloth wrapping. The slender box was intricately carved with flowing knots and spirals entwined with

leaves, and she took a moment to admire the craftsman-
ship before opening the lid.

Nestled in a carefully shaped pad was a delicate spindle, exactly the size she preferred to use, and she lifted it
out. Only then did she see what was embedded in the
weighted whorl near the top of the shaft, and tears
sprang to her eyes. The last time she had seen the cracked
amber disc, it had still been knotted on the leather cord
that Triska had always worn. A pale and grieving Winternight had shown it to her after the last Mage Storm, the
one that had caught Triska in a Change Circle and led to
her death. The spindle was clearly the work of one of the
hertasi artisans, so Nightblade must have asked them to
incorporate the pendant. She assumed that Kikara, Triska's eldest, would have kept it—and had been willing to
part with it.

Turning the spindle in her hands, she saw that the
hook at the top of the shaft linked into what looked like
a jumble of loops of twisted silver. When she held it up,
she saw that it was a chain with a post and loop from
which the spindle could hang. Hooked in that loop, the
spindle would spin freely, without a cord twisting or
knotting up on itself.

Stardance smiled, fond warmth at his thoughtfulness
filling her like an embrace from within. Although she
didn't need to, she liked to use a spindle when working
with the earth energies. It acted as a focus, making it easier for her to blend the threads of magic into a strong
line, but she would frequently need to interrupt her work
to untwist the physical spindle from whatever cord she
was using to hold it. Nightblade, who often assigned himself as her guard when she worked outside the Vale, must
have noticed her irritation and worked out this clever

solution. With the linked chain, she could start the spindle twirling and work with the magic without pausing. A subtle question nagged at the back of her mind, a flash of memory of the expression in Nightblade's dark eyes when he had pressed the box into her hands, but she couldn't connect the thoughts. Replacing the spindle back in the box, she set it on the center of the table and returned to her unpacking.

The *hertasi* guided Stardance to the stone workrooms where Deermoon and his apprentices had gathered. Entering the outer chamber, she eyed them in turn as they studied her. Silverheart had indicated that Deermoon was only a few years older than she, but his appearance was that of a much older man. Thin and worn, he seemed even more frail than Winternight, the most senior Mage and Elder of k'Veyas. His students, on the other hand, were quite a bit younger than Stardance, and they shifted in their seats as she took the open seat beside Deermoon.

"What is it that ails the earth here? How long has it been this way?" Stardance's question was blunt, and Deermoon let out a raspy chuckle, his hands twisting stiffly on the end of his walking stick.

"You are Silverheart's pupil, that is certain. She never used two words when one would do." He coughed, and Stardance's own Healing Gift recognized what the k'Lissa Healers had seen. His body did not seem truly ill but was suffering a deep exhaustion. Small wonder, then, that the Healers had been unable to provide more than temporary aid.

"We don't know either answer," he replied at last. "At some time in the last year or two, my work became more and more tiring, and I could not hold my focus for as long as I used to. I thought little of it when I noticed it, for I am no longer young. Instead, I concentrated on finding and training any Healing-talented Mages among k'Lissa. As I taught more, I went beyond the Veil to work less. When I did, I found it even more fatiguing, but again, did not think it unusual."

He paused, then shook his head. "It was always so easy to explain away the exhaustion as overwork, as distraction, as something simple. But now I've noticed that, in this last six-month, my students are tiring rapidly, and that their focus and control is less than it used to be. That was the first time I thought there might be something else behind this. With even the apprentices affected, the Healing work of the Tayledras is all but halted. Until we find what is causing this, we can make but little progress. K'Veyas is one of the closest Vales to us, and I know Silverheart better than the senior Healer-Mages of the others. It was logical to call upon her for aid, and Firewind supported the idea in the Council. Some wanted to go to k'Onsoya as well, but Firewind left first, as soon as there were signs of spring. When the weather turned so fierce, the Council decided to wait on his return. Now that you are here . . ." He shrugged. "The Council will likely wait to see if you are able to assist us before they ask for any other help."

Deermoon's mention that the apprentices had been weakened caught Stardance's attention. "Have any of the other Mages been affected, those who are not Healing-Mages, especially those who support your work? Even here in the Vale, I can feel the undertone of whatever it is, although the Veil mutes it. Though they do not draw on the Heartstone as once they did, do they notice the change? Or did it happen too gradually?"

Deermoon shook his head. "K'Lissa has never been noted for its great Mages—we mostly have skilled Masters. Your father is one of our few Adepts, and he has said nothing. Our Mages are very capable, but not sensitive to this subtle degree, which is partly why they are limited in reorganizing the threads of magic. Whatever this is, it has its greatest effect at the lowest level of the earth energies, and the dissolving of the great magics after the Mage Storms made this smaller change even less noticeable."

Stardance frowned at the mention of the storms. "Is it possible that this is something from the Mage-Storms themselves?"

Deermoon shook his head again, so firmly the feathers in his white braids fluttered. "I shouldn't think so. Why would something like this only appear now, years later, when all the other effects were so immediate? And would not other Clans or Outlander Mages be noticing this, if it were a broad effect of the Storms?"

Stardance sought other possibilities. "Might there be another Mage who is drawing on the lines of power, some sort of invader?" She would think the odds would be against something like that happening in k'Lissa, since k'Onsoya or even k'Veyas were closer to the edges of the Tayledras territories, but it was something to be considered.

"That is the most likely answer and what I suspect," Deermoon replied. "Such a Mage would have had to pass one of the other Vales unnoticed, but it is not impossible."

Stardance frowned, green eyes narrowing as she sorted through her options. "So. I will take some time to observe, first. Since I am newly come here, I should be less affected by this, and might be able to see what has gone wrong more readily. Until we can determine what is happening, and stop it if we can, I will not attempt to do anything with the earth energies. The last thing your Clan needs is another ill and exhausted Healing-Mage." *I think I'm in over my head*, she thought, her stomach knotting. *An Outland Mage capable of disturbing the earth energy around a Vale? Does Deermoon truly realize how serious this could be? Did Silverheart suspect it? Do they really expect an apprentice, a Journeyman, to be able to fix whatever has gone wrong here?*

Stardance began her study of the earth energy around k'Lissa from the carefully shielded Workroom. Sitting near the Heartstone, feeling its faint pulse of warmth, she sifted through the web of lines feeding it; a Journeyman could See the lines, even if she could not safely use them. Within the Veil, all was in order, but when her focus reached the border of the Veil, she detected a subtle shift, a fraying of the lines. In her own work, she would say that the lines had not been twisted securely enough and what held them together was beginning to loosen, but Deermoon's craft was different. Instead of the spun threads of magic that she produced, his lines had a sense of water to them. He created channels like riverbeds that led the droplets of energy into larger and larger rivulets.

The rippling of the magic outside of those courses seemed to be the strongest at the southern boundary of the Veil, so she left the Workroom. A *hertasi* appeared from the foliage beside her, and she asked him to guide her to that area. Kir flapped and soared overhead as they walked, familiar with her mistress' routines, even in this strange place. When Stardance found a sheltered seat just within the Veil, the falcon came to a nearby roost to wait, and the *hertasi* disappeared back down the path.

When she sank into Trance and opened herself to the earth, Stardance was glad she was still within the borders of the shielding Veil, for the strange blurring of the energy unsettled her. This close to it, she didn't have to strain her Mage Sense and could focus instead on the feel of the power. The hazy mist of magic seemed somehow confused, as though it wanted to flow to the Heartstone in the channels that Deermoon had so carefully crafted, but the stream of power wavered with another pull, like a lodestone from beyond the Veil.

It was this pull that Stardance now attempted to track, although she couldn't sense it directly herself. It was like chasing the wind without actually feeling it, knowing where it had been only by the movement of the leaves. She let her awareness drift, seeking the place where the power was most disordered and following that disorder farther into deeper unease and chaos, until she felt that she had placed it. To mark the spot, she let a tiny bit of her personal energy sink into the earth, trailing a spidersilk-fine strand of Power behind it, linked to her as she emerged from her Trance.

She stood and stretched, then moved back down the path toward the center of the Vale. Amberlight, the senior Elder of k'Lissa, had suggested she seek out Sunsong when she needed to go beyond the Veil. The scout could guide her through the physical surroundings of the k'Lissa territory while she followed that silvery thread. That bit of her personal magic was how they could find what was at the center of that muddle of energy—or find out if she needed to go still farther.

Only effort of will kept the contents of Stardance's stomach in their proper place. Now that she faced what was producing it, the *wrong* was so intense that she could barely keep her composure to study it.

:It feels like Blood Magic.:

Her eyes flicked over to the tree next to the one that concealed her. She could not see Sunsong's blond head, but she knew he was there. It was a good thing he had been chosen to assist her, because he could project Mindspeech to those who were not similarly Gifted, and she had practiced "thinking" back to him as they had moved through the trees toward the rocky outcropping on the southern edge of k'Lissa's cleared territory. They had started on the paths, but some instinct had led them to go up to the trees, "walking" from branch to branch.

:You know it?: She wasn't sure she wanted to know how.

:After the Storms, a scouting party came upon a lost and desperate Rethwellan Mage who had turned to it. I'm not that Gifted, but even I could feel the pain, the nasty stench to the Power she'd raised, when we interrupted her.: He didn't elaborate, and she didn't ask further, turning her attention back to the creature in front of the cave.

In appearance, it looked like a small basilisk with shimmering dark gray scales, all lizardlike torpor, but leaner, with longer legs. It seemed to be sunning itself, basking in the late spring sun, but something about it gave Stardance pause. This was no mere nap, and she made sure her shields were securely layered and doubled before shifting her vision to See the earth energies around them.

The nausea swelled again as she did so, and she pressed her forehead against the tree's cool bark to calm herself. With deep breaths, she steadied until she could concentrate on the nebulous wisps of life energy around her. Those tiny tendrils should have been gathering into droplets of power and feeding the intricate web of ley-lines, the foundation worked by Deermoon and his apprentices.

This area, according to the maps of k'Lissa, had been cleared soon after the Storms, and the ley-lines and loci that would become nodes should by now have been firmly established. But that web was muddied, the rivulets pulled out of their channels toward the cave. Toward the creature in front of the cave. Stardance could See the tendrils and lines flowing to the ground under the creature, then disappearing. To Mage Sight, the strange creature might have been any other creature, filled with the glow of life. To a Healer-Mage, however, the color and feel of that life was dark and unpleasant. Stardance shuddered as she released her Mage Sense and slowly straightened from her perch in the branches.

:Back to the Vale,: Stardance said to Sunsong. *:I've seen enough for now.:*

Moving in silence, the two of them began their slow tree-walking return.

"I don't know how our scouts could have so often missed so large a creature, even if the caverns are a bit hidden." That was Fallingwater, the young leader of the scouts, who clearly took the creature's presence as a personal affront.

Stardance shifted in her seat. "It is not so surprising. On one of the occasions Sunsong and I observed it, one of the large forest cats came down along the river. The creature hid in the cave long before the cat was near, despite its larger size. A scout would be a much greater presence in the web of earth-energies than the cat, so the thing would have vanished before a scout could even guess it was there. We could only observe from a distance, up in the trees, so that we would not be perceived as a threat. Too close, or on the ground, and it would hide at once."

"No matter how it was missed, what are we to do about it? If it is anything like a basilisk, those are not easily dealt with." Amberlight's words caused several of the Council to grimace as they remembered a previous encounter.

"If it has been concealing itself, I think it is not a true basilisk," Stardance pointed out. "They fear nothing." She paused. "I think we were too far away to tell if it *smells* like one. At least, I did not notice any foul stench."

"No, we were well within smelling range," Sunsong replied with a wry smile, and the same Councilors who had grimaced earlier now sighed with relief.

"Would that make it reasonable to just kill the thing? If it seems to be less tough than a basilisk and wouldn't have the horrible odor?" Firewind's suggestion was met with several nods. From what Stardance had seen, his name was accurate, for he always favored a blaze of swift action, and his influence on the Council was great. "It would be simple to gather enough warriors, and we could use some illusion or other to bring it out from the caves." He gestured, the full sleeves of his Mage robe rippling through the air.

"Considering how connected to magic it seems to be, its death could disrupt the web of power as much as its life already has," Stardance replied, her voice thoughtful. "It has distorted the web Deermoon has created, and I don't know if that power will simply sink back to Deermoon's channels if the creature is killed, or if the magic will go wild. Deermoon and I will need to discuss what might happen and what can be done about it. In the meantime, perhaps the scouts can monitor the area more often than Sunsong and I have been able to? They can see if the creature becomes active by night, if it hunts, if there is anything unusual that we have not noticed. The thing has probably been here for some time, I would guess at least as long as Deermoon has been noticeably weakened. A little while longer will not make much difference."

When the reports of the scouts came, they were encouraging. The Blood Beast, as Sunsong had named it, didn't seem to hunt at all, and the animals of the forest did not seem much disturbed by its presence. It always retreated into the caverns if the scouts crossed the invisible threshold it considered a safe distance. Even better, the scouts never observed it using the ability of the basilisk to fascinate a prey creature, and those who got closer to the rocky outcropping confirmed that there was no foul stench. Only those most sensitive to magic reported the unpleasant wrongness, the feel of Blood Magic that Stardance and Sunsong had noticed.

"It would appear that it lives just by absorbing energy from the earth around it," Stardance said, and Deermoon nodded. They sat at the side of the Workroom, observing the practice of Deermoon's apprentices. At Stardance's suggestion, the students were doing what they could to strengthen the web that fed the ley-lines of the southern edge of the Vale, rather than looking to expand the perimeter of the k'Lissa territory. "I've observed it, the scouts have watched it, and no one has seen anything unusual about it. We don't know if it has a tough skin or any strong defenses, but its claws and teeth are no more fierce than any other lizard's, just larger to match its size. I think Firewind is right, and we can attempt to kill it where it is. A true basilisk could be lured or driven to some other area, but I would never want to send this thing elsewhere to wreak havoc with the web of power. Even to the Uncleansed Lands."

"Because if it goes to the Uncleansed Lands, sooner or later a Tayledras is going to have to face it," Deermoon replied, his smile crinkling the corners of his blue eyes.

"And probably sooner rather than later," Stardance continued. "I suspect the beast would only be attracted to another Vale if it was driven away from k'Lissa. As the Tayledras reshape and organize the ley-lines, we create nice, juicy 'food' for such a creature." She grinned, then sobered. "At least basilisks have been around since the Mage Wars, and we are accustomed to them. This thing . . ." She let her words trail off. *New monsters are never a good thing,* she thought.

The plan that Stardance and Deermoon presented to the k'Lissa Council and Elders was simple. She would go to the outcropping with a warrior party and a few Mages. The Mages, as Firewind had suggested, would use illusion to drive the Change-Creature into the open, where the fighters could take it on. Stardance herself would monitor the web of magic and try to weaken the creature by slowing or blocking the flow of the earth energy toward it. Beyond that, they set no particular strategies, keeping in mind the Shin'a'in proverb: *Plans seldom survive first contact with the enemy.*

*   *   *

The day of the intended ambush dawned clear. Stardance carefully tucked the wooden box with her precious amber-whorl spindle into her belt pouch, then joined the group. The call from the Council had resulted in a flurry of volunteers, more than could ever have been needed, and Amberlight and Deermoon had selected from among them. Three Mages would go, including Firewind, and a dozen scouts, some of the most skilled with bow and arrow and thrown spears as well as those most capable with sword and dagger. They would try to kill from a distance first but would close with the creature if necessary.

Stardance held up her hand to signal the first stop, and the group gathered around her. "I will stay here," she said. "There is a locus here into which I can feed the power, and the locus links to one of the larger channels to the Vale. That line of trees ahead is where Sunsong and I first saw the creature, so from here I should be able to work with the energy without disturbing the thing too much. At least at first."

She sat and took out the amber-whorl spindle and chain, Kir shifting on her shoulder as she entered her Trance. Several of the scouts stayed with her as a guard, while the rest moved forward.

With her Mage Sense, Stardance could See the others as large shapes of life energy, moving slowly and cautiously toward the outcropping. Sinking into the earth, she let her breathing slow, closing off the protests of her mind to the sense of *wrong* that came from the creature ahead of her. Her first step was to set another layer of secure shields on the locus, adding to those Deermoon had created years ago. These shields were what prevented the creature from directly drawing on the Heartstone as well, for Deermoon had locked the magic so only Tayledras could use it. Her shields built on his, binding the magic around the locus tightly to her, so that nothing could wrest it from her. Working with a locus was just past the edge of a Journeyman's ability, but simply shielding and feeding the lines that went to it was far easier than making use of the power it held.

When she was satisfied with her shields, she set the spindle in motion with a deft flick. Stardance began her work, gathering the nebulous power with delicate fingertips and drafting it out, linking it to the twirling spindle until it held together, then binding that strand to the locus. With deliberate movements, she collected more, drawing the muddied energy toward her. To Mage Sense, the tendrils of power wavered as they were torn between the gentle flow of Deermoon's channels and the roiling pull toward the Blood Beast. With a gentle nudge, she drew on those diffuse bits, reminding them of their natural course, to run into the lines that fed toward the Heartstone. Each bit of energy she captured glowed as she blended it into the coil of power that trailed from the shaft of her spindle down to the locus.

Her awareness of the Mages and scouts ahead of her sharpened when she felt Firewind begin to build his first illusion, the web shivering around her as he drew on another nearby locus. The plan had called for him to create an illusion of a threat of some sort in the cavern *behind* the creature, to drive it forward. If that failed, one of the other Mages would try to lure it. She hadn't bothered to ask what they would use as a lure, considering that the creature didn't seem to eat anything. Her concern was just to hold the magic away from the thing.

It was her own actions, though, that finally elicited a reaction from the Blood Beast. Through the web, she had felt the Mages in turn creating their illusions, for most of them were drawing on the lines or one of the loci. From what she could sense, though, there had been no response from the creature to any of their efforts. A small part of her mind, one not occupied with the spinning whirl of power she held in her hands, wondered if the creature's connection to magic meant that it could see through illusions.

She had been drawing on ever-stronger pieces of power, first clearing the muddled surface energy, then carefully nudging the smallest rivulets to feed back into the locus below her. It was when she gently teased the tendrils of one of the larger lines out of its new route, guiding it back to the original channel that Deermoon had created for it, that she felt a response through the web.

In her Mage Sense, the creature was a dark, roiling mass as it emerged from the cavern and headed unerringly in her direction. The bright life energies of the scouts and warriors surrounded it, but she had no perception of whether their attacks affected it.

Stardance was caught in a struggle of her own, as the Blood Beast now *pulled* on the lines, trying to wrest them from her. She grounded herself even more firmly in the earth, flicking her spindle so it flew, and held to the nebulous strands of power she had regathered, feeding them ever more rapidly to the shielded locus below her.

Sweat gathered on her brow, stinging her eyes as she

worked, but her grip never wavered as the creature struggled to steal the lines of magic from her. Its efforts grew weaker, and she guessed that the fighting party was succeeding. A distant shout of triumph reached her ears, and she Felt the beast's death through the lines that it had been pulling at.

With a snap of backlash, the creature's hoarded Power flooded out, a dark blaze of chaos that threatened to drown her, connected as she was to the lines that had fed it. Fire rippled through her veins, singeing the ends of her nerves. Gasping for air, she strained to hold the surge of energy, the amber spindle bouncing crazily as she struggled to channel the power down toward the locus before it burned her mind. So great was the flood of Power, she reached to the locus and past it, to the greater lines, desperate to keep the energy moving without burning either her or her surroundings. The larger lines were white-hot, but somehow smoother and easier for her to handle than the raw power that the Change-Creature had released, and she battled to keep the threads of magic blended, to keep the flow moving toward the Heartstone. Through the chaos in her mind, she was vaguely aware of Kir, mantling on her shoulder and shrieking a warning.

Stardance had no sense of how long she struggled with the seething, turbulent magic, until at last the flaming tide ebbed, her spindle slowing as the flood of energy dwindled. With a new confidence, she held the lines, testing them and feeling their flow, until she was satisfied that they should return to Deermoon's channels without immediate guidance. Only then did she release her shields, letting her spindle drift to a stop, and emerged from Trance, her body slumping.

Most of the original group now stood around her,

concern in their eyes as Kir chittered at her. "It will be well," Stardance managed in a croaking voice, and Firewind handed her a flask.

It was the mineral drink favored by those suffering magical exhaustion, and Stardance drained it, then leaned back against a nearby tree. Slowly, the drink began to cool her overheated mind.

"Will *you* be well?" her father asked, taking back his flask with a frown. "Should we send for a *dyheli*? You've been working for candlemarks since we killed the thing."

Stardance shook her head to clear it. Kir had calmed, nibbling at her ear, and she reached up a quivering hand to stroke the soft underfeathers of her white-barred breast.

"I will be well enough," she replied, her voice raspy. She glanced up toward the sun. "I just need a little more time." The edges of her mind felt vaguely scorched, and she didn't even think she could concentrate long enough to replenish herself from the earth.

Stardance wound off the last length of spun thread from her spindle onto one of the tapered wooden storage rods, tying the end with a light knot so the strand wouldn't drift back to loose fibers before she could ply it with another length. Even though she used the spindle every time she worked with the subtle drifts of Mage energy, she never failed to find working with fiber a calming pastime. Her thread would never be as smooth as a true artisan's and was certainly nowhere near as fine as Triska's had been, but still it gave her pleasure to have something of substance to hold after a session with her spindle.

The physical task also helped her to think, clearing her mind and aiding her focus. The k'Lissa Council had asked her to stay longer, to help Deermoon and his apprentices continue to restore balance around the Vale, and she needed to make a decision. She had been here for several moons already, assisting them after the death of the Change-Creature, but did she feel she was still needed? Would she prefer to remain? She knew her father wanted her to stay, to become part of k'Lissa entirely. But while she had enjoyed meeting her half-siblings and her cousins, she couldn't think of them as family. Her thoughts drifted back to k'Veyas, to Silverheart and Windwhisperer and Nightblade. Images of each filled her mind: Silverheart's round face and efficient manner, Windwhisperer's warm brown eyes and calm advice, Nightblade's darker eyes and sharp features.

Reaching for the box to store the spindle, she traced the knotwork details of the delicately carved lid with a finger before opening it. She assumed Nightblade had done the carving himself—as she enjoyed spinning, even though the *hertasi* artisans were more skilled, he enjoyed woodworking. She opened the lid and placed the tapered spindle in the shaped liner, and her fingers caught a corner of the fabric. A flicker of *something* underneath it reflected a glimmer of light into her eyes. Realizing that the corner was actually folded to pull on, she set the spindle on the small table and gently lifted out the padding.

In shocked silence Stardance stared at what was tucked underneath, until at last she reached out with a hand that actually trembled. Her fingers traced the crystal-decorated shaft of a kestrel's rusty brown tail-feather, gliding along it to pick up the beaded chain and hold it dangling in front of her. Green stones glittered in the narrow ribbon of sunlight that angled through the window of the guest-*ekele*, the feather twisting in the air from her sharp, rapid breaths.

Her pulse raced while her mind scattered from thought to thought. She had exchanged flowers a few times with the young men of k'Veyas—and had gently refused those from Sunsong here in k'Lissa—but never had Nightblade offered her a flower. He had never courted anyone, that she could recall. He was older, and she assumed he thought of her as a younger sister, nothing more ...

Stardance let that thought trail off as her mind crowded with images. She remembered how Nightblade seemed to have always been there when she needed assistance, even back to those hard days after Triska's death. She recalled how he always assigned himself to guard her, how his eyes always seemed to seek her out, how he always knew where she was, even in a crowd—and how she usually knew where he was. She thought of the consideration shown by the gift of the spindle itself and the clever linked chain so that she could use it as her focus more easily. She remembered the strange expression in his eyes when the visitors had first come to k'Veyas and again when he had said his abrupt farewell to her, and the pieces began to make sense.

She frowned at the feather. *Why* would he have done it in this manner? To offer this when there had been no previous relationship, or even any overt indication of desire? And not to properly *offer* the feather, but to conceal it where she might never have noticed it? And then to tell her not to open the gift until she was at k'Lissa, far from k'Veyas and the ability to ask him anything about it?

The frown turned into a burst of laughter. That made the most sense of all. Nightblade had never been one to take kindly to questions—and certainly not from her. *What good would it do to interrogate him, anyway?* she thought, a soft half-smile still lighting her eyes as she gently brushed her finger along the feather's delicate inner vane. The feather itself, despite the peculiar circumstance, was perfectly clear. The only questions that needed answering were the ones she had to ask of herself.

As Stardance had expected, when she joined the Council the next morning, her father's eyes were immediately drawn to the sparkling of the crystals on the feather woven into her hair, the red-brown vanes almost blending with russet braids streaked with white. She saw a flash of speculation in his expression, and she could almost *see* him wondering if Sunsong might have earned her favor.

"Have you made your decision, Stardance?" Amberlight asked, and she nodded.

"Yes, Elder. It is time for me to return home, before the autumn rains make it too difficult." A moment of silence, then a flurry of protests, in which her father's voice was loudest, until Amberlight held up his hand for silence so she could continue.

"It has been nearly three full moons since the death of the Change-Creature, and the energy where it had been is well on its way to balance. Deermoon's strength is a little slower to recover, but his focus is much improved. His apprentices should be able to continue the work in the area well enough under such supervision as he can now provide. I need to return home to k'Veyas, to Silverheart, and to my responsibilities there."

"But surely Deermoon can supervise your Mastery Trial—and with only the apprentices, will the Vale be safe should something like the Blood Beast return?" Her father again, but she could see nods of concerned agreement among the Council.

Stardance shook her head, the feather in her hair brushing lightly against her cheek, a reminder that more than responsibility to Silverheart and the Clan awaited her. "If, as we believe, the creature was a product of the Mage Storms, it is a wonder that it survived unnoticed for the years since then. It would be doubly a wonder if there should have been two. And as for the Mastery Trial," she actually chuckled a little, "Silverheart is cleverer than all of us. This *was* my Trial. Ask Deermoon, if you doubt me," she continued, gesturing to the older Mage, who had sat silent throughout. "Only a Master Healing-Mage at full strength could have dealt with the discordance to the earth energies that *thing* created."

The rest of the Council now turned and watched Deermoon, who barely leaned on his stick when he stood. "Stardance is correct. Her ability and control have surpassed what Mastery requires." His blue eyes narrowed briefly as he studied her. "If there were more magic gathered for her to use, she would be likely to soon be Adept."

Chatter erupted around them, once again hushed by Amberlight. "Is she also correct in her estimation of your apprentices?" he asked Deermoon, leaving unspoken the question of Deermoon's own capacity.

"They have control enough to do what is needed now that the major imbalance is righted. My own strength will continue to grow, as it has already begun." The Healer-Mage replied to both the spoken and silent questions.

Amberlight turned back to Stardance. "We shall certainly be sorry to see you leave, Stardance, for you have been a welcome addition to k'Lissa." He glanced over at Firewind, then continued. "But it has always been your decision to make. Scouts will accompany you to k'Veyas whenever you wish to depart."

At last, Stardance met her father's eyes. In their green depths, she saw resigned disappointment. It would not have been lost on him that she had referred to k'Veyas as *home*, and deep within her she knew that it always would be.

As they neared the edge of the k'Veyas territory, where they could expect a greeting from whichever scout patrolled this border, Stardance's eye was caught by a bondbird circling overhead that was soon joined by a soaring Kir. She squinted and eyed the bird, then gave a tiny smile. It was a large gray goshawk, and she was not surprised to see Nightblade standing before them when they moved farther along the forest path.

Although his arms were casually folded, she read a subtle unease around him, and she hid another smile. With a fluid movement, she dismounted, leaving the *dyheli* with the k'Lissa scouts and taking a few steps forward, then stopping and waiting, her eyes on him.

Nightblade had straightened, no longer trying to disguise the tension radiating from him. A light breeze sprang up, riffling her hair and the beaded feather braided into it, and from the change in his stance she realized that he hadn't seen it, so well did it match her red-brown hair. Now it was his turn to move, measured strides bringing him to stand in front of her, his focus shifting from the feather in her braids to her waiting gaze.

As though he didn't quite believe his eyes, he lifted one hand to trace along the crystal-beaded chain, his fingertips then tenderly gliding down her cheek.

Stardance released a breath she didn't even know she held, sighing and pressing her cheek into his hand, which gently curved around her jaw. For long moments dark brown eyes held gray-green, then Nightblade folded her into his arms, her head tucked in the crook of his neck.

"Welcome home, *ashke*," he whispered against her hair, and Stardance smiled.

Weavings
Diana L. Paxson

Deira had always found weaving soothing. Once the upright loom was braced against the wall that faced the hearth and the warp attached, you could lose yourself in drawing the shuttle back and forth and beating up the thread. Weaving was something you could *control*.

But not today.

As she jerked the shuttle past the last group of warps, the thread snapped, and she swore. Why was she surprised, on a day that had begun with a fight with Selaine about taking a turn at the loom? Her daughter had reached the age when any parental order produced a protest. In the end, Deira had sent her to the mill beyond the village for some of the flour with which the miller was paying for a length of wool.

Brushing back a lock of hair that the years had darkened to old gold, she allowed herself to remember being sixteen, the last year before the war. Instead of the loom, she saw the house by the bridge, and in the next breath, flame. Suppressing the memory, she replaced the image with the snug surroundings of her cottage. Net bags suspended from the hewn beams held shuttles wound with thread and hanks of yarn, or flax needing combing, or lengths of wool roving waiting to be spun. The thick rug was patterned in a lozenge and stripe design, and crisp linen curtains fluttered at the window that looked across the meadow to the river and the road. It was better to live without memories.

She fluffed out the broken ends of the thread and joined them, then rolled them together between thumb and forefinger, willing the tiny hooks in the strands to link and hold. Wool fibers *wanted* to cling together. When you were weaving flax, a broken thread was a disaster. It was only a serious annoyance with wool. The clay warp weights clinked and swung as she carefully eased the repaired thread up against the weft and pushed it tightly into place. Then she looped it around the edge and began once more.

"Mother, Mother!"

Deira jerked as the door slammed open and felt the thread snap again.

"How many times—" The words died as she saw Selaine's face, hazel eyes wide and fair curls standing on end.

"There was an attack on Highbarrow farm yester'eve," gasped the girl. Beyond the village the ground rose steeply, and a number of farmsteads were tucked into the folds between the hills.

"Raiders?" asked Deira, her anger congealing into a cold lump of fear. She blinked away memories of screaming and firelight on a lifted sword.

"Dunno—Farmer Dorn's boy Tad saw smoke when he was driving sheep up t' the meadow. At least one body—" She reached for the box of medicines by the hearth.

"Where do you think you're going?" A swift step put Deira between her daughter and the door.

"They'll need help—if there's any still alive—"

"Not from you, my girl. Your place is right here!"

"*Mother!* I'm not a child!"

"Nor a warrior nor a Healer neither! What you *are* is a lass who hasn't finished the work you promised. I'll think about giving you a woman's rights when you've learned how to get a job done!" She pointed to the loom. For a long moment they traded glares. Then Selaine sighed, replaced the medicine box, and began to mend the broken thread.

The grouped warp threads hung from the card-woven band at the top in stripes of cream and beige and brown and all the shades of new green that dappled the surrounding hills. The thread to be woven in was in the same colors, but more randomly arranged. The muted colors would have bored the Tayledras or Shin'a'in, but the folk of Evenleigh loved their tumbled hills, and when winter came, the blanket would comfort the spirit with a memory of the season when the blanket had been made.

"Don't raiders usually burn a holding when they're done?" asked Selaine. She beat the reunited thread up into place, moving with a coltish grace before the loom. "Tad said th'house was torn apart, not burned, an' trails of sticky stuff left all 'round."

So, our enemy is not men, but monsters, thought Deira, easing into the wicker chair. After Westerbridge burned, her only thought had been to put as much distance as possible between herself and the Karsite border. She knew too much about reavers. She'd been willing to take her chances with the strange creatures folk sometimes sighted in these hills.

"Headman says whatever 'twas is bound to strike again," the girl went on with a kind of nervous glee.

"Wants folk t' refuge in th' village 'til they can hunt 'em down. He's sent to the Roadguard down at Donleigh to ask for a Herald, says uncanny beasts is more than we can manage on our own!"

I know too much about Heralds, too. . . .

Deira's gaze fixed on the girl, already tall, like her father. She watched Selaine ease the shuttle between the sheds and let it go, saw the shuttle trail thread as it floated through the space to the other edge where she caught it, just as Deira had once seen a spear jerk free from the fist of a Karsite mercenary and fly to Herald Aldren's waiting hand . . .

Deira woke, shuddering, from dreams in which she was working at a loom that had no end. When she tried to turn away, she found herself surrounded by veils of fabric that flapped and clung. There was something she was seeking, but she could not remember its name. She knew only frustration and an aching sense of loss.

She opened her eyes to a dappling of morning light through the shutters and her daughter's anxious gaze.

"Are you all right?" Selaine helped Deira free herself from the tangle of sheet and blanket.

"Bad dreams, and I'd bet I'm not the only one . . ."

Only the young found danger exciting. This talk of monsters was like a blow that set an old wound throbbing with remembered pain. Deira told herself that nothing that might come out of the Pelagir wilderness was as fearful as the evil that hid in the hearts of men.

Mint tea with a little lemon-balm, scalding hot, took the fur from her tongue, and movement some of the ache from her limbs, but the feeling of helpless dread remained. When the miller's boy came knocking to tell them that the monsters had destroyed another farm, she was not surprised.

In the next few days two more steadings were attacked, all in the same way. By now, taking refuge in the village seemed good advice to many, and most families were sheltering one or more refugees. Deira thought the palisade would be little protection from a creature that could pluck the roof from a cottage, and putting all the people together only made them easier to attack. She knew what it was like to be hunted through the streets. Walls that did not keep predators out could still keep in their prey.

The weaver's little house was set a short way down the road on the other side of the village from the afflicted farms. When Headman Bartom sent to offer them a place in his house, Deira refused, but she no longer objected when Selaine went to help with the refugees. The girl had a gift for calming hysterical children, and a calming touch when the Healer was treating wounds.

Deira dropped the shuttle and whirled as the clangor of the tocsin assaulted her ears. Through the open door of the cottage streamed the light of a golden afternoon. The creatures had never attacked during daylight before. A few steps brought her to the porch. The village was hidden by a stand of oak trees, but smoke was rising from beyond.

Her heart clenched again. She had given Selaine permission to go to the village this morning. *"Get out! Come home!"* her spirit cried, but she knew her daughter would not come even if she could have heard.

And would you want her to be the sort of person who would run when she was needed? a small voice spoke within. There were sure to be those who needed help now.

We should have fled when the monsters first came! she answered. She had not wanted to leave all she had built here, but the essential tools were the knowledge in her head and the skill in her hands. She knew how to start from scratch. She had done it before.

Without conscious decision, she found herself reaching for a bundle of absorbent wool roving and clean rags to bind wounds, a sharp needle and a spool of strong linen thread. She added packets of powdered willowbark and goldenseal. She put her sharpest knife into the basket, though it would do little good if something got within knife range. Then she tied a kerchief over her hair, grabbed her shawl, and set off down the road.

The village had been built in a bend of the river. By the time Deira crossed the bridge, she could hear screaming and the sound of rending wood. She paused, blood running cold as something like a huge, jointed claw lifted above the angled roofs. Then she pushed past the swinging gate and went in.

Evenleigh had never been more than a few streets surrounding the shrine and a small square. The homes on the east side of the village were untouched, but when she reached the square, she saw that the western side had become a tangle of beams and bits of building, daubed with some pale substance that glistened in the sun. Inside, something dark was moving. From time to time she glimpsed a jointed limb, and once, a stinger the size of a warrior's spear.

A small group of villagers still milled about before the barrier, shooting arrows that disappeared without effect or were caught by the sticky bands. Half of them were wearing cloth that she had woven. She saw Headman Bartom among the others, thinning hair awry, and beyond him a familiar knotwork shawl and a head of bright hair.

"Selaine!" she shouted, hurrying forward. "Selaine!" In the next moment, her child was in her arms. *Flesh of my flesh* ... Deira gripped with all the strength of her fear, confirming the tangible reality of strong young limbs, the scent of Selaine's hair.

Then a flicker of movement made her recoil; she dragged the girl back as a sticky rope arched over the barrier, caught one of the villagers, and dragged him away. For a moment she saw the beast entire— fanged head, segmented body, and two pincers that darted outward, rolled the victim neatly in sticky silk, and plucked it back over the barrier.

A spider, she thought numbly as they all gave ground, or some obscene combination of spider and scorpion, with more legs than any creature that size had a right to own.

"It's building a nest . . ." she whispered.

"And stocking it—" her daughter replied in a shaking voice. "Tommet is the third man it's captured that way."

It's a mother, thought Deira. *I might even be sympathetic, if the creature were not threatening my child.*

Some smoke still rose, but apparently the spider-stuff stifled flame. They stared, listening to the sounds of cracking wood. The screams were more muffled now. Even the villagers were growing still in the face of this invulnerable enemy.

As silence fell, they heard clearly the sweet, silvery shimmer of harness bells.

*   *   *

"Herald Garaval at your service—I am sorry I took so long."

It was not *him*. This Herald's voice was a pleasant tenor, and his shape was wrong, shoulders too broad, and the hair too dark a brown. And too young—he looked barely past his internship year. He swung down from his Companion's back and gave her shining neck a pat.

"I came as soon as I got word, and Nienna goes like the wind, but not swiftly enough, I see." Garaval cast a dubious glance toward the growing rubble pile. "The message was not very informative. What, exactly, do we have here?"

Deira began to edge backward, still gripping Selaine, as the men started trying to explain.

"Mother, let go! I want to know!"

"It's under control," Deira said tightly. "The Herald has come. They don't need us here."

The girl continued to protest as her mother dragged her back down the road. Once there, the older woman began to methodically sort through chests and bags. This little house had seemed such a refuge. It felt like a trap to her now.

"What are you doing?"

"Packing." Deira forced herself to meet Selaine's troubled gaze. "You must do the same. One basket, a shoulder bag. No more than you can carry."

"But *why?* The Herald's come. He'll kill the spider-thing."

"Or she will kill him, and her eggs will hatch. Either way, Evenleigh is done."

Selaine flushed red, then paled. "I don't believe you! Being dragged from place to place was the first life I knew. Then we came here, and they let us stay, and we had a *home!* When our friends are in trouble is no time to abandon them!" Shaking her head, she darted toward the door.

The fringes of her knotted shawl slipped through Deira's fingers. She made a despairing grab as Selaine lifted the latch. Her fingers hooked into the web, but suddenly there was no resistance. Selaine had halted in the doorway, and she was laughing.

Deira let go of the shawl. A crowd of people had gathered in the meadow between the cottage and the road. Others were coming up the path—Kel the miller and Anellie who ran the inn and a dozen more. In the lead was Headman Bartom, with the Herald at his side.

"The Hawkbrothers might have a name for it, but it's no creature the Heralds have ever seen."

Deira sniffed as she recognized the frustration in Herald Garaval's tone, and she reached into one of the net bags for a shuttle. She had not been able to keep the villagers from taking over her cottage for their meeting, but she could make her refusal to have anything to do with this clear. With half an eye still on the others, she worked the thread between the warps, set the heddle rod against the frame and let the front warp swing back, looped the shuttle around, and worked it back once more.

"But ye've got magic to fight it, d'ye not?" asked the headman. His wisps of white hair quivered like the topknot of a demented bird.

Garaval shook his head. "Valdemar has not had a Herald-Mage since Vanyel Ashkevron's time. My Gifts are Mindspeech and Foresight, but even if I were a Fire-starter, it would not help since you say the Creature's web-stuff does not burn."

The hearthfire leaped as if in ironic commentary, glowing on the Herald's whites and gleaming on Se-laine's bright hair. Deira frowned. When the girl looked at Garaval, there was entirely too much admiration in her hazel eyes. He was young, good-looking enough to catch a girl's eye even without the glamour of a Herald's uniform. Falling in love with a Herald was only too easy, if one forgot that they only cared for their own kind.

"We could build a new village . . ." said the headman. "Downstream . . ."

"And who would grind yer grain? The flow's not strong enough to turn the mill wheel there," growled Kel.

"When the creature's eggs hatch, there will be no safety anywhere in these hills—" the Herald replied.

"Send to the Hawkbrothers—" said Anellie.

"And what do we do 'til they arrive?" exclaimed Farmer Dorn. "If we don't get the fields planted soon, we might as well let the creature eat us now, for we'll starve when winter comes!"

"D'ye say we should give up, then? Leave our homes and our fields and run away?" They had already loaded the elderly and smaller children into wagons and sent them down the road to Donleigh.

That's what I *had to do,* Deira exchanged shuttle for weaving sword and beat up the thread into the weft, eve-ning, tightening, until it was smooth. *Sometimes that's the only way to survive.*

"Fetch help from the Hawkbrothers, then!" Headman Martom gestured northward. "Isn't dealing with the beasties that escape from the Pelagirs their job?"

"That might take weeks!" interrupted the miller. "Ye can't just ride off and leave us to deal with this monster alone!"

"Couldn't your Companion carry a message?" asked Anellie.

Silence fell as the Herald's gaze went inward. After a moment he sighed and focused once more. "Nienna says she can do that, but it will take time . . ."

"'Til then, how'll we live?" asked Dorn.

"If the Creature is making a nest in the village, perhaps it will no longer hunt the hills," said Deira. "You might be safer back at your farms—" *And out of my house*, she thought.

That sparked a new round of debate. Homes might be in ruins, but the fields were waiting. The farmers were grateful for any encouragement to return to them.

They have their work, she thought, touching the polished upright of the loom, *and I have mine. Though mine is more portable.* But now that the human involvement she had hoped to escape had come to her, it no longer seemed so urgent to leave.

"And I'd best be getting back down th' hill to see what my daughters've done to the soup I set going over th' fire," said Anellie.

The knowledge that she was not somehow expected to feed all these people eased another of Deira's worries. She contributed some old potatoes to the pot and bid them farewell with a semblance of courtesy.

"I am sorry we had to invade your home," the Herald said quietly as the others began to leave. "We could have had this discussion in the meadow, but the folk are on the edge of hysteria, and we needed privacy. Also, I think their leaders needed to see a whole roof and your work at the loom. It reaffirms their belief that there's order in the world."

Deira stared at the loom without seeing it. "A pity they're wrong," she said grimly.

"You came here from somewhere else, didn't you?" he asked, with an inward look, as if he were trying to place the accent she had tried so hard to lose.

"And it looks as if I will be going somewhere else soon," she snapped, turning away as she pulled the heddle rod forward and let it click into the slot at the bracket's end. She suppressed a bitter smile as she heard him sigh, and then his polite farewell.

"Why don't you like the Herald?" asked Selaine when Garaval had gone. "He's come all this way t' help us—"

"Oh, yes," Deira said bitterly. "And he'll be on his way just as quickly once it's clear there's nothing he can do. Easy enough for a Herald to escape, wearing those pretty white clothes that he doesn't dare get dirty!" For a moment, memory showed her a white uniform stained with blood, but bitterness forced her on. "Galloping away on his pretty white not-a-horse and leaving us to deal . . . !" She caught her breath on a sob. For a time, her struggle to control her breathing was the only sound in the room.

"The Companion's going, but Herald Garaval's staying *here*. . . ." Selaine said softly. "An' you yourself wove him into the web." She pointed, and Deira saw that the shuttle she had snatched up earlier must have been from the wrong bag. A broad band of Herald white now ran through the fabric on the loom.

Deira dreamed that she stood on the graceful stone arch that gave the town of Westerbridge, where she had grown up, its name. The Herald was beside her, commenting on the beauty of the evening as the setting sun turned the clouds to flame. Basking in the sense of safety she felt when he was near, she scarcely noted his words. The sky dimmed, and he wrapped his cloak around her as the clouds released the first spatterings of rain.

Then, suddenly, the wind was roaring. Furious gusts lashed the river to a froth. They dashed for shelter, but now it was the new Herald, Garaval, who ran at her side.

"The storm is coming!" he cried, "The town will be washed away!"

And then the flood crashed over them, and she woke, gasping, to lie in a tangle of bedclothes, listening to the pattering of rain.

The rain did not last long, but when Deira stepped out of her doorway, she saw clouds like sodden rovings of gray wool stretched across the sky. As she moved about making breakfast, Selaine eyed her uneasily. Deira wanted to reassure the girl, but something was stirring just below awareness. Something related to her dream.

"Fill up the big pot," she said finally. "They'll be cold and damp down there. We'll take them some tea."

Selaine's eyes widened, but she did not argue. *There was this to be said for disaster,* thought her mother—*a situation sufficiently dire stilled even adolescent rebellion.* Deira did not try to explain—could not have explained how somehow during the night she had gone from wanting to flee the village to looking for a way to save it.

Anellie had boiled up some porridge for the refugees' breakfast, but the tea was welcomed all the same. As it was passed, Deira seated herself by the Herald.

"You said your Gift was Foresight," she said as Garaval looked up in surprise. "Does it work for weather?"

"Good question," he answered. "If it's going to storm, we'll need to fix up some shelter here." He closed his eyes, and her sense of his presence suddenly dimmed. After a few moments, he looked back at her, shivering.

"You were right. A storm is coming, a big one! But you get heavy rains every year—why did I see a flood sweeping through the town?"

Deira closed her own eyes, images flickering into place behind them as they did when she was designing a tapestry.

"The creature is stronger than we are, and we cannot use fire," she said slowly. "But nothing stands before a flood. The creature is nesting right where the river bends around the village. If we could gather the waters and then release them, they might sweep it away."

"Mill's a wreck, but there's nothing wrong with th' millpond," said the miller from behind them. "Plenty of broken timbers there to make a dam."

"We make it so when one board is knocked loose it gives way—" said the Herald, and Deira remembered that building was one of the things they taught at Herald's Collegium.

"Village wall's down at that corner already!" said someone.

"Th' flood'll carry the creature away!" Now everyone was talking.

The eggs would go, certainly, thought Deira, *but the creature might be able to hold on.* Images wove in and out in her brain.

"If the creature doesn't drown," she said at last, "it would be better if we could capture it. My daughter and

I—" she nodded at Selaine, "make nets as well as cloth. Bring me rope—all the ropes you can find—and we will show this beast that she is not the only web-weaver in Valdemar!"

That first day, everyone with the strength for the work joined in dismantling the wreckage of the mill. They came back with scrapes and splinters, but they were smiling, even when the rain began to fall. Except for two boys who had ventured too close while trying to observe the creature, there were no more deaths, and the people who remained had crowded into the houses on the eastern side of the village, so they had shelter. The nimble-fingered members of the community worked on the netting, led by Deira and a woman who had grown up in a fishing village on Lake Evendim.

Even if this doesn't work, in times to come these people will hold their heads up knowing that at least they tried, thought Deira. *And Selaine and I will feel easier because we tried to help them.* She laid her fingers over those of the miller's wife, showing her once more how to make a sheet bend that would securely join a rope that was thick to one that was thin.

She had run away before. Flight had brought her no peace, and even the safety had been an illusion. Time to see what fighting back would do.

By the end of the second day, the men had erected a framework for the dam. As the days passed, and they wove planks or ropes together, the lumpy pile of netting grew and the level of the millpond began to rise. Day by day, the volume of water passing beneath the bridge dwindled, despite the rain.

On the morning of the fifth day, Deira was whipping

the end of a rope before tying the final knot on one of the edges of the net when a shadow fell across the work, and she looked up to see Herald Garaval standing there. He had clearly been working hard. His leathers would need a session in the bleaching vats before they were either white or pretty again, while she doubted that even her clever needle could salvage the cloth.

"How close are you to finishing?" he asked. His voice was hoarse, and beneath the mud on his cheek she glimpsed the flush of fever.

"By this evening we'll be done," she answered, "and so will you, my lad, if you don't take care. You wouldn't be the first Herald I've had to nurse because he burned himself to a stub trying to save the world. We need you alive and strong! Ask my daughter for some white willow tea, and get some rest, in the Lady's name!"

"Soon . . ." Garaval said vaguely, as if even the thought of rest had distracted him. Then his gaze focused again. "I've been Foreseeing. The rain will stop soon. For a few hours we'll have run-off, but only the gods know how long before the eggs hatch and we have a dozen creatures to catch instead of one. Tomorrow we have to break the dam."

When he had gone, Deira closed her eyes, seeing in memory the hollow-cheeked features of another man who had thought that the desire to serve could substitute when the body's strength was gone. How could he have abandoned her?

He didn't . . . Certainty blasted through her barriers from somewhere deep within. *Heralds are neither invulnerable nor immortal. Something happened to keep him away.*

"Mother, why are you weeping?" Selaine's voice recalled her to herself again.

Deira opened her eyes and managed a smile. "Weeping? Why should I weep? No, my love, it's only the rain."

The rain had ceased during the night, but the watery sunlight was veiled by thinning clouds, the outlines of wood and field blurred by mist rising from saturated ground. On the bridge, a ripple of tension ran through the waiting crowd. Compulsively, Deira stroked the harsh hemp rope she held. She and Selaine and most of the other women were holding down the ends of the net on each shore while the men used stout branches to suspend the middle from the bridge, ready to drop it over their prey. The Herald and the strongest of the men had gone to free the linchpin holding the dam.

From upriver came a long horn call. For a moment, the only other sound was the chuckle of water in the stream. Then, senses were assaulted by the shriek of rending wood. A vibration shook the bridge as beyond the village planks and water sprayed into the sky. In the next instant, all gave way to a roar as the pent waters burst free.

Another burst of spray fountained high as the flood hit the edge of the village, sending everything the creature had not already destroyed hurtling downstream. Logs from the palisade, furniture and beams and thatching surged toward them, and tumbling in the churning mass they glimpsed the egg-sacs' gelid gleam. An ear-shattering screech pierced the river's roar.

"She's coming!" shouted someone.

The mass approached with terrifying speed. Deira

tightened her grip on the rope as a knobbed claw flailed. As the first debris passed under the bridge she could see the curve of the carapace heaving upward. With a shout the men on the bridge let the net drop and shoved the other edge outward. The bridge shook as the wreckage crashed into it, and the people on the shores braced as the ends they had tied to trees or pegged into the earth took the strain.

The creature had reached the top of the tangle. The net heaved as she struggled to break free. Someone screamed, knocked aside as a tree was jerked from the soaked ground. Across the river two more ropes gave way. Deira swore as the one she gripped tore from her fingers. Still reaching, she heard Selaine grunt and then, impossibly, saw the rope end curve back toward them, to be grasped by a dozen eager hands. Deira turned to her daughter, saw Selaine's eyes roll up in her head, and caught her as she fell.

"Mama, I'm sorry . . . I know ye don't like me t' move things with my mind."

The whisper brought Deira upright from where she had been dozing, leaning against her daughter's bed. The house was full of people, talking, tending the injured, brewing tea over the fire, but there was only one voice she wanted to hear.

"Oh, darling—" Deira gave her daughter a quick hug. "I never said—"

"Your face said," Selaine replied, "but I *had* to—"

"And you saved us," said a new voice. They looked up to see Herald Garaval, gaunt and muddied, but triumphant. "Without that rope, the net would have given way." He turned to Deira. "Your daughter has a rare talent, Mistress Deira. She should go to Haven, where she can be trained."

"And be snapped up by the Heralds and lost to me?" the response was automatic, a fear born the first time she had seen Selaine call a fallen toy to her hand, but it lost force as she looked at the exhausted Herald standing there.

"We've burned the last of th' egg-sacs." Headman Martom came bustling up before Garaval could reply. "We've got th' creature tied down proper t' wait 'til th' Hawkbrothers come," he went on, "thanks t' you, Mistress Westerbridge, and your girl."

"Westerbridge?" Garaval frowned.

"She came from a big town called Westerbridge," the Headman boasted, "a widow with a little lass. She's th' best weaver from here t' Rethwellan!"

"Then *you're* the one Aldren met when he served on the border . . ." breathed the Herald. He looked from her to Selaine and back again. "Of course!" he exclaimed. "The girl has your hair, but his eyes. How proud he would be."

"He's dead, then?" Deira whispered. "He told me that Heralds are not supposed to get involved with local girls, but I loved him, and when we were hiding from the Karsite raiders, I let him love me. And then he rode back to the battles, and there was no way to let him know I was with child."

"He meant to come back," said Garaval. "But he had to go where he was needed. By the time he returned to Westerbridge, the town had been destroyed."

Deira nodded. "I was one of the few who escaped when the Karsites came again. I kept running. I thought we could live in peace here."

"Why didn't you bring your child to Haven?" exclaimed Garaval. "The Heralds would have taken care of you!"

Deira shook her head. "At first I was crazed with fear. I thought Aldren would reject me, or the Heralds would not believe me, or they would punish him for having loved me. And then I saw that Selaine was Gifted, and I thought they would take her away. But there's no escape, is there?"

"You can't run from fear, only fight it," Garaval said softly. "Haven't you found that out, these past days? Herald Aldren taught me that. He was my mentor. In a year and a half riding Circuit, he taught me the meaning of all my instructors' noble words. And later, when he lay dying . . ." he swallowed, "he asked me to keep looking for you."

Deira could not pretend, this time, that the tears that left burning trails down her cheeks were rain. *He loved me. . .* she thought. But it was hard to give up the anger and the fear.

"And now," she said, "I suppose you will take my child away . . ."

"Doesn't anyone care what *I* want?" They both looked over as Selaine pushed herself up in the bed, scowling. "If Valdemar needs my help, th' Companions know where t' find me. Right now, seems to me the place I'm needed most is here."

Behind Selaine, the green and brown blanket with the white band running through it still hung on the loom.

All these years, I have been weaving, thought Deira. *But even the most skillful weaver can only lay down one thread at a time.* "With each choice, each action, we set a thread into the cloth," her mother had once said. "It's the

*sum total of all those threads, all those choices, that decide
what the weaving will be . . ."*

She reached up to grip her daughter's hand, then let
it go.

"You will weave your own story, Selaine."

A Wake of Vultures
Elisabeth Waters

"The vultures are unhappy," Lena murmured, almost to herself.

"What vultures?" Herald Samira looked up at the sky.

"The ones ahead of us," Lena said absently.

"Where?"

"We can't see them yet . . ." Lena's voice trailed off as she tried to pick up more detail. The utility of her gift depended on the ability of the animal to focus its thoughts, so what she received often varied a great deal.

They rounded the bend, and Herald Robin said faintly, "Oh. *Those* vultures." He was turning a delicate shade of green, but Lena didn't hold it against him. He had just gone into Whites and was on his first Circuit, under Samira's supervision. Samira's task was first to train and then to supervise him, and she had years more experience—not to mention much more exposure to people with Animal Mindspeech and the strange changes in outlook caused by their gift.

Lena looked from the bodies on the ground to the vultures ranged about them. One body was a male human—five days dead, the vultures told her—but remarkably undecayed and untouched by the local predators.

The second body was that of a vulture who, judging by the mess around it, had eaten something that violently disagreed with it.

"That's odd," Herald Samira remarked. "I didn't know there was a poison that could kill a vulture."

"There isn't," Lena replied grimly. "A vulture can digest anthrax, let alone anything more common and less deadly." She started toward the bodies and stopped abruptly as the protests of the surviving vultures coalesced into a scream inside her head. She realized that she was mind-linked with *all* of them, and, in some peculiar fashion, the dead body was tied into the link as well. Her knees buckled, Samira stepped forward to support her, and vultures swooped down from the trees to make a physical wall between them and the bodies.

"What is it?" Samira asked, dragging Lena backward out of the apparent danger area.

"I don't know. I've never seen anything like this before."

"What do the vultures say?" While all Heralds had at least some magic, Animal Mindspeech was not one of Samira's gifts. Lena, on the other hand, had it to a high degree. She was a novice at the Temple of Thenoth, Lord of the Beasts, in Haven.

"They say it's death," Lena replied faintly, still feeling odd. She tried to break off the Mindspeech with the vultures so she could concentrate on talking to the humans. She couldn't; she and the vultures were still firmly linked.

"Well, of course it's dead," Samira said. "It's a corpse."

"No," Lena corrected, "not dead. They said *death*."

The King still had hopes of arranging a suitable marriage for Lena, who was both the last surviving member of her highborn family and the King's ward, so he required her occasional attendance at Court, and when most high-born families retired to their country estates, he arranged for her to visit those who had been friends of her parents. This meant that all too often she was visiting people she didn't know well, if at all. She was currently on her way to stay with a friend of her late father's near the border Valdemar shared with Rethwellan.

Robin, with visible effort, looked at the body. "You know," he said, "I think he's from Rethwellan."

"Who is?"

"The body. I can tell by the clothes." Robin had been part of a troupe of traveling Players before being Chosen, so he was probably right.

"How far are we from the border?" Lena asked.

"Less than two miles," Robin replied promptly. "I've studied maps of this area until I felt as if I would go cross-eyed."

"So he could have been dying, staggered across the border, and died on this side," Samira said.

"Yes, he did," Lena said promptly. "At least the vultures think he was already dying when he crossed the border, and they're probably pretty good judges of that."

"But what killed him?" The two Heralds moved closer to study the body—or at least as close as the vultures would allow.

Lena stayed back with the Companions, thankful that finding out who the young man was and why he was dead was not her responsibility. Not that she wouldn't help as much as she could, but nobody was going to blame her for not knowing.

"It's odd, though," she said.

"This whole situation is incredible, so what is it that strikes you as odd?" Samira asked.

"Why are we the first ones to find him—assuming we are? He's barely off the road, and the vultures are quite visible."

"Possibly more to you than to most people, but that's a good point." Samira turned to Robin. "You stay here and watch the body. Don't try to be clever; just make sure that nobody gets too close to it, especially you and your Companion. I'm going to escort Lena the rest of the way to the estate. Lord Tobias is the local magistrate. And given that we're almost on his property, he should know if anyone found the body before we came upon it."

"Bodies," Lena pointed out. "There's a vulture dead, too."

"True, and I'm sorry for it, but I think most people are going to be more upset about the human." Samira sighed. "And here I was thinking this couldn't be anywhere near as bad as your last visit to the country."

"Well," Lena said as she studied the body, "I'm pretty sure that he wasn't shot by the local magistrate in an idiotic hunting accident."

"And he's not dressed like a deer," Samira agreed. "Really, what sane person wears brown leather to go hunting?"

"The late Lord Kristion, unfortunately." Lena sighed. "I really hope that this visit goes better."

"If things get worse than they already are," Samira pointed out, "we have serious trouble."

At first, things didn't seem too bad. Lord Tobias, her host, went off with Samira to view the body. He was a widower, and his daughter, Agneta, who was only a few years older than Lena, ran the household. She showed Lena to a guest chamber and suggested that she rest until dinner "to recover from the terrible shock." Lena refrained from telling her that anyone who lived at the Temple of Thenoth, spent time at the royal court in Haven, and numbered several Heralds among her closest friends was not all that easily shocked. It was nice to be pampered occasionally.

She lay down and tried to rest but found that she couldn't do more than nap fitfully. Her mind was still connected to the vultures, and she was as twitchy as they were.

When she and Agneta went down for dinner, Lord Tobias and the Heralds had returned. Conversation at the table did not dwell on the dead body other than to say that nobody in the area recognized him. The vultures were not mentioned, but Lena was still linked to them, both the ones watching the body and the ones leaving the group to eat. And while she would not have called herself particularly squeamish, Lena did find that this was destroying her appetite. She shoved food around her plate, took small bites and swallowed them quickly, and sipped her wine.

After dinner, they went to the drawing room, and while Agneta poured tea, Samira took her cup, sat down next to Lena, and asked bluntly, "What's wrong? I've never seen you go off your food like that."

"I don't know," Lena sighed. "I can't seem to break the link with the vultures. I'm still connected to the entire wake."

Samira choked on her tea. "A *wake* of vultures?" she asked when she got her breath back. "Is that really what they're called?"

Her voice was loud enough for everyone in the room

to hear, and Robin started laughing. "A wake of vultures! That's a good one—and, in this case, quite appropriate."

Lena looked at her host, who looked bemused, and his daughter, who looked appalled. "He doesn't mean any disrespect to the dead," she explained hastily. "It's a sort of game at the Temple: learning the names for groups of animals."

"Like a murder of crows?" Lord Tobias asked.

"That's one name for them," Lena said, "but we call ours a storytelling of crows, especially since they saved Samira's life. We also have a charm of finches and a leash of greyhounds."

"Your Temple must be an interesting place," Agneta said.

"It can be dull," Samira said with a grin, "but it's been my experience that it doesn't happen often. There is, of course, the Peace of the God, but that's different."

Lena didn't hear the rest of the conversation because her attention was suddenly completely captured by the vultures, who were watching a woman approach them—or rather the body they were protecting everyone from. They flew toward her to chase her away, but lightning sparked from her fingertips as she sought to drive them back. They swooped in dizzying circles, trying to avoid the attack while still keeping her away from the body, but a bolt grazed one of them: a searing pain across the top of its wing.

Lena cried out, clapping a hand to her bare arm and then screamed when she touched it. Her vision was doubled between the roadside where the birds were and the room where her body was, but she could dimly see a burn across her arm.

"What is it?" Samira said urgently.

"Help them!" Lena gasped. "She's trying to kill them!"

"The vultures?"

Lena managed to nod. She heard Robin and Samira run from the room and caught the edge of Samira's Mindcall to her Companion. Then she fainted.

When she came to, Lena was lying on the sofa, with a pillow beneath her head and a blanket covering most of her body. Her burned arm was outside the blanket, and Agneta was gently pressing a cold cloth against the injury. The cold felt good. The pressure didn't. The pain made her feel sick—and thankful she hadn't eaten much at dinner. And the shouting didn't help.

Apparently Samira, Robin, and their Companions had managed to subdue the stranger and had dragged her back to Lord Tobias to answer for the attack.

"—and what you did to the King's ward!" Lord Tobias finished angrily.

"All I did was try to deal with the vermin feasting on my son's body!" the stranger shouted back.

"Vultures are *not* vermin!" Lena might feel ill, but she wasn't taking *that* lying down. She pushed herself to a seated position, letting the cloth fall from her burned arm. "And they were not *feasting* on anyone!"

"My son's body is still lying by the side of the road, surrounded by those flesh eaters! Has nobody here the decency to pick up the dead and lay them out in a seemly fashion, someplace where they are *not* food for the vultures?"

"I don't know why your son died," Lena said, "but I'm guessing you didn't see the dead vulture next to him—or notice how uncorrupt his body is. Anything that touched him—or tried to eat something that touched him—died. The vultures guard the body so that nobody else dies; they chased us back when we first saw him. They were trying to save you from whatever killed him—and you tried to kill them in return." She turned anxiously to Samira. "How many—"

"None dead," Samira said reassuringly. "A few singed feathers, the one burned wing, and your matching arm."

"Is that creature your familiar, then?" the woman asked.

"I don't know what a familiar is," Lena said wearily. As her anger subsided, the pain was becoming more noticeable. "I have Animal Mindspeech, and I'm linked to all of them right now. They're not happy."

"Neither am I," the woman said grimly. She looked around nervously—as if, Lena thought, there were people in the room that none of them could see.

"I don't believe any of us is happy right now," Lord Tobias said. "And I am sorry for your loss. Having seen your son's body, however, I must say that Lena is correct. The vultures have not touched it, and neither have the normal processes of decay."

"You don't know how long he's been dead," the woman pointed out.

"Lena?" Lord Tobias looked at her.

"Five days," she replied. "That's what the vultures say."

"He can't possibly have been dead that long!" the stranger protested.

"When did you last see him?" Samira asked.

"A week ago."

"Then he could very well have been dead for that long," Lena said. "You don't know. You were not there, and the vultures were. They saw him die."

"You don't know that."

"Yes, I do. It's my Gift." Lena sagged wearily against the sofa. *Ladylike posture can go hang.*

"Father," Agneta said. "I really think she belongs in bed."

"She does," Lord Tobias agreed. "Didn't you send for a Healer?"

"Yes, but she doesn't need to be awake for that."

"Lead the way, Lady Agneta," Robin said, lifting Lena carefully into his arms. "I'll carry her upstairs."

Lena's arm was fine when she woke in the morning, and she was hungry, so obviously a Healer had treated her while she slept. Unfortunately, while her arm was healed, except for an area of reddened skin, the Mindspeech with the vultures continued unabated. She was glad that some of them were asleep and the rest were on guard, which meant that none of them was eating. This enabled her to eat a large breakfast troubled by nothing other than doubled vision, which she could cope with as long as she was otherwise healthy.

Lena and Agneta were sipping tea and nibbling fruit-filled pastries when the rest of the household joined them. Samira and Robin had the stranger between them, and she was looking about wildly as if she were trying to see things the rest of them couldn't.

"Girls," Lord Tobias said, "I don't believe you were properly introduced to our guest last night. This is Mage Photine, who lives just over the border in Rethwellan."

Both girls murmured conventional replies, as the rest of the group sat down and began to eat. Photine seemed nervous, and she kept looking around the room. "Do you have secret passages and spyholes in the walls here?" she asked.

"Probably," Lord Tobias said. "This is an old castle, and it was built to guard the border."

"Do your servants use them?" Photine shuddered. "I can *feel* the eyes watching me!"

Robin chuckled. "My mother always used to say that Vanyel's eyes were always watching us—I think she was trying to make sure we didn't get into too much trouble when *her* eyes weren't on us."

" 'Vanyel's eyes are watching you'—I think that's a song," Lena said. "It sounds familiar, somehow."

"Yes," Agneta agreed. "I think I've heard it too."

"Before we become immersed in ancient ballads," Lord Tobias said with a fond look at his daughter, "we need to deal with our current problems."

"We should make a list," Samira said. "Lena, are you still Mindspeaking to the wake?"

"I'm not actively speaking to them," Lena said, "but I'm still linked, and I can't break it. Ever since we saw them on the road, I've been linked to all of them."

"So Lena is bound to the vultures," Samira said.

"And my son is dead." Photine appeared to find that more important.

"Dead and uncorrupt," Samira pointed out, "which is not natural. Do you have any idea how that could have happened?"

"He was working on spells to increase his magical ability, I believe."

"Does he have older siblings who are more powerful?" Robin asked. He was more familiar with sibling dynamics than Lena, who had not been blessed with siblings—or even friends—her own age.

"Younger ones," Photine said dryly. "Eskil was my oldest child, and very obviously the least talented.

Everyone in the family knew that. I think the dog has more magical ability."

"He probably did something stupid," Lena said. "Young men tend to . . ." her voice trailed off, as she remembered that her older brother had done something stupid—not to mention blasphemous—and ended up dead at about the same age as Eskil.

"Is there a spell in Rethwellan to increase one's magical power?" Agneta asked.

"Several, actually," Photine admitted, "but they wouldn't work here in Valdemar. There's no magic here."

Lena frowned in thought. "So if he tried some sort of spell that absorbed ambient magic . . ."

Photine sighed. "He would go for maximum power— I caught his little sister teasing him when I was home last—but his body wouldn't be strong or trained enough to handle it."

"At which point he would cross over to Valdemar in order to stop the spell," Samira said.

"But it didn't stop," Lena objected. She turned to Photine. "I've heard that evil Mages used to get power by killing people. Does that mean that life force, whatever it is that keeps us alive, works like magic?"

"I supposed it could," Photine said reluctantly, "but any spell he was using should have stopped at the border. Everyone knows you can't do magic in Valdemar."

"Wasn't what you did to the vultures magic?" Lena asked. "There was fire shooting out of your fingertips."

"Levin-bolts," Photine corrected absentmindedly. "They're more like lightning than fire."

"Well, I can assure you that they burn," Lena said, looking pointedly at the still-reddened area on her arm. "But the point is that you *can* do magic in Valdemar."

"Vanyel's Eyes!" Agneta said suddenly. "That's what I was trying to remember. They guard against the sort of magic foreign Mages do. That's why you feel that you're being watched; as soon as you used offensive magic within our borders, they started to gather."

"Started?" Photine said nervously. "What happens *after* that?"

"It's an old ballad," Agneta said, "not a recipe book."

"The point is," Lord Tobias said, "that magic does work in Valdemar, so whatever spell your son was attempting would not have stopped at the border."

"I think it's still active," Lena said. "I didn't notice at the time because I was distracted, but your ... levin-bolts ... were pulled toward the body. That's why you had trouble hitting the vultures. And I think that anything that touches the body has its life energy pulled from it to the body."

"The grass!" Robin said suddenly. "When I was guarding the body yesterday I noticed that the grass around it was dead."

"You don't get energy from *grass*," Photine said scornfully.

"It was alive, and now it's dead," Lena pointed out. "A vulture ate a rat that touched the body and fell away from it as it died, and the vulture died as well. The vultures have kept anything alive from touching it since then—aside from the grass."

"And you say it was sucking in levin-bolts?" Photine asked.

"Not completely." Lena said, "From what I picked up from what the vultures were seeing, it seemed more like it was trying to draw the bolts in, but you were trying to hit the birds, so it just pulled them toward it. I don't know what would happen if they actually reached the body. And the vultures appear to be convinced that any human that touches it will die. That's why they're staying there and keeping guard over it." She looked at Photine. "*Would* it kill a human who touched it?"

"Quite possibly," Photine said. "We would need to experiment to be sure."

"Not with my people you don't," Lord Tobias said firmly.

"No," Photine sighed. "That would be much too dangerous."

Samira, who had apparently been pondering the various possibilities, asked, "Could the spell be what's holding the vultures and Lena together?"

"Gifts aren't Rethwellan's sort of magic," Lena said, "but they can't be *entirely* natural or everyone would have them. And if the spell on the body is pulling energy from grass, maybe it could be trying to pull it from the link."

"Which means we really need to do something about the body," Lord Tobias said grimly. "It obviously can't be buried where it is now. Can you transport it back to Rethwellan? What do you normally do in a case like this?"

"We don't normally *have* 'a case like this'," Photine said crossly, "and I'm not certain what it would take to transport my son's body safely." She scowled. "I believe our best option is to destroy it here."

"Cremation?" Robin asked. "If we piled wood around it as close as we could get, and you used your levin-bolts to amplify the flames?"

"No," Lena shook her head violently. "Poisonous smoke."

"You don't know that," Robin objected.

"Do you want to risk it?" Lena demanded.

"The girl has a point," Photine said. "If we don't know whether the smoke will be poisonous, this is not a spell I can ethically use." She fell silent, apparently lost in thought. "Not Fire," she murmured, "apparently not Earth, using Air would have the same problems as Fire, but maybe Water. . . ."

"Elemental transformation spells?" Lena asked. She had always been a bit of a bookworm, and the Palace and Collegia in Haven had large libraries. She had read some books on foreign magic, and she remembered that there were systems that used four elements: Earth, Air, Fire, and Water.

"Something of the sort," Photine replied, "and Water is my strongest element. Let's see: 'Let this skin and all within be changed to purest Water'—if I specify purity in the spell, that should transform whatever might be poisonous."

"But that doesn't cover anything outside of his skin," Lena objected. "There's still his hair, his clothes—would that spell even change his fingernails?"

Photine looked first startled, and then approving. "It's a shame I can't take you home for training. You obviously have the mind for it, and apparently some natural ability. How would you word the spell then?"

"Well, I'd test whatever I came up with on the dead vulture first. If turning it to water doesn't damage the area around it, then we know the spell is probably safe to use on a human. And if the spell doesn't work properly, at least it will be on a much smaller scale."

Photine nodded approvingly. "And the wording?"

"May garb, hair, skin, and all within be changed to

purest water," replied Lena. "He's wearing gloves, so using 'garb' would include fingernails and anything else covered by his clothing, and his clothing needs to be destroyed anyway. For the vulture, I'd substitute 'claws, beak, feathers, skin' for 'may garb, hair, skin'—I think that would work."

"I think so, too." Photine said.

They all went to the roadside; Photine was needed for the spells, Lena had to explain what was happening to the vultures and get their cooperation for the test spell, and everyone else was either concerned about Lena's safety, curious, or both.

It took a while for Lena to persuade the vultures to allow a foreign Mage to destroy one of their wake, even if it was dead. But once they agreed, the test spell proceeded flawlessly. The body of the vulture turned to water, and the water ran along both the dead grass and the grass that was still green. They observed the area for some time, during which the green grass remained that way, and the area with the dead grass started to sprout new growth. Photine, however, became more agitated.

"Yes, the spell works," she snapped, "but those wretched Eyes appear to have called in all their friends to watch. They're even more unnerving than the vultures!"

Lena, meanwhile, was discovering that the dead body that had anchored her link to the wake was the vulture, not the human. Her Animal Mindspeech was now back under her own control. The vultures, however, still perched in the trees, keeping watch over Eskil's body.

"Can you do the second spell?" she asked Photine, "even with the Eyes watching?"

"Yes," Photine said through gritted teeth. "Remind me of the words again, just to be safe."

"May garb, hair, skin, and all within be changed to purest water," Lena recited.

The Mage repeated the spell, and the body dissolved into water, washing the surrounding area clean. Lena could tell that the vultures were satisfied even before they started to fly away. In a few moments, all that remained were the humans and a patch of damp grass and earth.

"Now that I know my son is properly at rest," Photine said with profound relief, "I can go home and get away from all these Eyes!"

Maiden's Hope
Michele Lang

Spring had finally returned to the Northern village of Longfall. Sparrow walked silently through the edge of the Forest of Sorrows, where only shadowed patches of old snow remained, clinging to the darkness under the shade of the great evergreens.

The air smelled of tender, green new leaves, and she inhaled their fragrance like a tonic. Sparrow knew the forest held many unknown and hidden dangers—her old dad had been careful to warn her about them—but the air smelled so sweet, and the dappled sunlight warmed her face so deliciously that she couldn't imagine anything dangerous happening to her on this sunny morning. Still, just in case, Sparrow carried a stout walking staff for defense.

Besides, she needed the healing herb trefoil, needed it badly and the villagers had picked the beds closest to the village clean. Sparrow's mother had died for lack of trefoil during the long winter just past, and she'd be hanged before she lost her father, too.

This morning, his face had looked gray and drawn. Her mother had looked exactly like that before the symptoms of snow fever had closed in, shutting down

her lungs and killing her. It was spring, but only just . . .
the danger of winter sickness still lurked. Sparrow's father didn't realize the snow fever had returned to claim
him, but Sparrow saw the shadows over his face.

She just *knew*.

So trefoil she must have, no matter how far into the
forest she must venture to claim it. After her morning
chores were done, she'd dressed for a long forage, wore
her oldest homespun skirt, her winter shoes. Carried the
family herb basket, its wicker handle rubbed smooth by
her dear mother's fingertips. And, recklessly, she wore
the berry-red sash Sparrow herself had woven and embroidered through the endless, gray winter.

Her villagers, virtuous, sober, and hardworking, preferred the dove-gray of homespun, with light blue veils
for ladies for festivals, faires, and hearth celebrations. So
the red was bold. But Sparrow so craved a splash of color
in that endless Northern gray that her father had given
her the berry dye himself, kind man. The sash had distracted her through long, closed-in days when the
weather was too bitter and violent for her and her family
to emerge from their cottage. And during the nightmarish nights, when Sparrow tended her mother in her last
illness, she'd desperately contemplated the stitching, the
leaf border, how she would finish the tassels at the end.
Anything to distract her from the cruel, indisputable fact
that her mother was slowly dying under Sparrow's patient fingers.

So she wore her red sash today in defiance of the gray,
in defiance of sickness and of death. And it was the red
sash that ended up changing the world that morning.

Still and all, defiance alone wouldn't find Sparrow her
trefoil. Only a deep foray could do that, a long hike deep

into the heart of the forest, her thick shoes slipping in mud and her hands untangling her skirts from thorny brambles.

By midmorning, Sparrow's tenacity was rewarded. She found a clearing hidden deep within a circle of broken boulders, ringed inside a dense clump of bluefurr trees. A bluebird shot over the circle and safely past, and its progress reassured her that no spell, not even a benevolent one, hovered over the silent, watching stones.

She gingerly touched the nearest greenish stone, and no hum of magic warmed her palms. But as she slipped between the stones and entered the circle to harvest the trefoil, Sparrow wondered.

The trefoil swept in a gaudy carpet between the stones, sparkling with droplets of morning dew. The bluebird, hidden within swaying branches over her head, broke into a virtuoso song so beautiful that it thrilled Sparrow to the marrow. Spring had come, new life had returned to the North. The moment contained pure magic, crystallized out of time, and Sparrow uptilted her face to the sun, greedily soaking up sunlight and gratitude both.

But the sublime moment passed, as such moments always do, leaving Sparrow alone in the hidden glade. Her fears returned, and the gray shadows in her father's face evoked memories, too fresh, of the darkness that had already stolen her mother. She had a job to do.

With a sigh, Sparrow bent to the purplish-silver trefoil, the bottoms of her skirts soaking up the cool dew as she began harvesting. But a sudden rustle in the underbrush past the clearing brought her upright again, trembling. She scanned the encroaching forest for the dangers her dad had warned her against. Downwind, no scent of bear. No muffled roar of a Mountain Cat or screech of a Great Eagle or other magical, malevolent winged beast.

Sparrow strained her eyes staring into the undulating shadows underneath the swaying evergreen branches, searching for pair or two of hunters' eyes. But no.

She feared the hidden tribes even more than the beasts of prey that hunted in the untamed forest. When Sparrow was a tiny mite, her best friend, a sturdy five-year-old named Brock, had been carried away by a tribe — or so her parents had told her, in an effort to scare her from wandering away from the village and into the woods the way Brock had loved to do.

Fear held Sparrow now in its grip. She could see nothing, sense nothing, but an inner knowing insisted that *something* was coming out of the cool darkness.

Coming for her.

Sparrow glanced at her walking stick, propped against the side of one of the stones, and then forced herself to harvest the trefoil once more. Standing tall, flashing her red sash, wasn't going to protect her from that creeping fear edging along her spine. Or from bears, either.

And secretly, in her heart of hearts, she was so sick of waiting. Waiting for her mother to die no matter how hard Sparrow fought to keep her in this life. Waiting for spring to finally arrive. Waiting, waiting. Afraid, afraid . . .

She refused to wait for that unknown magic to leap out of the forest and grab her. Refused to fear it, even. Sparrow had trefoil to pick.

She bent again to her task, gratefully inhaling the flowerlike fragrance of the herb carpet as she worked. Gently, she stripped the mature leaves from the stem, leaving the tender, growing buds intact. The repetitive motion and the peaceful stillness of the glade soon soothed Sparrow's jangled nerves and she sighed in relief. Like the surface of a cool lake, the ripples of her fear edged out to shore and away, and the natural tranquility of her spirit surfaced once more.

Another rustle, unmistakable this time, and Sparrow rose again, ready to run. But where? If she chose wrong, she might well leap into the jaws of a hidden hunter.

The bluebird shot out from the tree branches, trilling its magnificent song. The bird was clearly not frightened—it swooped overhead, singing, as if announcing an important visitor.

The bird alighted on the boulder nearest to Sparrow, scarcely a hands-breadth away. She held her breath, half in fear, half in wonder, and watched the antics of the bright little creature with growing amazement.

The bluebird cocked its head, focused one bright eye upon her. And then it burst into an intricate little chorale of joy, as if trying desperately to convey some compelling news.

He sang the same series of notes again, a wind rose in the clearing, and then he cocked his head the other direction, shot into the sky and away. Sparrow watched him go, even as he disappeared and the rustling grew louder.

She had not understood the specifics of his song, but the bluebird had brought her glad tidings.

Sparrow took a deep breath, ready now to face whatever emerged from the forest, the bird's song still echoing in her ears. She no longer feared predators, but she did not know quite what to expect.

What emerged from the deep shadows under the trees struck Sparrow with absolute, starkest amazement.

A scent of spices wafted along the breeze, and in the next moment an enormous white stallion, richly caparisoned, leaped out of the darkness and into the golden sunlight of the clearing.

Sparrow's knees went soft, and she almost fell into the herbs, so great was her shock. She had seen horses before—traders' hacks, donkeys. But never such a noble steed, with such velvet-smooth haunches and beautifully expressive sapphire eyes.

The steed strode forward impatiently, scuffing at the moss outside the ring of boulders. Answering his call, Sparrow stepped hesitantly out of the circle, her mother's herb basket overflowing with fragrant trefoil.

As she drew near, for the first time she noticed the young man on horseback, bent over the stallion's glorious snow-white mane. His fingers interlocked deeply within the long, glossy strands. His face was turned away from her, seemingly oblivious to her approach.

He wore the tunics and the leggings of the tribes who hid within the forest, and who of late had been engaging more and more in trade with the villagers of the North. Brilliant embroidery bordered his sleeves and cuffs, and the feathers and plumage embroidered on his sleeves and across his back dazzled her eye with color, as if a fantastic tropical bird had emerged from the green darkness in search of the bluebird.

His appearance thrilled her, and yet, despite the finery of both horse and rider, the hairs on Sparrow's nape prickled in warning. Her fingertips tingled with a sudden rush of fear. She looked him up and down again, from the shock of his white-blond hair, down the length of his slim, wiry body, to the clenched fists buried in mane, and then ending at his feet.

Bare feet.

Sparrow took a step back. It was too soon in the season, the mud and the bare underbrush too unforgiving, to go about without shoes at all. Aside from that, this prosperous-looking young man had no provisions rolled up behind him, no saddlebags, no water, nothing. And he had clearly ridden far, in such outlandish foreign dress.

These were no hunters. But something was terribly wrong here.

Gingerly, Sparrow forced herself forward, and she dared to look the stallion in the eye. He whickered gently and waved his nose at her, as if beckoning her to approach. Her mouth went dry, but step by step she grew closer to this spectacular creature.

He must be a Companion. No mere horse would carry a slumping rider for so long without becoming spooked and attempting to drop him.

She reached out a trembling hand, and the Companion tapped her fingers with his velvety nose. At his touch, her fear completely melted away, and new confidence rose inside of her like a secret spring.

She gently moved to the Companion's right side in order to peer into the young man's face. His eyes were shrunken and looked sealed shut, and pockmarks marred his cheeks and chin. His thin lips moved soundlessly, as if he were whispering a secret spell under his breath, but he seemed to take no notice of Sparrow, his surroundings, or even of his Companion.

From what little Sparrow knew of Companions, only

their Chosen may ride. But this bent over creature was surely no Herald ...

Without thinking, Sparrow reached into her mother's herb basket and pulled out a trefoil leaf. Gently, she rubbed the silver foil from the purplish leaf's underside over the boy's pitted, scarred face, knowing that the silvery pollen held the greatest concentration of the herb's healing qualities. If only she could steep a tea and get it into him!

:Thank you,: a voice whispered inside Sparrow's mind. *:We finally found you ... your beautiful red sash was like a flare in the forest.:*

Her fear whipped up again, so sharp it sliced her like a knife. Her heart beat hard enough to pound in her throat. She knew instantly that it was the beautiful white beast who spoke.

:Do not be afraid,: the voice whispered, so lovingly that her heart pulled back from a full gallop into a canter. *:We have been seeking you, Sparrow.:*

"Me?" she squeaked aloud. "But why? This boy needs a Master Healer, one trained by Keisha herself, if possible. And how did you know my name? I am just the goat farmer's daughter."

:You are Sparrow. And Brock needs you ... only you. This boy is Brock.:

With a cry, Sparrow sprang to the boy's side, reached up to give him an awkward hug from far below. Brock! Her beloved childhood friend, somehow returned.

But she hadn't recognized him, he was so grievously changed.

"I don't understand, sir. He needs more healing than I could ever do."

:He does not need healing. He needs you. Besides, do you not realize your calling?:

And in an inner whisper, the Companion shared his name, Abilard, a precious gift. Sparrow knew enough to understand that such direct communication with a Companion only occurred with their Chosen.

But she knew just as certainly, in her heart of hearts, that she was not the Chosen one here. It was Brock, somehow, even maimed and silent as he was . . .

:He is Brock, but his Clan calls him Cloudbrother. He needs you to call him out from the clouds, back here to me.:

Chills rippled up and down her spine. "Call him out of the clouds? I don't know how to do that . . ." she whispered.

:I know. But I believe you will.:

Abilard quickly made it clear that he wanted them all to return to Longfall without delay. After tying her mother's herb basket to the Companion's tack, Sparrow used one of the smaller rocks to climb up behind Cloudbrother. And after only a moment's hesitation, she left her walking staff behind. She was safe with Abilard.

Sparrow had ridden a horse astride before, but in her skirts she was forced to ride sidesaddle. Once the Companion made sure she was ready, he leaped forward down the pathway back to the village. Abilard's stride was so huge and smooth that Sparrow relaxed after a few moments, resting her head against Cloudbrother's back. And tried her best to be sensible and to think.

Cloudbrother. She was glad to call Brock that new name, because she saw hardly a trace of her old friend in this new, strange form. She remembered a busy, funny, always moving little boy with a restless, wandering spirit.

This silent, distant, closed-off person held no resemblance to that boy who had been lost to the forest so long ago.

It was no matter; Sparrow would still do her best to reach him. But her healing skills were rudimentary at best, and her belief in her ability had been deeply shaken by her mother's fatal illness. If she could not heal her own mother, Sparrow doubted she would be of much use to this young man.

And yet . . . Abilard, the most wondrous being Sparrow had ever met, clearly had unshakable belief in her. She was used to being the invisible one, the helper, the sweet one. Her older brother, a big, brawny fellow and the secret object of admiration of all the other girls in the village, had gone all the way to Haven to serve in the army there. Her brother was the star of the family, not her. Sparrow's role was to make sure that everybody around her was safe, well fed and happy. Her father's nickname for her, "Little Mother," suited her well, and Sparrow had been more than happy to assume that role . . . until today.

But the appearance of this strange boy and his magnificent Companion had thrown her completely out of her old life.

Sparrow sighed, held on tightly to Cloudbrother's waist, and tried her best to relax and enjoy the extraordinary sensation of flying through the air on Abilard's strong back. Somehow, all would come out right. She hoped.

Their arrival in the village of Longfall caused a great sensation. The little children who watched the flocks of sheep on the meadows outside the village took up the cry first, and by the time Abilard galloped to the tiny

central square (more of a lawn, really) in front of the
mayor's handsome house, almost all the village had gathered to see what all the fuss was about.

Sparrow's father, Hari, stood at the front of the crowd,
an anxious expression wrinkling his face. When he saw
her, his face softened in relief. But the shadows of sickness haunting him had only deepened since she had left
to find the herbs, and the sight sent a chill deep into the
pit of Sparrow's stomach.

She hid her trepidation, though, and slid off Abilard's
back as gracefully as she could without a mounting
block. "It's Brock!" she called to her father. "He's been
Chosen! And returned."

A low murmur rippled through the small crowd.
Brock's parents, heartbroken at his loss, had left years
ago to live with relatives in Errold's Grove, a bigger village not too far away. Terreen, the washerwoman, muttered under her breath just loud enough for Sparrow to
hear, "Good thing his parents aren't here to see this."

Sparrow looked over her shoulder at the boy on his
steed, blind, white-haired, and bent. About to protest
Terreen's harsh judgment, she held back from a harsh
reply. Instead, Sparrow said, "His tribe calls him Cloudbrother. I guess you can see why . . ."

The mayor pushed through the crowd, and Sparrow
relaxed a trifle. Mayor Undor was a good man, kind and
shrewd both, and she expected he would take her part
and welcome Brock home.

But his expression was grave. "Sparrow, dear. This boy
looks sick. Really sick."

His fear was well-founded. In years past, the tribes
who traded with the villagers sometimes inadvertently
brought disease with them, plagues the villagers had no

defense against. This past winter had been brutal and hard, and while no clan members had visited in the heavy snows, many people had sickened like her mother.

Mayor Undor was charged with protecting the village. But Sparrow wasn't about to stand by and let the mayor send her old friend away.

"He isn't contagious," she blurted, her cheeks flushing. "Look, he was sick a while ago. His Companion tells me he needs no healing, and plenty of traders visit us here with no harm. He is no danger to us."

Terreen crossed her meaty arms across her chest. "He sure looks sick to me. And how does a horse talk?"

"No, this ain't no horse," Mayor Undor quickly said. "This is a true Companion, no doubt." He bowed to Abilard. "Welcome, sir, to our village of Longfall. You've met Sparrow, of course, and I am Mayor Undor."

Abilard snorted and whinnied his approval.

Mayor Undor shot her a quick glance. "The Companion told you? He spoke within your mind? Don't that mean he just Chose you?"

A shocked silence passed over the crowd. And it bothered Sparrow. She knew she wasn't Chosen, but did all of these people think the prospect was so shocking? Was she that invisible? She took a deep breath, reminded herself not to jump to conclusions.

"No, Mayor," she said slowly. "He spoke to me in my mind, yes, though not to Choose me. But to ask for my help."

Hari stepped forward and bowed deeply to the Companion. "Thank you for watching out for my girl Sparrow. I'm her dad, and you are both welcome in my home." He looked around, daring anybody from the village to protest.

The mayor shook Hari's hand. "I can open my larder for the guests too, Hari. Anything you need, just send Sparrow over, and we'll get it for you."

Mayor Undor brushed his too-long forelock of hair out of his eyes and smiled. "Sparrow, you're a good-hearted girl. If your Companion there says this boy is safe to stay, I'll believe him. You go take care of him like you do."

A flood of warmth passed through Sparrow, a cascade of gratitude. "Thank you, sir," she said. "I'll take care of Cloudbrother at home. And that's how it should be."

The mayor smiled, nodded, stepped back. But Sparrow could see he was still worried.

Hari helped her ease Cloudbrother off his mount and into the house. Together, they tucked him into the second featherbed, and covered him with old quilts, though he had no fever. "He looks like a leaf getting ready to blow away," her father remarked, and he was right.

In the bed, he looked profoundly peaceful, milky-pale, asleep. *Who would want to return from floating in the clouds?* Sparrow wondered, thinking ruefully of all the chores that waited for her every morning.

But Abilard needed her to call him back. How would she reach him?

She returned outside, where the Companion patiently waited. "You must be starved after such a run," she said. "Can I bring you over to the mayor's house to get a bite to eat? He's got the nicest stables in the village by a long way." She was too shy to admit that she and her father had no stable at all, only a goat pen where Hari daily milked the goats. Abilard was too royal a creature to set foot in such a place.

Abilard whickered his consent, and they set off for the mayor's place.

:You do not need to Heal him,: the Companion assured her again. *:Only call him back ... :*

But wouldn't that require healing far beyond any skill Sparrow possessed? She sighed instead of voicing her concerns, and together they walked. Suddenly the village looked too small and muddy and gray for a magnificent being like Abilard.

The mayor himself received the Companion kindly, and Sparrow took the herb basket back to tend to both of her charges. Before she left, Abilard whickered at her once more, gentleness radiating from his beautiful sapphire eyes.

He knows I am afraid, Sparrow thought in a quiet wonder. *And yet he still believes in me ...*

When she arrived at her cottage, her mother's herb basket swinging from its handle over her bent elbow, Hari was waiting at the threshold.

He looked at the basket, overflowing with healing trefoil, and sighed. "I know why you went to so much fuss," he said, his scratchy voice breaking over the words. "It's me, right? You always were quick to see trouble coming. Poor little mother. Always worrying about everybody else first."

By now, Sparrow saw the symptoms had passed from a foreboding shadow to physical effects her father could feel. His voice was thick with sickness now ... if she could not heal him herself or get him help, he would not last two weeks.

But winter had retreated, and spring had finally come. Sparrow had plenty of trefoil, and better yet, the trading paths had opened again. The mayor could send word to the Healers who rode Circuit in the area, and they would not be alone in their battle against sickness. It was still early enough for Hari to survive the snow fever.

Sparrow memorized the sight of her father standing in the doorway, his shoulders rounded but still strong, a smile creasing his face. Even haunted with shadow, Sparrow still adored the sight of him.

She had the sudden sense she would not see him again in their doorway, not for a very long time.

"Look, Dad," she said, her voice choked too, not with illness, but with emotion, "Mama's herb basket is full to overflowing."

Hari tilted his head and took a step toward her. "It's not Mama's herb basket anymore, Sparrow girl. It's yours."

Sparrow didn't know what to do with the storm of emotions whirling inside her . . . fear for her father warred with the wonder of Abilard and his ability to speak in her mind, and worry for Cloudbrother threatened to rob her of her memory of Brock, and her ability to see past his hurts to his true self.

She knew better than to stay within that storm and stew. Instead, Sparrow got to work, and, as always, taking care of the business in front of her helped soothe the worry inside.

Her father had already tended to the hearth fire, and Sparrow set a steep of the trefoil to boil. While the tea strengthened, Sparrow crushed a double handful of trefoil in her mortar and pestle to make a poultice and splashed it with some witch hazel to brighten it.

She hurried to Cloudbrother's side. He still slept, apparently exhausted from the long journey through the forest with Abilard. His hair, light and airy as a blown dandelion puff, rested on his forehead.

Sparrow felt again for fever. Thank the great Mother, nothing. She gently lowered the quilt, watched the easy breathing of his chest, rising and falling without strain. Abilard was right . . . he suffered from no plague, not now.

Still, the trefoil couldn't hurt, and hopefully the increased stimulation of his system could help. Blushing, she scooped the poultice mash from the mortar with her bare fingers, and reaching inside his untied tunic, she spread the mixture over his half-bared chest. The poultice tingled under Sparrow's fingers, strengthening her as well as Cloudbrother, and she took refuge in that warm tingle, took it in from her hands to strengthen her vitality in her core.

A great lassitude took her at the same time, and Sparrow found herself kneeling by the side of his bed, her fingertips resting over Cloudbrother's heart, her own heart slowing to beat in concert with his.

She shook off her sleep long enough to look behind her, back to the hearth where Hari waited. He was watching her . . . and smiling.

"I know how to serve tea, girl," he said, stifling a cough with the back of a balled fist. "Go ahead, I'll have a little rest here." And quite deliberately, Hari turned his chair so he faced away from the back room where Cloudbrother rested.

The tea's gentle fragrance wafted over to Sparrow, relaxing and strengthening her still more. Gratefully, she returned her attention to her charge, still sleeping under her fingers.

A small smile now curved the young man's lips, and a

rush of color had filled his cheeks. He no longer looked like a marble carving, but a living, breathing man.

Tears prickled at Sparrow's eyes, but she was too busy to give in to them, at least not yet. Instead she rested her forehead on the soft quilt and closed her eyes, took a deep breath.

Immediately her consciousness swept into a swiftly moving current of thought, as if she had turned into a sparrow for true and shot into the sky like the bluebird. Far away, her body waited for her, and Sparrow sensed that though her mind insisted she should be frightened, nothing would hurt her in this new place.

She soared into the whiteness, focused her sight, and saw that she flew through a great vastness of light, filtered through shifting carpets of white and gray.

Clouds.

"Brock," she said in this place, and the air vibrated around her, sending ripples through the billowing white. "Please come."

Instantly he appeared. In this plane of being his eyes were open, sparkling with life and vitality, his shoulders broad. He wore the same tunic as back in Longfall, his legs stretched long and straight, the gorgeous plumage of his embroidered trews and tunic shining through the whiteness like a beacon.

"No fear, Sparrow," he said, his face shining with happiness. "I missed you! And here we are, together again. After the fever, I searched for you here, but never could find you."

Sparrow wanted to laugh with joy, fly through the endless white with Brock, and forget all that waited for them below. But she remembered why she had come here to seek Brock, the master of the clouds.

"Abilard needs you," she said. "Is there any way you can come back with me? To speak with the people around you?"

He shrugged, and while the smile never faded from his face, it grew a little sad. "I never left. My brothers just couldn't find me up here. Even the Masters who came to find me . . . they sensed me, but I couldn't speak to them! But you . . ."

Brock's sadness faded away. "You knew me before I became Cloudbrother, you know me to the root. And Sparrow, you always could fly . . . just you'd forget before you woke up again. We'd fly like this together, as children. I missed you. Plenty of folks here to talk to, but none of them knew Brock. And you do."

With a shock of recognition, Sparrow remembered. How they'd flown together at night as children, after going to sleep in their respective cottages. No need to swear a secret because they'd never spoken of it in the daytime.

"Come closer," she said. "If I stay with you, could you speak to your brothers on the ground?"

He glided to her, took her dream-hands in his. "If you stay with me, I think we'll find a new country to explore. I can go ahead, you can report back."

Sparrow half-laughed, half-sobbed, "But I can't stay here forever, Brock! My dad needs me, and we'll all starve to death if somebody doesn't cook the eggs or milk the goats!"

She could never leave Longfall, not for long. Sparrow had never considered the possibility, not even to leave her home in dreams.

Brock's expression grew solemn. "Sparrow, a lot of people can milk goats and comb wool and tend house.

You have a gift for all that, too, and it's a noble calling. But not a lot of folks can fly up to the clouds with somebody like me, then come back to earth and report back to folks like your dad. Or Abilard. Or the Heralds."

"But you've been Chosen, Brock. That always happens for a reason. I'm here to help you now, and that's all that matters."

"Oh, it matters all right. It matters a lot. But not for the reasons you think it does. I've already been Chosen, it doesn't matter what happens to me next. But, Sparrow . . . Longfall can mind its goats without you."

His words thundered through her mind and echoed there, endlessly. They weren't talking about Cloudbrother and his being Chosen, and she knew it. They were talking about her. All her life, she'd forced herself to wake up before she could fully remember the visions, the adventures she and Brock would have in the white.

She remembered now. And how she'd held herself back from her Gifts because she was afraid to leave the world she knew behind.

"You think you are up here to find *me*," Brock went on. "But you're wrong about that, too. Abilard came for you as much as he came for me."

"But I'm not Chosen!" she blurted out, as if to insist the door stayed closed.

"Not the way I am, by a Companion. But your Gifts are waiting for you to say yes. Say yes, Sparrow . . . I'll make sure you come to no harm. Come to the Collegium with me. We'll learn together."

"But—what about Dad?"

"No fear," Brock said again, and a bolt of pure peace and golden light shot through her air-heart, filling her with a quiet jubilation. "No fear. Your dad can head into the Vale . . . I'll go call my brothers, and they will send a scout to take him. You won't believe how beautiful the Vales are, Sparrow, but if you come with me you'll see it for yourself someday. He'll stay with my brothers until he's healed. You can come visit him there, and when he feels strong enough, he can come back here if he wants. And you can visit him here too, just as your brother does."

One last time Sparrow hesitated. "But how will he get on?"

"Fine. Just because you head forward into your Gifts doesn't mean you leave love behind. Love is like this, Sparrow . . . it can follow you anywhere, across dream, mountain, or forest. Even death, Sparrow. I'll come back down with you, near as I can anyway. But you'll see what I mean, soon. I'll show you everything."

The next thing she knew, Sparrow had woken up next to Cloudbrother's bed, tears streaming down her face. He was right. Sparrow had to leave the memory of winter behind and head forward into the spring.

She glanced at the table next to the bed. A small bouquet of Maiden's Hope rested there, little white flowers blooming early in the season. A little note propped up there from her father. *For You.*

Sparrow blinked, looked again. The villagers of Longfall often sent message-bouquets to their loved ones, messages of romantic love, mourning, grief. Or hope.

Her dad must have picked them this morning, before she had returned home. Picked them in the hope that she would return out of the dark forest to find them by her bedside. Her father had hoped Sparrow would come home, to him and to herself. And her father's hope, and Sparrow's, had been rewarded.

She sighed in pure relief, then whispered, in her ordinary old voice, "Can you hear me, Brock?"

And far away, with a tiny whisper of a breath, Brock answered. *"Almost."*

The next morning, Sparrow and Cloudbrother both walked down the winding, narrow path to the mayor's house, holding hands. Her friend was still blind, but he was steady on his feet and walking straight, the way Sparrow had seen him in the clouds.

Hari had given Sparrow his blessing, and he had agreed to go with the scouts to healing sanctuary in the K'Valdemar Vale once they came in answer to Cloudbrother's call. "I'll be here when you get back from the Collegium," her father told her. "I promise. No snow fever for me . . . you've seen to that, Sparrow dear."

He didn't call her Little Mother, and Sparrow noticed. She reached up to kiss his weathered, wrinkly cheek. "Thank you," she whispered.

She tucked the little white bouquet of Maiden's Hope into her red sash, the sweet fragrance of home surrounding her. And she left with Cloudbrother by her side.

Sparrow was about to leave the only home she'd ever known. And yet, strangely enough, she knew her true homecoming was only about to begin. She was coming home to her Gifts, and offering those Gifts in service to a higher cause. And even her father and the village of Longfall would be the better for it.

Abilard stood outside the mayor's house waiting for them, as if he knew they'd already set off to meet him.

He looked at them with those wise, luminous deep blue eyes.

    :Welcome, Chosen one, welcome back to this plane of life. And Sparrow, thank you for bringing my Chosen one to me. You have found your true Gift and your calling.:

    :Your adventure is about to begin . . . :

Ex Libris
Fiona Patton

The first hint of spring came to Valdemar's capital as the promise of warm rain on the breeze. On any other day, Sergeant Hektor Dann of the Haven City Watch would have breathed it in with pleasure as he followed his twelve-year-old brother, Padreic, through the streets. On any other day, he would have made some attempt to keep up with the stream of words—official messages, gossip, speculations on the messages and the gossip, greetings to passersby, mild curses at the condition of the cobblestones—issuing from the boy's lips at high speed as he expertly navigated the market-day crowds. This day, however, Hektor had other things on his mind.

... Ismy smilin' up at him from across the saddler's shop counter, from across the table in her small kitchen, from across his desk in his tiny office in the Iron Street Watch House. Ismy, the girl he'd loved at thirteen, lost and found again eight years later. Ismy, who would soon be dressed all in white, with flowers in her hair, smilin' up at him from ...

"—all together in the garden."

He blinked. "What?"

Paddy gave him a speculative grin, then apparently

deciding that discretion was the better part of avoiding a smack to the back of the head, schooled his expression to one of neutral formality more in keeping with his rank of Watch House Runner.

"All together in the garden?" he repeated.

"What?"

"All over the house?"

Hektor's mystified expression remained, and his brother gave a dramatic sigh.

"Daedrus says," he began again, "that he thinks it's been goin' on for a couple of months now maybe. He wasn't even sure that it was theft at first, because his library isn't what you might call organized or anythin', and by library he means his books, all of 'em, and not just the ones in the room he calls the library. They're all over the house, see, because he'll pick one up with the idea of puttin' it back where it belongs, start readin' it on the way, get thinkin' about somethin' else, put it down, pick up a different one, and end up readin' a third book altogether in the garden."

"But he's sure now, that some of them are missin' and not just mislaid?"

"Mostly certain. It's actually kinda more complicated than that."

"Kinda?"

"Yeah, well . . ." Paddy shrugged. "He's old, isn't he? Stuff gets muddled up."

"My dear Sergeant, it's been so long! Come in, come in!"

Retired Artificer Daedrus beamed as he drew them into his long and cluttered front hallway. "Thank you, Padreic. That was very fast indeed," he continued. "I hadn't expected you back so soon. I was going to jot down my thoughts, but I seem to have misplaced my notebook, and now here you are. I imagine Padreic has already filled you in on my little dilemma, Sergeant?"

"Some of it."

"Good, good. We'll just have a cup of tea first, then. If I can find the kettle, that is. Come into the parlor!

"Now, my children, sing peacefully, the way Kasiath taught you!" he called as Hektor braced himself for the usual cacophony of noise that greeted his visits. Instead, a single note from a single bird thrilled out, then as, one by one, the little yellow birds and finches residing in Daedrus' dozen ornate bird cages added their voices to the first. The music swelled and lifted until it seemed as if the very air vibrated with song; then, one by one, they dropped out, until only the first bird continued to sing. When it too fell silent, Daedrus beamed at Hektor's thirteen-year-old sister, standing in the window with three of the birds perched on her shoulder and one on her head. She wore the light blue tunic of an Unaffiliated student over her light blue and gray watch house messenger bird apprentice uniform, and Hektor noted that both were already dusted with yellow feathers.

"Kasiath taught them to do that in less than a fortnight," Daedrus stated, his rheumy blue eyes sparkling with pleasure. "Her teacher's very proud of her, and so am I. You know she takes lessons with Master Clevin here these days?"

Shaking off the birds' spell with some difficulty, Hektor nodded. Believing Kassie had the gift of Bird Speech, before he'd died three months ago, their grandfather had arranged for her to take lessons as a Blue—an Unaffiliated student—at the Collegium next to the Palace itself. But the crowds of highborn youths had been too overwhelming for the shy girl from a watchman's family, and so Daedrus, an old friend of her teacher, had stepped in, opening up his house for lessons for her and a few other like-minded students. He'd waved off any and all thanks; he enjoyed the company, he said, and so in return, the Dann family had taken it upon themselves to keep an eye on the aging Artificer. While Hektor and their oldest brother Aiden, himself a corporal at the Iron Street watch house, made sure Haven's petty criminals kept their distance, Paddy ran Daedrus' errands, Kassie saw to his birds, their middle brothers, Jakon and Raik, who stood the night watch, escorted him home from his various evening events, and their mother and sister-in-law, Suli, saw to his mending.

Paddy maneuvered himself between his brother and the crammed bookcases lining the wall by the door. "I'll make the tea if you like, Daedrus," he offered. "I think I saw the kettle in the hall. That way, you can catch Hek— I mean Sergeant Dann," he corrected smoothly as Hektor turned a frown on him, "up on what happened with yer books."

"Thank you, Padreic," Daedrus replied. "I think the tea tin is in the garden."

"Why is it . . . never mind," Kassie said. "I'll fetch it."

"The thing is, you see, books come and go about the house," Daedrus explained once Paddy had brought the tea and Kassie had returned to his birds. "Almost as if they had a life of their own, but I'm generally aware if they come and go out of the house. You know how it is— you lend a book here, or you lend one to a friend there, and you don't miss them until you need them, and if your memory isn't what it used to be, well, there you have it. Take *The Life and Works of the Great Master Artificer*

Brayce of Travale, for instance. I lent it to my friend, Destrian, nearly twenty years ago now. Last spring I wanted to look up something Brayce had taken particular note of, and, well, Destrian had died just the week before, which was probably what brought Brayce to mind in the first place . . . Anyway, it was very awkward asking for its return, as you can imagine, and in the end I just borrowed a copy from the Artificer's Guild library. Come to think of it, that needs to go back . . ."

"But in this case . . ." Hektor prompted before Daedrus could head off on another tangent.

"Oh yes. In this case, well it's the Willot, you see."

"The . . . Will . . . ?"

"*Lady Willot's Guide to the Wildflowers of the Forest of Sorrows.*" Daedrus picked up a small, green book bound in leather from the pile beside his chair. "It isn't mine, you see."

"So, people are stealin' his books and replacin' 'em with other books?"

Seated around the Dann family table that evening, Aiden gave him a disbelieving look from over his four-year-old son, Egan's, head. "One oatcake in the mouth at a time, little man," he added sternly, moving the plate out of arm's reach. "You know better'n that."

Egan smiled an innocent mouthful of food at him as Hektor shrugged.

"Maybe."

"Were they valuable books?"

"Not as such." Hektor took a bite of meat pie, opened his mouth at Egan when Aiden wasn't looking, then shrugged again as the boy broke into peals of delighted laughter. "One might be about spinnin' wheels and the other might be about weight-driven clocks," he said, pretending not to see Suli's exasperated frown as she and Aiden's year-old daughter, Leila, pointed at her uncle and laughed as loudly as Egan.

"Might be?"

"Yeah, well, he thinks he remembers where he saw 'em last, but they might have moved."

"Moved?"

"Moved."

"So, they might not be missin' at all?"

Hektor sighed. "No."

"Did you check for any signs of a break-in?"

"Top to bottom. Nothin'. Likely the thief just walked in an' walked out again."

"Who would have that kind of easy access?"

"Plenty of folk," Paddy offered through a mouthful of spring peas. "So far this week there's been Hadon, Linton's apprentice, Deen, the butcher's boy, the herbalist's girl, her name's Marti, I think . . ." As Kassie nodded, he continued. "Three book binders, they're older folk, I don't know their names, two book sellers, four gardeners, the chimney sweep with two helpers, the dustbin man an' his son, Rik, the privy cleaner, he was by himself, the sweet spring water delivery man and his apprentice, Mern, and me. An' that's jus' the trades. There's been Kassie with these two other students, Janee an' Alix, an' their teacher, right, Kas?"

His sister nodded again, and Paddy continued. "Then we got the highborns: his niece Adele an' her friends, plus his own friends—Artificers, Bards, Healers, Scholars. His house has more comin' an' goin' than the Palace, I reckon."

"So, couldn't one of them have borrowed the books

and left that wildflower one behind on one of their own visits?" Aiden pressed.

Hektor shook his head. "Daedrus says not. He showed it to me. There's a plate inside the front cover that reads . . ." He squeezed his eyes shut as he called the words to mind. "Gifted from the Private Collection of Lady Willot to her nephew, the Herald Navene."

"Who lives where?"

"He has an estate north of the city near Westmark, an' he hasn't been near Daedrus' house for years. Apparently he's kind of a shut-in now."

"Right, so it ain't him. What a surprise," Jakon noted, spearing an oatcake with the end of his knife. "Why would anyone steal books, anyway? There's lots more valuable things scattered all over his house that'd be a lot easier to pocket."

"An' a lot easier to sell," Raik agreed, deftly scooping the oatcake off his brother's knife with his own.

"Not in front of Egan, Raik," his mother admonished.

"Sorry, Ma." Raik set the cake onto his twin's plate with a contrite air, then scooped it back up with his fingers. "Better?"

"Not really, no."

"Not really at all," Jakon added, snatching it back. "Get yer own."

"All the booksellers past Breakneedle Street know each other," Paddy observed, bringing the subject back to the missing books. "An' they all know Daedrus an' what he buys, so they all know his collection. A stranger tryin' to sell stolen books there would stick out like a sore thumb, an' the secondhand shops nearer the outer gates haven't the market for 'em."

"So, someone must be takin' them for their own collection," Hektor mused.

"Which is also suspect," Aiden argued. "Anyone with
a book collection of their own'd be a friend to Daedrus.
Why would they thieve from him?" He turned a stern
gaze on the two youngest Danns. "Neither of you have
borrowed any books, have you? Even with his permission? I know how you both love to read."

Both Kassie and Paddy glared back at him. "No,"
Paddy retorted. "Hek made it plain when we first started
goin' up there: be polite, be friendly, but keep a professional distance, and don't accept nothin' more'n a cup of
tea an' a biscuit."

"You have to keep sayin' no to him; he gifts things to
people all the time," Kassie added somberly. "Sometimes
they quietly put 'em back when he's not lookin'."

Their mother set another plate of oatcakes into the
center of the table, then returned to her seat with a
thoughtful expression. "Many of his friends are his own
age," She noted. "Do you think he might have gifted
these missin' books to someone and forgotten, and they
left the other book in its place forgetting it wasn't his?"

"Maybe," Kassie allowed, but her tone was doubtful.
"He an' his friends talk books all the time, and most of
'em carry 'em about—"

"Daedrus says he thinks a couple of his friends might
have had the same thing happen to them," Paddy interrupted. "Books missin' and other books mysteriously
showin' up."

"But why would any of them just slip one of their own
books into someone else's house an' not tell 'im about
it?" Kasey shook her head. "It doesn't make sense."

"Then most likely it didn't happen at all," Aiden answered. "Daedrus'll probably find the two he's missin' in the privy." Handing Egan to Suli, he stood. "I'm be downstairs, puttin' a few hours in on the new flat 'afore bed. I could use your help, Hek, if you've the time."

Hektor started. "I . . . suppose."

A smile cracked Aiden's usually frowning demeanor. "But you were plannin' on callin' on Ismy, yeah?"

"Yeah."

"Give me a few minutes help buildin' Egan's new bed frame, an' I'll let you loose with plenty of time left to get over to Saddler's Row 'afore dark. Deal?"

"Deal."

As the two oldest Dann boys made for the door, Hektor paused to glance back at the rest of the family still seated about the table, talking, laughing, and eating. His mother rose to straighten his collar, then gave him a fond smile.

"What are you thinking about so seriously?" she asked.

He shook his head. "Nothin' really. I was just tryin' to keep this memory in my head. With Aiden and Suli movin' downstairs with the twins this week, it's gonna be lot quieter around here."

"Well, then, you and Ismy will just have to fill it up again. It's high time I had more grandbabies, anyway."

Hektor reddened. "I don't think we're ready for that just yet, Ma."

"We'll see. Give her my love."

"I . . . yes, Ma."

"You look tired."

Ismy Smith glanced up at Hektor as they walked

along Saddler's Row together, and he felt his head begin to spin with the same sense of lightheaded elation he'd felt since he'd been reunited with her last autumn.

"No, not tired, just . . ."

"Just . . . ?"

"Worried a bit. It's Daedrus."

"Your family's Artificer friend. Is he all right?"

When Hektor filled her in, she frowned. "It sounds like you're worried that his mind is failing?" she noted.

"A little, maybe. He's old and forgetful, an', well, you know how it is."

"Perhaps, but I might remind you, Hektor Dann," she answered sternly, "that not all that long ago, you—all of you—thought my father was gettin' old and forgetful just because he was missin' items from his shop and believed that people might be stealin' them."

"And it turned out his own granddaughter, Zoe, was playin' shopkeeper with his things right under his nose. That doesn't make me feel any better, Ismy."

"It's not meant to make you feel better, it's meant to remind you to take your friend's concerns seriously, whatever his age."

"I am."

"Good." As they turned onto Iron Street, she bumped him slightly with her hip. "And speakin' of my father . . ."

Hektor felt an involuntary thrill of if not fear then at least foreboding travel up his spine.

"Yeah?"

"Judee wants us all to have a meal together 'afore the weddin'."

He gave a faint snort. "So Edzel doesn't think she's stealin' from him anymore either?" he asked. The rows between Edzel Smith and Ismy's third ex-stepmother were legendary in the area, and both Hektor and Aiden had been called in to referee on numerous occasions.

Ismy dismissed the question with a flick of one hand. "Of course he doesn't. They're gettin' along just fine these days for Zoe's sake an' for the sake of our weddin'," she added. .

Hektor raised one amused eyebrow at her. "You don't mind if I doubt that last part, do you?" he asked. "Edzel's never liked me."

"Maybe not, but he loves me and wants me to be happy." Her tone brooked no rebuttal, from either him or her father, and Hektor smiled.

"True enough," he allowed. "So, how soon 'afore the weddin' was she wantin' this dinner?"

"The night before."

"Oh."

"Is that all right?"

He sighed. "Yeah, sure." As Ismy tucked her arm more securely in his, he bent down to kiss the top of her head, breathing in the scent of her hair with an intoxicated smile. "Course it is."

"Unless I get buried under a mountain of reports before then," he sighed, glancing around at the untidy piles stacked all over his office the next morning. "Makes me wish I'd never learned to read."

A knock interrupted his grumbling, and he smoothed his expression quickly as Paddy put his head in the door.

"Capt'n wants you, Hek—I mean, Sarge."

Captain Travin Torell glanced up as Hektor entered his office, then finished the report he was reading before setting it carefully on the top of a very neatly stacked pile.

Promoted from a far more affluent watch house just over a year ago, it had taken the highborn captain some months to recognize that competency as well as tradition had seen generations of Danns at the Iron Street Watch House, and it had taken an equal number of months for the decidedly tight-knit community of locally born watchmen to trust their *outsider* commander. Now both managed a restrained formality that was only just beginning to meld into a smoothly running unit, due in no small part to the efforts of Day Sergeant Hektor Dann, the captain's first, if at the time, somewhat reluctant, promotion.

"I understand you've been to see Daedrus, Sergeant. Something about missing books?" he asked.

Hektor eyed his commander thoughtfully. The captain and Daedrus were friends; the two often dined together at the White Lily, an inn so far above Hektor's station that he'd never even seen the inside of it. The captain hadn't mentioned the Dann family's relationship with the old Artificer, but Hektor had no doubt that he knew all about it. Mostly, he admitted silently, because Daedrus was a dreadful gossip.

"Yes, sir," he answered, opting for a neutral tone.

"And . . . ?"

"Investigations are proceeding, sir."

"Proceeding how?"

"Sir?"

The Captain frowned. "What have you discovered, Sergeant?"

"More questions than answers, sir." Hektor admitted. "Ordinarily we'd be makin' inquiries with the other householders in the area as well as the local booksellers, but . . ."

"But?"

"Well, sir, Daedrus' home and the booksellers stalls are in Breakneedle Street's jurisdiction. I wouldn't want to . . ." He paused, uncertain of what words to use to the former Breakneedle Street officer without giving offence.

The captain nodded. "I'll speak with Captain Rilade. His officers can interview the householders. They're known, many of them are younger sons who come from the local surroundings. As they do here," he added wryly.

"Yes, sir."

"Your brother, Padreic, often accompanies Daedrus to the booksellers, yes?" the captain continued.

"He does, sir. When he's off shift, he goes with him to carry his packages."

"Well. then, perhaps he can make those inquiries for us." The captain inclined his head stiffly. "It will be good experience for him when he's ready to move up to lance constable."

Hektor allowed a faint smile to cross his lips. "He'll be thrilled at the opportunity, sir," he noted. "And fully discreet."

"I'm sure he will be." The captain met his gaze sternly. "And, Sergeant, if your inquiries turn up nothing more than say . . . an old man's forgetful nature, I would appreciate it if you would keep it between us. I'm very fond of Daedrus, as you may know. He was a brilliant Artificer in his day, and I would hate for his reputation to suffer now that he's getting on in years."

"I understand, Captain." Snapping off a rigidly formal salute, Hektor made for the door, then decided to simply speak his mind. "The Danns are very fond of him too, sir," he said, turning back to meet the captain's gaze no less firmly. "An' we don't let the people we care about get hurt."

For the first time, the captain gave him a tight but genuine smile. "I'm sure you don't, Sergeant. Very well then, I'll leave the investigation in your capable hands. Let me know what you find out."

"Yes, sir."

The next day, Paddy stood beside Daedrus in Booksellers Row, gently leafing through a volume of street ball stories while the Artificer flipped through a bin of engineering manuals.

"Our young watchman can read very fast indeed, can't he, Michen?" the neighboring bookseller called out, winking at the stall owner, who was eyeing Paddy suspiciously. "Why, I've seen him polish off most of a Rethwellan epic poem before Daedrus had finished passing the time of day."

"Well, it's a good thing he's careful with them, or I might expect him to buy one for a change, Ivarra!" Michen snapped back. "Get back to work, Erlan, you lazy wretch!" He aimed a swipe at his twelve-year-old son standing beside Paddy. The boy danced out of the way with a grin, a book on griffins clutched in one hand.

"I was dusting it, Papa," he protested, winking at Paddy.

"I'll dust you! I swear if I sold apples, I'd have no stock left! Younglings! It's a wonder I can make any kind of a living with the amount of trade they read for free!"

Setting the book down carefully, Paddy backed up a step, his face burning. "Er, do a lot of folk just read 'em an' put 'em back?" he asked, trying to mask his embarrassment with an attempt at an official question.

Michen gave an unimpressed snort as he straightened the books on the counter. "Enough! The Scholars are the worst!"

"You can chase them off while they're still students," Ivarra explained at Paddy's confused expression, "but once they come into their own, it's harder to demand payment without giving offence and risk losing their trade for a time."

"Only for a time?"

"Where else are they going to go?" Erlan answered, elbowing the other boy in the ribs as he pointed out an elderly woman so absorbed in a copy of *The Myths of Valdemar* that she hardly blinked as she dropped a coin into Ivarra's hand.

"Buying books is like buying sweets, lad, so beware," Michen said with a hideous scowl. "Once you've gained a taste for it, you'll never stop wanting more. Forever."

"Some collectors'll buy books before they buy food," Erlan added, then burst out laughing at Paddy's appalled expression.

"Mind you," Ivarra allowed as the woman wandered off, still reading. "Most of us don't mind if the reader is careful with the books. There are some, students mostly, who can't afford to buy very often, but they can't stay away either. They'll come every day just to snatch up a few pages before lessons, and sometimes, if it's obvious they love the book so much that it would just about kill them if someone else bought it before they reached the end, we'll tuck it behind the counter until they've finished with it."

"And sometimes we might take another in trade, if it's been kept clean and undamaged," Erlan added. "Right, Aunt Ivarra?"

"That's right, lad."

Paddy frowned. "Take another in trade?"

Michen snorted again. "I've had some try to trade me my own books back again, week after week, as if I could afford to sell naught but one volume every three months!"

"It does help if they move around between us," Ivarra admitted, "so that no one stall gets touched up too often."

"Moves around?"

Michen glared at Paddy as if he suspected he was poking fun at them. "Have you got a hearing problem, boy?" he demanded.

"No, sir," Paddy stammered. "I were just thinkin' out loud."

"A bad habit to get into."

"Yes, sir."

"Anyway, looks like Daedrus has made his choices today, so get gone."

Paddy turned to see Erlan wrapping up a dozen manuals for the Artificer, who handed over his money with much the same expression as the woman had, then turned back, his own expression torn.

"I, um, was wondering . . . how much is the street ball book?" he asked casually.

Michen wordlessly held it up to show him the price prominently displayed on the back cover and Paddy's face fell. "Oh, um, thank you. Maybe next week." As the boy accepted Daedrus' parcels, Michen rolled his eyes, then deliberately tucked the book behind the counter.

"What!?" he demanded of his son who was now openly grinning at him. "Get back to work, or you'll find yourself apprenticed to the very next swineherd who passes by!"

The boy's smile grew. "Yes, Papa, just as soon as I fin-ish this one last story, all right?"

"One. Only."

"Thanks, Papa."

"So, I thought maybe the thief starts out by just snatchin' a bit of readin' here an' there," Paddy explained to the three other on-duty Danns gathered in Hektor's office later that afternoon. "But finally the waitin' to finish gets to be too much for 'im an he borrows one, brings it back right away the next time, does it again, an' again, an' then he does it at someone else's house, only this time he brings the wrong book back to Daedrus' because he's got 'em all mixed up."

"Seems a bit complicated," Aiden pointed out. "Be-sides, these weren't storybooks, they were books on what things are or how they work."

Paddy shrugged. "Readin's readin.'"

Beside him, Kassie nodded.

"So we're lookin' at someone who has regular weekly, or monthly access to more than one private library, no money to buy his own books, and no chance to ask for the loan of one," Hektor summed up.

"And has a few moments alone to read without being detected," Aiden included.

Kassie and Paddy put their heads together for a mo-ment.

"Well, it can't be a privy cleaner, chimney sweep, gar-dener, or dustbin man," Paddy noted. "They'd leave marks on the books."

"And it can't be Hadon, Deen, or Marti," Kassie added. "Because they're not there long enough."

"And they're only ever in the pantry, anyway."

"And it can't be Janee or Alix, because they could ask Daedrus to lend them anything they were interested in."

"An' it can't be one of the book folk, because it would hurt their trade with Daedrus, an' their apprentices can read all they want at their masters' own stalls without payin' a single pennybit."

"That leaves Mern. Daedrus has water jugs all over his house that need fillin'."

Both brother and sister shared a triumphant smile that quickly became stricken expressions.

"Oh, poor Mern," Kassie breathed.

Hektor glanced from one to the other. "Why poor Mern?"

"Well, because . . ." His sister shrugged. "Because he's nice."

Paddy nodded. "He's from Sweetsprings. He wanted to be a Scholar but had to quit lessons when his older brother died, an' he had to start workin' deliveries with his Da."

"He's smart, too," Kassie added. "He thinks about things before he says 'em."

"Doesn't sound like he thinks about things before he does 'em, though," Aiden observed.

"I guess not. But if it is him stealin' books, I'll bet he just means to borrow 'em for a bit an' then bring 'em right back."

Aiden gave her a stern look. "That's how it always starts, Kasiath," he said, not unkindly.

She sighed. "I know."

"But it might not even be him," Paddy argued. "We don't know anywhere near all the folk who come and go at Daedrus' house."

"No, you don't, but I trust your instincts," Hektor

answered. "You've both been hanging around the watch house your whole lives. You know how people act. So, you tell me, as watchmen, has Mern been actin' in any way in the last few weeks that might make you think he was guilty of somethin'?"

Kassie and Paddy exchanged a look, then they both nodded glumly.

"I'll talk to Daedrus."

"No! Under no circumstances do I want him arrested, Sergeant!"

Three days later, Hektor stood in Daedrus' front parlor, trying to make the old Artificer see sense while his birds filled the air with a cacophony of agitated shrieking.

"But, sir—"

Daedrus fixed the much younger man with an indignant glare. "Don't you 'sir' me, Hektor Dann," he snapped. "I'm to attend your wedding in less than a fortnight, so we can just dispense with such formalities right here and now."

"Fine. Daedrus . . ."

"No. You brought this to my attention, just as you should have, and I've spoken with the boy, and he's admitted the whole thing to both myself and to his father. His choice of materials shows he has a discerning mind and a keen intelligence, as do the others."

"Others?"

Daedrus waved a dismiss hand at him. "He's been sharing my books with a few others in his home village. They have no hope of gaining access to such works, since they are so far from the capital," he continued before Hektor could voice another protest. "He did have access, so it only made sense that he be the one to do the procuring. Now, I've arranged for certain volumes to be regularly lent out, all above board, all with the complete knowledge of myself and the other participants, so you needn't worry about that."

"Other participants?"

"Yes, yes, yes. The boy gave me a list of libraries that he'd been particularly tempted by, and since they all belong to close friends of mine, I've taken the liberty of discussing with them the setting up of a formal lending library, and they are all quite excited about the project. As the great Artificer Brayce once said: 'No advance or invention ever came from knowledge hoarded, but only from knowledge sprinkled into fertile minds. Then it can move mountains.'" Daedrus paused. "Or something like that, I forget the actual quote. And for that matter, who said it. Now that I think of it, it might have been Isora, King Valdemar's Head Gardener back in the day. My point is that young Mern is wasted as a sweet waterseller. He shows excellent organizational skills, or he will, once he's trained up a bit. Now that he doesn't have to do the lending in a clandestine manner, he's free to tweak it. I think we'll put him in charge."

"Sir!"

"A bit of proper responsibility is just what he needs."

"You'll have no library left!"

"Don't be silly, my boy, that's not how it works at all. No, no, you leave it to me. All is in good hands." Daedrus pushed Hektor gently but firmly toward the door. "Paddy tells me that Aiden and Suli are moving into their new flat today, and they'll need you to help them before you're to meet with the watch house tailor to have your new dress uniform fitted for your wedding, so off you go, Sergeant!"

"But . . ." Hektor tried once more. "I have to report what I found to the captain."

"Quite right. Tell him I'm hosting the first meeting of the Friends of Haven's Public Library Association here tonight, and we'd welcome a volume or two from his own collection if he has a mind to offer them. I have a list here somewhere of works that might suit. Ah yes, here it is!" Daedrus pressed a piece of paper into Hektor's unresisting hand.

"Now, if you would be so kind as to ask Kasiath to drop by a bit early tomorrow before lessons if she could. I'm afraid my children have gotten a little unsettled by all of this," he continued, wincing as the cacophony continued. "And they could use some calming down. Give your mother my regards, and tell young Jakon and Raik that I'm escorting my dear friend, Annise, to the third year Bardic Trainees' concert at the Virgin and Stars Tavern next week. Annise needs two canes to get around these days, so we'll be taking chairs instead of walking. They needn't accompany us unless they want to. I know they worry—quite unnecessarily by the way—about my being out of doors late at night, but they might enjoy the music. So, love to all, good afternoon!"

Hektor found himself on the front step with the door closed very firmly behind him before he could get another word in edgewise. He stood a moment, trying to sort out what had just happened, then headed for the watch house with a resigned air. As the breeze sent the first few drops of a warm, spring rain spattering across his face, his thoughts returned to Ismy.

Ismy looking up at him with a smile, her arm tucked securely in his. Ismy . . . mentioning a prewedding dinner with her violent and unpredictable father.

His steps faltered as he wondered what the likelihood of him actually surviving until the wedding was. Maybe he could convince his brothers to come with him as backup. For that matter, maybe he could convince the entire watch house to come with him as backup . . .

He quickened his pace, and as the capital's bells began to chime the hour, he turned onto Iron Street a few moments later, already lost in thought as to what kind of report he could possibly write about all of this.

A Dream Reborn
Dylan Birtolo

Sera sat at the edge of the road, leaning back against the inn's stone wall. It was hard and rough, with points that bit into her muscles, but she was used to the discomfort. She shifted to make it as bearable as possible but continued watching people as they passed by on their way to Wineboro's central market. She was close enough to smell the freshly baked bread, and it made her stomach rumble.

The inn's location, on the borders of the town and along the road to Tindale, forced all traffic from the East to pass by its door. By serving as a beacon to late night travelers and offering succor without the need to search through the narrower town streets, it had prospered, and the innkeeper had built expansions onto it twice, judging by the different colored stones used. The location also served Sera's purposes, letting her keep an eye out for any new travelers with coin to spare.

Some of the local residents glanced her way as they walked past, but most simply ignored her. A select few who considered themselves of higher stature went the extra measure to sneer in her direction before leaving her behind. It was almost time to leave this place and look for a new town to make her livelihood. Beggars were not welcome in one place for long, and it seemed that she was at the point of overstaying her welcome. Sera pulled her ragged cloak tight around her. She might as well make one last attempt at picking up some traveling coin before taking to the road again.

As if in answer to her thoughts, a suitable mark crested the hill to the east, near the horizon. Even from this distance, the traveler's wealth was obvious. He—at least Sera assumed it was a he, based on the style of dress—had two horses trailing behind his own, both hauling bags bulging with goods. His clothes were bright, with dyed colors designed to catch the eye and capture attention.

Sera took a deep breath and waited for him to arrive. As he got closer, she scanned the street to make sure the stage would be set for her performance. He glanced up at the inn when he was a few strides away, but he refocused on the road in front of him. It didn't look as though he would stop. Sera used her hand to push herself up from the wall, trying to keep her back hunched and looking weak as she stumbled in front of his horse.

He pulled hard on the reins, making his horse whinny as it stopped hard on its front feet. The animal snorted at her, and she felt warm, wet breath against her face, blowing her hood back. The merchant looked down at her, concern etched on his face. When he saw her ragged cloak, dirty clothes, and bare feet, his lips tightened into a sneer.

"Out of the way, beggar." He jerked his reins hard, yanking his horse's head to the side. He gave his mount a harsh kick, trying to urge it to move around her.

"Please, just a little bit of coin for a meal." Sera held

out a wooden bowl that she had deliberately chipped and beaten up to add to the image.

The merchant grumbled and reached into the purse tied to his belt. He pulled out a couple of coins, barely enough for a crust of bread and watered ale, and dropped them into her bowl. They hit the bottom with a *clink* and bounced into the dirt at the horse's feet.

As they did, Sera reached out, using her Gift. It wasn't powerful enough for her to Mindspeak, but she pressed on him a sense of pity and sorrow. She willed him to look at her again, to see the dirty young girl with skin stretched tight over her cheekbones from lack of food. She brought to mind every aspect of her pitiful appearance, down to her raw fingers with dirt caked under the little nails that remained from scrabbling for roots to feast on.

He turned away from the road to look back at her. His eyebrows furrowed together, and he frowned, as if seeing her for the first time. His shoulders slumped, and the morning light glistened in eyes beginning to tear up. Untying the purse from his belt, he leaned out of the saddle to hand it to her.

"You need this far more than I do. Please, get some food, a room, and a bath."

Sera smiled, dropping her gaze as she mumbled her thanks. When she looked up, the merchant smiled and nodded at her before nudging his horse and team to go around her. She pocketed the purse, tucking it inside her rags and out of sight. She stooped to pick up the coins in the dirt, sliding them inside the purse. She hobbled back over to the wall, in case anyone was watching, before resuming her watch.

*   *   *

Over the rest of the day, Sera didn't find another mark as lucrative as her first. She doubted that the other three combined would equal the wealth of her first take. It was getting close to sunset, and most of the people traveling to market had already left. She saw familiar faces as they passed by, and Sera made sure to hide her face and avoid eye contact. It had never been a problem before, but an ounce of caution was worth more than a pound of trouble.

It was about time for her to retire, take a long bath, and then leave before anyone took notice of her sudden wealth. She was sure the innkeeper wouldn't mind, especially if she left a healthy tip. But she did not want to wait long enough to have people asking questions.

She climbed the first few steps to the inn's front door when she heard the quick patter of hoof beats on the packed dirt as a horse galloped toward her. Sera turned and froze as she saw a woman riding up on the most gorgeous all-white horse she had ever seen. She had heard of the Companions, but she had never seen one in person before. The descriptions of their grace and beauty paled in comparison to the reality. She could only watch, transfixed, as the Herald rode up to the front entrance of the inn and stopped just a few feet from her.

Sera made eye contact with the Companion and got lost in the deep blue gaze of the animal, which was clearly not just an animal. She felt as though the Companion could see into her soul, and saw all that she had done. While it did not judge her, it knew and did not approve. Sera felt a sense of guilt rise up in her, but she stamped it down. What did it know about needing to survive anyway? Sera's bitterness gave her the strength to tear her gaze away. She felt the Companion staring at her, and it made the skin between her shoulder blades itch. She walked toward the center of town, searching for another inn. She wouldn't be denied her bath and hot meal because of a horse. After she got cleaned up and ate, she'd return to her hideout. Wineboro suddenly felt very small.

Calling it a hideout stretched the definition of the word, at best. It was a small clearing in the woods, a place that Sera knew she would be able to recognize again. The thick trees curled out from each other, giving the area the appearance of two giant hands cupped together, fingers spread and stretched to the sky, ready to catch the moon. Sera paused for a moment, leaning against one of the trees and enjoying the relative quiet. Insects provided an incessant hum, but it was nothing compared to the constant bustle of the town.

Walking to a large root that arched up from the ground, she dug up her stash underneath it, taking her latest prizes and tucking them into the sack. It didn't look like much, but it had nicer clothes, some food, and enough wealth to live comfortably for several weeks. Perhaps that was what she would do at the next town: change clothes before she arrived and stay at the best rooms the inn had for a few days before moving on. That had been her cycle of late; living comfortably for a while until her funds nearly ran out, then moving on and earning more until she was no longer welcome.

Sera put down her sack and walked around, collecting twigs for a fire. As she moved around, she couldn't help but think back to the Companion's stare. She clenched her jaw and squeezed the branches so tight that some of them snapped in her grip. She began talking to herself, a habit she'd picked up from spending so much time alone.

"It isn't like I'm stealing anything. They give me the money on their own. I just give them a little nudge. I'm not forcing them to do anything. Besides, it doesn't always work."

She tossed the sticks into the center of the clearing with a loud clatter. She snatched up the branches, arranging them into a pile as she muttered to herself.

"Besides, what does a Companion know about anything? They get to live at Haven with Heralds, and have everything they need given to them. They don't know what it's like to be working all day in the street with your mother, trying to entertain people enough to eat for the first time in weeks."

Sera froze, holding a twig a few inches above the kindle pile as her mind shot back through the years. She pictured her mother's face, long and sad as she counted the coins in their collection bowl, realizing there wouldn't be enough for them both to eat. She would smile, trying to hide her sadness from her daughter with that jongleur's mask, but Sera saw through it even at that age. She couldn't remember the last time she saw her mother smile for real.

Both of Sera's parents had been street performers. When they'd learned that Sera had a Gift and could influence others when she sang, they hoped she would be able to go to the Bardic College in Haven. But that dream faded long before it ever had a chance to become reality. Her father died from illness before ever learning the truth. Sera didn't have the Bardic Gift; it was just weak Mind-magic that let her strengthen emotions others already possessed. For the hundredth time, Sera cursed her Gift for being so trivial. Perhaps if it had been more, she could have used it to make enough money to save her father.

After he died, Sera and her mother lived as best as they were able, but her father had been the true performer. Even on those rare occasions where they were able to scrounge up enough coin for two meals, burly men with ugly scars would show up and demand a "tax." At first, Sera's mother had refused, but the men were more than willing to show their propensity for violence. Sera learned to hide the coin, never revealing how much they had in the hope that they'd be able to hang onto it.

And then one day, the men didn't believe Sera's mother when she turned over everything she had. Thinking she was holding back, they tried to beat her into giving them more. She gave up every last coin she had, but it still wasn't enough. Her mother died that day, and Sera didn't even know the names of the men who killed her.

Sera wiped her face, the fresh tears from a long, never-healed wound leaving tracks in the dirt on her cheeks. With renewed fervor, she set to work on the fire. As it started to blaze, she paced around it, kicking at the dirt until there was an obvious circular path. When she ran out of energy she collapsed, propping herself up on her arms as she watched the flames dance and listened to the wood pop. Tomorrow was another day, and she was still alive. That was all she could do, just keep living one day at a time, no matter what she had to do.

The next day, Sera took the road east, heading toward Tindale. Not that it mattered much—one town was the same as any other to her. She wore her beggar's rags while traveling. Once she got closer to civilization, she would change. But experience had taught her well that it was better to appear poor and carry a simple sack than to openly display one's fortune.

She passed a few people throughout the day, most working on their farms. Sera made sure to keep her eyes down and her shoulders slumped, an act practiced so often that it felt more natural than walking tall. It also allowed her the luxury of ruminating over her own thoughts as she traveled. Every once in a while, her mind wandered back to the Companion and the way it had stared at her. Even a good night's rest hadn't released the tension knotted between her shoulders.

A scream jolted Sera back to the present, and her gaze snapped up. Ahead, a couple stood close together in a field, their backs to each other and sheltering a small girl. Based on how they were dressed, they were farmers who had been hard at work. The girl was the one who had screamed. Her mother held a hand behind her, trying to calm the youngster.

Three men on horseback rode at a walk around the farmers, their mounts trampling the plants just starting to sprout. They carried weapons—two with gnarled clubs and one with a sword—and wore rough, ragged clothes with leather patches haphazardly sewn on.

"Lookin' good, Triel. Lookin' real good. Looks like you been eatin' fat all winter while me an' my men starved. That ain't right, is it?" One of the men reined in his horse in front of the father.

Sera passed even with the group, and one of the bandits looked her way. She snapped her stare back to the dirt in front of her. It wasn't her problem. Besides, it wasn't as though she could do anything. The farmers could spare a bit of food.

"I already gave you a whole pig. It was my last one, you know that." Triel's voice was strained. Sera could tell he was trying to be brave, but failing. The bandits probably knew it, too.

"Maybe you been holdin' out on us."

The words sent a chill down Sera's spine, and she froze. They were too familiar. Even if these weren't the same men, they were the same type.

"Maybe you just need some convincin'."

Sera glanced back and saw the leader dismount in front of the mother and reach out to grab her. Triel shouted and grabbed the man's wrist, yanking it away. The bandit responded with a harsh backhand that cracked against the man's cheekbone. He dropped to the dirt, and his wife and daughter ran to him. The bandit leader shook his hand.

"That was stupid, Triel."

The bandit drew his sword, metal rasping against leather as it came free. The other men on the horses chuckled and leaned forward, resting their arms on the front of their saddles. The mother covered her daughter and Triel with her body, looking away with eyes tightly shut.

"NO!"

Sera was as surprised as the others to hear her own voice. Everything seemed to grow quiet as all attention was drawn to her. The bandit leader recovered first, tilting his head to look at her as if she were an oddity, something he had never seen before.

"This don't involve you, beggar girl. Walk on, or you're next."

Sera's anger raged inside of her, and she clenched her fists at her side hard enough to cut into her palms. She took a step toward the bandits, and then another. She didn't know what she was doing. Conscious thought had left her actions. She only thought of the hurt these men caused. The suffering. The horrible events that they brought to pass and the amount of pain that covered their hands. Tears filled the corners of her eyes. A strange heat filled every inch of her body, and her head felt as though it would split under the pressure. The emotion could not be contained.

She crossed inside the circle made by the bandits' horses and stood next to the huddled family. When she spoke, each word was filled with suppressed fury, and accentuated with another step. "You will not hurt anyone any more."

They all stared at her in silence. The bandit leader shifted his feet and took a half step backward. He laughed, but it sounded as forced as Triel's earlier attempt at bravery.

"Who's gonna stop us? You?"

"You aren't even human," she replied. "You can't be. You're just beasts—mindless animals. All you do is prey on those weaker than you, because you're afraid. You're afraid that someone stronger than you is going to take everything away, because that's the only thing you understand."

Eyes wide, the bandit leader took a step away and glanced over his shoulders. His hand started to shake, and he fumbled his sword back into its scabbard. She heard one of the men behind her whimper. The third bandit jerked on his reins, trying to turn around and get away. His horse whinnied in protest at the harsh treatment. Even the bandit leader's horse was cowed, dropping its head and digging furrows in the dirt as it backed away.

"All you know is pain," she continued. "That's all you can give. And when you're gone, everyone else will be better off. You are *nothing*."

Sera collapsed to her knees with the effort of the speech, slumping forward and catching herself with her hands. The bandit leader turned and ran, not even bothering to mount his horse. The other two bandits took off as well, the sound of their retreat fading into the distance.

Sera was still slouched, staring at her knees, when she felt a soft hand on her shoulder. She looked up into Triel's eyes—one of which was swollen shut. But the smile on his face carried a warmth she hadn't felt in years.

"Thank you. I can't say it enough. Thank you."

Sera took his hand and let him help her to a standing position.

"Please, come to our home and share our dinner. It's the least we can do."

Sera nodded, incapable of doing anything more. Her feet dragged through the dirt as she followed the family in her own daze, trying to understand what had happened. It felt as though she had used her Gift, but so much more. She'd never been able to make others feel something they hadn't already felt before. What did this mean? She longed to figure it out, but the effort of remaining upright took all of her mental abilities. Her mind felt burned out.

The young girl came back and grabbed Sera's hand as they walked. "Are you a Herald?"

After the meal with Triel and his family, Sera refused their offer of a bed for the night and continued her journey. Only this time, she traveled west, returning the way she had come. Along the way she changed clothes, discarding her beggar's rags and wearing comfortable travel clothes. Now that she stood at the edge of Wineboro, she had a momentary pause. She took a deep breath and shifted her sack on her shoulder. There was no point in delay. She knew what she had to do.

As she walked up to the inn, she was surprised to see the Herald standing outside of it, leaning against the wall where Sera had been just two mornings ago. Her Companion stood next to her, watching her approach with those deep blue eyes. Sera stopped when she was a few feet away and offered a slight curtsy as way of greeting.

"Herald, there's something I need to talk to you about, if you have a moment."

The Herald grinned. "My name's Helene, and Myron said you'd be coming back."

When Sera raised an eyebrow, Helene gestured toward her Companion.

"Ah, yes." Sera dropped her gaze to stare at her feet, shuffling them back and forth as she tried to get the words out. "I wish to turn myself in. I'm a criminal."

"Oh? And what crimes have you committed?"

Sera couldn't be sure, but it almost sounded as if Helene was mocking her. She flushed and was glad it was dark. "I'm a thief."

She held out the sack containing all of the goods and

coin that she had left. It was all money she had per-
suaded others to give her.

"Didn't they give that to you? You didn't steal it from
them. They reached into their pockets and handed it to
you of their own free will, right?"

Sera looked up and her mouth hung open as she
searched for words.

*:Helene, stop playing with the girl and making this
more difficult than it needs to be. You can see how uncomfortable you're making her.:*

Helene sighed, and the mischievous grin left her face.
She opened her mouth to say something, but Sera found
her voice and cut her off.

"He can talk?" Her eyes widened, and she stepped
forward until her face was only inches from Myron.

She heard a warm chuckle in her mind. *:Of course I
can speak, child. How else would I have told Helene to
wait here for your return?:*

"But . . . how did you know?"

*:You have a good, if injured, heart. I saw it when we
met. I knew you'd return. If not today, then tomorrow, or
the next day.:*

Sera's shoulder slumped, and she looked at the sack.
"What I did was wrong. I don't even know how to go
about fixing it."

"You could always donate the money to Haven. We
would see that it is put to good use," Helene said.

Sera held out the sack, trying to be rid of it as if it
were a bag of venomous snakes. Helene took it, and the
grin appeared on her face again.

"Besides, you can use it as payment to enroll in the
Collegium."

It took a moment for the words to sink in. When they

did, Sera glanced back and forth between the Herald and her Companion.

"You mean . . ." She couldn't finish the sentence. It felt as if giving the fragile hope any real form would cause it to shatter.

:You have Gifts, child, and with the proper teaching, you could bring much good to the world.:

"We leave first thing in the morning," Helene said with a wink.

Forget Me Never
Cedric Johnson

Spring had come early to Rethwellan. The last traces of winter had vanished in a fortnight, and in another fortnight all the land seemed to be in full bloom. The streets of Petras were filled with the fragrances from every flower, bush, and tree in the city, as well as a cacophony of birdsong from the returning migrant flocks.

Few were immune to the distractions of this glorious season, least of all the young. Students had it doubly hard, being trapped indoors with the temptations of the season just out of reach. Each class could not end soon enough.

Karinda wasn't the only Bardic Trainee yearning for freedom that afternoon. Every one of her peers half-heartedly paid attention while their Master droned on about proper care of stringed instruments. Karinda had her belongings neatly piled up at her feet like many others, ready to pick up everything and be out the door the moment the Master Bard dismissed them. She plucked at each string of her lyre, not giving a tinker's damn what each note sounded like.

Finally the elder signaled that the lesson was over. Karinda grabbed her things quickly and made for the door, eager as the rest to enjoy a few minutes of freedom outside before the next class.

"Karinda!"

She winced at hearing her name, but stopped in her tracks. *Of all the days to get called on,* she thought, *it had to be the one when I didn't want to be.* Karinda waited until the last of the Trainees were well out of the room before approaching the teacher. "Yes, Master?" she asked cautiously.

It took another minute for the old man to respond. Karinda tried not to fidget as the Master put away his instrument and collecting the parchments next to him. Finally, the Bard looked up and started to call her name again, but stopped when he caught Karinda's gaze.

"Well, I see you've finally decided to grace my class-room with your presence," he said briskly.

Karinda clenched her jaw. "I've not missed a day, Master."

The Bard scowled, but rather than call her out on this, he continued in a brisk tone. "Quite frankly, young lady, I don't know why you bother at all." Karinda scowled in return but held her tongue. "Your work is mediocre at best. Despite a year of training, your skill with the lyre would lead anyone to think you'd picked up the instru-ment for the first time yesterday. And your compositions are uninspired at best. Care to revise your statement about not having missed a day?"

Karinda turned bright red. Not from embarrassment but from anger. Not all of it was directed at the elder Bard, though. His words were true, even if the reasons for them weren't. Karinda hadn't lied. She really hadn't missed a single class. But she couldn't put it all on her negligent trainer, either. No matter how hard she studied and practiced, the true skills of a Bard eluded her. Her playing never got better, all but the simplest of songs slipped from memory, and the less said about her own songwriting attempts, the better.

The redness passed from Karinda's face, but the anger remained. "What would you have me do, Master?" she asked quietly.

The Master Bard sighed and looked at her with genuine sympathy. "Honestly, child, I would strongly urge you to consider if the path of the Bard is truly yours to follow. Despite your family's rather—generous donation to the Bards, your heart really isn't in it. Your lack of retention and attendance make that abundantly clear."

A bit of anger crept into Karinda's voice. "But I said—"

The Master help up his hand. "There's no point in denying it. The other Masters—the ones that can remember you, anyway—feel the same way. I'm not telling you to leave our school, Karinda . . ."

No, of course not, she thought bitterly. *You still want my father's coin.*

". . . but I do think it's in everyone's best interest for you to think long and hard on whether being a Bard *is* in your interest."

Karinda nodded silently. There was no point in arguing with the Master. It was equally clear that he'd already made up his mind on what her answer should be. She left the room just as quietly, since the Master Bard had already gone back to his work as if she'd already gone. She walked down the corridor and into the courtyard, passing small gatherings of students chatting merrily and enjoying both the weather and the company.

Karinda found an unoccupied stone bench under a

tree not too far from a half-dozen students, so as not to appear to be withdrawing from the rest, but not eager to be included. *Not that it matters*, she thought, glancing at a nearby group of girls her age with no small envy. *No one had ever invited me to join them*. It had been like this from the moment she donned the Trainee robes; teachers and fellow students alike acted like she was never there.

The Master Bard's words echoed in her thoughts. The longer Karinda thought about them, the more she agreed. She had no real drive to become a Bard, other than not disappointing her parents, who had given the Bards a considerable "gift" in return for accepting her. Even if she had the drive, it wouldn't change the fact that she felt just plain unwelcome as a student—and when she got right down to it, as a person.

No, not unwelcome. That implies people know you exist and don't want you around. No one here seems to know I'm around . . .

As if to emphasize the point, the summoning bell rang for the next classes. The two dozen students in the courtyard called out to each other to hurry up and not be late, but none of them called out to Karinda, even though she sat unmoving. In a few minutes, the courtyard was empty except for her, and for the first time she would be late for a class.

Karinda got to her feet and sighed. But after only a few steps, she stopped. She looked back over her shoulder toward the archway that led out to the streets of Petras and the world beyond. As she did, a wild thought entered her head.

No one here would notice me if I stayed, so nobody would notice if I left. I can walk right out of this city, and the forest beyond, and it would be as though I were never here . . .

She was now facing the archway, tightly clutching the neck of her lyre in a way that would have made the Strings Master livid.

I wasn't meant to be a Bard, she thought with conviction. *Somewhere out there is something I'm good at, something that will make people notice me. There has to be. But I'm not going to find it in here.*

Karinda's feet were taking her through the archway before she had finished the thought. "Forgive me, Papa, Mama," she said to the walls of the school. "This might not be right for you, but it's right for me."

The single call of a songbird was her only answer. It was all she needed.

As thankful as she was for the passing trade cart a few hours into her journey, Karinda was just as thankful to get off of it. After two days of what had to be the bumpiest road in all of Velgarth, without any breaks to speak of, every muscle ached. Still, her drivers were gracious enough to leave her alone, not asking questions or for compensation, so she had little reason to complain. Right now all Karinda cared about was the inn in front of her and the hope of a soft bed.

Quite a few people found themselves at this inn tonight, but it wasn't busy. Regardless, Karinda stood at the bar with growing impatience at the housemaster as he went about his business with everyone but her. It wasn't until she clumsily cleared her throat that the man finally turned his attention her way.

"Ah. Welcome, young miss. Didn't see you standing

there. Night approaches, and if you seek a place to lay your burdens, you're in luck. I've one bed left."

Karinda let out as quiet a sigh as she could manage. Even this one lucky break was enough to lift her spirits.

"I'll certainly take it, sir," she said, careful not to sound too grateful. "And a bit of whatever is in the kitchen, as well."

The housemaster nodded and barked an order for food and drink to the nearest servant boy. "Not that it's any of my concern," he said, returning to his work, "but where would a young woman such as yourself be headed to alone? Somewhere here in Vitimish, or points beyond?"

Karina froze for a moment. *Be confident*, she thought. *Don't show them any weakness, and don't agree to anything that costs you more money. That's what Papa always said.*

"I'll find out when I get there," she said with a shrug. "All I want to do is get far away from here and start anew."

"You'll want north for sure, then," the housemaster replied. "North lies Valdemar, and if you want new, that's the place for it. You would be like so many others, making the life they want how they want."

The housemaster paused to let the servant boy place a tray of stew, bread, and cheese in front of Karinda. Before she could get started on her meal, the housemaster leaned in to talk in a lower voice.

"But you don't want to be like all the others, I can tell. You want some adventure, yes? Something to be remembered by."

Karinda furrowed her brow. "And what if I do?" she asked.

The housemaster grinned. "Then I know of something that could give you all of that and more. It's only a rumor, but I've heard it enough from the right kind of people." He pointed over Karinda's shoulder. "The road north will get you to Valdemar, but if you turn west as the road turns to the east, deep into the Pelagiris Forest you'll find a forgotten ruin, and there you'll find an Adept Mage guarding a living node."

Karinda didn't know much about magic, having seen very little in her childhood and none at all in the last few years, but she knew enough to know why she hadn't seen any—and that this man was lying.

"That's impossible," she said. "Even if a node had survived the Storms, with all that energy it would have been found right away, and many would have braved the deep woods for that grand a treasure. Excuse me sir, my stew is getting cold."

The housemaster didn't act offended by the brush-off. "I did say it was only a rumor. But imagine if it were true? That 'treasure' could grant you any life you desire. Just something to think about."

And she did think about it; all through her meal, during her idle strumming by the hearth, and as she lay in bed, Karinda pondered *what if . . . what if . . . ?*

The next morning, the sun had barely peeked above the horizon when Karinda set off for the Pelagiris Forest. It was the only thing she could do to stop thinking about it.

The fifth morning in the forest, Karinda was regretting everything, starting with her last day of school. To her credit, she hadn't just dashed off like a crazy person. She had bartered and bought suitable clothes and supplies for the hike from other early-rising traders, but even so, Karinda was at her limit. Four nights with no fire, sleeping in trees and not stopping during the day was more than enough. Not to mention that she had no idea where she was going.

Her caution had paid off, at least. Other than distant sounds of movement, there had been no signs of the horrors that were said to dwell in the Pelagiris Forest. Karinda decided that earned her some rest. Still mindful of her surroundings, she leaned against a tree and took the weight off of her feet in turn.

In the relative silence, Karinda picked up the faint sound of running water in the direction she'd been heading. The fresh water was much needed and gave her something to move toward. When her feet had quieted to a dull grumble, Karinda stretched and started toward the water.

Not more than a dozen steps later, Karinda stopped to look at an unusual rock that caught her eye. It was tall, skinny, and looked to be placed in the ground rather than exposed by weather. It would have been no more than a curiosity if there hadn't been another one of similar shape a few meters ahead. Stepping up to that one revealed several more farther down by a trail hugging a small river.

Karinda forgot the stones and the ancient path long enough to drink her fill, replenish her waterskins, and wash off the worst of the grime. A full clean could wait until she knew the area. Refreshed, Karinda resumed following the path of stones.

Five minutes along the river, the path turned from dirt into paving stones, wide enough for a single oxcart. The trees were particularly thick along this part, giving the ancient path a closed-off feeling save for the sky.

The path opened up as abruptly as it had appeared. Instead of disappearing back into dirt, the paving stones expanded out into what looked like the remains of a small village. There were four piles of stones still more or less in the shape of dwellings and at least two more that weren't even that. A large circular platform stood where the river became a lake. Whatever had once been held up by the seven stone pillars around the platform was long gone as well.

On top of the decay of time, most of the stone was covered in moss and vines. Karinda paused to take it all in. This, she accepted silently, was probably all she would ever find in the Pelagiris Forest—including a way out. *Better enjoy it for what it's worth*, she thought.

It didn't last long. Despite the primordial beauty of this place, Karinda quickly realized that something had disturbed it. There were trails through the pavement's moss that didn't meander like an animal would. They went from structure to structure, with purpose. Someone—or some*thing*—was living here.

She got her answer almost right away. Two structures over from the platform, a robed figure stumbled out of a doorway, holding a large staff in front of him like a torch. Karinda took a deep breath and hid behind the nearest pillar, willing herself to be smaller.

"I know you're out there!" the man shouted. "I can see the ripples of your passing! You cannot hide from magic!"

Despite her animal instinct to flee, Karinda believed what she'd been told. *If this man is the rumored Adept, he probably has the power to do anything he promises.* The thought was rational enough to prompt her to step out into the open. She slowly walked forward, her hands open at her sides. At the count of ten, she stopped.

There was still about twenty meters between them. Karinda could see now that he was an old man in tattered, stained robes. *If he is an Adept, he didn't let it go to his head*, she thought. *Or he did, in the wrong way . . .*

Even though she could clearly see the old man, he showed no sign of seeing her. Was he blind? The staff pointed at her several times, but never for more than a second. There was only one thing left to do.

"I come peacefully," Karinda announced. "I hold no weapon. Say the word, and I will leave in peace."

There was no doubt that the old man saw her then. The staff swung directly at her as he came forward. "No weapon? You'll leave in pieces that way!" He cackled. "It's a wonder you made it this far undamaged."

A strange glint appeared in the Mage's eye. "Or is it, hm? You certainly are a clever one, and a real spark of talent, too. No . . ." He took two more steps closer, a revolting smile crawling onto his face. "I don't think you've made it this far just to leave that quickly. There's something here you want. Say it."

Karinda stayed calm, despite the shudder running through her spine. "It's . . . a rumor," she answered slowly. "A rumor of a magic node."

The end of the staff was now uncomfortably close. "So . . . you're here for power. I have enough power here alone to end your life. Would that be enough to satisfy you?"

"If you wish to end my life, there's nothing I can do to stop you." Karinda lowered her head but kept her eyes open and swallowed hard.

The old man took a step back and pulled the staff to his side. "You will do well to remember that, Clever. You're not the first to have tried and failed."

Karinda nodded deeply. "I will, sir. I'm Ka—"

"You are Clever," the old man said sharply. "Until you have learned all that you can learn here, you will be Clever. Understood?" The girl nodded. "Very good. Here, I am called Bellgrove."

Karinda raised her head. "Should I call you Master Bellgrove, or Adept?"

Bellgrove's face went red and anger contorted his features. "You should all be calling me GRANDEST Adept!" The staff went up again, the old man's knuckles going white. But as suddenly as it appeared, his anger vanished. "But no. There are no titles before the Greater Power. I am Bellgrove, just as you are Clever. Come, we will begin."

Bellgrove turned around and headed back toward the structure from which he'd appeared. Karinda stayed silent for a minute, then asked, "May I ask a question, Bellgrove?"

"Just one, for now."

"Were you going to channel your magic through the staff to kill me?"

The old man barked out a laugh. "Don't be ridiculous. I was going to beat you with it if you got too close. Waste of perfectly good magic, besides. No, no, don't want to damage you if at all possible . . ."

Karinda furrowed her brow. "What do you m—"

Bellgrove held up a finger. "One. No more. All will be known when it is meant to be known."

Which means you'll tell me if you feel like it, Karinda thought. *I already know more about you than I want to. Why am I even putting up with this?*

At least I'm not alone anymore. At least he still knows I'm here . . .

The rest of the walk went by in silence. The structure Bellgrove led her to was the one he was living in. It was surprisingly functional, and it even had most of a roof. Maybe she would get lucky and one of the other buildings would have mostly intact cover. Maybe.

Bellgrove made himself busy inside his ramshackle dwelling. Karinda watched him most of the time and had no idea what he was doing at all. She was starting to wonder if *he* did.

"I want to know everything you were told about this place," Bellgrove finally said. "And everything about me. We must begin by separating the truth from the lies."

Karinda waited for a moment to see if Bellgrove would turn his attention to her, but it was obvious he wasn't going to. "The truth of it is that I wasn't told much of anything. I was told that there was a rumor of a magic node that survived the Storms and an Adept guarding it. I thought it ridiculous at first, to be honest."

"And yet here you are. A part of you wanted to know the truth." The smile that made Karinda shudder crawled back onto the old man's face. "Or maybe it wanted something . . . more."

There was no holding back the shudder from that one. Bellgrove simply cackled. "It is no mere node or ley-line that resides here. No, this place belongs to a Greater Power. I will teach you to weave great magic through it, but it may very well beyond your grasp entirely."

"I will give it my all," Karinda said with real conviction.

Bellgrove arched an eyebrow. "Will you, now? There is another path to this power. Quicker, easier. And definitely more entertaining."

The leer on the old man's face was unmistakable. Karinda felt ill and then horrified. Not by what Bellgrove was offering or how he offered it—though that by itself was disturbing enough—but by the realization of who he thought he was offering it to.

Karinda hadn't bathed for the better part of a week, after heavy hiking. Her traveling clothes were slightly too big, just as grimy as the rest of her and not the least bit feminine. Karinda had always kept her hair short, and despite the fact that she was closer to being an adult than a child, her body had yet to catch up.

Just my luck. Of all the Mages left in the world with any magic, I find the one who's not only likely insane, but a boylover . . .

Karinda managed to keep her stomach down. She didn't know how to answer Bellgrove's offer, so she quietly shook her head.

"Suit yourself," he said. "Then we will start with the simple magics, what you would call kitchen magic or hedge magic. Show your skill with that, and we will move on. Tomorrow at first light, you will begin."

By first light, thought Karinda, *I'll be heading north as fast as I can. To the Abyss with you.*

It couldn't properly be called dawn yet, and Karinda was already covered in a thin sheen of sweat. She rolled over in her makeshift bed, wiped her face with the hem of her shirt, and got to her feet. She padded over to the doorway, looked around for signs of movement, grabbed the cloth bundle waiting there, and went to the lake's edge.

Karinda looked around once more out of habit, dropped the bundle on the bank, and slipped into the water. Her clothes instantly clung to her skin and her teeth chattered, but the cold would pass soon enough. It would be warmer later, but this was the best time for bathing. Bellgrove slept in later the hotter the days became, which suited her fine.

This had been her routine for nearly two months now. It was the only time she had without Bellgrove's unwanted attention. Always attentive of her every move, always leering. Never once did he try to touch her, but that didn't make things any less revolting.

Karinda sighed. "Why do I stay, then?" she asked the fading ripples, though she already knew the answer.

Bellgrove hadn't been bluffing about being a Mage. Karinda had been prepared to head out into the forest that next morning, but she wasn't expecting the old man to make good on his promise of first light. He had been standing on the platform with the pillars, looking over the lake. Bellgrove's forearms were wreathed in orange flame to match the sunrise. As the sun cast more rays across the water, Bellgrove would flick a wrist and the rays became colored flame upon the lake.

Karinda vowed to become a Mage then and there, no matter how long it took.

The only problem was, after two months she was as proficient with magic as she had ever been as a Bardic Trainee. Which was to say, hardly at all. All Karinda could manage was the simplest of kitchen magic; anything more complicated than lighting tinder or stirring pots eluded her.

Bellgrove would act the same way every day. He cackled viciously at every failure, never actually teaching her anything, but flamboyantly showing off on a whim to humiliate. Leering, watching, always suggesting the "quick and easy" path.

Karinda took a deep breath and ducked under the water. Submerged, her thoughts turned to the latter. Even in two months, there had been plenty of times when Karinda was ready to give in to the old pervert's desires—even if it turned out she wasn't what he expected—for the smallest amount of real magic. And she hated herself more every time she got to that point.

But she refused to give in. She wouldn't give Bellgrove the satisfaction. So she toiled all day, fixing Bellgrove's hut and hers, cooking meals, mending clothes, and in the spare moments putting all of her effort into tapping some of the ley energy that was supposed to be here.

Karinda surfaced and pulled herself out of the lake. She quickly swapped her soaked clothes for the spares in the bundle and headed back to her hut. With the sun now breaking over the treeline, Karinda almost didn't see Bellgrove standing in front of her doorway until she almost ran into him.

"Good morning, Bellgrove," she said quietly, backing away from the old man and averting her eyes.

"Yes, Clever," Bellgrove answered, "It's quite a good morning, indeed. You've bathed, excellent. You are as prepared as you need to be. This is the morning your wait is over."

It was then that Karinda noticed Bellgrove was wearing robes she had never seen before. These were immaculate, deep crimson with silver thread. A thought popped into her head then, too horrible to ignore.

"You . . . you're . . . This is Blood Magic!"

Bellgrove laughed. "Nothing so crude and painful, Clever. No, these are to honor the Splendid One." He took a step forward, but he made no move to touch her. "I've told you many times that a Greater Power dwells here. This morning, you will meet It and give yourself to It. Come, to the pillars."

Karinda followed, mesmerized by the hidden promises in Bellgrove's words. A voice in the back of her mind told her this was wrong, to run away. But Karinda wasn't listening.

Bellgrove led her to the pillared platform, where an intricate pattern of shiny dust had been laid out in the center. As Karinda crossed through the pillars, Bellgrove held up his hand, and she stopped.

The Mage entered the dust pattern and stood in the middle. Lifting his staff above his head, he began chanting in what Karinda was hard pressed to call a language. It hurt her ears and dulled her other senses. Bellgrove's voice rose to a commanding tone as he began thrusting the staff in random directions, contorting in ways Karinda wouldn't have imagined his old body capable of, and somehow not disturbing the dust at all.

Karinda had no idea how long this lasted, but the moment the sun cleared the trees, Bellgrove slammed the butt of the staff down onto the pattern. The dust erupted into silver flame and just as quickly died away. As it died, a great wind picked up from across the lake, creating a thick mist that swirled around the pillars. Karinda squinted to keep the mist out of her eyes, and the ancient platform took on the appearance of swirling white walls.

And in the middle of one of those walls, a doorway appeared. Bellgrove held the staff out with both hands and bowed his head. What appeared a second later was the most beautiful person Karinda had ever seen. He—she? it seemed both, and neither—had hair like a flowing river and wore crimson robes identical to Bellgrove's. Karinda's heart pounded fiercely just from the sight, and her breath was snatched away when It smiled and spoke to Bellgrove.

"Has another Solstice arrived already?" It asked. Karinda "felt" the words in her skull bones more than hearing them. *"The time goes too quickly, my disciple."*

Bellgrove gave one deep bow and answered, "Indeed it does, Splendid One. As does your boon. But I am patient, as you commanded. We may begin the Solstice offering."

There was a moment of tense silence. "I see no offering, my disciple," It said. "Do you mean to give yourself to me completely?"

"What? No!" Bellgrove looked around in panic.

Karinda froze. She was close to one of the pillars, but not close enough for the mist to obscure her—unless Bellgrove really was half blind. But the "Splendid One" as well? There was no time for questions.

Bellgrove pleaded, "Splendid One, I don't understand this! I was ready! SHE was ready! Some other magic is at work here!"

"She"? So he did *know,* Karinda thought, despite the situation. *Not that it matters, now . . .*

The Splendid One stepped away from the doorway, his gaze intent on Bellgrove. The glamour started to melt away. It was still beautiful, but now there was an unmistakably ugly *evil* beneath the beauty. "Explain yourself, then, my disciple. You give me many offerings, and now this. Why do you delay?"

"I do not delay!" Bellgrove stammered. "She was here, I swear it! And now—"

At those words, there was a flash of light visible through the mist. All three turned to look. Through the thick white, two shapes were barely visible. The Splendid

One waved a hand, and the mist thinned enough to see. It was clear now that it was two horses, one riderless. They stood at the end of the path that Karinda had first discovered so many weeks ago now.

The rider raised a hand as well, and a moment later the sun seemed to brighten until everything was turning white. Karinda and Bellgrove squinted to shield their eyes, but the Splendid One howled in pain.

"Greedy little insect!" it roared at Bellgrove. "This is your 'other magic at work'?" The Splendid One grabbed the old man's throat and lifted him high in the air. "You brought them here! I give you more power than any one man has left in the world, and this is your thanks!"

"This one is mine!" it shouted to the figures on the path. "He may have brought you here, but I claim this one as my offering! Even your kind cannot stop that!" The air was suddenly filled with a noise that made Bellgrove's chanting seem melodic. The mist walls burst into flame as the shiny dust had, and when the flames died, the mist, Bellgrove, and his "Splendid One" were gone.

The sun's brightness quickly returned to normal, and save for scorched stones and an old, cracked walking staff, there was no sign that anything had been to these ruins since its original inhabitants left.

Karinda craned her neck to see if the newcomers had gone as well, but in fact they were much closer, and Karinda's breath was taken away again. Two truly beautiful white horses walked into the circle of pillars. One of them bore a rider, his attire and bearing something Karinda had only seen in paintings and illustrations. But she knew them, and she stood in awe—and a little fear.

The Herald took a good look around at the remains

of the ritual. "Well, that was an unfortunate thing to witness," he said to no one in particular. "Why people continue to think they can outwit demons is beyond me. Now, where's this young lady we're here for?"

Not him, too! Karinda thought with a quiet groan.

The Herald seemed to hear that and scanned the area, looking slightly confused. It wasn't until the riderless horse nickered at him and nodded directly at Karinda that he finally locked eyes with the girl. He gave a start but quickly followed it with a smile.

"Arissa was right—you are a hard person to find, even when you know where to look."

Karinda blinked, but quickly found her voice. "Who is Arissa?"

:That would be me, dearest.:

It took a moment for Karinda's confused mind to acknowledge the fact that it was the lone horse that had answered. It took another to realize that the horse had answered *inside her head*.

:And I have been looking for you for a long time, Karinda,: Arissa continued, a feeling of warmth radiating throughout her words.

A hundred questions bubbled up inside Karinda, and the first one to come out was, "How can I hear you? I don't have this 'Gift' your people have."

The Herald let out a polite laugh. "It's not just 'our' Gift, love. Anyone can be born with it. Admittedly, from what Arissa has told me, your Gift is rather unique."

:And your *Gift is being rude,:* interjected the Companion bearing the Herald. *:Introduce us to the young lady first. Then we can continue.:*

The Herald grinned, a bit red in the cheeks. "You're

absolutely right, Ashlen. My apologies to all." He gave a slight bow. "Herald Anselm at your call, my lady."

"I'm hardly a lady," Karinda said with a blush of her own. "And what's this about having your . . . this Gift?"

:Yes, you possess a Gift of the mind, Karinda,: Arissa said. *:And as Anselm said, it is one we have never seen before, and we really don't know what to call it.:*

:I'm still partial to "Never Mind", myself . . . : quipped Ashlen with a whinny.

Karinda cracked a smile and didn't bother to hide it. " 'Never Mind'? What does that mean?"

Anselm replied, "You caught a glimpse of it just before I first spoke to you. That look, as if I couldn't see you, even though you were right in front of me? I saw you, but as soon as I did, your mind told mine that you were . . . well . . ."

"Irrelevant," Karinda answered before Anselm could find a word. "Unimportant, too much so to even remember seeing."

Arissa snorted. *:You mustn't think like that, dearest. You are anything but!:*

Karinda shook her head. "No, I don't mean it as an insult. It's true. I've dealt with this since I was a child . . . this explains so much."

"You don't have to deal with it alone anymore, Karinda," said Anselm. "Now that you know about it, we can train you to control it and use it responsibly."

Karinda looked confused. "Responsibly?" She held up a finger. "Wait, no, before that . . . Train me? You mean to be a . . ."

:Yes, dearest. A Herald.: Arissa lowered her head and looked her chosen in the eye. *:A Gift like yours needs*

guidance, and a pure heart. Even on the surface of your thoughts, I can see glimpses of what you were put through. But you were resolute to the end. The purity of your body and soul remained untouched despite the temptations. I would have sought you out for that alone, dearest.:

"You have the potential, love," Anselm said, "Do you have the desire?"

I have the desire for a hot bath and a real bed. Karinda thought. *We can negotiate from there.*

:I like her already,: said Ashlen, and the three had a quiet laugh at Karinda's blush. *:My apologies, young lady. I shan't listen further unless asked.:*

Karinda shook her head with a smile. Anselm returned it and said, "Everything we have said is an offer only. It is for you to choose. What say you, Karinda?"

For the first time since the beginning of the ritual, Karinda took a step forward, and another, until she was close enough to rest a hand on Arissa's muzzle. Silently, the Companion sank to her knees. Karinda kept her hand on Arissa's neck until she had mounted. Arissa rose, and Karinda knew—as if she'd always known—that her Companion would never let her fall.

Karinda had nothing to say. Words weren't needed. She knew that from now on, there would be someone who would always know she was there.

Beyond the Fires
Louisa Swann

Morning sun chased the night's chill from her bones as Liana eased herself down onto a gnarled root, ran a hand over her rounded belly, and stared up into the arching canopy overhead. Broad elm leaves, still spring-fresh and untarnished by the summer heat yet to come, glowed a light green against the spiky, dark fir and pine needles. The scent of damp earth and moss rose from the brook she'd just stumbled through, the burbling waters a peaceful counterpoint to the battle raging more than a day behind her.

The trees and bushes were a welcome change from the gorse-covered hills she'd passed through late yesterday. She felt like a spider clinging to its web, suspended between the peace flowing through the forest and the violence that had been her life ever since her fourteenth birthday, less than a year ago.

Liana sighed and rubbed her aching back. Peace was only an illusion, and though the skin-crawling stink of blood and death was far behind her, the clashing swords and screaming men reduced to faint background noise, even the toughest web could be torn, leaving the spider vulnerable.

A black-tailed squirrel chittered at her from a nearby tree as a raven swooped down and landed on her knee. The bird tilted its head to the side, peering at her first with one eye, then with the other before ruffling its ebony feathers and letting out a hoarse croak.

"Ya know as well as I do there ain't nothing in me pockets," Liana told it. "Ya sussed out all the crumbs last night."

The raven ruffled its feathers again, and Liana scowled. "Yer the one's got me into this mess, and now yer tellin' me ye never figgered out how we gonna eat?"

The raven's indignant croak almost brought a smile to Liana's lips. The movement felt strange, using muscles that hadn't been exercised in what felt like an eternity. She studied the mischievous bird, the almost-smile fading into blankness.

She hadn't planned on escaping when the mercenaries left the main camp. All the men, including the boys old enough to fight, had marched out to attack Valdemar, leaving behind their women and almost a thousand children of varying ages.

Liana had gone down to the river to fetch water for cooking. She'd been numb, eight months with child and exhausted beyond caring. Instead of filling the bucket in her hands, she'd found herself following a raven as it flew upstream, its ebony reflection rippling across the river's surface, then flattening out, then rippling again. When she finally realized how far she'd wandered, she'd almost panicked. Almost turned back.

But the raven had drawn her on.

Every step took her farther from camp. With each of those steps she could feel hard eyes watching her. With each of those steps her shoulders had tensed, anticipating the blow of a heavy hand.

No one escaped the Tedrel mercenaries.

No one.

Until now.

A fly tickled Liana's arm, and she gently brushed it away in wonder. She no longer felt numb. Since waking this morning, everything seemed fresh and untainted.

Then she shivered. In spite of the peaceful setting, she wasn't safe. Not yet.

The raven lifted gracefully into the air as Liana shoved herself off the root, standing with a muffled groan. The child in her belly kicked hard enough to make her gasp. She growled low in her throat, torn between hating the beast growing within her and wanting to believe the baby she'd give birth to in another month or so wasn't really a monster. Fear washed over her as strong as a river current, the same fear that threatened to choke her every time she thought about the impending childbirth.

Fear snuffed the peace from the air like wind blowing out a candle. The shadows seemed deeper, more menacing, and the sun burned instead of soothed. Something splashed in the brook behind her. Liana's heart thudded against her ribs as she glanced over her shoulder, certain she would see her captor standing there, a predatory smile on his scarred face, his enormous fists clenched and ready to beat her into submission.

But Grunt wasn't there.

A doe stood ankle deep in the brook, its brown eyes soft and inquisitive. Liana hadn't seen a live deer since she'd been captured, and this one seemed small, almost delicate. The doe flicked its enormous ears backward, then forward as it licked its muzzle, then dipped its head and drank.

Liana swallowed, trying to work moisture back into her suddenly dry mouth. She turned to waddle after the raven . . .

And found herself belly to muzzle with an enormous white horse.

Liana stumbled back, too startled to even shriek. Once again fear bubbled in her throat, a different fear this time, a fear born of Karsite tales, told around the cook fires, of white, blue-eyed demons that committed the most horrible acts . . .

The fear disappeared almost as quickly as it had come. If this . . . horse . . . truly was a demon, what it did to her couldn't be any worse than being Grunt's slave. Besides, it didn't look like a demon, in spite of the sapphire-blue eyes. Eyes that looked . . . intelligent.

A memory tickled at the back of her mind—a woman with hair the color of sunshine smiling down at her, weaving fantastic tales of Heralds and Companions . . .

The horse snorted, splattering the tenuous vision before Liana could grab onto it. The images disappeared into the fabric of her mind like water on a dry stone, leaving behind a vague sense of irritation, like an itch that couldn't be scratched.

"What ye on about then?" The words were out of Liana's mouth before she realized it. She cringed and clasped a hand over her mouth, startled by the tone of her voice.

She'd used that tone once after her capture. She'd been both terrified—and stupid. She should have known better, after seeing her father knifed and her mother burned alive. But she was only fourteen, barely old enough to be married and still innocent in the ways of the world. The man who'd carried her off had kept her in his tent, isolated from the other children. When she'd dared to defy him, he'd grabbed her beneath one massive arm, carried her into the men's tent, and left her to be raped over and over and over until she felt like a piece of meat that had been tossed into a pack of ravenous dogs.

When he returned for her, there was no fight left. Only a limp body that had once belonged to a young girl who'd once dared to dream.

The horse stomped a hoof, then swung around as if to leave.

That's when she saw the raven perched on the horse's back.

Liana's mouth dropped open. This was all getting much too strange. Would she wake to find her escape had been only a dream, a nightmare sent to taunt her with the thought, the taste of freedom, only to have that freedom taken away as soon as she woke at daybreak? How could life be so cruel? That would be like showing candy to a child, then snatching the treat away as soon as the child reached for it.

She squashed the thought like an annoying insect. She'd stopped praying for help months ago. No matter how hard she'd prayed at first, no savior had shown up to save her from the clutches of those insatiable men, no miracle had delivered her from Grunt's violent desires.

There were a lot of younger children in camp, ignored by the mercenaries until they were old enough to train for battle or to breed, and those youngsters had tried to convince her that better times were coming, that she only needed to hang on and have faith. Liana had tried to believe as the children believed, that Ghost Horses and White Riders would someday come and take them all to safety.

That belief, tenuous at best, died a slow death as her belly grew day by agonizing day, and Grunt's beatings got worse . . .

Puzzled, Liana stared at the white horse serving as the raven's new perch. Was this a Ghost Horse, then? Had the youngsters gotten it right after all?

Then she snorted. Startled, the raven flapped awkwardly off the horse's back and up into a tree. The horse looked at her over its shoulder, its blue eyes shining with something that almost looked like humor.

Liana shook her head at her own foolishness. The horse might be white, but it was only a horse, and if the raven was a White Rider, she'd . . . well, she didn't know what she'd do, but something . . .

The horse moved off down the path. After a moment, the raven glided down from the tree, taking up its position on the horse's back again. Then the bird croaked and tilted its head, watching her.

Liana sighed. "All right, then. I jes' hope ye have food waitin' wherever yer takin' us." She waddled after the pair, feeling like a lumbering mule.

Luckily, they didn't have far to go. Liana frowned as she struggled up a hill, concentrating on putting one bare foot in front of the other, dully watching dust from the dry woodland path curl up between her toes with each step. The swirling dust mingled with the scent of vanilla and pitch oozing from the fir and pine trees towering over her. Pain stabbed her ribs with each breath, wrapping around her belly.

She paused beside the pair waiting for her at the top. Her feet felt as swollen as her belly, and she couldn't seem to catch her breath. She put her hands on her back, stretching first forward, then back, trying to relieve the ache that wouldn't go away. Her head spun and her stomach growled. Not only did she need food, she needed water. She felt like a shriveled raisin. That couldn't be good for the baby.

The baby.

Why was she suddenly concerned about the monster growing in her belly?

Ignoring the question, she edged her way around the horse, trying to see why they'd stopped. They stood at the edge of a grassy clearing. There appeared to be some sort of cabin made of stone and rough-hewn wood nestled among the trees on the far side. It looked like someone was sitting in front of the door.

Waiting.

The raven rose into the air at the same time the horse broke into a run, racing across the clearing and coming to a stop just in front of the cabin. The raven perched on the thatched roof and looked back at her.

Liana gritted her teeth and moved forward through the knee-high grass in the meadow. The grass was soft and smelled of mint, with blades that bent under her feet, then sprang upright, leaving only a faint trace to show where she'd walked. She put her hand on the horse's shoulder as she passed and stopped without looking at the cabin's owner. Keeping her eyes on the ground, she chewed her lip in growing panic, trying not to grimace at the copper taste of blood.

Why didn't the man say anything? Why didn't he demand to know why they were here?

The ache in her back had grown into agonizing pain, and Liana wasn't sure how much longer she'd be able to stand. "Beggin' yer pardon. But we be needin' a place to rest for the night, and . . ."

She'd almost said, *and the horse thought maybe you'd help us,* but that probably wouldn't make a good impression, and Liana didn't want to be turned away because the man thought she was crazy.

The man didn't say a word.

A sudden shove sent her stumbling forward, and Liana glanced up, horrified that she'd somehow offend . . .

She froze as she recognized the Tedrel sitting against the door, a man she'd seen off and on around camp. Dried blood caked his lean, dark face and he didn't appear to be conscious, though she could see his chest rise and fall beneath the leather vest. The stench of camp surrounded her in memories, wood smoke mingled with sweat and blood.

Terror billowed inside Liana's chest, blocking her throat until she couldn't breathe. This was a man she didn't really know, yet when she looked at his face and smelled the stink rising from his body, reality seemed to morph, and she saw Grunt instead, with his leering grin and greedy, pig-eyed stare.

Hate sparked deep in her chest, then burst into full flame, no longer smothered by the coat of numbness she'd wrapped herself in for so long. With a snarl, she lunged at the man, searching first his vest and then his trews for a knife, a weapon of some sort . . .

:He is not your enemy. Reneth is not a mercenary. He's a Herald from Valdemar.:

A chill raced down Liana's spine. The voice hadn't come from someone close by.

It had been inside her head.

Slowly, she turned, looking first at the raven staring

down at her, then around at the horse standing close to her back. The unconscious man groaned as the horse stomped an enormous front hoof, sending vibrations thundering through the ground.

Something was going on here, something she didn't understand. Liana sank down onto her heels and wrapped her arms around her stomach, so tired she could hardly think.

:He needs your help.:

Again the voice in her head, but this time she knew it had to be coming from the horse. He towered over her, piercing her with those startlingly blue eyes.

And there was no one else around except the unconscious man.

:Inside you'll find supplies, among which is an emergency kit. Bring it outside, and I'll tell you what to do.:

Liana staggered to her feet, heart fluttering in her chest like a wounded bird. She stepped around the unconscious Tedrel and pulled the latch string, letting the cabin door swing open.

Pain shot through Liana's belly, tightening her muscles. Her breath caught in her throat as she fought to stay on her feet. She needed to rest, to get off her feet . . .

The horse—the *Companion?*—snorted, and she automatically moved, taking a deep breath as the pressure around her belly lessened. She'd spent the last year surviving in a slave camp. There'd been no relief in her duties just because she was with child. She'd hauled water, cooked, washed dishes, done laundry, and carried around children hardly smaller than herself. No reason she couldn't put this *Herald* to bed.

She found a hunting knife inside along with several other tools, a fair supply of beans that looked to be good, flint for lighting a fire, and the emergency kit filled with herbs and salves the Companion had asked for.

Liana found herself falling into her old routine, automatically following orders, her mind gone numb and uncaring while her body did what was needed. She carried water from a well behind the cabin, lit a fire, made a poultice from some herbs in the kit, and tended the Herald's wounds. As far as she could tell, his injuries weren't all that severe. Probably just suffering from a hard bash on the head.

After she'd seen to the Herald, she'd filled the bed frame with soft grass and covered the grass with blankets that had somehow managed to stay free of mice. She'd even made a bed for herself.

And she'd done it all before the sun disappeared for the night.

Now all she had to do was get the unconscious man inside.

Liana positioned herself behind the Herald and reached down to grab his shoulders. She'd have to drag him . . .

:You've done your part, and done it well,: the Companion said. *:Now I'll do mine.:*

She straightened with a groan and stepped aside, wondering how such a big animal thought he was going to fit through a door meant for a man.

Evidently, the Companion had a different plan. The huge white horse stood still, staring at the Herald, blue eyes so intent they glowed. The world seemed to hold its breath. Even the gnats that had been buzzing around Liana's head grew quiet.

The Herald groaned.

The Companion stepped closer and nuzzled the man,

softly at first, then more insistently. To Liana's surprise, the Herald reached up and scratched the horse's nose, muttering something in a language she couldn't understand. Then the Herald opened his eyes and looked at her. Liana stood, transfixed by the emerald gaze, a gaze more intense than the Companion's.

"Bolan says I'm supposed to thank you for taking care of me," the Herald said in Karsite.

"'E's the one you should be thankin'—"

A shrill cry split the air, and the raven sailed over Liana's head so close she could feel the breeze tickle her hair as he passed. The raven cried again. A squirrel took up the alarm from somewhere high in the trees behind the cabin.

:Get inside.:

Liana helped the Herald to his feet, pulled him into the cabin, and sat him down on the bed. She turned to bolt the door, catching a glimpse of white as the Companion spun on his haunches. Beyond the white horse, a horde of mercenaries flooded into the clearing, their swords gleaming in the fading light.

Liana pressed the back of her hand against her mouth and tried not to scream, fighting against the urge to tear the door open and run for her life.

Before she'd been taken, she used to be one of the fastest runners in her village, delighting in racing around town, her red hair blowing about so freely her mother likened her to a wild flame.

A sob choked her throat. She leaned the top of her head against the door and wrapped her arms around her stomach. Her mother was dead, burned alive after her father's throat had been slashed. *She* was the mother now, a girl barely old enough to be called woman.

She *could* run, though she wouldn't be as swift as she used to be. While the Tedrels were distracted by the Companion, she could slip out the door and around the side of the cabin, disappear among the trees.

"It's okay if you want to go."

Liana's heart skipped a beat, and her face grew hot. Could the Herald read her mind?

"Bolan can handle these thugs, and I'll be all right now that I've got my head back on straight."

Liana stared at him. "Yer still not right in the noggin, suggestin' I leave ye here ta fight with nothing but a horse and an itty-bitty knife."

The Herald's laugh made her feel as though she'd said something foolish. Liana glared over her shoulder at the man sitting on the bed she'd so carefully prepared. He jerked his chin at the door. "Take a look."

Only a fool would open the door with a battle going on outside, and she never had been a fool. Innocent, yes, but never a fool.

The Herald's face went blank for a second, then he gave her a lopsided grin. "Go ahead and take a look."

Liana frowned as she opened the door just enough to peer out. She blinked, trying to understand what she was seeing.

Over a dozen men surrounded the Companion near the center of the clearing. As she watched, one flew through the air as if he'd been thrown. Another went down as though he'd been struck by a falling boulder.

The legends are right, she realized. The Companion was a whirling, biting, kicking *demon*, head snaking out to bite as his hooves slashed through the air, catching one attacker in the chest, another in the head, then spinning impossibly fast to catch the other attackers before they could reach him with their swords.

Hope surged through her, so hot and sweet her eyes began to burn, a feeling she hadn't felt in way too long. She turned back to the Herald, then stopped as she saw a new group of Tedrels pour into the clearing.

The hope melted away, replaced by an anger so fierce Liana felt as if she'd turned into a different person. "Ain't fair," she growled, glaring out the door at the newcomers. There had to be something she could do.

The Herald stood up, all traces of laughter gone from his face. He grabbed the hunting knife and headed toward her.

As if answering her anger, pain grabbed Liana in its fierce grip, doubling her over. The room spun and memories flashed through her mind—visions of a laughing child she almost didn't recognize as herself, playing with the forest animals and never getting lost or being scared.

Understanding stabbed her mind as the pain deepened. She pictured the raven who'd led her away from the camp and sent out a wordless plea.

The image faded along with the memories, leaving her alone with the pain.

"Maybe you should sit down," the Herald said. Liana looked down at his hand on her arm. She took a deep breath and straightened.

"I'll be okay. I still got a month ta go."

He gave a quick nod, his grim face pale as his Companion's hide. "Move aside. Bolan needs me."

Liana shifted her weight and moved away from the door. The Herald cracked it open and uttered a cry.

Screams came through the open door, sounds of

terror and pain. Human sounds mingled with sounds she couldn't quite identify. Liana tried to see around the Herald, but the man wasn't moving. She finally reached around him and pulled the door open wider.

A cloud of black feathers, sharp beaks, and sharper claws had descended on the newcomers. Liana stared in astonishment as the birds—blackbirds, ravens and crows—chased one screaming man from the clearing, then another, in a violent dance that ended almost as abruptly as it had started.

She slipped outside before the Herald could stop her and instinctively held out her arm.

Feathers whispered in the air, and the raven landed, gently gripping her arm with bloodied claws. He tilted his head and peered at Liana with first one eye and then the other.

Liana tilted her head, mimicking his movement. "Thank ye," she whispered. The raven bobbed his head, then took flight, circling once before flying off into the trees.

The rest of the birds followed.

Even in the growing dark, the clearing looked and smelled like a battlefield, with bodies scattered throughout the trampled grass, the scent of fresh blood lingering in the air. Bolan trotted to them, his tail raised like a proud flag. Scarlet blood striped his white coat in several places, but the Herald reported that all the Companion's wounds were superficial.

Liana stared at the blood, memories flashing through her mind once again—gaping wounds, pools of darkened blood, the gagging stench of burning flesh . . . memories that had haunted her for almost a year. She gasped and bent over as pain burned through her belly, pressing both hands tight to her ribs. Out of the corner of her eye she could see alarm spread over the Herald's face.

"Is it time?" he asked, his voice slightly shaky.

Liana shook her head, trying to steady her breathing and failing. It felt as though someone had filled a kirtle with coals, wrapped it around her belly, and yanked hard on the laces. Panic grabbed her throat, threatening to strangle her.

It couldn't be her time. Not yet. She still had a month to go. Besides, she needed a midwife to attend her. A priest to bear witness. Otherwise she would die.

The pain eased, allowing Liana to stand straight. She tried to smile. "Too much ..."

Another pain knifed through her belly and she gasped, unable to hold back a small cry. Warmth flooded down her legs. She stared at the puddle growing on the floor, then looked up at the Herald in confusion. "I think ..."

The world faded to a single point of pure white agony, unlike any pain she'd ever felt before, and suddenly, Liana wasn't in the tiny cabin, she was back in her village ...

... Gleaming swords streaked with scarlet ...

... Her uncle sprawled in the dirt next to her father ...

... Hands—her hands—coated in the blood flowing from Father's throat ...

Someone screamed in the distance as Liana watched the puddle surrounding her feet spread across the stone floor. Another scream grew louder and louder until she realized that she was the one screaming. Panic flared in her chest.

She was dying.

The monster that'd been growing inside her for eight months was eating her from the inside out. Liana tore at

her shift with broken fingernails, trying to loosen the
pressure that stole the very breath from her body.

She'd seen a girl not much older than she was die in
childbirth two months ago, a girl who'd been raped and
beaten until she moved around camp like a scared dog,
never looking anyone in the eye, never smiling.

Liana had been raped and beaten the way that girl
had been, and now she would die the way that girl had
died, bloody and alone.

A hand fell on her arm, and she screamed again, shov-
ing away from the man looming in front of her. His
mouth moved, but she couldn't hear his words, just the
noise pouring from her own mouth, mingling with her
fear, her horror. She tasted the blood in her mouth,
smelled Death hiding close by . . .

:Stop.:

The command jolted through her body, staying Liana's hand and silencing her screams. She blinked, clearing her eyes as if wakening from sleep.

"It's going to be all right," the Herald said.

She glanced around, confused to find herself in a
small cabin . . .

:A Waystation.:

. . . with a strange man . . .

:Herald Reneth. You need to walk.:

Liana frowned down at her hands and slowly let go of
her shift.

The Herald smiled at her, his emerald eyes gleaming. "If
Bolan says you should walk, you should probably walk."

Walk? "Tell *Bolan*, that 'e can go—" Again, pain
grabbed Liana in its white-hot grip, crushing her belly
into a boulder. Pressure mounted between her legs, and
she found herself squatting in the middle of the room.

"It's killing me . . ." she gasped. Not only was she giving birth to a monster, her own body had turned traitor. Too much more of this, and her guts would be joining the wet puddle on the floor.

Suddenly she had an insane vision of Grunt as tall as the trees, reaching down through the roof of the cabin, grabbing her around the belly, and squeezing the life out of her.

The beast had killed a chicken in front of her. Picked the poor bird up in one hand and squeezed its neck until its wings stopped flapping and its feet stopped kicking and the bird dangled lifelessly in his hand.

Then he'd carelessly tossed it in her lap and left . . .

Liana's throat closed. She took a great, shuddering breath and almost choked on her own stench—the stink of sweat mingled with a terror she could barely contain. Her hands tingled, and she couldn't catch her breath, and suddenly she was living the nightmare she'd had ever since the baby's first kick—giving birth to a monster that looked like Grunt, only it had two heads and a forked tail, a monster that would follow in the footsteps of its father, growing up to pillage villages, raping children and devouring babies . . .

:You worry for naught,: the voice said. *:I would teach you to let go of your fear, but there is no time. I will help— if you'll let me.:*

A knot untied somewhere inside her, and Liana felt herself drifting. A soft blanket draped down over the nightmare, blotting out the terror and wrapping her in warmth.

And through the warmth she felt a presence . . . innocent and scared. And behind that presence was another, also innocent and scared.

:Not a two-headed monster. Twins.:

Twins?

Time melted into a blur of muted pain, interspersed with flashes of Herald Reneth bending over her. The voice kept her calm and somehow helped with the pain.

When she heard the first weak cry, Liana mumbled something about not being able to do it again, and once again everything blurred.

She'd almost given up hope when she finally heard the second cry.

Then the crying stopped.

Liana fought to clear the fog from her mind, frantic to find—to hold—her babies.

A warm bundle slipped into her arms, then another.

She *felt* the innocence deep in her bones.

Looked into one wrinkled red face, then the other.

And slipped into a deep, peaceful sleep.

A Brand from the Burning

Rosemary Edghill and Rebecca Fox

The western heights of Karse were poor and windy. Fields were small, their yields meager. The few scattered villages of the district eked out their livings through the sheep and goats they herded, and the Sunpriests who lived among them lived as simply as they.

Save for the Hierophant. The Hierophant Virtulias' Palace was an enormous manor house, and the attached Chapel of the Sun had a roof covered in pure gold. And yet, for all the pomp and glory of the Hierophant's Palace, all Virtulias' flock knew that a bowl of bread and milk would be readily given to any who asked at the kitchen door, and his household was filled with foundlings he had rescued.

He did it because he was a good man, even though he was a Priest-Mage. He did it because he believed that the Writ and the Rule were simple truth. He did it for love of Vkandis Sunlord. And he would never know that in saving one child, he had saved not only all of Karse but perhaps all of Velgarth as well . . .

It was early on a midsummer's morning when word reached Hierophant Virtulias that Artiolarces, Son of the

Sun, lay dying. The message summoned Virtulias to Sunhame at once, for the Conclave must gather to choose
Artiolarces' successor.

The messenger had come to the refectory, where Virtulias was presiding over the household's morning meal:
priests and servants and novices and postulants and acolytes. In the evening, Virtulias dined off linen and gold,
as custom said a Sunpriest was entitled to. In the mornings, he ate from wood and pewter and looked happier.

When Virtulias dismissed the messenger to his rest
and his household to their daily tasks, three souls remained: his housekeeper, Hettes, and the two youngest
novices under his care. Every Sunpriest had a responsibility to gather up the promising young boys in their domain to train them up as the next generation of Vkandis'
priesthood—Virtulias (said his colleagues) took the responsibility of training new Sunpriests to unreasonable
extremes. Virtulias simply smiled and went on sheltering
the weak and the helpless.

"Is it true we're all going to Sunhame?" Solaris asked
eagerly. Even though she was a girl, not a boy, somehow
no one spoke out against Solaris being taught among—
and *as*—one of the novices.

"Not all of us," Virtulias said with a fond smile.

"*But*—" Solaris protested.

"*But*," Virtulias went on, "I see no reason why you
and Karchanek should not come with us. It will teach the
acolytes humility, if nothing else. Now off with the both
of you, before Father Aetius takes a switch to you for
dallying when you should be at your lessons."

Hettes gave Virtulias a long look when they were alone.
She had been the first of his foundlings. Decades ago, a

very young Sunpriest had saved an even younger orphan girl from the Fires; he had sworn (regardless of whether it was true or not) that Hettes had no visions and heard no voices and was merely a termagant girl.

For the gift of her life, she had rewarded him with years of loyalty and devotion. Far more than a mere housekeeper, she had agents throughout his domain and allies beyond, and there was no gossip, no bit of information Virtulias needed to hear that Hettes did not bring to him.

"I don't suppose you could just not go to Sunhame, Father," Hettes offered. "I'm sure the Conclave wouldn't miss you."

Virtulias chuckled softly and shook his head, a sad smile creasing his weathered face. His brown eyes were filled with kindness. He patted the bench beside him, just as he had when Hettes was a little girl. She sat down carefully and looked up at him, wondering when he—when *they*—had gotten old.

"It will make no difference, in the end, if I stay home," Virtulias said gently. "If Lastern or Siralchant or Lumillian takes the Sun Throne, I will be summoned to Sunhame to face charges of heresy. Vkandis Sunlord may call Priest-Mages to his service, but the Solarium as a whole trusts us even less than we trust each other."

"Not that Lastern or Siralchant or Lumillian—or for that matter, half the Solarium Excelsis—aren't black-robes as well," Hettes grumbled.

But there was a deeper reason Virtulias meant to go to the Conclave in Sunhame, for they both knew charges of heresy could be bribed away—if one knew whom to bribe. Virtulias' presence certainly wasn't wanted in Sunhame, for he'd been a thorn in the Solarium's side for decades now, quietly but firmly holding to the Writ and the Rule. For that reason, the hopeful, the naive, and the desperate among the ranks of the Sunpriests and their adherents now hoped to see him chosen as Son of the Sun—and it was for that reason Virtulias intended to go. The rot among the priesthood had been growing for generations, deafening both red-robes and black-robes to Vkandis' whispered words. Only the Son of the Sun—*a* Son of the Sun—could have the power and authority to sweep it all away.

"All the more reason for me to go," Virtulias said brightly, patting her knee. "And who knows? By Vkandis' grace, I might be the next ruler of the Solarium."

"Just as you say, of course, Father," Hettes said sourly. *By Vkandis' grace? It will take all His grace to let us survive the election, let alone win it!*

Sunhame was exactly as it was described in the scrolls Karchanek had read and nothing at all like he expected.

Even from a distance, Karchanek could see the great Temple of the Sun rising like some vast gold-gleaming Presence over the city. Upon closer approach, the broad, marble-paved avenue leading to the Hierophant's Palace in which Virtulias and his party were to be lodged (one of twelve, all identically broad and fine) did indeed radiate out from the Temple like a ray of the Sun in Glory. The air was filled with spices and incense, and the avenue was indeed lined with the great, gleaming bronze statues.

Karchanek gawked at all of it, until Father Aetius frowned terrifyingly and the acolytes riding in the cart with them snickered and nudged each other. But somehow, it was still a disappointment. Whenever Father Virtulias spoke of Vkandis, Karchanek always imagined the Sunlord—and Sunhame—filled and surrounded by the same sort of warm, golden light that softened the wheat fields in the fall just before the harvest. (Maybe, he'd once whispered to Solaris while they sat sleepily waiting for the dawn service to begin, Vkandis *was* light.) But the light that filled Sunhame wasn't like that at all.

This light was cold.

Unsettled, Karchanek looked over at Solaris. Her eyes were hooded, and she was frowning. It was one of those weirdly grown-up looks she sometimes got. In spite of the heat of the day, his arms prickled with goose-flesh.

"'And lo, I was a stranger, and in a strange realm, and no man knew me,'" Solaris murmured softly.

"It'll be different when Vkandis makes Father Virtulias Son of the Sun," Karchanek said loyally. "You'll see."

"Little Novice Karchanek thinks Vkandis picks the Son of the Sun." Acolyte Tobias smirked. "Boy, does he ever have a lot to learn!"

Even the younger Sunpriests riding with them looked amused, and Karchanek glanced at Solaris in surprise.

She looked sad.

The Hierophant's Palace is very grand, Hettes thought, *but like any place with no master, what belongs to many is the responsibility of none.* She had barely terrorized the kitchens into some semblance of order when word came that Virtulias was entertaining an important visitor and had called for refreshment.

Not trusting any of the Palace staff, Hettes took charge of the matter personally.

She would have anyway.

*   *   *

"How good it is that you have come back to Sunhame in our hour of greatest need, Father," Lumillian said smoothly.

Hettes fought back a smile as she cleared away the delicate glassware. Lumillian's annoyance hung between the two men like a cloud of smoke. He'd been a thin-skinned, sour-faced child in the days when he served Virtulias as an acolyte, and he hadn't changed much since.

"It is the duty of whole of the Solarium Excelsis to attend the Conclave," Father Virtulias said after taking a sip of his tea, "and to act in Vkandis' name to choose a new Son of the Sun."

"Ah," Lumillian said, "but with the right backing, you know, you might become Son of the Sun. These are dark times in Karse. Holy war looms over us. We are in grave need of good men to lead us. Good men like you, Father."

Hettes had heard whispers that Karse meant to declare a holy war upon neighboring Valdemar and take its lands for her own (all in the name of Vkandis, Prince of Peace, of course). It was disturbing to hear Lumillian speak of it so openly.

"Eh," Virtulias said with a phlegmatic shrug, "with the right backing, the village priest's goat could become Son of the Sun."

"I come offering the hand of friendship to my old teacher, yet he mocks me." Lumillian's tone was light, but there was a dark undertone to his voice. "Who else can lead us with the consent of all? Siralchant is ambitious, but he's young—who wants a Son of the Sun barely out of priests' robes? Cronturin is greedy and hasn't the brains Vkandis gave a sheep—you know as well as I do he's nothing but a puppet of the old men who pretend to advise him. And Lastern . . . well. The streets of Sunhame would be crawling with demons inside of a year. Our true choices are few."

"Hm," Virtulias said noncommittally. "And what would the Solarium Excelsis see in an old man from the country—one who is widely thought to be entirely too traditional for his own well-being?"

Lumillian sighed softly. "I'm only trying to help you help us all, Father. Out of respect."

It was a lovely show, but that was all it was. Outwardly, the priesthood bewailed their God's long absence: they declared fasts, made sacrifices, demanded penance from the people. But no *Good* power would ever intrude where it wasn't asked and wanted, and it had been a very long time since the Sunlord had appeared to his people. Hettes was sure that if Lumillian got his way, the wait would be longer still.

"You've always been a good boy," Virtulias said in the same gentle voice he used on particularly difficult children and frightened animals. "And certainly you've given me much to think about."

"If you change your mind, you know where to find me," Lumillian said in clipped tones.

Hettes waited until the sharp report of his footsteps had faded before she dared to look up. There were lines of worry in Virtulias' face, but he found a small smile for her when she met his eyes.

"Lumillian never did like being told he couldn't have what he wanted," he said gently. "What did you think of his offer?"

Hettes raised her eyebrows. "That depends, Father. Would you prefer the politic answer or the honest one?" she asked, settling the tiny glass plates on a silver tray.

Virtulias laughed. "Always so careful, is my Firecat. If I wanted the politic answer, I could ask almost anyone here. I'm asking you."

"I wish you wouldn't call me that," Hettes said without rancor. It had been a very long time indeed since a true Firecat had walked the streets of Sunhame. She spared a moment to wish they still did; Father Virtulias could certainly use the help right now. But there were ways, Hettes supposed, that she could be of more use to Father Virtulias than a Firecat might have been.

"There are forty-eight Hierophants of the Solarium Excelsis, and according to the Writ, any one of you might become the next Son of the Sun," she said, seemingly at random.

"The Writ teaches that such decisions are in the hands of the Sunlord," Virtulias answered placidly.

Hettes couldn't help but snort softly. "In reality, only five Hierophants have any chance at all of getting enough backing, and that includes you. I think that worries Lumillian a great deal. He was a lying weasel as a child, and he's a lying weasel still. He'd make you into another Cronturin, only instead of being the voice of many, you'd be the voice of . . . Lumillian."

"I did not come to Sunhame to speak the words of another," Virtulias said simply.

As a girl, she'd dreamed endlessly about coming to Sunhame, about seeing the gleaming Palace of the Sun, about standing in the ancient temple where Vkandis Sunlord's voice had once echoed. Now that she was here, all Hettes wanted was to go back to bleating goats and grazing sheep and fields of wheat waving in the endless west wind.

Virtulias still had not returned from the Conclave. It was late enough—well past the end of the midnight service—that Hettes had dismissed the acolytes who served him as well as the other servants. She was starting to worry that the Conclave would run all night when at last the door opened and Father Virtulias appeared. The lines around his mouth looked deeper than they had even a sennight ago.

"There's tea ready," she said, taking his heavy embroidered mantle, "and bread and fruit and cheese. You should eat."

His smile was both tender and rueful. "Ah, my little Firecat. I'm not entirely sure how I'd survive without you to look after me."

"You'd have to rely on novices to bring your supper and fetch your slippers," she said dryly, pouring two cups of tea. "Certainly you'd either die of starvation or exposure before the year was out."

That at least drew a weak chuckle from him. "Perhaps I was too hasty in dismissing Lumillian's offer." He picked up a piece of bread and was regarding it as if he weren't sure what to do with it. "If nothing happens to break this deadlock, we'll be here another six months, and there will still be no Son of the Sun."

"Perhaps then the Sunlord will grow tired of waiting and simply choose someone Himself." Hettes took the bread from Virtulias' hand, spread it with soft cheese, and handed it back. "Eat."

"We can but hope," Virtulias said with a sigh. "The way things are going, no one has any chance of getting a majority. If it weren't for Lumillian and Siralchant, Lastern would already be Son of the Sun, and we'd be going home. If it were a choice between me and him, there would also be no question; no one really wants Lastern, but what they want even less is a moralizing old man. But Siralchant and Lumillian give the ones who can't quite stomach Lastern other options. And so we endlessly debate."

Hettes glared meaningfully at him. Looking somewhat abashed, Virtulias took a bite of the bread he was holding, smiled, and took another.

"Lumillian is still willing, so he says, to withdraw and back me," Virtulias went on, "which might give me a majority. But I'm fairly certain I'd never be able to conscience whatever he'll undoubtedly want in return."

"Only 'fairly,' Father?" Hettes asked, and took another sip of her tea. "You know what he will want. And you are as ready to give it as you were the day we arrived here."

Virtulias sighed ruefully, shaking his head. "Tell me, wise little Firecat, what do you think I should do?" He sounded so very weary, as if Sunhame were wearing him away little by little, the way a trickle of water might wear away a stone.

"You already know what I think, Father," Hettes answered gently. "It's simply that you don't care for it."

"Hettes," Virtulias said, his voice full of quiet rebuke. "How could I face the Sunlord knowing that I had abandoned His people to a man like Lastern—or even one like Lumillian—out of a desire to save my own skin?"

Something inside her chest tightened, and she looked away, swallowing hard. He put a gentle hand on her shoulder. "I know you say this out of love. But—"

"But what of the child?" Hettes asked, looking out at

the stars, at the floor, anywhere but at Virtulias. "What of Solaris?" They had never spoken of her, not even on the day Hettes brought her home in her market basket, but she was sure he felt it too. Solaris was . . . special.

"I have faith that you will always do what is needed to keep her safe," Virtulias said in a quiet voice.

Hettes shivered in spite of the heat.

She had known since before they came to Sunhame what she must do to keep Solaris safe.

Karchanek had never imagined there could be so many people in one place—and all of them very busy, with no time for a small boy. Solaris spent most of her time in the Great Temple, watching the ceremonies that occupied every candlemark of the day, but, devout as he was, Karchanek found them boring after a while. Nobody had any time for him. Even Father Aetius had told him to run along and amuse himself today!

With a sigh of relief, Karchanek stepped into the coolness of the garden. The place had become his refuge, for the garden of the Hierophant's Palace was little used. The fountain at the center of the garden lay just ahead, but it was a moment before he realized he wasn't alone here. Through its dancing spray he could see two figures standing on its far side. He could not see them clearly, but he could hear their voices—a man's tenor and a woman's low alto. Through the sound of the plashing water he could make out a few names. Lumillian. Lastern. They were names everybody was talking about lately, and Karchanek quickly lost interest in the conversation. Then he heard a name he recognized: Virtulias.

It was enough to make him creep forward and try to hear more. As he came closer, he could see them clearly.

The man had his back to Karchanek, but he was wearing a Hierophant's gold robes. The woman was wearing an embroidered gown of a deep red. She was veiled, as many wealthy women were. Karchanek wondered who she was and why she was talking to this man. Perhaps she was one of the nobles of Karse? Father Aetius said that Karse was a "nominal" kingdom. But Father Aetius also said that the King might reign, but the Son of the Sun ruled.

The Hierophant suddenly looked around.

"We are not alone, madame," he said.

Karchanek fled.

Each of the embroidered silken veils was as delicate as a butterfly's wing and worth more than a mere house-keeper might hope to earn in a year. Removing them felt rather like shedding an outworn skin—though it was a skin she had donned many times in the past. Hettes folded them carefully and tucked them away in a small spring-loaded drawer concealed in the lid of her largest trunk. The crimson dress, thick with embroidery, was folded into a plain blanket of light wool and put away with the linens. Hettes stuffed the little gold slippers inside a pair of scuffed boots, then simply stood for a moment, savoring the coolness of the air against her bare skin. Finally, with a little sigh of regret, she pulled a shift of plain white cotton over her head.

She regarded herself soberly in the mirror as she wiped away the kohl she'd used to line her eyes, and then carefully tucked her hair under a tidy linen kerchief. Siralchant had taken her for a high official's wife, who clearly had access to her husband's vast network of spies and informants, and an interest in seeing a young man with ample reason to be grateful ascend the Sun Throne.

While the story suited Hettes' purposes nicely, almost none of what she'd told Hierophant Siralchant (in strictest confidence) was true.

It would, however, break the deadlock in the Conclave.

Father Aetius shepherded the novices, the acolytes, and the postulants to sunset service each evening—as well as the younger priests in Father Virtulias' household—and Hettes went along, as she always did. Their rooms were usually empty when they returned, but tonight Father Virtulias was waiting for them.

At first Karchanek didn't see him—and did not expect to, for what would Father Virtulias be doing sitting in the novices' common room? But Hettes gasped softly and ran forward, and suddenly Karchanek saw Virtulias, sitting slump-shouldered on one of the hard little wooden chairs.

"Father!" Hettes cried, kneeling at his feet while the acolytes and novices looked at each other in alarm. "What is it?" She glared at the two acolytes who normally served Father Virtulias and said: "Make yourselves useful and bring him some wine."

Karchanek thought he saw the ghost of a smile pass across Father Virtulias' face, but it was gone again as quickly as it came. "It is done," he finally said in a voice like dry leaves. "Karse has a new Son of the Sun."

Karchanek felt cold all over. He reached for Solaris' hand.

"Hierophant Lumillian was found dead this morning," Father Virtulias said in the same colorless voice.

"The Conclave has brought charges of murder and heresy against Hierophant Siralchant. Both Lumillian's and Siralchant's supporters were only too quick to transfer their allegiance to Lastern, lest anyone think they might be . . . *involved*."

"The Conclave would have been in a hurry to settle the matter, I'm sure," Father Aetius said in an uncharacteristically dark voice. "I suppose we all must now do honor to Radiance Lastern."

"It is our duty," Father Virtulias agreed wearily.

Karchanek shivered and glanced at Solaris. Her hand was as ice-cold as his. But she wasn't looking at Father Virtulias at all.

She was looking at Hettes.

By the time Hettes stumbled up the stairs to her little chamber the following evening, weary in body and bruised in soul, it was that time of night that always left her doubting—just a bit—the sun would ever rise again. The day had been filled with hurried ceremonies: Lastern was not slow to take up the reins of power, and the Solarium Excelsis was just as quick to display its prudent loyalty.

But at last Hettes could seek her bed, here in the wolf hour. It brought back memories. She remembered kneeling on the flagstone floor of the Chapel of the Sun in the bone-deep cold of Longest Night, a child younger even than little Solaris was now, weeping with terror at the thought the darkness would endure forever. Father Virtulias had gathered her close, and leaned down to whisper in her ear. "Morning always comes," he'd said. A promise in the darkness, just for her. His coarse robes had smelled of sunlight and spices.

"Morning always comes," she murmured under her breath now as she pushed the heavy door open. She was halfway across the threshold when some instinct—some half-heard rustle, some sense of something out of place—stopped her.

She let the little knife slip from the sleeve of her tunic into her hand (Virtulias had frowned fiercely when he first learned she carried it, but he'd never forbidden it) and raised the candle she carried so that it cast its feeble light into the room. All Hettes could make out were shadows, but she didn't need to see any more to identify her nocturnal visitor. It was the girl-child Solaris, sitting as still and as patient as a priest keeping vigil in the temple. Hettes felt a tiny shiver crawl along her spine—how long had the girl been waiting here alone in the darkness?

"Solaris," Hettes said in mild reproof. "If Father Aetius finds you out of bed, he'll take a switch to you." It was a foolish thing to say, but a part of Hettes shied away from giving voice to what she felt hanging in the air between her and the child.

Solaris made a scoffing noise. Such an adult sound should have sounded ludicrous coming from a girl so young, but it didn't. Hettes' breath caught in her throat.

"It's late, child," Hettes said more gently. In the dim and wavering light, she imagined she could see greatness flickering around the child like a crown of flames. "You should go back to bed."

She stepped carefully into the room and shut the door behind her. The smoke from Artiolarces' funeral pyre still clung to her clothes. With a new Son of the Sun enthroned, they had been able to burn the poor old man at last. But Lastern had burned him at sunset, not at dawn.

Hettes wondered what that meant, and she was afraid she knew. The sooner they could all leave Sunhame, the better. The changes that were coming were not good ones.

She set the candle and the little knife down on the lid of her largest chest and reached up to unpin the kerchief that covered her hair.

"You were supposed to get Virtulias chosen as Son of the Sun," Solaris said in a very even voice. The candle flickered and guttered. "He trusted you. We *all* trusted you. But you helped Lastern instead! Karchanek told me he saw a woman dressed in red talking to Hierophant Siralchant the day before Hierophant Siralchant was accused of killing Hierophant Lumillian. I know it was you."

"You weren't there to see, and Karchanek doesn't know what he saw," Hettes said in a gentle voice. It wasn't *quite* a lie.

Solaris folded her arms and gave Hettes a searching look, and for a moment—perhaps it was a trick of the shadows and the flickering candlelight—Hettes didn't see a child at all. She saw a woman, tall and stern and decked in gold and jewels. A woman she'd seen in a dream many years ago: the night before she brought home an abandoned babe in her market basket and begged Father Virtulias to take in the child.

"He doesn't know it was you, but I do. And I trust him. He wouldn't say he'd seen something if he hadn't," Solaris said implacably. "It was you. You were there. In disguise."

"You think I betrayed you," Hettes said softly. If Solaris told Father Virtulias what she knew, it would break his heart.

"Didn't you?" Solaris asked. She hadn't raised her voice above a level suited for pleasant, private conversation, and yet somehow it filled the room. "Lastern is a black-robe," Solaris said, her voice still cold and adult.

"As is Father Virtulias," Hettes pointed out steadily.

"Lastern will—"

"How long do you think Father Virtulias would have survived as Son of the Sun?" Hettes asked. "He is a good man, a pious man, and Sunhame grinds good and pious men into dust. Lastern would still be Radiance Lastern before the seasons changed." It was more difficult than she expected to keep her voice even.

"My people—!" Solaris' voice was filled with quiet anguish. She scrubbed impatiently at her eyes, her voice wavering.

It was a matter of a few steps for Hettes to cross the room and gather the little girl up in her arms, just as she had so many times before. Solaris leaned into her, trembling.

"It's better this way," Hettes murmured against Solaris' hair. "Radiance Lastern is the Son of the Sun Karse has chosen. And he will live and reign for many years, as he is much like Artiolarces—yes, and like Siralchant and Lumillian and most of the rest of the Solarium Excelsis—and he knows how to gain power, and keep it, and keep it from being taken from him. As Father Virtulias does not. And Father Virtulias will return home, and we with him, and there we will follow the Writ and the Rule for the greater glory of Vkandis Sunlord, just as we always have. But Radiance Lastern will not live forever, and the day will come when a new Radiance must be chosen." She stroked the child's hair carefully, gently. "And I think that one will be wise, and will have learned a great lesson from the time she has spent here in Sunhame, and will have worked very carefully for many years to find good men and make strong alliances. And, so, when she reaches out her hand and says, 'in Vkandis' Name,' she will not find herself given to the flames as a madwoman, a heretic, or simply someone . . . inconvenient . . . before she can say it a second time."

Solaris looked up at her, brow knitted in consideration. "Girls can't be Sunpriests," she said. "Everybody says it says so in the Writ. Even Father Aetius says so."

But Father Aetius was wrong. Hettes knew that. So did Virtulias. The Writ said nothing at all about women being barred from the priesthood. It was only that the Writ didn't mention Sun*priestesses* at all. The trouble, Virtulias always said, was that without Vkandis declaring his intentions before all in the Temple, the Writ was subject to interpretation.

And revision, by those in power. In the name of clarity. Or simple convenience.

"Rebellion against tyranny and corruption doesn't come from the top. It comes from the bottom. Or else it doesn't last," Hettes continued, as if Solaris hadn't spoken. "You must remember that—when you are Son of the Sun."

Solaris went utterly still, and her gaze sharpened even as her eyes widened.

"Who *are* you?" Solaris asked. In her voice Hettes could hear the woman she would become and fought the urge to kneel.

"You have known me since you were a babe, my darling," Hettes said quietly. "You know I am nothing more than Virtulias' housekeeper."

* * *

The Robing had been but the first of the ceremonies surrounding the elevation of a new Son of the Sun; today was the last of them, and it was a relief for Hettes to follow Virtulias back to their rooms when it was over, to send Solaris and Karchanek off under Father Aetius' care.

Sunhame was no place for innocence.

"Now—at last—we can return home," Virtulias said, turning to her. Servants lifted the heavy, gold-trimmed robes from his shoulders as Hettes undid the elaborate fastenings down their front; beneath them, he wore the simple homespun priest's habit he usually wore at home. "We will leave tomorrow—the day after at the latest." In the morning light, his face looked careworn and heavily lined.

"I'm sure the children will be glad to return to their studies," she said, looking away. "And I for one will be grateful to sleep in my own bed again."

Gently, so gently, he cupped her cheek in one of his big, gnarled hands. Startled, she looked up and met his eyes. The sadness she saw there made her want to look away again. "I know you did your best for me, my little Firecat," Virtulias said softly. "But even your skill could not make me Son of the Sun."

For a moment, all Hettes could think of was how grief-stricken he looked. He had come to Sunhame hoping to gain the power to do great good, and those hopes had been dashed. Even if he had known what Solaris had been born to be, he would still have wished to try.

But your task is a far harder one, my dear friend. She thought of the years Vkandis' true daughter would need to gather up the power that would let her survive what Virtulias could never have survived. The power she could gain in a Hierophant's household, living under his protection. The power to fulfill Virtulias' hopes and dreams and those of Vkandis' people. *And I do not know if you will live to know what you have done. I can only pray you will.*

"Yes, Father," she said around the lump in her throat. "I did my best. For you, and for Karse."

Vixen
Mercedes Lackey

The inn near the Pelagiris Forest was bustling this morning, with horses being saddled and loaded and people bustling out of the stable and inn doors, but Healer Vixen was getting priority help in starting on the next leg of her own journey. Already in the saddle, she was arranging things on her horse's back from in place; Brownie was an exceedingly tall horse, and it was much easier if someone was atop him to make sure everything was secure. A boy from the stable had been assigned to her alone, just to help her get her bay hunter saddled, bridled, and loaded up, and the innkeeper himself had just now brought a nice selection of pocket pies for her to eat on the road. Those were stowed in the saddlebags that hung over the bay's shoulders, in place and fastened shut, though the smell coming from the left-hand one was enough to try her willpower and tempt her into a second breakfast.

Then again, while everyone was glad to see Vixen arrive in a hamlet or village, they were also happy to see her leave as quickly as possible once her job was done, which was probably why the innkeeper was doing his level best to get her on the road. Her sharp tongue was

the stuff of legend, and no one wanted to be on the re
ceiving end of it. She encouraged this, to be honest. She
didn't much care for people. Healthy people, that is. She
was generally able to muster *some* compassion for sick
ones, but she much preferred her own company to that
of anyone else. She not only did not suffer fools gladly
she didn't suffer them at all.

"Healer Vixen," that was what they called her, since
no one actually knew her real name anymore. She'd have
gone by "Healer" and nothing more, but at one point
someone who'd had the dubious benefit of the sharp
edge of her tongue had dubbed her "that Healer-vixen,
and the name had stuck.

Some might have resented it, but Vixen was just as
glad, actually, that she'd gotten a name that no one would
ever have associated with her past. She didn't look any
thing like she had as a child, and the last thing she wanted
was for anyone to connect her with *that girl*.

Especially when she spotted someone who might
have known *that girl*, as she had just now.

She sat quietly in the saddle of her enormous horse –
really, he was as big or bigger than the mounts fully ar
mored knights used – and watched a fellow unload a
wagon in the thin morning sunshine out of the corner of
her eye. He was across the village square from her, and
she couldn't tell exactly what his wagon carried. Sacks of
something. Flour? Marrows? It could be anything. She
knew him, though; he had been one of the boys who had
tormented "Rosie" unmercifully, in another hamlet, long
ago, a place much smaller than this village but within two
day's ride of here.

So that's what's become of you, Digby.

He clearly didn't recognize her except as what she

was now, which was exactly as she wanted it. He'd gone past her six times now, and only once had he said anything, when he made her horse snort and back up a pace. "Beg pardon, Healer Vixen," he'd said, and tugged at the rim of his hat apologetically. Her throat had tightened, and she'd felt a sickness in the pit of her stomach when she'd first spotted him, but as it became clear he didn't recognize her, the fear had turned to something else. Anger, a little. Some self-satisfaction, the sort you get when you see someone who deserves it in misfortune. There really should have been a word for that.

The inn's boy heaved the wicker panniers holding her Healing supplies over Brownie's rump, and while he fastened the belly strap, she tied them to the back of the saddle. She made sure that the lids were tied down tight, feeling both accomplishment and bitterness.

Well, there it was, *he* hadn't changed; he looked like the same bullying dullard who'd thought it was so funny to run after her, chanting, "Where's your Companion, Herald Rosie?" with the others. He looked shabby, work-worn, and duller than he had been as a boy. She wondered how he'd ended up here, right on the Border and within a shout of the Pelagiris Forest. He'd certainly thought he was the cock of the walk back in the day: blond, strong, wide-shouldered, and if he wasn't handsome, he also wasn't homely. He'd been sure he was destined for a fine and easy life. It looked as if he was a carter now, hauling loads between the villages, which was a hard way to earn a living.

Maybe his older brothers had run him off the farm but granted him a horse and a cart so he didn't starve. Well, if so, it served him right, since he and his friends had been part of why *she'd* scarpered off as soon as she was old enough to do so.

Her hunter snorted at the sight of the innkeeper's boy
bringing the saddlebags holding her personal posses-
sions. He knew that meant they were about to leave. She
patted his neck and then turned in the saddle to help the
boy fasten them properly behind the panniers.

Brownie flicked his ears back at her. *:Go soon?:* she
heard in her mind.

:Soon,: she promised. Unlike every other Healer she
knew, besides the Healing Gift, she had Animal Mindspeech. Mostly it was a nuisance, though occasionally it
was useful. It happened to be quite sensitive, and unless
she kept her—well, they weren't *shields,* exactly, they
were more like sieves, or cloth filters—up, she was subject to all sorts of background nonsense. It was a lot like
being in an enormous crowd, where everyone was
talking at once. Fortunately, the Animal Mindspeech
Gift had not started out nearly that sensitive, so she'd
had time to learn how to put up protections that kept the
babble at bay and let in only the important things. She'd
learned to welcome the winter woods, with so much of
the wildlife gone or hibernating. Absolutely the worst
were busy farms, with not only farm animals but also
flocks of sparrows in the thatch, hordes of starlings in the
trees, and armies of mice everywhere. By contrast, cities
were almost restful, because she couldn't hear people,
only animals.

She finished settling panniers, saddlebags, and all to
Brownie's satisfaction, making sure he was happy with
the load; after all, he was the one doing all the work on
the road, and he deserved to be comfortable. It didn't
take long; the two of them had been doing this routine
for four years now, and gods willing, Brownie was good
for another twenty at least. With a pat to his neck, she le

him set the pace out of the village and down the road toward the Pelagiris Forest. There were a lot of little villages and hamlets out here that had no resident Healer and would never see one if she hadn't taken this Circuit on. It was the same route the Herald assigned here took, but so far she'd managed to keep from running into him. That was by design, not accident, though she'd taken pains to keep *that* her own little secret.

For such a big horse, Brownie was very light-footed, and he preferred a brisk pace; his big hooves made solid *clops* on the dirt road as he set off on his ground-eating fast walk. Out of the village they paced, across the little stone bridge over the slender river that supplied the village's water, and then they were back on the main road, passing immediately under the first trees of the forest. There was no cultivated land this side of the river. The folk of the next hamlet on the route were hunters and gatherers rather than farmers. What they needed, they traded for.

But the sight of Digby had put her into a bad mood. And memories she didn't want bubbled up out of the past.

She was only four, and she had no idea why her parents were so excited. She only knew that she was getting to wear that pretty dress they almost never let her put on, and Ma had put a wreath of flowers on her head and they had all run out to the road. Everyone was craning their necks, and there was a sound like bells off in the distance. The sound got nearer and nearer, and then she saw what made it—the prettiest white horse she had ever seen, dancing its way toward them! Her parents got more and more excited the closer it came, and then it danced right past them all and off into the distance, and she wondered why her parents were suddenly so disappointed. They picked her up and took her back to the cottage, and Ma made her take off the dress and put her everyday tunic back on. "She's young for it yet," her pa said. "Next time, surely."

She hadn't understood, that first time, what had happened—or rather, what *hadn't* happened. Nor the next, nor the next. She'd only known that her parents would get excited, drag her out of whatever it was she was doing, dress her up as if for a festival, and make her stand by the side of the road, waiting for another white horse to come. And then they would be disappointed when it just raced on by. And look at her as if she had somehow done something wrong.

But eventually . . . eventually she learned. Learned that the white horses were Companions, that they Chose their Heralds, that Heralds were Very Important People, and that her parents *expected* her to become one. Not just hoped, but *expected,* as if they had the power to control the future. And by all the gods, they were going to dress her up, drag her to the road, and shove her under the nose of every Companion on Search that came through until she *did* become one. And every time the Companion passed on without Choosing someone, they were disappointed—in her.

It quickly became an embarrassment as well as a misery. Impossible in such a small hamlet for people not to know that her parents had such inflated ideas about what their offspring should become. She got pitying looks or snickers behind sheltering hands. And there was a pack of little bullies who tormented her about it every chance they got, running after her, calling her "Herald Rosie" and asking where her Companion was. Digby wasn't the chief, but he certainly relished the "fun" and egged the others on when they lost interest.

And meanwhile, her parents piled things on her that they reckoned would "improve" her: lesson on lesson, hours spent in schooling, and lots of correction, from her speech to her posture....

Some of those tormenting bullies got the bright idea to call false alarms, just to see her dragged into the house and dragged out again, dressed up in her finery, to stand between her parents, head hanging and miserable, waiting for Companions that didn't come.

Seeing Digby had brought all that up again, knotting her stomach with unhappiness until even those lovely pocket pies were more nauseating than tempting. She shoved the old memories away as best she could, but it wasn't easy. There wasn't much to distract her from her own thoughts. The winding, twisting road was completely empty, and by the state of the drifts of leaves on it, no one had been on it for a day or more. Bandits weren't much of a problem here; the forest itself was the danger. This was just on the edge of Hawkbrother territory, and strange things roamed under these trees.

That had never bothered Vixen. She could sense most of them long before they were close enough to be a danger, Brownie was big enough that most predators wouldn't even consider trying for her, and he was fast enough that so far he'd been able to outrun anything that did.

It would be winter soon. The trees were leafless, and the dead, fallen leaves themselves had all turned brown and lifeless, lying in drifts on the roadway and among the trees. Berries and nuts were gone, and anything that was going to hibernate had found a den or a cave or a hollow tree. The birds were far enough away that their mental chatter didn't bother her, so she allowed her protections

to thin. Brownie had a remarkably quiet mind; he enjoyed her company, he enjoyed his work, and he was enjoying this morning, and he managed to do all of that
without internally babbling, although she didn't know
many horses that babbled. Birds were the worst for that,
and chickens were the worst of the birds.

So it's a good thing I don't ride a chicken, I suppose.

Brownie had already grown out his shaggy winter
coat, so the cold breeze didn't trouble him at all. He was
staying alert, however; she could tell by the way his ears
were constantly moving. He knew this route, and he
knew there could be dangers on this road. His nose and
hearing were those of a prey animal; if by some chance
something out there was both dangerous and able to
hide itself from her Gift, Brownie would probably scent
or hear it. And while he stayed watchful, she wrestled
with her uncomfortable emotions until she had them all
clamped down and under control again. She told herself,
over and over, as the road wound on beneath the leafless
trees and a clear, cold sky, that Rosie was gone, and only
Vixen remained. And no one, *no one*, ever mocked
Vixen.

She wondered about her parents, though. She'd sent
them a single message, about six months after the Healers had taken her in. *I'm fine. Don't try to find me. I never
want to see you again.* Harsh, perhaps, but . . . true then,
and true now. What had they done with *their* lives once
she was gone? Did they have another child, or children,
and put those poor things through the same torture she'd
gone through, or had they learned their lesson?

She allowed Brownie to pick the place to pause for
their midday rest, right around noon. They had made
good time, and he deserved a break to browse on what

he could find beside a small stream that cut across the road. He wore a bitless bridle, so he was free to wander along the stream, cropping the last of the green grass, taking occasional drinks of water. She stayed in the saddle and had a meat pie and an apple pie, finding ones that were miraculously still warm at the bottom of her saddlebag, and enjoying them with water from the inn's well. She reckoned that at the rate they were going, they would easily reach the next hamlet before sundown. The wind had stilled, and the sun actually warmed her a bit as she ate.

Finally she took up the reins and got Brownie back on the road again. Refreshed by the halt, he took up his ground-eating fast walk again, and she settled into keeping watch for trouble and trying to keep from brooding. *Matya will probably put me up, unless one of her boys returned to the nest and claimed the spare bed.* Matya was one of the few people she counted as a friend. The old woman never chattered, had a refreshingly sardonic sense of humor, was practical, and good company. And . . . she cooked divinely. *Her nut porridge ought to be outlawed, it's so good.*

The hamlet they were heading for hardly justified having a name, but it did; Kettleford. She was well known there, and it was one of her favored stops on this circuit, even when there was no one there who needed her services.

It wasn't likely anyone from her old village of Hartrise would come that far and recognize her, so she always felt reasonably safe from detection there. Hartrise had its own Healer and wouldn't send anyone looking for the Healer on Circuit, no matter who was hurt or ill. As for people from Hartrise coming to Kettleford, the people of Kettleford shrewdly took their trade and sale goods to the larger village, rather than let anyone sharp them by offering less than the market value.

And no one ever questioned why she left Hartrise out of her Circuit.

The pure fact was, she never wanted to see it again.

Once again, her thoughts reverted to the past. It seemed even when she was determined *not* to think of it, the mere sight of Digby had triggered memories she'd hoped were long buried.

It had been a fine spring day, and she had been fifteen, when it finally got too much to bear. No matter how much she objected, her parents would not give over the charade. Not one, but two Companions had passed through in the same week, and twice more of being dragged out—and the taunting afterward by boys who, by now, should have been old enough to know better and should have by rights been too busy with work to take the time to find her and tease her—had been the straw that broke the cow's back.

By that point, she was an easy target for taunting; for years she'd been stuffing herself with anything she could get her hands on whenever the hurt got too bad. Food had turned into a source of comfort, and if it was salted with her tears, well, it was still consolation. But all that food had taken its own sort of toll. Now it was "Herald Fatty," not "Herald Rosie," with taunts about how she must have broken her Companion's back.

So that night, before she could lose her nerve, she packed up what she could carry and a big basket of food, and she ran away. By dawn, she was far enough away from Hartrise that she figured she'd outpaced her pursuit—she could walk for leagues when she put her mind to it, and she'd been determined to escape. She did have some skills she could use to make her way, thanks to all those lessons her parents had forced down her throat. She'd reckoned that if she could find some religious place or a House of Healing, she could go to work making copies of books or writing letters for those who couldn't. There was always room for a good scrivener. The one thing her parents' constant nagging had done was ensure she had excelled past just about anyone in the village except the local priest when it came to reading and writing and figures. Certainly far past the bullying boys who reckoned they didn't need to learn anything, since their strong shoulders and handsome faces were all they'd need. Marry a rich farmer's daughter, and live in clover, was their idea of how they would prosper.

That didn't work out so well for you, did it, Digby? she thought maliciously.

She'd come to a House of Healing first, but when she'd rung the bell and got no answer, then decided to go ahead and come in anyway, she discovered a scene out of a nightmare. There'd been an avalanche down onto the mining village of Stonetree, where a pile of tailings that had built up for generations had given way, and the place was full of smashed-up men, women, and children. She'd stood in the doorway of the main ward, transfixed with horror. There was blood everywhere, and the moans of the injured were somehow worse than screams. The Healers and their helpers had seen nothing in her but another pair of healthy hands; they'd snatched her things out of her hands and off her back, given her some rudimentary instruction, and shoved her at the least-injured, figuring anyone could bandage cuts and staunch the bleeding.

And then came the miracle she had never expected.

The moment her hands had touched the first child, she felt something flowing out of her, and before her own astonished eyes, the bleeding gashes down his arm and face stopped bleeding, closed, and sealed . . .

One of the Healers felt it happening, felt the flow of Healing energy suddenly surging out of her, and rushed to her. He was on his last legs, but she was fresh. He could muster enough energy to coach her in what she needed to do, though he was so spent he was just barely able to stay coherent.

Then came the second miracle, as she used up that store of fat she had built up, burning it off in a frenzy of Healing. By the end of the day, she was a full two stone lighter—and at the weight she should have been, if she hadn't been cramming food in her mouth all these years. That was when she learned that the energy to Heal generally came from the Healer herself, and that the store of fat she had built up over the years was the source of the fuel that had driven her to do more that day than any but the most experienced. She had an instinctive talent for Healing that more than made up for her lack of training. And that put her out of reach of any other demand. Even if her parents had shown up at the door and demanded her back, the Healers would never have let her go.

Rosie, calling herself "Ruby," had done her best to cover her trail so there was never a chance they'd find her in the first place. She'd spun a tale of being orphaned and looking for work, and the Healers didn't question her, not once in all the time of her being there.

They'd asked once if she wanted to go to Healers' Collegium in Haven. "And what can I learn there that you can't teach me?" she'd asked. Since the answer was "Nothing," she was spared having to face a horde of Companions, and Heralds, too, and be reminded how she had managed to fail over and over.

I'm not a failure, she told herself fiercely, as the wind stung her eyes and made them water. *I'm not. I was never meant to be a Herald in the first place. And I am a damn good Healer, so there.*

And just as she thought that . . . she heard the sound of bells and bell-like hooves racing toward her.

Brownie reacted to her start by stopping dead in his tracks, and before she could collect herself, the Companion whose hooves and bells she had heard rounded a bend of the road just ahead and skidded to a halt in front of her.

:Oh, thank goodness,: she heard, clearly, in her mind. *:I didn't think you were so close!:*

Vixen held back the half-dozen things she might have said, most of them angry retorts that would have upset the poor thing, and throttled back on all the emotions pouring through her. After all, absolutely *nothing* she had gone through as a child was the fault of any Companion, or Herald either. "I take it your Herald is injured? Ill?" She did let out a slight sigh of exasperation. After all, it would make a Healer's job a great deal easier if Heralds didn't persist in flinging themselves enthusiastically into danger at the drop of a hat.

:Injured. He broke his ankle this morning; a plank on a footbridge gave way under him.:

It was such a *prosaic* injury that it startled a laugh out of her. The Companion's head came up indignantly, but a moment later, she dropped her nose and shook her head ruefully.

:I know. It's terribly . . . ordinary. Isn't it?:

"Entirely. I assume he's in Kettleford?"

:Matya has him put up on a featherbed by the fire and she's warming the spare bed in the loft for you.: Well, that

was a most satisfactory answer. :*She said you were due today or tomorrow, but I didn't want to chance his ankle setting wrong and came to look for you.*:

"Then let's not dilly-dally around here any longer," she said firmly. "You're right; we don't want his ankle to set without proper tending, and I don't want to be caught out on the road anywhere near dark."

The Companion nodded in agreement, reared and pivoted gracefully on her hind hooves, and was off like a shot arrow. Brownie didn't need any urging to follow, and increased his pace to a trot. His feet thudded heavily on the turf-and-dirt of the road, and she pulled her cloak tight around her as the wind picked up again.

There was still light in the sky as they came out from under the trees and into the cleared land around the hamlet of Kettleford. There were only nine houses, five on one side of the road and four on the other. There was a watering trough and a well in a widened spot in the middle of the road. There was no inn, though the sign of a shock of wheat above the door of Old Taffy's house, and the presence of a couple of benches on either side of the door, would inform anyone passing through that he could get beer and something like a meal there. Locals would all gather in Taffy's parlor of a night for a drink and a chat and perhaps a game or two. Each of the houses had a little cottage garden where folks grew their vegetables, but for the most part, people here hunted or trapped, with a couple of those who knew what to look for supplementing their income by gathering rare herbs and dye plants. There were hides and furs staked out in various stages of curing in every yard and on every bit of wall. Some of the hides were of odd shapes or very peculiar patterns or colors. This was the edge of the Pelagiris Forest, after all, and odd things prowled the paths, creatures whose furs were highly desirable just on the basis of their rarity or oddity. Matya was the sole holdout among the hunters, although her husband had been one of them when he was alive. She raised chickens and rabbits and had three cows. The entire hamlet got their butter, eggs, and cheese from her, as well as their potherbs. She was no kind of Healer though; herbs for the kitchen, herbs for tanning, and herbs for dyeing were her specialty. In season, she'd get at least a visitor a week from all over this area to trade for what she produced.

Matya's cowshed was spacious—big enough for a half-dozen cows, though she only had three now. There was more than enough room for Brownie and the Companion. And like every building here, the word "shed" was something of a misnomer; it was built like a fortress, all of stone, with tiny windows that had heavy shutters, and a stout slate roof. Even the chicken coop and the rabbit hutch were built the same. It wasn't safe, otherwise. Matya herself came out, wiping her hands on her apron, her shawl wrapped firmly about her shoulders, at the sound of the Companion's bells.

"Nah, I told this one you'd be coming along shortly, Vixen," was Matya's greeting, as she opened the gate and let them into the yard with the shed in it. "But nothing would have it but that she go out looking for you."

"She told you that?" Vixen raised an eyebrow.

Matya bellowed a laugh, tossing her weathered head back. "Don't be daft! She mimed it, belike. Let's get these creatures both comfortable, then ye can see to the lad."

Together they untacked both Brownie and the Companion and let them find places for themselves among the cows, who amiably made way for them. Dividing the saddlebags and panniers equally, they closed a door built of planks a thumb-length thick, latched it up, and went in to the cottage.

Matya's cottage consisted of two rooms with a loft. One room—just big enough for her bed—was where she slept. The other served every other purpose. The loft was over the bedroom. The floor was wood, for warmth; half-logs laid in sand and pegged together, gaps filled with a combination of sawdust and glue. Matya had once told Vixen proudly that her husband had laid it himself, not wanting his bride to have to cope with a pounded-earth floor.

There was a little table, three half-log benches, one corner was a kitchen with a pantry, a cupboard, and a stone sink, and that was all the furnishing. Right now the most prominent thing in the room was the bed made up of furs and blankets beside the fire, and the far-too-handsome, pale-faced, black-haired young man in Herald's Whites lying in it. He raised himself up on his elbow and tried to smile, but it was obvious to Vixen he was in a lot of pain.

"You are a welcome sight, Healer Vixen," he said.

He didn't know her, of course; they'd never met, but they knew each other's names, since they shared the Circuit. "I imagine I am, Herald Vanyel," she said dryly. "Let's see what kind of mess you've made of yourself."

She laid her burdens down next to one of the benches, while Matya did the same, and pulled off her cloak and draped it over one of the panniers. She knelt at the foot of his improvised bed and pulled back the blankets. "Well, at least you got your boot off," she remarked, cupping her hands around the misshapen ankle.

"I got it off as soon as I realized I'd broken something," he replied. "I couldn't see how I would make it worse, and I didn't want to have to have it cut off."

She just grunted. He *could* have made it worse, but, fortunately, either by skill or accident, he hadn't. She closed her eyes, and . . . well, it was hard to describe what she did in words. She . . . *sensed* what was going on in there. It wasn't like seeing, and it wasn't like feeling; it was more like *knowing*.

Well, he had gotten lucky. The bone wasn't broken entirely, it was cracked. If he'd tried to walk on it, he certainly *would* have turned those cracks into breaks, but he'd had the wit not to try. "Not so bad," she said, opening her eyes. Then she went to her panniers for the plaster-powder and bandages. Only after she had the foot and ankle protected and immobilized did she cup her hands around the joint a second time and give the bones their first round of Healing.

And only after *that* did she make up a dose of pain-killing tea, which the Herald drank down without a face and without a complaint.

Meanwhile, Matya had taken her bags and stored them out of the way, extracted the cold pocket pies, and warmed them next to the fire. Vixen was ravenous after the Healing session, of course, and she ate three to Matya and the Herald's one each.

Then she sat with her back up against the warm stone of the right leg of the fireplace, cushioned by another thick fur, and sipped a cup of Matya's famous chamomile-and-bee-bait tea. The Herald went supine again as soon as he had finished eating, and she didn't blame him. That had to hurt, even with her nostrum in him.

"Terribly unheroic of me, I fear," he said, his eyes closed. "Did 'Fandes talk to you?"

"She told me a plank gave way under you on a foot-bridge," Vixen replied, as Matya settled down on one of the benches with some mending. "Your timing was good, anyway."

"What the young fool isn't telling you is that he did it in Ostcroft," Matya said, "Then got his boot off and rode all the way back here a-purpose to catch you."

That earned him a raised eyebrow from Vixen. Ost-croft . . . it would have taken her three days to get from here to there on Brownie. But then again, Companions were supposed to be ridiculously fast, and if he'd waited in Ostcroft for her, it could have been a week or more before she got there. "I hope you gave them a piece of your mind," she said, dryly. "It could have been a child . . . and it could have been a broken neck, if it's the bridge I'm thinking of."

Vanyel opened one eye, and she noted with a start that his eyes were silver. "No scolding for not paying attention to where I was going? Am I not going to feel the edge of the famous Vixen tongue?"

She snorted. "Not unless you tell me it was because you weren't paying attention to where you were going," she replied as Matya cackled. "Regardless of what you've heard, I don't generally assume the worst of someone unless I already know he's an idiot."

That got a wan chuckle out of him. "I'm relieved," he said, closing his eye again. "I was quaking with dread. Your reputation is formidable."

"She doesn't suffer fools gladly," Matya put in, her strong hands making neat little stitches as she applied a patch to—whatever it was she was fixing. It was hard to tell, just seeing the fabric resting in her lap.

"I don't suffer fools *at all,*" Vixen corrected. "But an honest accident is just bad luck."

"To make up for the good luck of finding Jensen's boy before he ran into something vicious," Vanyel sighed. "On the other hand, if the bad luck had to go to someone, I'd rather it was me."

Vixen rolled her eyes. "Well, maybe bad luck doesn't have to go to anyone," she pointed out. "Why aren't you sleeping yet?"

Vanyel managed a slight laugh. "Because I'm not sleepy. The ankle isn't hurting now, and I admit I'm more than a bit dizzy, but painkillers rarely put me to sleep, Healer. I'm odd that way."

She snorted. "I've never heard of a Herald I'd classify as *normal,*" she pointed out. Vanyel seemed to find this very funny. Then again, it might have been the tea she had given him; it made some people giddy rather than sleepy.

And so things might have stayed, the Herald slowly succumbing to sleep, Matya and Vixen exchanging a little gossip before going to their respective beds.

That, however, was not to be.

Vanyel was just opening his mouth to say something when the night air was split by a sound that raised every hair on the back of Vixen's neck.

It was something like a roar, and something like the sound made by tearing heavy canvas, and it sounded as if it was coming from the point where the road entered the village. In a flash, Matya was up and making sure the shutters over the windows were barred and blowing out all the lights. Vixen raced up the ladder to the loft and took a quick look out of the tiny window up there to see if she could spot anything.

The window had an excellent view of the road, and the full moon had just risen over the tops of the trees, pouring light down onto the village. The hideous sound ripped through the silence a second time, and ... something lurched into a pool of moonlight.

Vixen could only say, "something," because it wasn't like any creature she had ever seen before. It was definitely bigger than two Brownie-sized horses put together. It had four legs, each ending in terrifying talons. The head was blunt, with a mouth full of sharp, pointed teeth; in fact, it looked like a lizard, if a lizard happened to be covered in short, shaggy hair. As she watched, it made that terrible sound again. She closed the shutter over the window, barred it, and scuttled down the ladder again.

"Did you see it?" Matya whispered, as the three of them huddled close to the fire. Vixen nodded, and described it to them. Vanyel shook his head.

"I've never heard of anything like it," he breathed. "It must be some sort of Change-Creature out of the Pelagiris." He acted as if he was going to try and get up, and both Matya and Vixen both held him down.

"Where do you think you're going?" Vixen hissed. "You can't stand, and believe me, if you're a Herald-Mage, you *really* don't want to try any magic in your condition!"

"But—"

"Shut up and be quiet!" Matya and Vixen both said at the same time. They exchanged a look over the young man's head.

"I'm going back up to the window," Vixen whispered. "I'm going to see if it's got a mind I can read."

"Wait!" Vanyel interjected. "How—"

"Shhh!" Matya and Vixen hissed, and Vixen scrambled up the ladder again.

The creature was still down there, but now it was sniffing at the door of the cottage across the road. Vixen closed her eyes and let her mind go blank and lowered her shields.

She quickly picked up the nervous mutterings of the chickens in their coop, the frozen terror of the rabbits in their shed. Brownie was petrified, and so were the three cows, but the Companion was keeping them all quiet.

Whatever this thing was . . . it didn't have a mind like anything Vixen had ever encountered before.

Well . . . it looked like a lizard . . .

It was hard to describe what she did next, though the closest she could have gotten was to say she was "listening harder." Straining, trying to catch "notes" that were "lower" than she could usually hear, perhaps. Sometimes it worked.

This time, it did.

It wasn't words so much as feelings. Hunger. Anger that the things it could sense were walled away inside stone dens. But what alarmed her most was that she sensed this creature was *not* going to leave until it had dug out every last warm-blooded thing here and eaten it. So far as this beast was concerned, this was a storehouse of food, and it was going to find a way to get at that food. There was nothing there to reason with, as she sometimes could with predators; the creature was mostly instinct and recognized only its own needs. She also got some very chilling images from the thing's mind, memories of hunting humans. Armed humans. It had done spectacularly well against them; in those memories it was frighteningly fast.

She went back down the ladder and rejoined the Herald and Matya. "There's nothing I can 'talk' to," she reported grimly. "It's hungry, and it intends to eat us, and that's all there is to it."

She looked from Vanyel to Matya. "I don't think your hunters can kill it. It's fast, and it's strong, and it's *huge*. The only chance they might have is if they can fill it full of arrows for a long while — that might weaken it enough that a concerted attack by everyone in the village on it might succeed. But from what I picked up, that might take a long while. How well stocked are people for food and water?"

"I'm fine, I could hold out for a fortnight, and I have the pump to my well right here in the kitchen," Matya said after a moment of thought. "But the Corsons, the Lentoffs and the Derlys rely on the village well for water. And then there's the animals. More than a day and a night without food and water, and I'm going to lose some, maybe all of them. I'm not alone, there are other horses, donkeys, goats . . ."

"I get the idea," Vixen said.

Vanyel's brows furrowed, and his jaw clenched. He squeezed his eyes shut and was obviously trying to do . . . something. But after a moment, he let out his breath in a disgusted sigh and opened his eyes again. "How long does this potion of yours last?" he asked Vixen.

"Six, eight candlemarks—" She bit her lip. "It's not merely interfering a bit with your magic, is it?"

"I can't hold the power," he confirmed. "It's as if I'm trying to hold water in my hands. Until it wears off, the best I could do would be to shoot at the damned thing. And it's mucking up Mindspeech, too. I can barely talk to 'Fandes." But then, his eyes widened a little. "I can't reach anyone with Mindspeech who would be near enough to do us any good. But *you* can!"

Vixen stared at him. "I don't Mindspeak to—"

"Animal Mindspeech. The Hawkbrothers aren't that far from here, and a lot of them fly owls. Just send out a general call for help! If a bird gets it, he'll pass it on to his bondmate!"

Well, it wasn't the craziest idea she had ever heard.

"Meanwhile, Matya and I will figure out how to speak to and coordinate everyone in the village," Vanyel continued. "If you aren't able to reach anyone, well, we can wait until dawn, and maybe we *can* fill the thing full of arrows without risking anyone. By then, your potion will have worn off, and I'll be able to use magic again."

Vixen gave him a very skeptical look. Personally, she didn't think anyone would be able to use magic with a broken ankle. Everything she had ever heard said that magicians had to have very finely tuned concentration to use their powers, and how did he propose to concentrate when he was a scant breath from screaming with pain?

He apparently read that look and shrugged. "All right. *Maybe* I will be able to use magic again. But I'd rather try every possible approach than sit here and do nothing."

"Aye, so would I," Vixen agreed.

It felt as if she had been sitting there forever, trying all the ranges of Mindspeech she had ever tried before. Well, except one—she carefully avoided the one where she had sensed the thoughts of that monster. The last thing she wanted to do was to alert it further, maybe make it home in on Matya's cottage. The problem, of course, was that she had never Mindspoken with a Hawkbrother Bondbird; she had no idea what their minds were like. Like regular raptors? Probably not.

And then, just as she was about to give up on one range and try a new one, she got a faint but clear response. A beautiful, silvery Mindvoice like nothing she had ever encountered before, and *nothing* like an animal's. :*I hear, Healer! I hear! Hold fast, I am coming!*:

"I got an answer!" she exclaimed, her eyes popping open with the shock of how intelligent the responder had sounded.

"What was it?" Vanyel and Matya replied simultaneously. But she could only shake her head.

"I have no idea. But it sounded intelligent, and it said it was coming—" Then she faltered. "—but it was at the very edge of my range. And I have no idea how far that is. I never tested it before."

Vanyel frowned a little. "Probably not far. Mindspeech doesn't go all that far unless it's boosted by a Companion, so I imagine that Animal Mindspeech is the same. Maybe a league? It will depend on how fast—"

The thing roared again—but this time there was a definite note of anger and challenge in the sound! Vixen raced up the ladder again and looked out the window.

And nearly fainted. Because now, there wasn't a single monster on the road between the houses, there were two. And the second one was a spider as big as the first.

She had no time to think of anything except to pray to whatever gods were listening that the two of them would manage to kill each other, when the spider attacked.

She couldn't have told how long the battle raged. The spider was agile and fast, just as agile and fast as the hairy thing. And it could jump like nothing she had ever seen before, managing to keep its relatively fragile legs out of the way of talon-swipes by amazing leaps backward. This frustrated the lizard-creature no end, and that, eventually was its undoing.

That was when the spider struck.

It made a tremendous leap and landed for a moment on the lizard-thing's back. Its head bobbed, and two enormous fangs plunged into the lizard's neck on either side of the spine. Then it leaped off again as the lizard screamed in pain, and it paused three wagon-lengths away—

—waiting.

The lizard turned to face it, but it was moving as if it was dizzy or sick. It roared, or tried to, but the sound came out choked. Then it staggered toward the spider, taking only three steps, before it collapsed in the street, spasmed once, and died.

Oh, hellfires. Now we have an even worse problem—

But then, completely out of nowhere, came that silvery voice. *:It is safe to come out, Healer. The thing is dead.:*

She gasped—and the first thing that sprang up into her mind, after that burst of total astonishment, was that she had to get out into the street, *fast,* or there was no telling what the people in the other cottages might do to the weird creature that had turned out to be their savior.

She slid down the ladder, ran for the door, threw it open, and pelted out into the street, running past the carcass of the monster—and just in time. Old Taffy had emerged with a face full of fear and a torch and a pitchfork in his hands, and she flung herself between him and the spider, heedless of her own safety.

"Stop! You damn fool!" she shrilled, and spread-

eagled herself in front of the spider's strange face, right between two of the hairy legs. "This is a friend!"

Taffy's jaw dropped, as did the jaws of the other three men who had come, armed, out of their cottages. And for a long, silent moment, they all stood staring at each other, while the giant spider remained behind Vixen, not moving a muscle.

Finally Taffy lowered his pitchfork. "Damn, Healer," he finally said. "I allus knowed ye was strange, but ye bain't half as strange as yer friends!"

By the time dawn came, Vixen had spent most of the night "speaking" for the spider, who had gone from terror to heroine. When she began to shiver, someone had brought a brazier of coals she could hover over, as she told her short story in her silvery Mindvoice and Vixen related it.

It seemed that she, like a few other hunting spider species, could winter over if she had a cave deep enough. But she had lost hers when the entrance collapsed over the summer, and she had been searching desperately for another. She had just about given up finding one when she "heard" Vixen's call for help.

:*I thought—if I must die, at least I shall either die in combat saving you, or—at least die* having *saved you,*: she said solemnly. When Vixen related that, choking up a little and surprising herself with her stinging eyes, the entire hamlet rose up in protest.

"Nah, tell the darlin' we won't *let* her die, Healer!" Taffy protested. "We'll think of somethin'! Mebbe we can raise a barn afore it gets too cold—"

"Pa—" said his youngest son.

"Or mebbe we can fit 'er inter a cellar—"

"Pa—"

"Or—"

"Pa!"

"What?" Taffy spluttered.

"I know where there's a cave!" the boy crowed. "I kin show ye!"

It had to wait until dawn, though. In the meantime, warmed by the coals, the spider waited patiently. By that point, the potion had worn off, and Vanyel had managed to come out to see the marvel, hopping along on a pair of improvised crutches.

When dawn came, an odd procession formed up: Taffy's boy Grek in the lead, Vanyel on Yfandes following, and Taffy and everyone else behind them. Vixen and the spider followed behind. By this time they all had given the spider a name: Melody. Vixen had suggested it, the spider liked it, and the rest of the village agreed to it.

:This is . . . so kind of you all,: the spider said, in her beautiful Mindvoice. *:Even if it isn't suitable, I . . . no one has ever been so kind to me except the* tervardi.*:*

Vixen didn't know what a *tervardi* was, but evidently it was some other race living in the Pelagiris. *:If it isn't suitable, I have the suspicion that they'll get shovels and dig until it is,:* she told the spider. *:And you deserve nothing less.:*

She sensed that Melody was going to say something else, but at that point, Grek cried out, "Here 'tis!" and the crowd parted to let the two of them come up to the front.

It was mostly a wide crack in the rock of a hill, just big enough for an active boy to squeeze into . . . but there was a damp breath of air coming from it, and the spider seemed to perk up at that. The boy pointed to the top of

the hill, where a forest giant lay. "That there tree come
down in that big storm two moons ago, an' cracked open
yon rock," he said. "I squoze in, on'y went in as fur as I
could afore I lost light, but I *think* it goes back a good
long bit!"

:It ... might be suitable!: the spider said, hope and
doubt warring in her Mindvoice. *:I will look!:*

Nearly everyone's jaws dropped, as the enormous spider sidled up to the crack and somehow squeezed herself through it. There was a long silence, and a very long
time of waiting. Vixen's hope rose, the longer it took.

:It's perfect*!:* came the long awaited answer, which she
relayed.

The waiting crowd broke out in a cheer.

The spider squeezed herself back out again. Taffy approached her himself this time. "Miz Melody, I reckon I
can speechify for all of us. We'd ... we'd like ye to stay
around here. If ye'd be willin', that is." He looked round
at the others, who all nodded. "This ain't the first nasty
thing we've had turn up, an' it'd be a damn fine thing
t'hev our own critter that'd take on the bad 'uns. We'll
make sure this here cave never closes up, if ye'll stay."

The spider froze. *:They—want me? They really* want *me?:*

"They wouldn't offer if they didn't," Vixen pointed out.

Vanyel cleared his throat, and they all looked at him.
"The only difficulty I can see is communication once
Healer Vixen is gone," he said. "I've been thinking about
that, and I think I might have a solution." He closed his
eyes, and held out one hand for a moment, and a faint
blue glow appeared in the air, then settled over the spider and melded with it.

There was a long silence. Then, *"He—hello?"* came a
silvery little voice from just above the spider's head.

"Sorted," said Vanyel, and sighed. "It seems that is the *only* contribution I can make," he added, ruefully. "I hope word about this never gets around. It would not make a very good song."

Vixen didn't understand what that was all about, but everyone else seemed to find that hilarious. So while the men of the hamlet slightly—but only slightly—opened the crack and reinforced it so that it was unlikely to close up or collapse, the spider came back to the village and ... ate the monster. It was rather odd. It seemed the venom she had injected into it had liquefied the thing's insides and she was able to suck it dry, leaving mostly bones and skin. Vanyel excused himself. Vixen found it fascinating, and so did almost everyone else who came to watch. But then again, in a hamlet full of people who hunted the Pelagiris, there weren't likely to be too many people who were squeamish.

Someone carted off the hide and bones, which would presumably end up cured and traded at some point, and the spider, abdomen swollen with a meal that would easily see her through her hibernation, returned to the cave. She squeezed in again, and the last Vixen saw of her was a leg waving goodbye from the crack, and that silvery voice saying, *"Thank you, my good and true friends! I will see you in the spring!"*

By then, it was almost noon and everyone was exhausted. By common consent, the entire hamlet retreated to their cottages to sleep.

"What would you think about the two of us continuing the Circuit together?" Vanyel asked, a few days later.

By this time, of course, Vixen knew that he didn't mean anything other than that; it didn't take a Healer long to notice whether one of her patients was—what did they call it now?—ah, *shaych*.

"Why do you ask?" she replied, satisfied with the progress her Healing treatments were having. In a sennight or so, he'd be fit to ride, though she'd want him to wear a brace inside his boot for a while, just for safety's sake.

"If you come with me, you can use the Waystations," he pointed out. "The two of us can watch each others' backs. Your Animal Mindspeech will be more useful than any of my Gifts if there are any nasty Pelagiris creatures out there. And people often tell Healers things they won't tell a Herald. I don't mind holding our pace back so we don't tire out your horse."

He smiled charmingly at her. "You are both an excellent Healer and an excellent person in an emergency situation, Vixen. You're quite brave. You had no hesitation in throwing yourself between the humans and what anyone else would have considered a monster once you knew the truth of the matter. I'd trust your judgment, and I would trust you as a partner in any situation I can think of."

"Hmm," she replied, "Let me think this over...."

He had several good points. It *was* safer for two to ride this Circuit than one. Heralds were often summoned to places where Healers were needed—or would be needed. Being able to use the Waystations between villages and hamlets would be much more comfortable than camping—although he probably knew or guessed she had no compunction about using a Waystation anyway rather than camp in the open in the fall and winter. And people did tell Healers things they would never tell a Herald—things a Herald often needed to know.

"I can make sure we're here in good time to bring the spider out of her hibernation," he added.

But he would be riding the full Circuit. Which meant he would be stopping at Hartrise. . . .

She thought about that. Really stared the idea right in the proverbial eye. And slowly, she came to the conclusion that . . . she was all right with that. Or, at least, she wasn't going to let it stop her. In fact . . .

. . . in fact, it would do no harm, and might do a lot of good, for her to have a good look at the Healer in Hartrise and make sure he was up to snuff. He'd been coasting without having to account for what he was doing—or not doing—along enough. Maybe he was fine. Maybe he was excellent. But if he wasn't, well, it was about time he got a taste of a signature Vixen lecture.

And she'd have a *lot* of insights into Hartrise that might come in handy for the Herald as well.

"That's not a bad idea at all," she said, at last, looking up to see Vanyel's satisfied nod. "I think I'll take you up on it. Just remember, if you're an idiot, you'll get a piece of my mind about it."

"I wouldn't have it any other way," said Herald Vanyel.

About the Authors

Dylan Birtolo resides in the Pacific Northwest where he spends his time as a writer, a gamer, and a professional sword-swinger. His thoughts are filled with shape shifters, mythological demons, and epic battles. He's published a couple of fantasy novels and several short stories. He trains with the Seattle Knights, an acting troop that focuses on stage combat, and has performed in live shows, videos, and movies. He jousts, and yes, the armor is real—it weighs more than 100 pounds. You can read more about him and his works at www.dylanbirtolo. com or follow his twitter at @DylanBirtolo.

Jennifer Brozek is an award-winning editor, game designer, and author. She has been writing role-playing games and professionally publishing fiction since 2004. With the number of edited anthologies, fiction sales, RPG books, and nonfiction books under her belt, Jennifer is often considered a Renaissance woman, but she prefers to be known as a wordslinger and optimist. Read more about her at www.jenniferbrozek.com or follow her on Twitter at @JenniferBrozek.

Ron Collins' work has appeared in numerous magazines and anthologies, including *Dragon*, *Marion Zimmer*

Bradley's Fantasy Magazine, and *Flights of Fantasy* (edited by Mercedes Lackey). Last year he celebrated the publication of *Five Magics*, a short collection of his fantasy work. Of "Nwah," he writes: "Back in college I wrote an essay completely from the point of view of a leopard visiting a watering hole that has been lost to the nuances of time. I loved the feel of that piece, and always wanted to do it again. With 'Nwah,' I got that chance."

Brenda Cooper is a science fiction and fantasy writer, a technology professional, and a working futurist whose primary concern is the environment. Brenda lives in the Pacific Northwest in a family with many dogs and women. Her most recent novels are *The Creative Fire* and *The Diamond Deep*, both out from Pyr. Her next novel, *The Edge of Dark*, will also be published by Pyr. For more information, see www.brenda-cooper.com.

Dayle A. Dermatis has been called "one of the best writers working today" by *USA Today* bestselling author Dean Wesley Smith. Under various pseudonyms (and sometimes with co-authors), she's sold several novels and more than 100 short stories in multiple genres. Her latest novel is the urban fantasy *Ghosted*. She lives and works in California within scent of the ocean, and in her spare time follows Styx around the country and travels the world, all of which inspires her writing. She loves music, cats, Wales, TV, magic, laughter, and defying expectations. To find out where she is today, check out www.DayleDermatis.com.

Rosemary Edghill is the keeper of the Eddystone Light, corny as Kansas in August, normal as blueberry pie, and only a paper moon. She was found floating down the Amazon in a hatbox, and, because criminals are a cowardly and superstitious lot, she became a creature of the night (black, terrible). She began her professional career working as a time-traveling vampire killer and has never looked back. She's also a *New York Times* Bestselling Writer, and hangs out on Facebook a lot.

Rebecca Fox always wanted to be John Carter of Mars when she grew up, because of the giant birds. Since that career path didn't look like it was going to pan out anytime soon, she got her Ph.D. in Animal Behavior instead. She makes her home in Lexington, Kentucky, where she shares her life with three parrots, a Jack Russell terrier named Izzy, and the world's most opinionated chestnut mare. When she isn't writing, Rebecca teaches college biology and spends a lot of time outdoors doing research on bird behavior.

Cedric Johnson was born and raised in Lincoln, Nebraska, where he began writing short stories and poetry at an early age. He developed his writing, layout, and editing skills during high school, staffing its award-winning annual literary magazine *From the Depths*, before moving on to short stories and novels in the genres of fantasy, science fiction, and cyberpunk. He has contributed to the recent Elemental Masters anthologies *Elemental Magic* and *Elementary*. He currently resides in Commerce City, Colorado, where he continues to write while working with other forms of digital media, including 3D modeling and virtual world communications.

Michele Lang writes supernatural tales: the stories of witches, lawyers, goddesses, bankers, demons, and other magical creatures hidden in plain sight. She is the author of the apocalyptic adventure *Netherwood* and other stories set in the Netherwood universe, as well as the *Lady Lazarus* historical fantasy series. Michele lives in a small town on the North Shore of Long Island with her family and a rotating menagerie of cats, hermit crabs, and butterflies.

Fiona Patton was born in Calgary, Alberta, Canada and grew up in the United States. She now lives in rural Ontario with her partner, Tanya Huff, two glorious dogs, and a pride of very small lions. She has written seven fantasy novels for DAW Books, and is currently working on the first book of a new series entitled *The King's Eagle*.

Diana L. Paxson's first short story was published in *Isaac Asimov's Fantasy Magazine* in 1978. Since then she has published many others, including several in anthologies edited by Mercedes Lackey. She is also the author of twenty-nine novels, among them the *Chronicles of Westria*, *The White Raven* and the *Wodan's Children* trilogy. In addition to writing, she paints, plays the harp, and knows enough about weaving to realize that it is harder than it looks.

Kristin Schwengel lives near Milwaukee, Wisconsin, with her husband, the obligatory writer's cat (named Gandalf, of course), and a Darwinian garden in which only the strong survive. Her collection of hobby accoutrements includes several spindles, one of which has a whorl of green dragon's-vein agate, the inspiration for Stardance's treasured amber. Her writing has appeared in several previous Valdemar anthologies, and Stardance's story began with "Warp and Weft" in *Under the Vale.*

Stephanie D. Shaver lives in Southern California with her husband, daughter, and two geriatric cats. She works as a producer for Blizzard Entertainment, and spends her free time tinkering in the kitchen, camping out, and exploring new and exciting ways to kill plants in her garden. She should probably be working on a novel.

Louisa Swann was born on an Indian reservation in northern California, and spent the first six months of her life in a papoose carrier. Determined not to remain a basket case forever, she escaped the splintered confines finally settling down on a ranch where she spins tales that range from light to dark and back again. Louisa's writerly eccentricities have resulted in numerous short story publications in various anthologies. Find out more at www.louisaswann.com.

Elizabeth A. Vaughan is a *USA Today*-bestselling author who writes fantasy romance. Her first novel, *Warprize* was re-released in April, 2011. You can learn more about her books at www.eavwrites.com.

Elisabeth Waters sold her first story in 1980 to *The Keeper's Price*, the first of the Darkover anthologies. She went on to sell stories to a variety of anthologies. Her first novel, a fantasy called *Changing Fate*, was awarded the 1989 Gryphon Award. She is working on a sequel to it, in addition to her short-story writing and editorial work

She currently edits the *Sword and Sorceress* anthology series. She has also worked as a supernumerary with the San Francisco Opera, where she appeared in *La Gioconda, Manon Lescaut, Madama Butterfly, Khovanshchina, Das Rheingold, Werther*, and *Idomeneo*.

About the Editor

Mercedes Lackey is a full-time writer and has published numerous novels and works of short fiction, including the bestselling *Heralds of Valdemar* series. She is also a professional lyricist and a licensed wild bird rehabilitator. She lives in Oklahoma with her husband and collaborator, artist Larry Dixon, and their flock of parrots.

MERCEDES LACKEY
The Valdemar Anthologies

In the ancient land of Valdemar, beset by war and internal conflict, justice is dispensed by an elite force—the legendary Heralds. These unusual men and women, "Chosen" from all corners of the kingdom by their mysterious horselike Companions, undergo rigorous training and follow a rigid code of honor. Bonded for life with their Companions, the Heralds endeavor to keep the peace and, when necessary, defend their country in the name of the monarch.

With stories by authors such as Tanya Huff, Michelle Sagara West, Sarah Hoyt, Judith Tarr, Mickey Zucker Reichert, Diana Paxson, Larry Dixon, and, of course... stories and novellas by Mercedes Lackey.

To Order Call: 1-800-788-6262
www.dawbooks.com

DAW 157

MERCEDES LACKEY
The Novels of Valdemar

To Order Call: 1-800-788-6262

www.dawbooks.com

DAW 25

Mercedes Lackey & Larry Dixon

The Novels of Valdemar

"Lackey and Dixon always offer a well-told tale."
—*Booklist*

DARIAN'S TALE

OWLFLIGHT
978-0-88677-804-2

OWLSIGHT
978-0-88677-803-4

OWLKNIGHT
978-0-88677-916-2

THE MAGE WARS

THE BLACK GRYPHON
978-0-88677-804-2

THE WHITE GRYPHON
978-0-88677-682-1

THE SILVER GRYPHON
978-0-88677-685-6

To Order Call: 1-800-788-6262
www.dawbooks.com

MERCEDES LACKEY

The Dragon Jousters

JOUST
978-0-7564-0153-4

ALTA
978-0-7564-0257-3

SANCTUARY
978-0-7564-0341-3

AERIE
978-0-7564-0426-0

"A must-read for dragon lovers in particular and for fantasy fans in general." —*Publishers Weekly*

"It's fun to see a different spin on dragons...and as usual Lackey makes it all compelling."—*Locus*

To Order Call: 1-800-788-6262
www.dawbooks.com

MERCEDES LACKEY

Gwenhwyfar
The White Spirit

A classic tale of King Arthur's legendary queen. Gwenhwyfar moves in a world where gods walk among their pagan worshipers, where nebulous visions warn of future perils, and where there are two paths for a woman: the path of the Blessing, or the rarer path of the Warrior. Gwenhwyfar chosses the latter, giving up the power she is born to. But the daughter of a king is never truly free to follow her own calling...

978-0-7564-0585-4
Hardcover
978-0-7564-0629-5
Paperback

To Order Call: 1-800-788-6262
www.dawbooks.com

DAW 135

MERCEDES LACKEY

The Elemental Masters Series

"Her characteristic carefulness, narrative gifts, and attention to detail shape into an altogether superior fantasy."   —*Booklist*

"It's not lighthearted fluff, but rather a dark tale full of the pain and devastation of war, the growing class struggle, and changing sex roles, and a couple of wounded protagonists worth rooting for."   —*Locus*

"Putting a fresh face to a well-loved fairytale is not an easy task, but it is one that seems effortless to the prolific Lackey. Beautiful phrasing and a thorough grounding in the dress, mannerisms and history of the period help move the story along gracefully. This is a wonderful example of a new look at an old theme."   —*Publishers Weekly*

"Richly detailed historic backgrounds add flavor and richness to an already strong series that belongs in most fantasy collections. Highly recommended."   —*Library Journal*

To Order Call: 1-800-788-6262
www.dawbooks.com